The Youth Movement

Benjamin Garratt

ISBN: 9798722256294

Cover art by Angela Beatson Wood

PublishNation
www.publishnation.co.uk

Contents

Walsall, West Midlands, 10th October 2016

Flattery and non-promise

Geoffrey looked out upon the array of brightly coloured turbans and shuffled his notes. His mind was focused, but his hands were clammy and shaking a little from the previous evening's whiskies. Before him sat the senior members of his constituency's Sikh community in their newly built cultural centre. He knew what they wanted: a short, uncontroversial speech, peppered with enough praise to enable them to go home to their families suitably emboldened, and he knew he would not disappoint. He was so well-practised at delivering these vacuous speeches, the 'flattery and non-promise' as he liked to call them, that he was entirely unconcerned that the words about to pass through his lips were, until half an hour previously, new to him.

He looked down at his notes on top of the stubby lectern and launched into his flow. The room disappeared into a blur as his eyes bounced from face to face, to notes, to face, and his brain operated his mouth, throat and breathing directly without the intervention of thought. Years of experience had given his words enough playful rhythm to hide their lack of content. His audience, as he knew they would, enjoyed the praise, the lists of achievements, the namechecking and talk of togetherness. He enjoyed every word as it brought him closer to a drink.

As on all such occasions, as he reached his conclusion, he imitated the finale of Queen's 'Bohemian Rhapsody' and gave a long pause, before softly lingering over each last word. The final line rolled through his mind as his hosts applauded.

Twenty minutes later, having achieved his mission and offered his excuses, lying that he had one last engagement that evening, he walked out under the clear autumnal sky towards his car and pondered what takeaway to consume alongside a bottle of wine in his usual hotel, a cheap little place that fell inside the bounds of the ungenerous Parliamentary allowance. As he began his ritual shuffle hunt for his keys, his phone began to buzz. 'Daniel, how are you?'

North west London, 13ᵗʰ December 2053

The march to Trafalgar

With less than two hours to go until the main event, the street outside their garage was beginning to hum with activity. Seeing the first shadows of movement flicker past their scratched plastic window, Sira, Yanda and Frank each temporarily disconnected from their digital chats and entered a real-life argument with each other over which era's costumes to adopt for the festivities. As on almost all such occasions, Frank's assertion that they lacked the time to do anything new was initially ignored, then rejected and eventually accepted without acknowledgment.

As they reached for their replica Great War greatcoats, stolen a couple of years previously from one of the country's last woollen mills, Yanda and Sira promised themselves that next time they would finish their winter-marching look by matching the coats with some imported, replica Great War boots and perhaps real antique medals, if they could find some in the landfills left behind by the house demolitions. By way of compensation it was decided that, despite Frank's protests over a lack of continuity, they would add more drama to their look by displaying some family coats of arms on their faces, found on the internet and projected from small addendums to their implants, stuck just under their hairlines.

The clanging of pots began as they were putting the final touches to their skin displays, the sound sharp against the unforgiving steel-coated garages and makeshift sheds that lined the street. Sira left Frank and Yanda to finish up, Frank standing on tiptoe to complete the design on his taller friend's face. She put her face to their cloudy window, squinted through the smoke-filled air and saw their neighbours peering out of their doors to watch others from further up the hill march past, banging wooden spoons and metal ladles against pans and bin lids. Each neighbour stepped forward tentatively at first, cautious of the outsiders walking past, before relaxing and joining the flow moving down the road.

With her eyes, she followed a toddler dressed head to toe in a home-made, seventeenth-century naval officer's uniform as he emerged from a door down the street. She gasped as she saw him break away from his pack and skip excitedly into the crowd. Before Sira could run out to grab him, an older person from his home pulled him back into line by one of the golden epaulettes stitched onto the shoulders of his stiff tunic.

Sira stepped backwards into the garage and sat on the corner of their couch, enjoying the adrenalin shot that was passing coldly through her veins. 'It's all happening. We need to get out there!' she asserted.

Yanda laughed as he played with the settings on Frank's face. 'You always get like this. You always think this is going to be the big one. The start of the big revolution!'

'Well, Yanda, one day it will be!' she snapped back, standing up to join the other marchers.

In response, Frank tutted loudly, frustrated that that Yanda would now be distracted from finishing their costumes. He was right. Yanda waved him away and took advantage of Sira's excitement to sidle up close to her and peer through the window himself.

After Yanda had taken a quick look and exchanged some encrypted messages with Sira, he pulled at a handle he had previously attached to the side of a small wardrobe. He scraped it along the concrete floor to reveal a doorway in the breeze blocks and corrugated iron that made up the walls of their garage. They all stuck their heads outside into the street to get a proper look.

'See?' whispered Sira, while pushing dozens of photos of the scene outside into the two boys' digital libraries.

'Yes, Sira. It's definitely getting busy,' replied Frank with a sigh. He was looking forward to getting out there, mainly to get some space from the Yanda and Sira show.

Turning back inside, they hurried through the last of their preparations before climbing out of the doorway, covering it up from the outside with a sheet of plywood. Like their neighbours, who they acknowledged with small nods, they shuffled slowly at first; then, buoyed by the atmosphere, they started marching in lockstep, sharing images of the cheap food they hoped to find on sale along the route.

As the crowd along the road became denser, a group of ten or so teens incited sneers and yells as they joked about, jostling the crowd as they performed a re-enactment of a grenade being lobbed between them. As each caught the home-made smoking ball, they yelled and threw it onwards to a friend. This caused a small panic amongst a Red Army-costumed brigade passing at the same moment. Assuming the grenade was real, they began yelling in fear until one of the teenagers, as part the act, leapt on the grenade just before it released a thick cloud of smoke that billowed out from beneath him and mixed into the smog hanging above.

As the boy got back to his feet, hoping for applause, one of the Red Army soldiers punched him in the face before stepping back into the safety of his own gang. Sira sent a laughing face to her friends with the text: '*Too early for all that. Everyone clearly hungry!*'

Frank laughed loudly, enjoying the failure of the precocious boys.

'Don't, Frank. Keep silent or you'll get us punched too,' ordered Sira in the authoritarian tone she had been developing gradually in the months since they had all decided to leave their official homes and move to the shanty.

'*Yeah, Frank! What kind of name is that for a weed like you, anyway?*' flashed across Frank's and his friends' eyes. The message was sent by a grenadier as he walked past them, sneering.

'*Who's got their bloody systems open?*' messaged Sira.

'Sorry, Sira,' said Yanda. 'Forgot to reset.'

'I think it's Frank you should be apologising to.'

'Sorry, Frank. You'll be alright, won't you, mate? But he does have a point!'

'I'm not sure about that,' Frank retorted as he threw a photo of Yanda masturbating into the trio's chat.

5

Yanda walked off ahead in embarrassment. He kept his distance as they marched down the road for the next twenty minutes, until he saw Frank was in danger of getting them into another altercation.

In a doorway to their right stood an old man, maybe seventy, wearing a greatcoat like theirs. But his was wrapped around a woman of similar age who he was either kissing or penetrating. His remaining strands of dyed black hair were slicked back in mock re-enactment of a popular image of wartime embrace.

Frank's eyes were locked in fascination, following their gyrating arthritic movements, until Yanda stepped in to block the view. 'I'm not sure they'd like you staring, mate.'

'I don't know. I think that's what they're doing it for.'

'I don't think you know why people do anything, Frank. And I think you're going to get us in trouble.'

'Fine. Just tell me what to do and I'll try and be normal,' Frank shot back sarcastically.

--

As the marchers got further from their homes, they were joined at each intersection by hundreds more revellers from other neighbourhoods. They became energised. Bags of broken biscuits, bread and nuts were passed around, presumably brought by those from more affluent streets. Screeching rockets shot upwards, creating rainbow-coloured swirling patterns in the cold, polluted air and returned echoes of the crowd's high-pierced squeals and bawdy cheers.

Looking down the road, the trio saw that the minor acts they had already witnessed were, as they hoped, a mere taster of what was to come. Bands of boys, girls, men and a scattering of women erupted into rehearsed shows. Makeshift canons fired by uniformed Ottomans competed with perfectly crafted production lines of boiler-suited characters and tank shells, alongside augmented reality projections of cavalry charging into and through olive-green generals.

--

6

Sira and Yanda were watching a parade cross the flow of marchers when Frank's hand lifted towards the Victorian roofline to their right. He was pointing at something that was bringing a gradual hush to the crowd. Security crackdowns had occurred during previous festivities and everyone had heard stories of marchers being slaughtered in the street.

A row of men, all in black with sophisticated weapons hanging from their shoulders, bounded softly along the tiled slopes and apexes. They were joined, fifty metres down the route, by colleagues on the roofs to their left. At the turn in the road, near the entrance to north west London's only remaining underground station, Sira gripped Yanda's arm tightly and said she had glimpsed, between gaps in the smog, gun tripods and sandbags being set up. Others had seen the weapons too and began to step slowly backwards, trapping the toes of those behind them under the heels of their boots, causing a wave of people to stumble and fall.

Pulling Yanda along, with Frank scurrying closely behind, Sira sought to get a better view. She pushed through the panicking crowd towards some steps that led up to an old shop front. From her elevated position, she saw the body of an adult lying motionless, stretched out across the pavement ahead of her. She messaged her friends to ask if they thought he was drunk or dead.

At that moment, a series of shots rang out, pumping with loud claps into the dense masses.

'Stop!' Yanda heard Frank scream, appreciating that his friend's cowardice had stepped in where his own could not. But as he and Sira turned around, they saw the fear in Frank's face replaced by wide-eyed pleasure and heard the crowd break into applause.

Everyone stared upwards to the roof of the tube station, as a large, heavy, cloth banner edged in gold braid was unfurled from the gun emplacements. It read: *The committee welcomes your neighbourhood to the winter Trafalgar Square extravaganza.* In front of it, on a platform slowly being raised by a forklift truck, stood four men in fake-bloodstained white shirts flanked by women in tight nurse's uniforms. They were enjoying their moment of fame.

'What did you think of it?' asked a slightly smug voice behind the trio.

They turned rapidly, stunned that a stranger was addressing them verbally without giving a text warning first. It was a tall, bald, muscular man in his early twenties wearing only a vest to protect him from the wintry air.

'Hi, my name is Captain,' he said, reaching out and grabbing Sira's hand to shake it.

'Oh, hi! It was fun, I guess,' replied Sira, pulling her hand away. 'But perhaps a bit too involved,' she added nervously. 'The day is supposed to be about us, isn't it?'

'I think today is about many things,' said Captain, staring at her. 'Just because you can see the injustice around us doesn't mean others aren't only here for fun. Anyway, I saw it all a little differently with the new plugin I'm using. You'll be able to see it tested at the Square. Some friends and I developed it. Hopefully I'll see you there.'

'Yes, maybe.' Sira paused, hoping something interesting could be coaxed out of her dry mouth. But it was too late; Captain had already moved forward into the crowd. He remained visible for a few seconds owing to his height before he disappeared into the underground station.

'That was a bit presumptuous. Why does he think he knows why we're here?' asked Yanda, irritated by Captain's intrusion.

Sira was distracted by her brief interaction with the stranger and did not reply.

Yanda persevered to get her attention. 'Before Captain turned up, you messaged about a dead body, Sira. You said you saw a dead body in the road, didn't you? I don't think that would be part of the show, not a dead person! Don't you think we should tell someone?'

Sira finally looked away from where Captain had disappeared and turned back towards the doorstep. 'Someone must have done something about it – it's been moved,' she said absent-mindedly, pointing to a group of young girls standing where the body had been. 'Come on, let's keep moving.'

'Ignore her, she's clearly in an odd mood,' scrolled across Yanda's eyes, sent by Frank.

Yanda responded with a raised eyebrows emoji and dropped back a little to let Sira take the lead down into the warmth of the tube station.

The ceramic floor and wall tiles were wet and slippery because of the steam rising from the throng of marchers that had preceded them. All but the youngest were stepping carefully, not wanting to fall and join the army of cripples that adorned the city's doorways and archways. Children, however, were exploiting their low centres of gravity to race downwards, knocking adults off balance as they went.

As the trio shuffled forward, they were flanked by an immaculately dressed quartet of genetically-impaired drummer boys, each clanging plastic and tin instruments while they swung their legs forward and around their sides owing to their fixed knees. To his friends' embarrassment, Frank abandoned caution and fell in line behind them, swinging his legs mockingly until an older man in the crowd whacked him disapprovingly around the head, silencing him for a moment.

When they reached the bottom of the steps, the air on the platform was thick with humidity and infused with the acidic smell of unwashed flesh. Heavy coats and tunics were peeled off, including Sira's and her friends, uncovering stained and worn vests and shirts, as well as ornate undergarments in the case of the few wealthier revellers who had chosen to slum it with the masses. The bright, shiny faces of the better off stood out in the darkness of the tunnels; they were protected from the London smog by layers of precision-engineered oils and reflective plastics. Perhaps Captain was right, Sira thought: some people were only here for the entertainment.

Sira looked at the rich women's sculpted lips, noses, eyes and necks, angry that they were wasting the country's last remaining resources on vanity, while simultaneously jealous that they had the ability to design and polish their own appearance. The wealthy men who stood alongside them were animated and engaged in conversation, shielding their partners from the crowd. She imagined them living in decorated rooms, or even having private homes to themselves, surrounded by healthy children who had been reared to look after their parents in old age in exchange for comfortable early lives.

9

Yanda and Frank squeezed onto the platform behind her. A freight wagon, comprised of flatbed trailers each with at least three black-uniformed security personnel standing on it, rolled into the station.

Yanda put his hand hopefully on Sira's bare arm, but she shrugged it off angrily and remarked pointedly about how handsome the guards were.

'I didn't know there were so many of them,' said Frank, trying to diffuse the tension that Yanda had created. 'And this is just one neighbourhood. Imagine if every train in the city is secured like this! They must have brought soldiers in from right across the country.'

'When the guards performed their act outside, do you think they were spying on us?' asked Yanda.

'They weren't really guards,' mocked Frank. 'That was the point. It was an act, imbecile! Nobody was really shot!'

Yanda turned to look at him. 'Yes, I know they were acting Frank,' he said, exasperated. 'But my implant was – well, somewhere it shouldn't have been and it read their serial numbers. Either they had stolen real uniforms or numbers, which is unlikely, or they were a genuine elite force. I think if they'd seen what they wanted, they would have fired live rounds. And I think that's why there are so many guards on the train. They're looking for something.'

'Interesting that you kept this to yourself, Yanda, rather than warning us earlier. It's a bit late to turn back now!' sneered Sira, her eyes still locked on the guards.

'I didn't say they were coming for us. I don't think they'd turn out in such force for a few illegal hackers.'

'You think you know everything we're up to, Yanda? That's a bit arrogant!' shouted Sira over the screeching brakes of the train as it pulled to a halt. 'You think Frank and I aren't doing anything interesting that we haven't told you about? Things the police could be interested in? You have no idea what networks I'm involved in when I'm not trapped down here with you!'

Before the two boys could digest her anger, she pulled herself onto a flatbed and tapped one of the young guards on the arm, inches away from where his rifle was resting.

'Excuse me, sir,' she said with a coy smile, breathing deeply in a manner that she'd seen older women do with men in films. 'Do you know why there is so much security today?'

Yanda hooked his hand around Frank's arm and pulled him back a pace, his face frozen in a false grin.

'I'm sorry, miss, we aren't supposed to say. Have you seen something suspicious?'

'Well, it depends what you mean by suspicious, sir.' Sira pressed on, turning Yanda's false smile into a genuine grimace. 'I've seen a lot more security than I thought existed in the city. That's suspicious, isn't? Especially on a day of entertainment.'

'We are here for your safety, young lady. Not all the other young ladies here today are as community-minded as you,' he mumbled, lifting his eyes from her chest to her face and tilting his gun slightly.

'What's she playing at?' Yanda messaged Frank.

'She's making a point, that she can put you in danger too. I'll be over here,' Frank replied, shaking free Yanda's hand before pushing his way along the wagon to sit down at the end and let his legs hang over the coupling.

After a few minutes of their journey had passed in silence, Yanda shared a funny video of a London government official urinating into the mouth of a dog. They had all seen the clip before, but Yanda had put it to a soundtrack of canned laughter and had the camera zooming in and out of the dog's confused eyes. Frank and Sira shared smile stickers in response and then regrouped, putting the guard incident behind them.

--

Once the train stopped, the crowd climbed down from the flatbeds and up the steps of Green Park station. Each reveller could feel the slippery crunch of paper streamers and food cartons underfoot, piled so densely in some places that they found it difficult to walk without gripping the handrail, forcing them into an unsteady, shuffling line.

While Frank unnecessarily reminded his friends that Piccadilly, with its precincts, courtyards, park and grand arches, had once been a Mecca for the world's consumers, Sira

11

adjusted her implant to take account of the rubbish and the fact that the pavement was actually a foot lower than her device assumed. She shared the data openly with the crowd to hasten their collective progress.

With their balance steadied, everyone pressed forward towards the pillared frontage of the Ritz, which jutted from manmade dunes of refuse and filth. As they passed the iron gates of Green Park, they sought to stay clear of the arms of the homeless that hung through them, picking at the rubbish and the occasional unguarded pocket.

Their first sight of Trafalgar Square was a dense riot of colours, shapes and sizes mixed with the odour of urine-damp straw that had been laid on the ground. They could see that microphones and other staging were being tweaked at the top of the steps to the National Gallery which loomed down on the costumed audience, many of whom were waving small rainbow flags with the cross of St George. The crowd was at least ten times that of recent events, and infectious waves of laughter and hysteria were spreading. The city was ready for its fix.

They moved as far forward as they could without being split up or impaled on one of the more elaborate costumes. Frank opened his small bag to dole out a few swigs of alcohol and a cigarette. Six months earlier they had never tasted moonshine but, since they'd set themselves up in their first garage, they had begun distilling it in steel barrels and selling it to grateful neighbours. Like them, these neighbours associated the illegal alcohol with fortitude and heroism because of a scene from *The Great Escape*, a famous World War Two film that had regained popularity in recent years. Similarly rolling tobacco, and one's ability to collect it from old stubs on the ground, had become a symbol of resilience amongst young Londoners. The trio had become adept at it.

Feeling a little lightheaded on a cocktail of ethanol and nicotine, Sira looked over the heads in front. A stocky, stern and physically assertive middle-aged man, dressed in the full official regalia of the governing class, had stepped up to a microphone.

'Welcome to the Square!' he bellowed in a thick Cockney accent.

The audience fell silent.

'Welcome to the Trafalgar Square extravaganza, a gift to the strivers, fighters and procreators. Today we celebrate all we have achieved in the face of hardship. We glory in our anger at those who abandoned their duties in the past, forcing us to find our strength. We have triumphed, and they will be banished to the fourth plinth!'

Horns and flashing lights hanging from the sides of the plinth came to life, drawing thousands of eyes towards it. A few seconds later, its red velvet shroud fell to the ground in perfectly timed theatricality, revealing a handful of elderly men and women. A couple of them were gripping walking frames for support.

'Have no fear, beautiful and strong London,' bellowed the speaker. 'These criminals before you are not your relatives. You are not their children, grandchildren or great-grandchildren. How do we know? Because they have no children! They spent their lives in perpetual hedonism, selling out our country in exchange for luxuries, turning our former greatness into parties, clothes, whores and houses. Before you, you see captains of criminality. They deserve to hear your pain.'

The crowd was consumed by hateful vitriol, letting out screams, curses and howls as the organisers played 'Help' by the Beatles, a popular music track for videos that mocked the liberal generations. The trio joined in, yelling and singing until their voices were hoarse.

After the main attraction was over and the forlorn figures from the plinth had been led away, the mass of bodies started to unpack from its dense form. Waves of prodding and pushing created fault lines, allowing friends to regroup and explore their surroundings.

'It's a bit of a nonsense, isn't it?' asserted Sira. Frank and Yanda both nodded while trying to steady themselves. Everyone knew the politician, whoever he was, was only trying to save his own skin. This was all a distraction while he and his colleagues failed to agree on anything drastic enough to dig the country out of its hole.

'Come on, let's check out the stands and get some food,' yelled Frank, marching off as soon as the crowd had cleared enough.

The first shack they came to near one of Trafalgar Square's giant lion's paws was selling Crimean war-protein fats, 'immune from rotting and perfect for keeping the heat in', according to the label on the tin.

Selling the tins of meat grease were two shivering girls dressed in stockings and stilettos, and covered in make-up. Their lips and breasts appearing to be just as much on sale as their fatty produce. Yanda was straining to keep his eyes away from their exposed flesh in an effort to prove his maturity to Sira, but Sira didn't notice as she was staring at them too. She had watched a vlog recently about girls being stolen from communal homes and having their faces and bodies reshaped for sale, so she was looking for signs of scarring.

The next stand was selling software patches for the three most common implants in circulation. A row of ageing computer monitors displayed what could be achieved in one's field of vision if these patches were downloaded. The augmented reality software ranged from age and sexuality calculators that would supposedly help you find your mate, to games that turned your surroundings into surreal chess boards or watercolours.

Edging away from Sira and Frank, Yanda joined a semicircle of boys in assorted tunics. They were watching a flashy demonstration of an augmented reality anti-crime app that positioned a number and colour above everyone in one's sight to indicate their threat level, based on their race, age, clothing and, for extra money, their comms data.

As she waited for Yanda to get bored, Sira felt a heavy hand fall on her shoulder. She jumped with shock, turned and was confronted by a tall, heavy-set man in his early thirties wearing a German SS-type leather jacket and gloves.

'Are you Sira?' he asked after a long pause, his square jaw releasing the sound without any sign of movement.

'Err, me, yes,' Sira stuttered, taking a step back from the six-foot mound of flesh and sinews that somehow knew her name. She sent panicked *'help'* messages to her friends. 'Why?

Who are you? Is that a costume, or are you security or something?' she asked with loud mocking cockiness, attempting to mask her fear. She emphasised the word 'security', hoping it would bring her friends to her side.

Without answering, the stranger reached forward and clamped his gloved fingers around her arm, burning her skin as he pulled at her through her coat.

'Hey, what do you want?' called the boy who was leading the software demonstration and had noticed what was happening. This finally alerted Yanda, who stepped out of the crowd and swung an ineffectual punch into the stranger's chest. He only succeeded in having his own arm grabbed as well.

'You're coming with me,' the man said firmly, dragging them both across the square while they yelled out for and messaged Frank.

As they moved through the crowd, strangers tutted and grumbled as their toes were trampled on and their backs shoved, but none came forward to help. Frank was nowhere to be seen.

Just as Sira was considering linking to the police, they came to a halt before a familiar face. 'Hi, Sira, how are you?' asked Captain.

'What the fuck is this? Why the fuck do you think you can do this to me and my friend?' she shouted, pointing at Yanda who was being held up by his forearm, his legs crumpled beneath him.

'Did Mr Woods ... force you?' Captain asked, sounding surprised.

'You asked me to bring her, Captain,' replied the giant, dropping Yanda to the pavement.

'I'm so sorry,' said Captain. 'I saw you across the crowd but I was in the middle of something, so I asked my friend to invite you to join us. Now, thinking about it...'

'Yes, think about it, you prick,' shouted Yanda as he stood up, his coat torn at the side from being dragged over the rough ground.

'Thinking about it, I asked him to "get you". But obviously I didn't mean that literally,' Captain said with an apologetic smile. 'I don't know what he was thinking. Listen, let me make it up to you.'

'Us you mean?' Yanda yelled.

'Oh, I don't think this is really for you, little boy.' Then, as Yanda went to throw a punch, Captain and Sira dissolved into the crowd.

Soho, London,
10ᵗʰ October 2016

'Is there a Jewish version of that?'

'Is there a Jewish version of that?'

Daniel was no longer listening to the presentation on the 'Fair Society', but instead was scrawling mocking phrases in the margins of his cheap notepad. To his left sat Lara, who looked just as bemused as he did, though less incredulous. Opposite, across the 'narrow waist' of the table as he liked to think of it, was the chief executive of the UK's most vocal Jewish community organisation. In truth, it barely spoke for north London's Jewish community, let alone those Jews in the country's more peripheral areas.

'This brings us to the equality bill,' the head of the British Jewish Board was saying. 'When it was first proposed, before we saw the bill itself, we were all united in our support.'

'All' being the twelve or so people around the table, Daniel thought.

'We all want to see anti-Semitic discourse treated as seriously as any other racist slurs, especially on university campuses.'

This was obvious to Lara, Daniel assumed. Why would organisations formed to represent and protect Jews not be pleased with legislation designed to protect them? But Lara had missed the previous six months of meetings and handwringing over whether more equality would help or threaten the community.

Furthermore, Lara had missed out on a lifetime of Judaism. He could see that, as a result, she was confused by the idea of people, often the same individuals, arguing both for and against change at the same time. She was that increasingly common feature of 'the table', a pro-Israeli political and community activist who supported Israel and the Jewish community because she felt it was the 'right thing to do' as opposed to being part of the community herself. This was largely a product of the great many years the right had been in power. For those with political interests who were not inclined to become Communists or Conservatives, the progressive fight for Israel had become a rare home for liberal centrists.

Heads nodded slowly as the chair, again, set out the issues. The minds of the group whirred as they considered that, while they were proud of Jewish liberalism, they were not keen on opening it to all and sundry. There was a growing consensus that there was a difference between *showing* the way and *being* the way.

Daniel had come into this area of lobbying, as he liked to think of it, not because he was Jewish (he was Jew-ish at best) but because a friend in a pro-Israel organisation had taken him in when he was desperately looking for a new job a few years earlier. It was a life-changing decision that had thrust him into a mysterious world, fetishised by anti-Semites and Jewophiles alike. At first, he had been nervous that his lack of a religious upbringing would mark him out as a fraud, but he soon realised that the organised Jewish community did not discuss Judaism at all. It preferred to focus on issues it broadly agreed on and to leave the religious stuff to the rabbis.

This was all new to Lara. Daniel, as a fellow non-religious, was keen to show her the ropes, and hopefully find himself someone who would appreciate his dark sense of humour. However, their first post-work quick drink had not gone smoothly. Lara had responded to Daniel's sarcastic comments with a deep earnestness that he feared was genuine. She had proceeded to lecture him on the desperate need in Europe for the promotion of liberty, democracy and an understanding of Jewish people's right to national self-determination. Daniel did not need convincing of this; it was what he had spent every working day doing for the last three years but, following his failed explanation of his 'Is there a Jewish version of that?' joke, he knew there was no way back, not that evening at least.

--

18

'Daniel, how are you?'

'I'm good, Geoffrey. Good to speak to you,' Daniel said in his most fake, over-friendly, Westminster-darling manner. It was a manner that he found hard not to adopt, even when talking to long-time work acquaintances, or 'friends' as the politicians liked to call them.

'I wondered if you were coming back to London this evening, and whether you wanted to have a chat?' Daniel continued.

'Well, I'm in the constituency now, heading back to London tomorrow. Fancy coming over to the house for some dinner with me and Julia?' Geoffrey offered.

Daniel and Geoffrey had known each other for almost all of Daniel's three-year tenure as a professional Zionist. When he was feeling out of the loop, Geoffrey was the person he turned to. Not that Geoffrey was particularly powerful; in fact, he had explained to Daniel many times that he did not want to change the world and preferred to keep his head down. He spent most of his time in Parliament chairing the industry and innovation committee which, in his eyes, enabled him to do his bit to improve policy and hold the government to account whilst keeping a healthy distance from his party's utopian leader.

For Daniel's purposes, this meant that while Geoffrey would never make a loud pro-Israel intervention in the House of Commons, he would usually be able to connect him with the right people. He was also very fond of Geoffrey's wife who, like his own mother, had left the Jewish community to marry out and sometimes acquiesced to be a sounding board for his own unresolvable confusion. For Geoffrey, helping Daniel was another one in the eye for the leadership, which entertained him no end.

--

The following evening, Daniel emerged from the tube. Pushing through the light drizzle and navigating around umbrella stands inconveniently thrust onto the pavement from corner shops, he gravitated towards the nearest off-license, a typically disorganised London affair. This was something about

19

the capital that Daniel, as an outsider, felt he would spend his life pondering. In Manchester, where he had grown up, one could immediately tell what an area would be like by glancing at its streets and houses. London was different. While the core of the metropolis demonstrated its political and economic power through towers of glass and steel, Zone 2 and beyond were aesthetically and demographically lawless. Wealthy and poor families alike hid behind equally shabby facades served by shabby shops selling essentials, nick-nacks and blue plastic bags, alongside curbs lined by rows of Chelsea tractors, revamped 1960s' Mini classics and disintegrating transit vans.

The Browns' street and house were no different, though significantly better adorned than most on the inside. Despite being an MP for the same West Midlands constituency for twenty years, Geoffrey had never become sufficiently fond of the place to warrant leaving London and so his and his wife Julia's house was an actual home. London was where he was from, where he had met Julia and where they had brought up their muddled but successful half-Jewish, half-not-Jewish children. And now that the children had moved out, their London home had become the perfect place to grow apart.

Daniel turned up to their front door armed with a cheap bottle of red and the hope of getting his latest gripes about Jewish community politics and the Labour party off his chest. Geoffrey was more than happy to accommodate him, much preferring to continue his Westminster conversations into the evening than spend any time pondering the real world.

'Good evening, Daniel. Lovely to see you,' Julia said with a smile on her attractive sixty-plus face. She pulled her boyish guest into a hug and took the blue carrier bag into the kitchen. Geoffrey and Daniel shook hands and followed her to where they were confident they would find some hummus and crisps to chat over.

'So, what's new?' bellowed Geoffrey, hoping for some complex minutia in which to entangle his mind. Daniel, eager to please, filled him and Julia in on the current Jewish community arguments and machinations, while Julia periodically slid dips and finger food onto the table and refilled their glasses too frequently.

20

Over the course of two bottles of wine, the trio vented their frustrations over Labour's unwillingness to engage intellectually with the problems of the Middle East, and Daniel's donors' equal unwillingness to put their feet into the shoes of the average non-Jewish MP. Daniel was getting particularly frustrated with the refrain: 'How can they not support Israel? Do they not know Hamas throws gays off buildings?', especially since this argument was usually deployed by conservative geriatrics with questionable views on sexual equality.

As with previous versions of the same evening, Julia began to take offence at Daniel's more coarse remarks; Geoffrey began to flick through his colleagues' Twitter feeds and other Westminster gossip sources, hoping to get angry and fired up over the latest non-issue, and Daniel drank, oblivious and enjoying the company.

Daniel had grown up in a similar home to the one that Geoffrey and Julia had created for their children: 'mixed race', argumentative, questioning and unrestrictive. However, in Daniel's case his parents had focused their energies not on nurturing but on pulling him both ways, arguing about religion and culture over every dinner as though the two subjects were mandatory. As he explained once to his therapist, he was always destined to be a little offensive, a little dismissive of what others cared about, and a little more likely to offend by conjuring up slurs like: 'Some Jews spend all their time crawling around in the gutter hunting for anti-Semitism,' the quip that had angered Julia that evening.

'So, honey, what's being re-Tweeted tonight by your favourite bully boys?' Julia asked loudly, hoping to bring Geoffrey's mind back into the room and to end Daniel's latest bout of self-loathing.

'Oh, he's said something daft again, something to do with blaming big businesses for not employing enough people, so his mates − or someone's mates − are piling in to shut down the conversation. I just want the argument over with before any of our partners get pissed off. I'm going to have to make some calls, I'm afraid.

'Daniel,' Geoffrey barked, ending the evening, 'let's meet up for a coffee.'

--

'What on earth are you and your wankers up to?' Tom had called at 7am to fire expletives at Geoffrey. For at least the first ten minutes, Geoffrey was completely bemused about what lay behind the anger until he heard 'fucking micro fucking systems!'

Micro-systems had been working with Geoffrey's committee on policy ideas to support innovation in universities; in a few weeks, they were due to sponsor a seminar which, for once, the media were interested in. Geoffrey had worked on it for months and had been told by the 'Dear Leader's' people on many occasions how supportive he was of the initiative. What Geoffrey had failed to do, he now realised, was get the boss's support for the programme on the record. Now, having listened to Tom's rant and then the radio, he knew it was all too late.

'Getting more British graduates into the sector is vital' said the guest speaker, muffled by the bedside lamp the radio was turned towards owing to Geoffrey's inability to operate it properly and reduce the brightness of the display. 'We are delighted to be working with the government on this.'

'Shit, shit, shit!' Julia heard Geoffrey yell through the shower water that was pounding the top of her head.

'Keep it down, will you? It's too early for all that. What's wrong?' she shouted back, poking her head around the shower screen.

'Everything, fucking everything. I'll see you later!' Grabbing his crumpled suit thrown over the wicker chair the night before, Geoffrey got partially and damply dressed and marched out of the door, downing a quick coffee from their machine on the way.

22

Switzerland,
10th February 2005

First sighting

Dr Finegold's manner was always liable to irritate the director of the facility, something Finegold knew and yet failed to avoid despite her best efforts. The director had explained to Finegold many times how the way in which she approached discussions on important matters gave the impression that she was trivialising the concerns and responsibilities of others, especially those who had to account for major budget decisions. Finegold also suspected that the director was irritated by her unkempt hair and mild obesity, taking both as further evidence of a lack of preparation and self-control. On this day, the director's reaction to her presence was no different.

'We're going to need about twenty more, as soon as possible.'

'Sit down, Doctor. I take it that you have drafted a business case and are asking me to do you a favour by reviewing it?'

Finegold knew her boss was being sarcastic, just as the director knew Finegold had not written anything resembling a formal proposal since she had joined CERN five years earlier.

She took the sides of the soft, leather armchair in her hands and gradually lowered herself into it, noting that, despite the contrast with the cheap wheelie chair she spent most of her days sitting on, she could not wait to get out of its comfort. The chair, famous throughout the organisation, had appeared in the stark breeze-block room when the director was first appointed. Finegold assumed its luxury served a dual purpose of highlighting the director's importance whilst infantilising her subjects by casting them in the roles of tired old fogies in search of a warm fire and a pair of slippers.

'I'm afraid I haven't had the time, Rebecca. This has been a very interesting week. Did you read the email I sent on

Tuesday? We're going to need about twenty more people. Good ones.'

'If that is where you would like to start, Doctor, please tell me more,' the director said tersely, clearing agitated by being addressed by her first name.

Finegold took a deep breath and resigned herself to attempting to justify her efforts to achieve CERN's core mission to a manager who, she believed, should be supporting her, not demanding she slotted herself into a predefined template. She took a printed copy of the email from her corduroy jacket pocket and unfolded it onto the director's desk.

'I'm sorry that I haven't come to you with a full proposal.' Finegold attempted to smile with her eyes whilst biting her lip to replace mental with physical pain. 'I would, however, like to discuss something important with you,' she continued slowly, 'because I think we will need more resources, at least in the short term, to capitalise on this opportunity.'

'Yes, Doctor, that's where we started. And yes, I did receive your email but I would be lying if I thought it was clear enough to understand. You know my philosophy on this: if it isn't digestible by external audiences then it isn't worth writing.'

The director stared aggressively as she made this last comment, sending a shiver of sour panic on behalf of all humanity down the scientist's spine. Finegold took a moment to consider her options: 'get up, swear and slam door', or 'play the game', which she found difficult at the best of times. Either way, she knew that evening she would be adding 'renege again on previous promises to her husband by protesting about the inappropriateness of a PR manager holding the director's position'.

After a moment's pause, she fudged the decision by employing a little of each, trying to politely make her case while tapping the arms of her chair at an aggressive tempo. 'How about you come down with me and I show you?' invited Finegold, trying to appear hospitable.

'I have to say, Doctor, I find that quite insulting.'

Finegold paused, wondering whether the director, through her evil glare, had somehow extracted the thoughts from her brain. She sat perplexed and waited for her to continue.

'I have a very busy diary and I do not take kindly to people dropping things in it at the last minute. It is very unfair. Very inconsiderate.'

Finegold's brain tensed, so she took a deep breath and held it for a few seconds to calm her temper. 'I am very sorry, Director, but I am confident that you will understand the gravity of the situation down there if you see it for yourself. I apologise for the lack of notice, but we didn't plan to get such an interesting result at this time.' Sweat trickled between the cheeks of her bottom, which then relaxed a little in response to her successfully delivering a full sentence.

'Very well,' the director replied, grabbing a notepad and pen and marching out of the door before Finegold had the time to struggle out of the squishy chair.

The lift took five full minutes to descend beneath the mountain, during which time the pair stood in silence. When the doors opened, they walked out onto a steel gantry that appeared to be identical in both directions. Finegold walked towards her lab with the director following, clearly uncomfortable not to be leading the way herself.

'We have done a lot of work on the control room since we reopened,' explained Finegold with a proud smile as she stopped outside one of numerous anonymous doors. She held it open to invite in the director. As they entered, she grabbed her tablet from the bench where she had left it.

'Yes, I know, Doctor. I sign the cheques, remember?'

Now they were in Finegold's domain, the director's barbed comments glanced off her lightly. She imaged them being captured by the collider and slung into oblivion.

'We now have much more accurate data collection, as well as better imaging software to show us what is going on in a way that our eyes can interpret quickly. This was going perfectly until Tuesday, when we got this.' Finegold pointed to a cluster of colours on the tablet screen. 'We have done two cycles since and have had perfectly normal readings, so we hoped that this reading was a sensor glitch. However, the same image was produced by the backup system.'

Finegold paused for a few seconds to explain what was on the screen. 'What we are looking at across the centre of the image is the collision. You can see the familiar streams of energy coming off in every direction. However, if you look closely you can see that this stream of energy disappears,' Finegold tapped the tablet about an inch beyond the epicentre of the collision 'and then reappears here.' She pointed at a gap in the stream that was about one centimetre long, before walking further into her laboratory.

The director nodded and followed Finegold towards her workstation, at which point she was distracted by the mess. Disposable plastic water cups and a hairy, overweight colleague competed for attention with the world's most sophisticated apparatus.

'OK, cut to the chase Finegold,' she snapped. 'What do you think this is? You've clearly got a theory! Some kind of sensor blind spot? Because if it is, we're going to have to control this news very carefully after all the money we've spent on the upgrade!'

'No, it isn't that. We have tested that Director. But we do have a theory and, whilst PR isn't my area, I believe we are going to have to be much more careful in the way we explain this to people than if it were a technical error.'

Finegold turned to her colleague. 'Phil, play the CCTV film of this room at the moment we ran this collision.'

The director stood her ground, rather than following Finegold to the monitors. 'Doctor, is this going to take much longer? Perhaps you could send me an explanation by email? I have a conference call in thirty minutes that I was hoping to prepare for.'

'This won't take much longer. Please, come and look at this screen. It is CCTV footage on a loop.' The director walked to the bank of screens and the pair stood next to each other watching. In the footage, Dr Finegold and Dr Franks sat at their stations. They turned to each other in shock before swivelling back to their starting positions.

'What exactly am I looking at, Doctor?' the director asked.

'Phil, please zoom in on the clock on the wall.'

Dr Franks replayed the footage. A moment before the two white coats in the film looked at each other, the second hand on the clock on the wall jittered and ticked one second back.

26

'Did you see it, Director? I must have watched this nearly a hundred times and it is unmistakeable.'

'I don't understand. Are you telling me that the reason why you and Doctor, um, Franks look at each other in this film is because you saw the wall clock flicker? I don't see how. You aren't looking at the clock.'

'Correct, Director,' replied Dr Franks excitedly. 'We didn't see the flicker on the wall, we saw it on our screens.'

'Phil,' Finegold declared theatrically, 'please zoom in on our screen.'

The film replayed. While there was some light glare on the screen in the footage, the director could see the digital clock pause and then go one second back before continuing as usual.

'You think the two are related, Doctor? The gap in the energy from the collision you showed me and this flicker in the clocks?'

'Yes – and there was no gap in the collision.'

'Pardon?' The director stood tall and took a step towards Finegold. 'Are you trying to confuse me? This doesn't seem like a very scientific approach, Doctor. Please just give me the information straight.'

'Sorry,' said Finegold, genuinely this time. 'I'm simply trying to take you through this as close as I can to the way Dr Franks and I experienced it. Phil, please bring up four images on the screens. Top-left, the collision that's on my tablet; top-right, the collision captured by the back-up system; bottom left, the collision captured from the other side of the array; bottom right, the collision captured from the other side of the array with the back-up system.'

'Yes, boss.'

The images appeared. The director could see that those on the right-hand screens were identical to those on the left, and those on the bottom screens were a mirror image of those on top with the shapes and colours in reverse. However, looking more closely at the bottom screens, she could also see there was no gap in the coloured bars spreading out from the collision. 'I see, Doctor. What is your theory?'

'Something was in the collider; something that wasn't in there before or afterwards. All the same, it was a physical object that created a tiny barrier between the collision and the sensors on one side. The collision happened as usual, which we can see from the bottom images, but something got between the collision and sensors on this side. Whatever that thing was, it also did something to our clocks.'

'Any ideas what that thing was?'

'Yes, a wormhole,' Finegold explained proudly.

'What?' The director's intensity flicked back to anger and she slammed her hand on the desk. 'I thought that the black hole theory was debunked. We spent hours on this, Finegold, and we agreed it was over!'

The doctor took a step back out of genuine fear, and Dr Franks turned his chair to pretend to start working on something else.

'No, I'm afraid not. We,' Finegold stuttered, 'we debunked it in the media, but it is true. It is simply that there is no danger to the public of a microscopic black hole or wormhole appearing in the collider for a fraction of a second. What we have never considered or, as far as I am aware no one has ever considered, is that in that split second when a wormhole could appear, we could also establish a link – a visual link – to something … well, more interesting. What I mean is, when we performed the experiment, we didn't see the wormhole, we saw something on the other side of it. A glimpse of an object somewhere else in the universe. More accurately, for a fraction of a second something that is normally elsewhere in the universe was right here in our mountain. That is what is obscuring these images.'

The director laughed nervously through a grimace, pulled out her phone and began typing.

'For some reason, it also affected our clocks,' Finegold continued.

The director gave another nervous laugh and continued tapping away furiously at her phone.

'I have checked, and it affected every clock down here but there is no record of it occurring anywhere else on the planet,' said Finegold. 'It just happened here. When I went home that evening, my watch was one second behind the clock on my computer, but when I came back on Wednesday the two clocks had evened themselves out. That means that after the event the seconds down here became momentarily shorter, compressed, until they synched up with the rest of the planet.'

'OK, I'm leaving for my call in five minutes,' declared the director, finally glancing up from her phone. 'You came up to ask me for money. You and Doctor Franks are obviously going to have to put together a formal proposal in the usual way – but, quickly please. Explain what you think should be done.'

'Right, um. First things first, we need to repeat the experiment. The first goal would be to prove this thing exists. Maybe then we can consider what it is. Whatever we are glimpsing seems to be able to disrupt time, so there will be a lot of interest. However, as I said, we need to repeat the experiment and then maybe see if we can repeat it consistently. My view is that we don't want to cause a big fuss at this stage, not until we can show what we have and that it can't be pulled apart. If we get that far, all the money that has been poured into CERN will have been worth it, irrespective of anything else going on down here.'

Finegold paused, then continued. 'To ensure we don't cause a fuss, I don't think we should consider pulling anyone else off their projects. It would arouse too much suspicion. Since the upgrade, we have the lab space for a new independent team, so I think we should use one. That means paying to attract twenty or so of the best scientists from around the world to work under Dr Franks and me. No one else at CERN needs to know about this. We can even be careful about what we tell the new recruits at first. No need to talk about worm holes just yet, just gaps in readings.'

'Fine. I think you've convinced me,' the director said. 'Put it in a proposal for the board. You can present it yourself, Finegold. Now, which way to that lift?' She turned and marched back through the lab before disappearing into the corridor.

Finegold sat down on her barely cushioned chair and enjoyed its simplicity. She knew the director was angry because she was scared. She also knew that, once the director had got her head around it and spun the news angles, she would be delighted.

Lincoln, East Midlands, 17th April 1985

In-patient

The pressure had begun to build again around James's lower neck, pulling up towards the base of his skull. The pain had started in the early afternoon and now, with the sun fading between the cracks of the curtains, he imagined that its heat would soon burst through his head, leaving his self-loathing brain cells splattered across the arms of Dave's cream sofa.

He took some more codeine, downed a pint of warm tap water and arched his thin neck over the end of the sofa, attempting to cut off the supply of blood to his head. It would be dark soon, that might help, he thought to himself.

During waking moments, James had picked at the three different left-over curries from the night before, their foil containers neatly lined up alongside him on the floor so they could be reached with a single swing of his right arm across his body and down to the ash-stained carpet. The food was not helping his migraine. Sometimes it helped, but not today; nor did the water, or the gloomy light made orange and brown by Dave's curtains. Only time would tell whether this spell would pass or if he would continue to deal with it on this sofa or on the plastic bus perch at the nearby bus stop, armed with his sleeping bag and a pocket of worn socks, if Dave finally threw him out.

Dave had taken in James accidentally, in the same manner that all of James's friends had given him places to exist over the years since they left high school. Four nights previously, he had found himself in a relatively upbeat mood, free of headaches and nausea, and armed with some cash, some weed and a bottle of vodka after his disability payment had come through. It was Dave who James had decided to share this moment with. He knew that his oldest and most reliable friend would likely be at home and not, unlike many of James's newer acquaintances, sitting in a grimy pub or eating sugary supermarket sponge cakes on the bench outside the old cinema. No, James wanted a civilised evening of good conversation, getting gently spaced out and watching rented horror films; that made Dave the only sensible choice.

The plan had worked. Dave had told James about his recent promotion at work – he was now in charge of a small, three-person team at one of the call centres at the business park – and that he was finally going to move out of this tiny old flat and find somewhere with exposed beams and perhaps a small balcony. He was also going to ask his girlfriend to move in with him.

Following a few joints, the conversation moved to slagging off old school 'friends', and then to pointless questions about religion, politics and when they had last seen their parents. Dave waxed lyrical on this last topic, expressing guilt that he only spoke to his mother once a week at the most, and that this was due more often than not to his mother calling him. James, on the other hand saw, or more accurately argued, with his parents a few times a week. He skirted over the fact that he had last seen his mother two days earlier when he was checking out, or being discharged as the nurses insisted on calling it, from a twenty-four-hour stay in the local psychiatric ward.

Dave and James did not speak about this. James knew that Dave knew about his hospital stays and other crises and he suspected rightly that his friend was bored with hearing about them. So instead, James pretended that his last few days had been occupied by his growing desire for the girl in the local sandwich shop. She was hot, James had noticed that, though not enough that he cared. However, it was always nice to tread the boards and pretend to be normal once in a while.

The pair eventually crawled to their respective beds. Dave had offered James a place to stay and was kind enough not to mention the sleeping bag that James had arrived with.

The best part of a week later, still lying on the sofa, James was pretty sure that Dave regretted this act of generosity. Experience is always worse than foresight; if this were true for the positive things in life, it was doubly so for life's ordeals.

James knew that he was intolerable, but he had never cared sufficiently to do anything about it – not for the sake of others, anyway. He cared about himself, about 'getting better', whatever that meant, but that was all part of his self-loathing. It was not that he was a bad person but, given that he spent ninety percent of his prescription-drug-addled mental faculties thinking about feeling better, there was very little left for anyone else, for listening, for genuine friendship. There was certainly nothing left for productive relationships. Thinking about women did not impact upon his desires, it only made him more anxious about his state.

'Come on, get up,' Dave called out from the front door, which had just slammed shut.

The sound of the crashing wood pushed pain straight through the back of James's eyes like a nail gun. He smelled cordite. His skull was a vessel of trapped exhaust fumes.

'Come on, get up, James.' Dave was leaning over him, the paper-globe lamp shade above now emitting white searing light. He was holding two paracetamols, a mug of water and a banana.

'Have this. Your mum's coming over.'

Dave had clearly had enough, James thought to himself. He must have been stewing over the problem all day, if not all yesterday as well. 'My mum? What's she going to do? I'm alright, mate. I'm alright.'

'James,' Dave said mockingly, 'you need help. I know you always need some help, but I haven't seen you like this in a while. Get up. Eat this.'

The banana, now peeled and pungent, was placed in James's hand.

James's thoughts moved on to his mother as he tried to predict her moves. The high-pitched voice would come first, then the stern look and the talk of fresh air, shortly followed by something exasperated about how stressful work has been.

James rejected the pills, for fear of overdose, ate the banana, downed the water and got up. As he stood, the sleeping bag slowly peeled away from the sweat on his pale legs.

--

32

Sitting in the back of his mum's car, letting her lecture about not abusing friendships wash over him, James placed his cheek against the cold glass of the window for some relief. 'Where we going?'

'What?' his mother replied tersely, trying but failing to hide her anger.

'Where are we going?' James repeated.

'You're in charge James. You always are,' she hissed.

'Am I supposed to know that means? I was fine where I was.'

'You made your friend take you in. You made him look after you when you didn't leave. And now you're making me take you to the hospital. And now, you're still thinking of yourself!'

Her voice burned through his brain like a laser, heating his skull until he couldn't help letting out a scream of agony, causing his mum to swerve the car a little. He continued to yell and bang his head on the window long after the initial urge had passed.

'Finished, James? Well, we're still going to the hospital.'

He watched his mother aggressively rearranging the layers of wool and silk she was wrapped in, each tug at her scarf and jumper making the car wobble in the road. He knew she had not forgiven him for missing his dad's birthday dinner and then phoning during it to scream at her. James's dad was not angry, he didn't care about such things, but his mother had decided that this was symbolic, 'the final straw' as she put it, as she always put it.

It was their first fight over this that had pushed James into his most recent hospital stay and now he was going back to be put in the NHS-funded naughty room for undeveloped adults. The doctors wanted him to stay there all the time, so they were perfectly happy to be at his mother's beck and call.

At least he could get some proper painkillers, he thought, as the car swung his stomach around the fifth mini roundabout in the sprawling, badly-designed NHS complex.

--

33

Dr Pilkins, a tall, plain man, dressed in dull olive green, was waiting at the curb outside the reception when their car pulled up. Mrs Benson stayed put, tightly gripping the steering wheel while James pulled himself out. Dr Pilkins turned his head slightly to almost look at him, saving most of his half smile for no one in particular, or maybe for himself.

'Do you know what she is upset about?' he asked of the world, or maybe James.

'Who?'

'Your mother,' replied Dr Pilkins in a smooth, calm voice, a voice James imagined psychiatrists were taught in training, to dampen both patients' and doctors' nerves.

'I am a massive irritation, I guess.'

'I think she wants you to be happy,' said Pilkins. 'I think she wants you to feel better and learn to be more positive about life. Come with me.'

Before James could retrieve his bag from the boot of the car, the doctor had padded off smoothly into the hospital. James turned to look at his mother to share a smile over Pilkin's aloof behaviour, but she continued to ignore him.

He took his bag from the boot and she drove away.

--

'Mr Benson, it's time for your appointment with Dr Pilkins.' The nurse's shrill voice cut through his head, so he tried to drag his consciousness deeper inside himself to hide from it. He mumbled that he had only just seen the doctor.

'Mr Benson, rise and shine!' she repeated.

Before peeling back his eyelids James could tell that, once he did, the morning sun and intense joviality of the nurse would burn through him. This was one of his least favourite things about hospital: being woken at 6am with bright lights and enthusiastic clangs of metal, corn flakes and shouting.

'Mr Benson, I'm going to sit you up.'

Before he could take in enough breath to exhale a sound of protest, he was wrenched upright by the grinning, shouting nurse who was operating him like an adjustable car seat. 'That was yesterday Mr Benson,' she explained, having apparently heard his protest. 'While you're here, you will see the doctor every morning. You're first on the list. Come on, get up.'

'But it's early. Surely he isn't here yet,' James forced out from the dry tunnel of his throat.

'It's a new idea, Mr Benson. Speak to you when you're fresh and alert and before you've dived into another one of your stupors. Come on!'

Westminster, London, 12ᵗʰ October 2016

Shared interests

Standing on the tube squeezed between enviably bright-looking young people and staring longingly like a teenager himself at the model in the hair advert, Geoffrey thought about how these few minutes without phone reception would probably be the best of his day. These were exactly the sorts of days he hated, all the more for knowing that these were the days Tom and his fellow travellers loved: full of punitive aggression.

Resisting his brain's attempts to fire up, he gazed deep into the model's chest as though it were a magic-eye picture that would soon reveal its hidden truth. But, just as her patina seemed at its most willing, the train doors jerked open and he was unfurled with the crowd onto the platform and onwards to the escalators of the imposing towers of Westminster station. His phone buzzed in his pocket as soon as he reached the top. He pulled it out and, on seeing who it was, bounded up the steps onto the street to take the call rather than disappearing down the exclusive tunnel into the Parliamentary estate. 'Nice of you to call, Jane. What happened?'

'You've become my trusted adviser, Geoffrey, and I'm not used to getting attention from political journalists,' she responded cheerily.

Geoffrey clung to the edge of the street, trying to avoid the urge to leap in front of a bus or even a bicycle. He briefly replaced the sound of her voice with the white noise of the outside world.

'Are you there?' She sounded calm, as though nothing had happened. He tried to emulate her bouncy tone, telling her that he was busy and they would catch up another time. It did not work. She eventually demanded answers and he found himself pacing up and down Westminster Bridge Road trying to hide his increasingly red face as he aggressively explained that Micro Systems could not both be the main voice in his independent select committee report and have its CEO become a government tsar.

When he could tell that he would not get an apology, he ended the call. He looked up to see he had developed an audience of free-newspaper hawkers and uniformed pupils from the nearby private school. He turned away just in time to prevent the phone cameras capturing his scowl.

--

Geoffrey strolled into Tom's office, half greeting and half ignoring the latest of his vaguely attractive underage interns. Tom was on the phone, clenching it between the two milky rolls of fat of his cheek and a cheap off-the-rack suit. Geoffrey received a mild nod and half smile from Tom, who continued his inane phone conversation about some football match for an agitating length of time before finally hanging up.

'Geoffrey, how's the family?' It was such a vacuous question that Geoffrey could not resist asking Tom how his wife was, knowing full well that the *Mail* was correct in its assertion that she was fucking someone else, someone slimmer. As was Tom.

'Right, let's get straight to the problem, shall we?' Tom snarled, abruptly changing his mood for effect. 'Your fucking committee is being sponsored by the fucking Tories, right?'

'No, Tom, it isn't. It is a cross-party committee and we're running a regular inquiry, taking advice from a number of different organisations as usual. Some of them have been generous enough to introduce our colleagues to small, sanitised and grateful sections of the real world.' He felt ashamed to be talking down the plans that he and his clerk – mainly his clerk – had worked on so hard. But, after rapidly procuring advice from his increasingly small circle of politically savvy friends, he realised that saving his chairmanship meant he was going to have to back-pedal on his ambitions, not for the first time in his career. His caffeine-soaked prostate pulsed beneath him, sharing his irritation.

Bringing people together around him was what Geoffrey was in politics for. It was what he was good at and why he had spent five election campaigns walking through wind and rain, and if he were to admit it to himself, some sun as well. While some climbed the greasy pole, or flesh totem pole as Geoffrey saw it, he largely sought to avoid the fight and create his own rational universe to play in, full of fascinating 'strangers' as they were known in the Commons. This was Geoffrey's revolution, his ideology and, if it did not sound too pompous, his purpose. While others obsessed over where they sat in the stale broad church, his church stayed fresh and fluid.

If he could be located within a section of the party, it would be the 'new right' if that term meant anything to anyone anymore. He knew which way to fall when the big decisions were being made but, given his modus operandi, he was rarely drawn into internecine warfare with the utopian north-London leadership, or any other faction. He was also aware that his younger self would have been horrified that his left-wing student activism had given way to plodding pragmatism; however, he was wholly confident that he was in the right now and that, even at the time of his maiden speech, he used to be embarrassingly wrong.

But what next? Geoffrey pondered as he walked away from Tom's office and through Portcullis House, the Palace of Westminster's hub of activity and inertia in equal measure. Today, it was busy, populated by Geoffrey's tribe: MPs fuelled by meandering conversations and minor expenditures of campaign groups, colleagues and trades unions. Seeing these creatures in the large glass atrium, ironically designed to resemble a bubble, sparked one of Geoffrey's repetitive internal debates. He was well past the time of life for conjuring up original thoughts but he still enjoyed the next best option: fitting whatever was in front of him into one of his preconceived ideas.

He found himself musing on the idea that the politics that he and his generation had created were decades ahead of today's social-media milieu. Social media had sped everything up, allowing like-minded people to bounce off each other, spitting out the occasional cackle at whoever they had decided to team up against. Beyond its speed, there was nothing new or helpful about it. In contrast, the world he and his fellow baby boomers had created was one of crossing paths and mutual dependency. Whilst the highly curated world of social media resembled getting to know someone in profile, like men glancing at each other at the urinal, his generation had created real sharing, like swapping wives with your neighbour after a dinner party.

His eyes fell upon one of the large steel girders, which he imagined to be groaning under the weight of the building's self-belief, and saw his small, smooth-faced friend pushing his way through from the outside. Daniel kept his own hours so was probably only just arriving at 'work', after a long relaxing lie-in and no career-crushing arguments. But he knew Daniel had value. If you had a chat with a children's charity, the conversation would be about just that: children. Even if it strayed beyond this, it would rarely get further than the stale operations of your constituency's Citizens Advice Bureau. Daniel might give you his biased analysis of the Middle East, but he was just at adept at sharing the latest rumours from the world of political high-flyers and donors.

--

Daniel had not had an easy morning and he was entering the bubble in the hope that Geoffrey could offer his ego a pick-me-up. He was in the middle of planning his next delegation of MPs to Israel and was being pulled in ten different directions by his donors, the Israeli embassy and the politicians themselves. While he knew it was hopelessly naive, he was refusing to let go of his belief that it was the latter group's views which should matter most, especially since the others were consistently difficult and wrong. He had realised very early on in his job that if you want to explain Israel to a Brit, you shouldn't ask an Israeli. But, of course, the Israelis disagreed.

'Do you think you'd have a coffee with him, then?' Daniel was holding a frozen half-smile, refusing to look away like a salesman seconds from clinching the deal.

'With whom?' Geoffrey murmured through barely moving chapped lips, opening the stage in the negotiation that was never remarked upon in the self-help books. In the split-second Daniel prepared to remind Geoffrey of the conversation they had just had, the MP had conjured up an irrelevant monologue.

'He's a shit, isn't he?' Geoffrey blurted out rhetorically. 'He does it for all the wrong reasons. What is the point in all that campaigning, all those meaningless speeches to ungrateful audiences, all those awkward attempts to persuade people of arguments you don't believe in yourself, if you aren't going to do anything with it?'

This was one of Geoffrey's most frequently repeated rants; it always focused at the outset on whoever had annoyed him last and yet always led to the same point: 'We can achieve something good here if we rein in the nonsense. People just want us to govern in a not totally incompetent manner. And when we're in Opposition, they couldn't care less what we think so we need to get OUT of opposition. It's not rocket science. Anyway, why should I listen to that fat fuck? He's never created anything more than a sound-bite in his whole life!'

Daniel waited patiently for the storm inside Geoffrey's head to subside. He spent the time wondering how the MP and Julia had survived so many years of marriage. Geoffrey was like this at home too, ranting about his supposedly worthless colleagues who, despite their supposed worthlessness, got a lot more praise and attention than he did.

'I thought that it might be a good for you to sit down with this tech investor guy who's joined the scene,' Daniel persevered, not yet willing to give up on his latest kernel of an idea for getting a normal job.

'Oh yes. The one who knows Lord Brillsbury. What's his name again?' asked Geoffrey, finally acquiescing to being spoon fed.

'David Kaye. I've been told he wants to work with a politician on some kind of focus group idea.'

'What's the idea? What idea does he want tested? Why doesn't he go to a polling company?' machine gunned Geoffrey in response.

40

'No, the new type of focus groups *is* the idea. I don't have the details but it's clever, apparently. Something about helping councils to work out what residents want or care about.'

'I'm not a councillor, Daniel. What are you talking about?' Geoffrey sneered while stirring another packet of sugar into his coffee, clanging the spoon loudly against the cup.

'I thought you might be able to help him,' Daniel continued. 'Introduce him to some companies that work in politics. He loves Israel, of course, so he may well rant at you about the failings of your dear leader but I can help you with all of that.'

Geoffrey looked half at Daniel and half through him to an exhibition in the corner of the building that was inviting MPs to test their hearts. He necked his coffee, got up and yelled, 'Send me his email.' As he stalked off in the direction of the palace, the division bell rang across the estate.

--

'It's awful what happened in Athens, isn't it?' Daniel was struggling to listen to his attractive long-time acquaintance in the designer blouse and leather trousers. He was terrible at these early-morning community meetings. He was terrible at mornings in general, owing to his habitual red-wine drinking with his housemates. His sense of inadequacy was amplified by being surrounded by bright, alive, often tee-total faces bobbing above their expensive suits.

'Yes, Athens, awful,' he murmured to Jenny as he refilled his coffee cup.

'Those poor children, all locked up like that,' she opined breezily.

Daniel had no idea what she was talking about, which the blank expression on his face soon gave away.

'The container full of dead children they found in the port, Daniel. Trafficked, probably. Apparently, they had started to eat each other.'

'Not kosher then?' he joked in reply and received a sharp look of disdain from his acquaintance. She moved on quickly to talk to someone more important, or tasteful.

'A chairman has two jobs, and one of them is starting on time, so take your seats.' Daniel was never quite sure whether this familiar booming voice was waking him up or numbing his senses. While he would usually hope for the latter, given that he was about to enter a ninety-minute adventure into a thick undergrowth of tedium, this week David was there so he had a reason to struggle to keep his mind intact until the end.

As he was sitting down, the chairman continued, 'Isaac, please update us on where we are with the equalities legislation issue.'

The question pierced Daniel's morality barometer like a hooligan smashing a school fire alarm but, in an effort to not remain agitated, he blanked out what he was hearing. He slouched into his seat so that the glass mineral water bottles and steel cafetière hid his face from most of the table, and yet he could still make eye contact with Lara.

He re-engaged when they moved onto a genuinely pressing topic: the danger posed to the country's links with Israel by the rapidly growing coalition of the hard left, concerned Christians and the socially conscious and secular middle-classes. All those around the table had noticed a change in recent years, with talk of diplomacy, international forums, peace summits and hard political choices giving way to references to occupation, massacred children, justice and international law.

The problem was well understood. The end of the Cold War, the end of apartheid, the end of the American dream and the rise of China had left a chunk of the political spectrum with nowhere else to go. The same people who, if born sixty years ago, would have danced for a positive future, now hunted in real life and online for the next popular single-issue campaign and conspiracy theory. Unfortunately for the world's Jews, the campaign they had chosen was the undermining and eventual dissolution of the world's only Jewish state.

But Daniel knew that, even though those around the table has accurately analysed the problem, they were the wrong people to stop it. They lacked the connections beyond their community. While some of their non-Jewish friends took a mild interest in Israel's democracy, they were not especially keen on its religion – or religion anywhere, for that matter. The same people who Daniel could encourage to assert that 'a state has the right to defend itself from terror attacks' were nowhere to be found when he needed someone to defend Israel's right to define its own character as Jewish. Increasingly, that was where the fight was. This did not stop the newcomer having a go.

The chairman introduced David Kaye as the chair of London's new Jewish Cultural Centre. Daniel grimaced. From what he'd heard about David, the man understood the tech sector but knew little about what made liberal politicos tick.

'Well, we just need to tell them how liberal Israel is, don't we?' David declared to the table, receiving a Mexican wave of nods in return. 'And tell people, like, how good it is on gay rights and women's rights – and how bad Iran is! Anyone against sanctions on Iran and in favour of boycotts of Israel needs to be reminded that they are aligning themselves with people who stone gay people to death, rather than people who are pro-gay rights.'

Daniel felt another piece of himself die as David's intervention had the desired effect of making everyone feel better by demonising their enemies. As Julia liked to remind him when he was at his most defensively Zionist, the problem was that even if getting stoned means very different things in Tel Aviv and Tehran you cannot convince people to admire a liberalism they cannot take part in themselves.

With this ticking over in Daniel's mind, he found himself sneering at David and was horrified to realise that David had noticed. At that moment the chair abruptly brought the meeting to a close, and Daniel had nowhere to hide.

David was making his way towards him, shaking hands as he went. With each step he took, Daniel felt more of a failure. But, when David reached him, he patted him affectionately on the shoulder and invited him for a coffee.

Somewhere in London,
13th December 2053

Reset me!

Sira was pushed from the vehicle through a pair of heavy double doors and into a large lobby. Its unfamiliarity served to drive her panic up another notch. Her eyes raced across marble-coated floor and walls and a ceiling taller than anything she had ever seen before. Cracked ornate lampshades and copper trimming that would have once glistened now resembled the dusty green algae of the banks of the Thames. She had seen black-and-white photos of dancing in lobbies like this, as well as hidden-camera videos of early twenty-first-century festivals of wealth, but she had been told that those old venues had been smashed up and the dust repackaged to create the communal homes that she now tried so hard to avoid.

To her left stood an imposing broad desk occupied by an obese teenage boy, his hanging stomach partially supported by a straining Russian sailor's uniform. As she got closer to him, she was overwhelmed by relief. She was sure that he would rise to save her, but he did not twitch as she was pushed past by her captors.

She had been flanked by the same two men since she was forced into the tank-like vehicle that had rolled up to her and Captain at the edge of Trafalgar Square. The men, now each with a hand on her back, guided her forcefully up a wide, red-carpeted staircase. At the top, they turned on to a long narrow corridor with dozens of steel doors on each side housed in ornate wooden frames. By the time they reached a pair of velvet curtains that were held slightly apart by thick golden ropes, Sira was shivering with fear and exhaustion.

She was shoved into another cavernous space in which sat two more smartly dressed young men wearing the same style of Russian naval uniform. Between them sat someone in a different uniform giving orders. She saw his lips move but her head and ears had filled with white noise. When she did not respond, she was shoved sharply in the back.

'Sira, come in,' he repeated. 'Can you hear me?'

She nodded.

'We are so glad you could join us in our, our – little home,' the man said in a thick, fake-sounding German accent. 'I have heard so much about you. Please, take a seat.'

Sira was forced down onto a spindly, gold-painted wooden chair with a red, embroidered seat. It creaked as she put her small weight upon it and she positioned herself awkwardly, her legs and stomach tense, fearing that it might give way.

'So, what do you think?' the young man said enthusiastically, gesturing to their surroundings. He was maybe seventeen or eighteen.

Sira tried to take in the room but the longer she sat in silence, the more her focus clung to her interrogator. Everything around him shaded into darkness. He resembled someone she had seen before but he was shorter and not as good looking or well dressed as the image in her mind.

'It's very, um, big,' she finally stuttered.

'Did you ever think you would be somewhere so luxurious?'

She didn't respond. Instead, she tried to regain control of her breathing.

'Please, try and relax. Just tell me what you think.'

Sweat formed on her face and trickled down, stinging her eyes. 'Could I leave if I wanted to?' she asked, her voice breaking a little.

'Very direct! I like that. Maybe you're as clever as we've heard.'

She was angry with herself for it, but his compliment gave her a boost. 'I imagine, decades ago, lots of London looked like this,' she said, trying to project calm. 'All our wealth traded in for shiny trinkets by rich people trying to force their hand on others. To dominate. Is that what you're doing?'

'I would like to let you into a little secret, Sira,' the young man replied. 'This place is even nicer than you think.'

'Are you going to answer my question?' she persevered. 'Can I leave? Or maybe I should just walk out of here and find out what happens?' A buzz of white noise flooded her brain again as she spat out the words.

The boy laughed. He pressed a button on his desk and pain shot through her eyes. When it subsided, she was surrounded by brightly polished stone walls and there was a new interrogator – Captain. He was now wearing an elaborate, medal-adorned uniform. The air had become intense with mildew.

He started speaking before she could focus. 'It has been tried before, as you will know. But it never looked realistic. People always knew they weren't in the real world. Before, to get the programme, the mirage, to work quickly enough, you had to prepare it long in advance, which basically defeated the purpose. But we have been working on that and, I think you'll agree, we have ironed out most of the flaws. Test me! The touch and smell don't work quite as well as the sight and sound, but they are still pretty good.'

'I don't understand. Are you...? Did we meet earlier today?'

'No. You met someone else earlier but, like me, he didn't actually look like that either, I'm afraid. This is just what someone I met a long time ago looked like, and I copied him. It was early days in the project, so it took us a while.'

Sira sat in silence.

'But I guess in some ways I was there earlier. I saw and heard everything. Anyway, in answer to your question, you can leave but I think it will be pretty difficult without a door.'

Sira turned to look over her shoulder and saw that the parted curtains she had walked through had vanished. They had been replaced by an array of old-fashioned viewing screens, incongruous against the ancient stone wall.

'I remember where the doorway is. I can still just walk through it,' she asserted.

'Try.'

Sira stood up from her chair, which now felt luxurious and robust. She stepped up to the wall of screens and tried to reach beyond them, but all she felt was glass and the heat of the cathode tubes. She ran her hand down them until she reached the floor. She crouched down and tried to hold back a growing nausea that was bubbling in her stomach and throat. 'I don't understand,' she murmured between heavy breaths. 'This is

46

augmented reality, right? I should be able to leave this room. This isn't real.'

The interrogator stood and walked over to her hunched body. Proudly, he tapped the hollow glass of one of the screens to produce a deep echo. 'Very good Sira. The long corridor is still out there, yes, but your brain can't cope with the idea that your sense of touch isn't behaving correctly. It won't let you do anything other than apply pressure to the glass. Push hard enough and you will break the screen. You won't really cut yourself but it will still hurt, I promise. Unless you switch off the system.'

She turned around on the rough floor so that she could no longer see him. 'So switch it off!'

'I can't, I'm afraid, Sira. I could hack into you again and do it for you but it would be easier if you switched it off. You will need the code, though. It is your system. I can still see the door, plain as day. I am just keeping a track on what you can see though a sub monitor replicated on that lower left screen.'

She squinted at the curved blue and red glowing glass. It was showing a never-ending blur of a single image, which bent left and right as she rocked her body. It was an infinity image coming from a camera or a lens, her own lens.

'Bring up your settings and turn off your device.'

Sira, too scared to argue back, followed his orders. When she attempted to turn off the new 'augmentation' option, she received an error message. Before she could speak, Captain or whoever he was continued.

'That error message is only shown to people who don't have the keycode installed. I do, which is why I can move around and see what I choose. I'll give you a keycode – not mine obviously –to show you what I mean. Treat this like an old-style school lesson. I'm showing you just enough for you to understand.'

Captain fixed his gaze on her and brought up a rapid succession of submenus on Sira's internal display too quickly for her to keep track of where they were heading. After a few seconds, a black passcode entry field appeared before her, which proceeded to fill up with hidden characters. Upon entering the code, two options appeared: *Revert to previous settings* and *Retain setting*. A third message, *Disable device*, was greyed out and inoperative.

Sira chose the first and, with a short flash through her temples, the scene faded back to its previous incarnation.

'Now, you've got two choices,' he explained, pacing around her while she sat on the floor. 'Leave now, and we will see you soon, perhaps with a little more force next time, or stay and help us. We are the fastest growing gang in the country, and you would be a great addition to the team. We've been following your skills since we hacked you days ago. Choose that option, and we can find another poor soul for the tough stuff, okay?'

'So, I can go?' she murmured, gripping the edge of the curtain.

'Well, I think I've explained this as best as I can, Sira. I can't explain more unless we build up some trust. But yes, if you want to make a bad choice, you can go.'

--

The light in the corridor groaned with an audible buzz as she spat out the last of her vomit on the thick red carpet and meandered unsteadily away from the interrogation room. Not knowing whether this was real or manipulation, she opted to continue without further thought.

As she turned the first corner an avalanche of blood flowed over her, leaving an iron taste on her tongue but without pushing her body or dislodging her feet. Once it had dripped from her face, she could see that the steel doors that flanked her were now ajar. From each doorway came a low flash of lights from something happening beyond her vision. She stood still for a while getting her breath back and listened for activity. She heard the faint laughter of a child perhaps, and pressed on.

At the end of the corridor, where the hotel lobby had once been, she now saw another heavy door with *EXIT* written on it in a large green typeface. Pushing aside her fear that her vision would continue to be manipulated even outside the building, she ran down the corridor, her arms outstretched, picturing the crumbling London she longed to see on the other side.

Sira's eyes sprung open as gravity took her body forward over a heavy plastic crate into which she had blindly forced her toe. She scraped the palm of her hands on a brick wall, preventing her from cracking her head, and fell to the ground in a heap. There was no sign of the guards or opulent building, just a narrow alleyway littered with refuse and a few dead rodents or birds, she could not tell which. It was raining but, given that her clothes had just snapped from being dry to soaked, she knew she had either spent more time outside than her delusion had implied or something about the blood was real.

She sat on the curb and absent-mindedly scratched at the spot behind her ear where she assumed the signal had gone in. Everyone Sira knew relied on some sort of implant to navigate the day and so, like her, had not been fully natural since their first school or nursery class when basic versions were inserted. There had always been agitations against them from fringe groups but until now she had dismissed the protestors as simply lacking the competence to protect themselves. The implant was how they all cheated, ate, laughed and sheltered, but hers had now been turned against her, and she no longer knew who owned her organs, her eyes, brain or limbs.

Her fingers played with her hair and she briefly imagined that, if she pulled the right clump of strands hard enough, the implant would slide out. She knew this was nonsense, of course. The device lived deep in the centre of her brain, bridging the hemispheres for 'the cleanest signal and the fastest path to your goals', as her brand's feed jingle went.

A soft haze surrounded her vision, bending the light inwards in gentle undulations of panic and fatigue. Before she passed out, she ran a chemical-inducer programme she had made to boost her dopamine levels and cause her to spring-up, clear and refreshed. Checking the time, she reassured herself that she had not been out of the real world for more than an hour. She pointed her GPS towards the garage. Her system warned her that the panic would return when the hormones had worn off so she should avoid uncommon situations.

Soho, London,
13th October 2016

What will £500K achieve?

'What do you know about networks?' David asked, stirring some sugar into his coffee.

'You mean the aggregating software I keep hearing about?' replied Daniel.

'True. Sorry, I've given my spiel a lot recently, but I'm still not sure you get my point.'

Daniel felt his stomach and face getting hot, reminding him that he was not built for the stress of the unknown. He looked around the busy, chintzy café and pretended to be casually confident.

'I saw you looking – how should I say – a little sceptical about what I said back there. And I liked that, Daniel. It's good to be sceptical, and you're right. Maybe I don't know what I'm talking about some of the time.'

Daniel tried to get out a pointless denial, but the businessman ploughed on.

'My expertise isn't really in community politics. I simply fund some projects so I get to sit around the table, and the chair wanted me to say something. I'm sure you understand.'

Daniel was unsure as to why such a senior figure was defending himself to him.

'As you know, my expertise is in networks, telecoms – investing in them, anyway. In my view Daniel, the reason that meeting we were in earlier is effective is because we are a small network, a very small network of people like you and me, representing a relatively tight network of British, or even just North London, Jews. And what makes a successful network? It is one that is small enough to produce results and just big enough to gather fresh ideas.'

Daniel decided that it was best to sit back and listen, rather than question the 'fresh ideas' assertion.

'Yes, we're not getting very far on Israel but that isn't really the product of our network. That's just a mess we will be cleaning up endlessly because of the failure of Israel's own internal network. But if you look at our own success, born from our own ideas, we definitely punch above our weight. Look at your other networks, Daniel. You're Labour, aren't you?'

'Yes,' he mumbled.

'Labour, and all political parties for that matter, fail. Why?'

Daniel tried to answer but was cut off before he could think of anything clever to say.

'Because they are too large, contain too much dead weight, not enough talent and not enough money, and they maintain ridiculously broad goals. Yes, they will continue to exist but the increasingly complexity of today's society and the speed of our technologies means that, when successes are achieved, they are not the product of the parties themselves but small groups of people that happen to operate within them. On top of that, the parties actually hamper such successful networks from forming, insisting that everyone follows the leader.

'Look at successful social media campaigns. They always have specific goals created by a small, tight network. They either achieve their goal or don't. Either way, the campaign comes to an end and lessons are taken forward. That's the future!'

Daniel was now ready to step in, feeling that David had sufficiently crossed into a world he understood. 'That's fascinating, David, but do you not think a country run by a succession of social media campaigns would lead to chaos? Parties do add some stability.'

David let out a hearty laugh and put his hands across his belly, for the first time resembling a middle-aged, slightly portly man, not the younger man that Daniel had so far taken him to be.

'Why have the baby boomers failed, Daniel?'

Daniel was confused by the apparent jump in the conversation; his mind was stuck on the baby boomers' wealth in pensions and property that they had built up that sucked up cash from both older and younger generations. That did not seem like failure.

'They have failed because, when asked the question you just asked, they gave up on their ideas and stuck to milking the status quo. And if you keep trying to draw value from the same structures, the foundations of those structures will dry and crumble. The question is, why do we continue with government when organic networks are more successful? The Jews are a case in point. We are torn between our homes in our host countries and our increasingly unimpressive home from home. Would we not be better off, like most groups, if our network was just that: a standalone network or an evolution of networks for interacting with others?'

Such a grandiose lecture was not what Daniel had expected from the tech investor, but he decided to stick with it. He pushed David every now and then with questions and concerns, while sipping his now-cold coffee.

Eventually David's phone buzzed. He thrust a brochure into Daniel's hands before dropping some cash on the table and bursting out onto the street.

Checking that there was nobody around that he knew, Daniel walked briskly to the toilets, shed his coat and jacket. He armed himself with the brochure while his bowels began to punish him for his early start, caffeine overdose and stress. Now, with his body relaxed over white porcelain and appreciative of the upmarket cafe David had chosen, he absorbed the literature. It was four sides of glossy A4 designed for potential investors. Although that was not him, he read it anyway.

What has been the most successful growth service in the last 30 years? it read, answering, *information technology and software innovation.* And *Why?* it asked, answering, *Skills and culture – because those working in these new networks want to, and know how to, network across cultures, languages and borders.*

The document went on to give facts and figures, arguing that the value in tech was not simply in innovation and utility, but that tech went on to encourage further innovation and value in a never-ending snowball. That is why, it argued, older, vital industries like transport, farming and energy were failing in terms of sustainability: not because they were 'old industries' but because they were incorrectly networked and too tied to outdated national, family, corporate and physical structures.

The product, it transpired, was a piece of software for taking social networks a step forward beyond the realms of campaigns and marketing and into real decision making. It argued that, in a world of increasingly innovative and self-reliant small actors, what was needed was a way to create dense and yet adaptable relationships, to take the self-employed and the small and medium-sized businesses beyond their confines and bring them together.

At the end of the final page, written in biro presumably by David, were the words: *I don't know politics. You do. What will £500K achieve? Work for me.*

Lincoln, East Midlands, 18th June 1985

Care in the community

'Welcome, Mr Benson. Have a seat. Please, pick up your tools.' Dr Pilkins pointed towards an A5 hardback notepad and biro on the arm of the chair. 'Now, how long have we known each other James?'

'Oh, um, maybe four years.'

'Six now. I think I know you quite well.'

'Yes, I guess.'

'Well, shall I tell you what I've learned.'

'Okay, but, this is—'

'A bit different?'

'Yes, you normally—'

'Say I shouldn't put words in your mouth?'

'Um, yes, exactly.'

'Well, this won't take long and we can go back to that any time. But, as I said, I think I know you quite well, James. I think – and tell me if I'm wrong – that you've been coming up with new and interesting things to tell me in recent months just to have something to say. Am I right?'

James shifted, trying not to fall back to sleep in the early morning sun coming through the slats in the blinds. 'Well, yes, sometimes.'

'What that tells me is that you've told me enough. Time for a change of tack. I'll do some speaking, and then we'll discuss my thoughts. Okay?'

James sat back into the grainy, rough armchair and traced his eyes across the doctor, mapping his face. He looked younger this morning, perhaps as a result of the sunlight bleaching his wrinkles and yellowing his grey hair. He wore his usual strange combination of a not-quite-formal shirt, covered by a black anorak, this time paired with some not-quite-smart jeans and brown loafers. He could wear anything he wanted, and yet he went for both a lack of style and a lack of comfort. He spoke in a similarly incongruous manner, breaking his sentences at odd moments to stare at James or give a few drops of water to one of the potted plants on the floor.

'Please, go ahead,' said James, happy to not have to mobilise his brain so early in the morning.

'You're a geography graduate, yes?'

'Yes.'

'Sorry, James, that's just how I speak when I'm doing the speaking. As I've told you before, you can assume my questions are rhetorical unless I say so, yes?'

James stayed tight lipped, hoping this was not a trick. He felt irritable and sleep deprived and wanted the session over as quickly as possible.

'Very good. You're a geography student. You brought me your third-year dissertation once, yes? I've got it here.' The doctor waved a thick spiral-bound document.

'In it, you write about the connection between people and the land. How culture is unique and tied to place and that, as a result, communities communicate in unique and subtle ways. You also say that, with a little direction from within, communities can collaborate to achieve a greater good even when they have not decided upon their larger goals. I see in the assessment that your lecturers did not find fault with this but hinted that they were uncomfortable with your suggestion that modern societies had lost some of this ability, both as a result of immigration and an attempt to replace informal communication with the restrictive rules needed to run a democracy, yes?

'Well, I think that sounds quite sensible. I suggest that the reason you are unwell is because you are more sensitive to this predicament. You want to communicate more organically, and you don't think people pick up on what you're saying. It is why you drink and take drugs because you feel that this language becomes more intuitive among a group of intoxicated people. Yes? And it is why, even when you most hate yourself, you insist on being the centre of attention and trying to control everyone around you. Yes?'

James wondered whether his doctor was the drunk one, but he still wanted to get out of the room rather than learn the answer.

'Sorry, that was a real question,' the doctor said eventually.

'I don't think it's unusual for people to try to influence others.'

The doctor stared at him, before continuing. 'I think you're evading the question, James. Anyway, I took the liberty of discussing your thesis with some colleagues. Do you mind?' Pilkins gently patted the dissertation, pausing as though he liked he feel of the cheap, transparent-plastic cover.

'No, no. I mean, I never got it published but I want someone to read it, I guess. You didn't though, er, find typos, did you?' James felt an unhealthy acidity rising from his stomach, a guilty nausea for caring and knowing he shouldn't care.

'That's not what we're talking about is it, James? We've discussed this. Please go through the steps and we'll continue.'

James nodded, forced five rapid expulsions of breath with his diaphragm, looked straight through the doctor and pinched the skin over the scars on his wrist. Then fell silent for ten seconds and nodded again.

'Good, James, good. So, as I was saying, I have spoken to my colleagues and we feel there is something different about what you have written.'

'Which colleagues?' James asked, a little too loud and fast, feeling his error before he noticed the doctor raise his eyebrows. 'Sorry, would mind telling me which colleagues you are referring to? I ask because I wondered whether they have as much experience as you with, you know, people who have a history of—'

'Substance abuse?'

'Yes.'

'Well, it's interesting, James, because no, they don't. I spoke to three colleagues, one only briefly, so two full conversations with people who have read this. All three of them are outside my discipline. They weren't colleagues, fellow doctors, they were academics at the university where I am also a professor in humanities. One, like you, started in human geography and the other two in sociology, but they are quite cross-discipline these days, hence me knowing them. Very impressive people. They all found your work interesting, and liked the lines you traced between different areas, from post-war reconstruction and slum clearance to the formation of languages. But they agreed with me that you also had something quite unique to say about drug-induced spiritualism and the role of substances and their dealers in early society in creating new and unspoken power structures. That's why I ask about your drug taking. But that's not really what I wanted to talk you about.'

Dr Pilkins smiled as though he believed he was creating an unspoken connection between him and his patient. On seeing James frown, he pushed onwards. 'I wanted to ask you whether you think there are modern implications.'

'I'm making – I was making – an argument against using conventional policy or law to tackle thorny social issues,' James said. 'We don't know how society works. All we know is that it is complex, so we should stick to helping in ways that we do understand, such as offering healthcare and education. However, we shouldn't give up when social problems are complex but should look for equally complex ways of interacting with them. That's why I became interested in the role drugs and leadership can play in enabling people to interact on a different level.'

'Really fascinating, James.' Dr Pilkins leant forward, his eyes wide and earnest, setting off James's lack of cynicism alarm.

'I think maybe you are taking it a bit far, Doctor. Anyway, can I ask—?'

'Yes?'

'Are you just trying to get me to talk about something else. Like, not my mother? So I can't make things up as easily?'

'No, no! I wondered if here, and then maybe later in a place of your own, you'd want to carry on with it.'

'With what?'

'With your studies James.' The doctor leant back and smiled. 'Carry on with your hunt to find a complex way to interact with the complex? One of the colleagues I spoke about would be happy to supervise you, remotely if you wish. They're willing to support you in developing your ideas.'

James felt his eyelids pulling down and his skin becoming a little itchy. 'I think I need to sit down.'

'You are sitting down, James.'

'I mean, I think I need a break.'

'You've had enough breaks,' the doctor replied aggressively, his smile falling from his face and his small eyes hardening. 'Today I want you to write up a plan for continuing your work. We will discuss it tomorrow and develop the plan.'

'I really don't, um, really— I don't remember a lot of it. You know it more than me now. It was years ago. I'm very pleased you like it, that's nice, but I really think I need to—'

'Do what James? You're not doing anything. You're under my care and this is my treatment.'

'What is? Writing? Fine, I'll write something. But it will be awful. I don't know where to start. But fine, I'll,' James paused for breath, upset that he had conceded this far, 'I'll put some words on a page.'

'Good. I'm sure it will be good, James. I'll help you.'

'What?'

'I'll nudge you in the right direction.'

'Right,' James snapped, pinching his wrist to pull himself back a little. 'You're a psychiatrist. You don't know this material, beyond what you've read of my work. To be honest, it feels a little strange that you've gone from listening to putting words in my mouth – and now you're forcing me to write what you want.'

A cloud shifted the light outside, sending an irritating glare into James's eyes and making him sneeze and push at his temples in a vain attempt to dampen the pain. When he looked up, the doctor had changed. His clothes were different; maybe he had pulled on a jumper and had shaken off his anorak. He was giving off deep, soothing red now, not a cold blue.

'Do you want a tissue?' the doctor asked.

Two short, sharp bangs came from the other side of the glossy blue fire door.

'Yes.'

'Phone for you, Doctor," yelled the nurse through the door, "and then your next appointment.'

'Right, yes. We've run over. Look, James, I'm trying to help. No, more than that. What I am suggesting will help. This is my last comment and then you can go. I want to know about that middle layer you were talking about in your thesis. I want to know how you can combine your understanding of the basis of place and culture with activities that create an ambitious middle layer of life and reasoning. What can be done? An experiment, perhaps, where you create a model society, where you take their cultures and help them form a new, collective one, with a purpose, a direction. Where you don't just get direction, James, but give it!'

The doctor stood up and handed the dissertation to James, along with a card. 'That's for the university library. You're working now, James, and you need materials, don't you? Yes, you do. Good. Right, James, I'll see you tomorrow.'

James was still looking at the jumbled letters and numbers on the card when he heard the door click shut, and then he was alone.

Kennington, London, 13th October 2016

Just because you're into politics!

'What do you think?' Daniel asked.

Julia was pondering the vague concept that Daniel had just explained to her, perplexed about how she had now ended up listening to his rubbish before even Geoffrey had had the pleasure of hearing it. 'We are friends, aren't we, Daniel?' she asked.

They were sitting in Julia's and Geoffrey's lounge. On a summer's day, Daniel thought, they would have had this conversation perched on the curb, their feet massaged by litter gently scraping through the hot, dusty air. But he knew everything in autumn was colder.

'I understand why you may want my view on this, but I really don't see why you can't talk about it with Geoffrey. I know you see him enough. I'm actually very busy today with my own work, which I realise is too "boring" for your current affairs tastes, in which the great "pamphlet" with its five-minute sell-by date is considered to be the upper edge of intellectualism.' She had already spotted the glossy brochure on this lap.

'Sorry, Julia, maybe I didn't explain it well enough. I've had quite a confusing morning. For one thing, no one has ever offered me that much money before. More importantly, I don't know whether it's ethical.'

Julia let out a short, passive-aggressive laugh. 'Look, Daniel, you're an idealist, and that makes these decisions unnecessarily hard.'

'An idealist! I spent last Christmas briefing MPs on how many civilians had died each day in the air strikes in order to *defend* the air strikes!'

'That's my point. You're a perpetually confused idealist. No one else is who does your job, but you insist on giving it some higher meaning.'

'It does have meaning, Julia. I believe in this.'

'Yes, well, that's not necessarily a good thing. Hitler believed in a lot as well.'

'Julia, that's pretty low'.

Daniel had always admired the way Julia had crafted something unique for herself away from the community, focusing her archaeology career on pre-historic Europe and not Jerusalem. But it did concern him that, even with organised pogroms sweeping university campuses for Zionist scalps, she did not involve herself at all. She regarded his arguments as scaremongering. Occasionally she claimed that her lack of involvement on campus was for fear of entering a circus of de-legitimisers but, in moments like these, she let her true feelings show.

'Where is Geoffrey anyway?' Julia semi-snapped.

When he phoned on his way over from Westminster, Daniel had carefully implied – though not specified – that he believed Geoffrey would be home at a relatively sociable hour. It being a Thursday, and without any evening votes in the Commons, that seemed highly plausible. However, they both knew that it was just as plausible that he would be in Soho with the other London-based MPs, enjoying the hospitality of one of many middle-aged alcoholic senior lobbyists who had lost the ability to differentiate between influence and inebriation. Daniel would have been with a similar group himself if he had not been struggling to process his day.

'Sorry, Julia, I thought he would be home by now. So, how is your work going?' he asked, making eye contact, hoping that if he gave an impression of genuine interest, he could later steer the conversation back to his own predicament.

That afternoon he had been dwelling on whether David's proposal was liberating or manipulative. Would the content of emails and phone calls ultimately be packaged up and processed with the same ruthless efficiency as the stock market? And, if that were where this was going, did he have the single-mindedness to make the case, to commit? He was, as always, also encumbered by the equal and opposite anxiety: what if he, and he assumed Geoffrey as his partner, did not push ahead with this? Did he have an obligation to try for the sake of a good idea and his own stalling career? He was trying to hold back these thoughts from crashing against the sides of his brain whilst he calmly looked at Julia, hoping for some words of salvation.

'I'm busy finishing my latest paper, Daniel. Nothing special. And worrying as usual about who this one is going to annoy.' Julia had built a reputation of being amongst the spikiest of her global clique of diggers, not afraid of (or, as some accused, intent on) bringing down long-held theories and careers in dramatic fashion. She did not see it like this at all and simply tried, she said, to stick to the evidence.

'What if you could take the ego out of decision making?' Daniel replied. 'What if there was someone or, even better, something that was aware of all these disputes, differences, pieces of evidence and theories and could rationalise them? Something that could take out the pride, and alert those in the network to the genuine gaps, not just the areas that interest those with particular niches but the areas where the "conversation" should flow?'

'Is this something to do with Israel?' Julia asked in a patronising tone.

'No, definitely not! Well, it's definitely not to do with anything in particular at all!' The grin remained on Daniel's face until he saw all that his silence was producing confusion and disinterest in Julia. He added, 'It is a piece of software.'

'I am not really sure where you're going with this, Daniel, but let me have a go anyway. I do not think that it is possible to rationalise all thoughts or activities. I was against Communism and its attempt to lead from the top. While I hate to say it, I don't think that there is a much better alternative to the ongoing and divisive arguments our democracy delivers today. As long as we are not killing each other, and we allowed to pursue our own interests, I think that is probably as good as it gets.'

'Okay,' Daniel responded. 'What if I was not talking about control from above, about politics, but more about a social network?'

'Daniel, I'm pretty sure you aren't really asking about me and I'm tired. You're probably just scared of moving on,' she scolded, before getting up and running up the stairs, leaving him awkwardly alone.

After ten minutes sitting in silence, he let himself out.

Lincoln, East Midlands, 14th July 1985

Self-reliance

The bedsit James had found was perfectly adequate for the task in hand. He knew he would get frustrated with its size and mould smell within a few months, but he had coped with worse and, armed with a word processor, his stack of university books and some money in his pocket to buy meals for the two-burner stove, he had everything he needed to get started.

It had been a long journey to get his new place. It had taken him three days, alternating between the emergency hostel and the twenty-four-hour cafe with the sweet-smelling bacon, to clear his mind, and to differentiate between his anxieties, the tramps in the shelter who were genuinely trying to steal his things, and the large black car that never left his peripheral vision.

At first, the bacon and warmth provided comfort enough from the car and the thieves, especially after he'd been consumed for so long by the disinfectant and cold empty smell of the ward. However, as the days went on these distractions gave way to his desire to catch a glimpse of the driver of the car, or the face of the homeless man periodically collecting and delivering items through its fractionally open window. His fingers itched at the thought of it, bringing back memories of a friend at university he had longed to 'accidentally' touch. That dream came to an end when she did not return after Christmas in their second year; this latest one was snuffed out when the car gently clipped him one morning when he was jogging across the road to the hostel.

After that, he decided that completing his work was more important than risking death, so gathered up his things and went in search of security.

--

He woke to a distorted view of his bedsit, the angle giving the impression of a long tunnel, guiding him towards his goal. Half-eaten tins of food lined his route, like landing lights on a runway. Next to the television stood his small desk, accompanied by a stack of books and three full reporter's pads. He had made great progress since crafting this temporary cave. While he wrote, his ideas were reinforced by the sights and sounds coming from the portable TV he'd purchased from a second-hand shop on which, with the aid of a mini-aerial and a protruding curtain pole to hang it on, he could pick-up the BBC and, occasionally, Channel 4.

Live Aid had consumed his attention the evening before. While he knew millions around the world had joined him and each other in concern over the famine in Ethiopia, he was sure that donations were not the answer. As they kept being told, there was an abundance of food in the world, but it was in the wrong place. It simply needed shipping to the right place, with the help of a multitude of small donations.

However, the TV did not tell him how many other countries were suffering such problems, or about cases (which he was sure existed) where there was plenty of food within countries, but still it did not get to people's mouths. The show had also asked him to donate to help teach people to fish, rather than buy them fish, but when he looked out of the window he saw so many fat people in the street who had, he assumed, consumed plenty themselves without doing a day's fishing or farming in their lives.

Maybe, James thought, he was wrong and the time he had spent in the hospital had somehow erased his memories of fishing and farming in the streets of the city in which he'd grown up. He had heard of fish farms, but did not recall ever seeing or smelling one. He also remembered that, when travelling in Hanoi some years previously, he had seen couples in blue boiler suits crouched in their doorways appearing to conjure dinner out of nothing but small steel buckets and coals. Perhaps that was a type of farming. But whenever he was close to walking out of the building and exploring the streets for signs of agriculture, he remembered the large black car that followed him wherever he went.

For the first few days, he thought the most likely explanation was that his doctors wanted to keep an eye on him and that the attempt to run him over was an accident. However, this did not correspond with his experience of the NHS, which seemed to lack the resources for home visits, let alone surveillance. Furthermore, he knew that staying indoors was not healthy and was the last thing his doctors would have wanted, so why did these watchers not come up to see how he was doing? If they did, they would find him well fed, rested and working hard on his research, but they could not possibly tell this from lurking on the corner below behind a blacked-out windscreen.

This morning, however, he knew he would have to ignore the dark metal box. He needed to buy more food, food sourced in a shop located such a distance from his home that Bob Geldof, would be proud of his hunter-gathering. He was also low on tablets and needed to visit the pharmacy to exchange one of his repeat prescription sheets for whatever his doctors had put him on months ago. Despite the cold wet feeling they induced across his body, the tablets were gifting him clarity of thought for the first time in years. He grabbed his zip-up track-suit top from the back of the door and ambled down the unlit stairs, running the fingers of his left hand down the badly painted wall as he went.

Once on the street, the sun called on him to take his jacket off but he was concerned that, after he had picked up his shopping, he would have no free arms to defend himself should he need to. Furthermore, whilst he knew he needed to absorb some vitamin D, the bright sun was his enemy, making every car indistinguishable from the next.

He put his head down and kept walking. He had a duty to his family to recover and to his doctors and lecturers as well, who had so much faith him; he knew they would be very proud to see him crafting his new vision.

As he approached his nearest shop, he felt a pang of anxiety as he saw a familiar figure flickering in the white light. As he drew closer, he realised it was the unthreatening looking man he had seen a handful of times out of his window giving out colourful leaflets at the bus stop.

'Excuse me, citizen,' said the confident but slight figure as he leant forward to shake James's hand.

James kept his hands, and most of his arms, firmly wedged into his acrylic pockets. 'Yes, er,' he expelled under his breath, not used to conversation.

'Horris, my name is Horris,' the leafleteer said with a strong Eastern European accent. 'Have I seen you before, citizen?' he asked, a slight smile emerging from one corner of his mouth as he paused for breath before continuing. 'You must be out for a walk on this beautiful day. I have come out to meet people like you, intelligent people who are interested in taking control of their own lives.' He handed James a cheaply printed magazine with a green symbol on the cover.

'I came for the shop,' said James, his clarity increasing with every word. 'I'm out of food,' he continued, now using a little too much force.

'Please take the magazine, citizen. This one is free, and you can speak with me again if you want to learn more.' He patted James on the shoulder and walked off towards a busy-looking woman with shopping bags, who avoided his approach by crossing the road.

James hurriedly entered the shop before looking at the magazine. The front cover was a jumble of left-wing logos and headlines. In the corner was one that caught his eye: '*A new way of living. Scottish pioneers celebrate fifth anniversary*'

Victoria, London, 13th December 2053

Nice night for a walk

Sira crossed Victoria Street, vaguely heading north-westwards. Wherever she looked, she assumed they could look. Whatever she heard, they could hear. She wanted to be alone to process her trauma but, with the help of her implant, she fought to keep her fear locked down.

As she scraped her tired feet along the uneven pavement towards home, she knew that she was also getting closer to unleashing her new parasite on her friends. Her only consolation was the hope that there would be some benefit in sharing the pain.

As she got further away from the decaying pomp of Westminster, Sira entered one of her favourite parts of the city. She tried to use it as a distraction, focusing on the shadows that grew before her and then slipped silently behind grey facades.

An imposing concrete structure at the edge of the deserted government district emerged to her left. Its reinforced mushroom-shaped roof stood hunched yet proud with the muscular aggression of a generation long gone. While all the buildings in the area were empty, she thought this tower was made stronger rather than weaker by its lack of human contact, its lack of empathy with its gothic and parkland surroundings. Unlike most of London's old buildings, which were designed as peacocks to show off their fragile wealth, this monolith sought to dissuade interest.

She knew she had nowhere else to go other than to her friends in the garage, and she was jealous of this tower's lack of need for interaction. Hoping to be inspired, she kept it in her peripheral vision for as long as possible, imagining its proud, pillared foundations forcing the ground beneath to submit as volleys of intercontinental missiles burst through the clouds, setting the sky on fire and smashing concrete and steel all around her but failing to scratch this cold war relic.

Dusk was falling when Sira reached the park. She decided to ignore the risk posed by its malnourished beggars who had made it their home and take its overgrown paths as a shortcut, aiming for the tube station that she and her friends had emerged from earlier in the day.

As she climbed over its gates, she saw a faded sign telling her to share her pictures and discoveries from the day on the park's My Favourite account. She assumed that even if this social media network was still going, which she doubted, her day's experiences were not exactly what they were looking for. Anyway, sharing was not worth the risk. Since that sign had been erected, since the collapse of what people once naively called progress, it was no longer common practice to mark yourself out as 'having a nice day'. Loose talk costs lives, as the old poster and now popular meme dictated.

As she meandered her way towards the station, squinting in the darkness to navigate smouldering campfires, human faeces and uprooted trees, she wondered whether the collapsing society around her meant an inevitable return to the basics, to meeting in person as the only way to safely communicate. Maybe the offline beggars had it right. Technology had never been better or more individual, but maybe now they had gone full circle and it was time to re-join the world and let the networks wither and die.

During her parents' and grandparents' lives, technology had been almost solely focused on increasing direct communication and reducing commuting, with physical travel becoming the domain of holidaymakers and hit squads. It was well understood that an attempt to return to physical travel was what had brought everything crashing down. A typical act of hubris, she thought, from the baby boomers and their descendants who had an in-built obsession with creating something new without thinking through the consequences.

She recalled that she was about ten when rumours of physical dimension displacers began and, for a while, nobody could speak of anything else. At parties they drew them – strange shapes emerging around the mountains of Europe – and at school they acted them out, pretending to disappear into dust. Her older sister was encouraged by teachers to learn how they worked, despite that being a state secret. First, they were discussed in the language of science but eventually the languages of religion and philosophy took hold. In hindsight, imprecise speculation was clearly preferred by the elite.

She had read later that Rome, Jerusalem, Mecca and Utah were dead against it and had tried to shut down the idea, but they had been no match for the self-appointed commentators who made their profit from drawing out the debate to create shareable content. At first, governments were largely against it too but were later encouraged by the corporations to invest alongside them. When these partnerships began, it was assumed that the manufacturers of India and China would take the lead but a renewed coalition of old Western corporates and liberal and English-speaking governments meant that, to the world's amazement, it was the UK that came out in front, at least as the host.

The market stopped investing in implants (or anything else) as all the value in the world was poured into an unknown and supposedly better future. Sira and her generation remembered this as the time shops began closing and official implant updates dried up. But, to her parents and their generation who had suffered years of economic stagnation, it was an exciting time that presented the opportunity to 'change everything'. That became the most popular phrase of the day.

Nobody really knew how it would lead to new or better jobs, but that did not seem to matter. One popular assumption was that scientists, engineers and development and aid workers could travel back and speed up scientific discovery and human progress in the past, therefore pushing forward today's reality. Fears that this would snuff out reality were brushed aside. Sira remembered a neighbour telling her father, 'What is the point in worrying about the future if you can't earn and feed yourself today?' She hoped this man was now sleeping somewhere in the park she was traipsing through.

On the night that the first test animal was locked into its capsule, cities across the world stood still in silence to watch. Sira, her implant still working owing to a friend's coding

70

ingenuity, sat on the little wall that surrounded her communal home and watched comment and conversations crawling across the event. Others gathered around large screens in social rooms or city centres. They watched a white rabbit being squeezed into a jet-black container and, between adverts for gambling products and surgery and clips of the Moon landings, they saw the vessel vanish. The world cheered.

She was not clear about whether these were real memories or imagined ones, since she had watched the clips of the rabbit so many times. But she was sure that her memories from the night the world found out the truth were real. She could still taste the barbecue smoke in her mouth when she recalled the news alert that had flashed across her eyes, and the screams from the garden and buildings around her that had followed it. In a matter of hours, the world went from toasting its new fortune with factory-made alcohol, synthetic beef and smiles, to despair, rioting and religiously-inspired suicide.

Sira and her friends had stopped going to school. They had no knowledge of what jobs were, and quickly discarded any memories of living in private homes. While their parents mourned for what they would never have again including, ironically, affording basic physical travel, younger people who knew no different slipped into spending more time connected. Soon fixes for frozen implants appeared; the connected community grew and grew, and began educating itself about what had happened, how the baby boomers and their spiritual followers had caused it, and how they could survive.

Westminster, London, 22nd November 2016

The new guard

The narrow and overly fussy windowpanes gently rattled in the wind that pushed along the brown river behind Geoffrey, a reminder of the inhospitable outside world in which all their constituents were doomed to toil.

He was sitting on the sofa at the rear of the Pugin room, his favourite destination for publicly serious and private conversations, all conversations in Parliament being public to an extent. According to the logic buried deep in the brains of all MPs, there was no point in doing anything unless people could see that you were doing it.

From his table he watched a thick, brown, woollen suit awkwardly meander towards him. Timothy was a relatively new breed of politico, especially in Geoffrey's party, being first and foremost an academic and now a brain for hire or 'guru'. In Timothy's case, he had become bored of his communist toilet block of an educational institution, deserting it for the leader's office, where his low-grade theories on community capitalism were being feted as intellectual dynamite. It was this connection to the top that Geoffrey hoped to exploit to get his committee back in the good books. However, the way Timothy opened the exchange made him feel less sure this was the right approach.

'Do you know what I think we used to do wrong, Geoffrey?'

Geoffrey pondered whether to reply sarcastically, making it clear that the 'we' to which Timothy referred did not include Timothy at the time, but he decided better of it. 'No. Well, I have quite a few thoughts on that but no single one really, besides you-know-who failing to attract aspirational voters,' Geoffrey stuttered unconvincingly.

'Yes, that's a part of it,' Timothy said patronisingly. 'But I'll tell you what I think. I think it comes from your generation's lack of any real sense of ideology. You know – or knew – what you were *against*, poverty, inequality, grey bureaucracy but, since you couldn't really decide what you were *for*, your side of the party became thin and shallow. Your generation was political paint-stripper without the following paint job. That's what went wrong.'

Geoffrey gripped the oak trim of his seat, pushing their three election victories in a row to the back of his mind.

'When in power, we failed to understand how communities evolve. We failed to understand pluralism, or that we would end up trying to govern a country in which 'Mondeo-man' had begun working a few days a year in Dubai, 'Worcester woman' would get two part-time jobs, and in which the petty thief is pettily thieving from a hacked Bulgarian bank account off a girl since trafficked to a luxury club for the super-rich in Chelsea.'

Geoffrey started to glaze over at this Twitter inspired zeitgeistathon. His eyes wandered across the room of whispered conversations that he assumed were all more productive than his own, or at least might evolve into a few glasses of wine in Strangers' bar.

'So that's the question,' Timothy said, with an expression of honesty that suggested he thought Geoffrey was listening.

After a long pause, during which Geoffrey would have felt embarrassed if he were not used to giving the impression that he was gathering fascinating thoughts, a fatuous escape route came to him. 'I think that we need to talk in a language that people understand,' he said with a smile.

Timothy ploughed on. 'This realisation gives us space for a new ideological handle, a point to grip upon which allows us to be really FOR something. Whilst your generation' –

Geoffrey winced inside – 'was against things, and for less control. We have an opportunity to put in place a system of power that communities can really use. This is where we think your committee should fit in.'

Geoffrey, having long given up trying to understand where Timothy could possibly be going with all this, realised he had been given another opening. He took a large gulp of cold tea from the ornate bone china cup to clear his throat and embarked on his own lecture.

'So, as you may have heard, I have been working with Micro-Systems and several other major technology firms in recent months, strictly in a cross-party committee manner. And, as you also have probably heard, Tom stamped on the idea as he thought it looked like me bolstering a government announcement of some sort, which I completely understand since it may have caused a small story in a small paper on a small day. Anyway, that is the past, but what is not the past is the need for us to look like we care about business and jobs. The leader pouncing on my committee's considered recommendations, and grilling the government on delivery would have helped our credibility.' Geoffrey spoke assertively, now feeling as though he had found his feet. 'Now that boat has sailed, we need a new approach. Before I launch into anything else, probably my last new project before I am deselected, I wanted your ideas on what is safe territory.'

Timothy looked pensive, unsure of his footing and a little surprised about the aggressive tone that the MP was taking. Geoffrey could see that he was much more used to fielding and critiquing the detailed plans of others rather than conjuring up his own.

'Well, that is exactly what I am saying,' declared Timothy falsely. 'We need something Labour, something that addresses our previous flaws with regards to recognising our changing communities, and something that injects some real left–right energy into the debate.'

The men smiled at each other, both trying to give the impression that they were seeing eye to eye. After a long pause, Geoffrey decided to buy some thinking time with a platitude and his own allusion to an idea. 'I think that is spot on, Tim. We need to talk about business in a way that works not just for stocks and shares but for communities, too, helping them as they adapt. For example, while northern mill towns were built around static industries that have long since gone, we need to support these towns with new businesses that wrap around people's needs, and which share their hardworking values.' Geoffrey felt pleased with himself, proud that he had just joined over a hundred and fifty years of meaningless history made in this room.

'Exactly,' asserted Timothy. 'I think that means there is interesting work to be done here, interesting work that fits your agenda – assuming any recommendations you produce are,' he looked for a clear formulation that would keep Geoffrey on a short leash, 'for the whole country.' He proceeded to wish Geoffrey's family well, which both men knew Timothy knew nothing about, and walked out of the room, making a slight show on the way that he was paying for their subsidised drinks.

The MP remained seated for a few more minutes, his pen hovering over a blank piece of paper and his mind whirring in an effort to extract any tangible points from their conversation. He jotted down: *gather together small number of businesses working in the 'ethical' field, perhaps 'community' energy generation or food production*, then dropped the pen as he felt a wave of exhaustion sinking down from his shoulders into his hollow stomach.

North west London, 13th December 2053

Welcome home

'Nice walk?' Frank was slouched on an old couch with a smug look on his face, which Sira rightly assumed was in reference to her rain-drenched clothes and hair. 'Imagine if you were porous! You'd be sloshed all over the pavement like some oil slick, just your teeth and matted hair for evidence.' He laughed to himself, whilst Yanda looked at him incredulously before wrapping Sira in an old floral curtain.

Sira shivered, collecting her energy to respond before telling Frank to fuck off and slumping on a large, hard cushion in the corner, sending a bitter cloud of dust into the air.

'Sorry. We were a bit bloody worried, that's all. You just disappeared with those goons – or they disappeared you. And then nothing, not a message!'

During her long walk home, she had found that the only way to avoid blind panic was to try to game ways of re-hacking her mind. At no point had she thought about how she would explain the situation when she reached her destination. As a result, she found herself sitting silent while Frank stood over her, firing questions.

'We – and I don't know why us – have an issue,' she finally explained with such unusual sincerity that her friends thought she was joking.

Her second attempt to begin to explain was no more successful. Struggling to find the words, she recalled a time when, after two nights without sleep and food, she had experienced a painful delusion that the back of her skull had become unsealed and grown into a long open-ended tunnel, crawling down her back looking for herself. Once again, she realised she lacked the ability to sense her edges.

Seeing that her eyes were watering, Yanda meekly slouched over, hugged her and whispered that he was sorry. He felt Sira's muscles relax and supported her downwards into a foetal position. She fell asleep.

Frank and Yanda shrugged at each other before returning to their previous poses. Yanda sat on the couch watching a 2030s' movie remake of a vintage series from ten years previously about a group of friends living together in the same old London building. They were trying to get jobs from robot interviewers between sleeping with each other and arguing with other anarchists and greens in the local alcohol vending gallery. The story had recently had a second resurgence in popularity, with snippets of the film appearing segments and strewn across profiles and blogs owing to the wealth of angry one-liners against the liberals who surrounded the story's protagonists.

Yanda liked to think of himself as Roberto, a South Londoner of Italian descent, who is constantly berated by friends and family for working and earning a pittance rather than joining them in planning the revolution. He gets his revenge at the end of the story when the police smash up all the local political meetings and houses of young people who are suspected of harbouring activists. Owing to the bribes he has saved up for, Roberto and his hard-working friends are protected and, the following day, are able to drink in peace.

Frank stayed at his makeshift desk, an old car bonnet folded at the sides to create squat legs and raised off the floor on two cardboard boxes filled with pieces of brick. On this contraption stood a computer station; his friends mocked him for it, since it had far less power than his implant and had to be viewed through a restored flat screen that made everything look green or blue tinted. He had built the computer himself from recovered parts, insisting that it gave a more authentic experience than the modern equivalent, not that he was ever able explain what 'authentic' meant in this context.

Both had their screens turned down low, allowing them to half focus and half snooze, each wrapped in their greatcoats after the day's trek. Their relaxation was occasionally interrupted by Sira's sporadic snoring and murmuring. If it was not for their shared obsession with her, they would have ignored the low sounds coming from within the old curtain; however, with each tiny sonic burst their vision was drawn away from their screens towards the soft curve of her back through the fabric and the rich, tangled dark-brown hair that flowed out of the top of the cloth tube she had rolled herself in.

Frank occasionally looked away from both Sira and the program he was writing to catch Yanda's confident and relaxed smile hanging over her with a sense of ownership.

Soho, London,
24th November 2016

The idealist

Daniel was waiting in the small, crisply expensive reception area of one his principal donor's offices, preparing to give a brief report on his activity over the last few months and, hopefully, secure the cash for flights for a couple of MPs he wanted to take to Washington. Before this simple conversation could happen, though, he had to wait whilst his nineteenth-century benefactor and some property investors finished their meeting. He knew their topic of conversation because he could hear their fat booming voices down the corridor, sharing anecdotes on the state of the gambling market.

As the investors left, he watched them shake hands with his appointment and pat each other on the back before squeezing into the renovated building's unrenovated lift. Daniel imagined them emerging on the ground floor with their rolls of rich fat imprinted with the diamond shapes of the lift's metal shutters.

--

'I see what you are saying, Daniel, but I don't think it will work.'

Daniel sat in Isaac's office, frustrated that to secure the resources to convince a small group of MPs to like Israel a little more he had to justify his methods repeatedly to those who grew up knowing that they were right, not just about Israel but, in Isaac's case, about everything.

'It's the biggest pro-Israel conference on the planet. If we are to show our friends a bit of love and introduce them to people who see their political views positively rather than through the eyes of International Criminal Court judges, this will be money more than well spent.' He waited patiently for another response, now confident that he would walk out of the office empty-handed. Isaac looked at him, slowly nodding, contemplating how such a visit could best work in his favour; how it could be used to bolster his prowess at any number of dinners over the coming weeks and shift the balance of power towards him and his enlarging belly and away from a long-time friend whom he now detested for being knighted.

'I can think of one of two MPs that fit that bill Daniel, and I think you're exactly right. But, to get the most out of the relationship at home, we need them to understand who made this happen,' he explained to the converted.

'Yes, Isaac,' Daniel agreed. 'We need to get them more involved in the Israel debate following the conference, whilst the experience is fresh in their minds.'

Isaac shifted his weight on his creaking desk chair and moved to reply, and yet only let out a low, indistinct hum. He looked severely into Daniel's eyes as though he were trying to ascertain some truth which they were hiding or some traitorous instinct in the younger man.

'This is not just about Israel,' he finally asserted, pausing again before manoeuvring himself towards his final speech. 'We need to deepen their involvement with the whole community, not just on Israel. THAT is why I should take them.'

As Daniel was about to let out a short insolent gasp, one of Isaac's partners walked in and immediately started a conversation with her boss without acknowledging his presence. He tried to turn his blood down from a boil to a gentle simmer. It had been a while since he had been gazumped by a donor. He recalled that last time this had happened it had also concerned an international visit with an MP – to Israel. On that occasion, he was eventually relieved to be disarmed, much preferring to have a week in the office than compete for egos on a minibus. But this time it was different: this time he was being pushed off a visit that meant more to him and, crucially, more to everyone else. Those he ultimately wished to impress in his career, wherever that took him, would always be more so by a visit to swampy Washington DC than dusty Jerusalem.

--

Leaving Isaac's office, and yet feeling still trapped by it, he decided not to go back to his own office. Instead he wandered down Charing Cross, joining its strange inhabitants as they busily performed their roles on the cultural fringes of Soho, shifting boxes of books and exotic items from small vans and trollies into gloomy shop fronts. It would surely be difficult, he imagined, to care too much about Israel and Washington when neither were compatible with the ridiculous combinations of tweed and glitter before him.

As he approached the cafes and open spaces of Trafalgar Square, he took a seat on the steps and let his junior colleague and intern in the office assume whatever he wanted. There was a lot to do to prepare for party conference season and to honour pledges made to less egotistical donors but this, he knew, was exactly the chain of thought that had solidified his position as dogsbody. He knew that those who paid for his job were not, in their minds, buying in skills they respected; they were buying what they regarded as cheaper than 'proper' lobbying.

He pulled his phone from his pocket and scrolled through his numbers looking for inspiration. David's number, he knew, would shine out in garish lights, but he was not in the right frame of mind for that. Instead he texted an old university friend who he had been feeling guilty about not seeing for a while. *Hey, John. How are you? Long-time eh? Fancy drink?*

While waiting for a reply, he walked back towards Soho to an old music shop with a strange poster in the window he had noticed many times. On inspection, it turned out to be a clown doing a handstand and not a woman with two heads as he had always thought. The shop reminded him of ones his sister would peer into as a child and, if their mother allowed, enter through the glass door smothered in stickers and fitted with a small bell. Once inside, he would be trapped as his sister pawed over the books of unintelligible scrawling and curved symbols, the opposite of their brightly coloured front covers. Dishonest, he thought.

North west London, 14th December 2053

Time to leave

The trio woke with a start. As they had done many times in the past, they grabbed their coats and blankets before piling into a large wooden cupboard at the back of the room. Frank held the door open for the others and finally climbed in after Sira and Yanda had shuffled sideways to make sufficient room. Once they were sitting next to each other, they gripped each other's hands for support and kept their knees tucked in to avoid accidentally kicking open the tin-foil lined chipboard door. To their side were some bottles of water and dry snacks, placed there for emergencies. It was a preparatory measure they had taken after they had nearly passed out from dehydration a year earlier in a different garage.

'Shit, shit, shit!' flashed repeatedly across Sira's and Yanda's eyes, broadcast by Frank who sat between them and had begun to shake in fear.

There were three more loud thumps on the front door before the fourth brought it down off its hinges. It slammed flat against the floor, sending a light shower of dust in all directions including between the cracks of their cocoon.

'What is that? How much do you think we can get for that?' barked the first voice they heard.

Sira held Frank's hand, knowing that they could only be talking about his computer.

'Forget it. It's a piece of junk!' laughed a second, higher-pitched voice coming from nearer the open doorway.

'Even better,' yelled the first voice, before a smash of metal vibrated across the room.

Frank winced and held Sira's hand tighter as a series of thumps and pops firmly signalled the end of his labours.

The trio watched the time creep forward. Sira's adrenalin was replaced by maddening sleep deprivation that pushed like pistons through her crumpled body. Hearing her breathing becoming increasingly heavy, Yanda took her other hand and started running his fingertips up and down her palm to help shift her concentration, whilst sharing some locally-saved meditation sounds from his implant to hers. If it was not for her kidnapping, she would have snatched her hand back at such an encroachment; given the vinegar tracing through her body, however, she acquiesced.

They stayed in their tense crouches for twenty minutes, hearing metal crashing and twisting against plastic, wood and brick until the sounds eventually stopped.

After sitting in silence for ten minutes, Yanda pushed the plywood door aside and levered himself out.

'How bad is it?' whispered Sira.

'I guess we still have our implants,' Yanda yelled back.

'Really? Nothing?' Frank messaged, unable to open his dry throat.

'Lego, Frank. Remember that box we found a couple of years ago full of small, grimy, colourful bricks? It said Lego on the side. It looks a bit like that.'

'Yanda, try and be a bit sensitive, will you?' implored Sira, removing her hands from her face and gripping Frank's hand as he started to sob.

'Sorry, Frank,' said Yanda. 'But we either sweep up and start again, or go somewhere else and start again. There is nothing left.'

'I'm not starting again without protection,' Yanda added, while kicking broken rubbish along the floor. 'It would be a waste of time.'

Sira finally heaved herself out of the cupboard, pulling Frank with her, to see the devastation. In the middle of it, Yanda was brandishing a length of metal tubing that had one been a part of their furniture. 'We need to protect ourselves,' he yelled, pretending to fence with an imaginary opponent.

'Maybe you're right,' agreed Sira, kicking some broken pieces of plastic towards Yanda. 'But I don't think you'd last five minutes.'

Yanda's face went red with anger and embarrassment and he sat down on the floor, hitting his metal implement against the concrete floor.

'I need to tell you what happened,' Sira said.

'We know what happened, Sira. We got robbed,' scrolled in front of her eyes from Frank.

She ignored her friends' self-absorption and sat in the corner, writing them a long message so they could not interrupt her. She told them how she had been trapped and manipulated by someone who may or may not have been the Captain they'd met on the march, and how he had a gang of adults, and maybe children, unless they were all fictions he or someone had concocted for her mind.

When she sent the message, Frank and Yanda read it silently for a few minutes, then walked over to her, both looking sheepish for not having asked before.

Sira ignored the plea for forgiveness in their eyes and continued verbally, explaining how her captors wanted her to join them and had threatened her if she didn't.

'We need to buy them off, Sira,' asserted Yanda.

'Very bold. But we've got nothing that they don't have already except this.' Sira tapped her finger on the side of her head, each tap knocking a tear from her eye. 'We – or I – either risk being taken by them or we get away from this city. Even if they don't catch up with us, we aren't safe. They're the only ones who can protect us, but I don't want to pay the price.'

'Do you think it was them and not the gangs that trashed our things?' asked Frank.

'Frank, will you listen to her and forget about your stupid computer?' Yanda interjected.

'I don't know, Frank,' Sira said. 'I think maybe they *are* the gang. It could all be one gang now, or maybe the one that took me was just a big one. But I think something's changed.'

'We have to leave then,' murmured Frank, playing with plastic debris on the floor. 'We can't do this again. It's such a waste.'

'You're scared,' Yanda taunted. 'You just like playing with this stuff. You've never had your heart in it.'

'Heart in what? Hacking?'

'Exactly. That's how you see it, Frank. Do you think those bastards that took Sira see it in such unambitious terms? No! And now they're after us, unless we can think of something, some leverage.'

'Yanda, if you had seen what I'd seen today you wouldn't be coming up with such nonsense,' Sira interjected. 'They are light years ahead of us. Yes, I'm sure the government would put us all in the same bracket, and we all agree that it's down to us to create a life in this mess. But these guys are in a different league. Maybe they are gearing up to take over, not just to make some money or survive but to run the place!'

Yanda wandered across the garage and whacked his 'sword' against broken pieces of chipboard hanging from the wall where some cupboards had been. 'Just hear me out,' he begged. 'We keep marching for strong leadership, but maybe they are it? Or maybe, if we cross the bar they have set, we can be *it* too, with them, maybe? Aren't you sick of everyone agreeing we need a new regime? Everyone agreeing that all this supposed freedom and choice has just led to poverty and corruption – and yet no one is stepping in to lead?'

'We need a proud leadership, not *any* leadership, Yanda,' Sira spat back, angered that he was talking about joining her kidnappers. She grabbed the piece of curtain she'd been wrapped in earlier, made herself a pillow and pushed her face into it block him out.

Frank shot Yanda a look of incredulity. 'Whatever we do, we need to stick together, Yanda. And first, we need a safe space, which isn't here. That's the priority.'

'Fine. I agree. Whatever we choose, we can't start anything in this mess. Let's find somewhere new tomorrow. I'll go out for food and then we can get some rest.'

'Yes, Yanda, but what about her.' Frank pointed to Sira sobbing on the floor. He thought about giving her a hug but felt too awkward.

'They've been in her head, Yanda. They are probably still in her head. Even if they didn't smash our place up, they probably monitored the whole thing through her. We need to get them out – out of her, out of her head.'

85

Yanda put his weapon down and sat with his head in his heads. 'You think they heard my plan to join or depose them?'

'I doubt anyone else apart from you thinks it's a plan, Yanda. A rant, perhaps.'

'Right. OK, you got any ideas Frank?'

'A few, but I'm not sure if any of them will work.'

'I think you're enjoying this. Spill the beans.'

'OK, we need food and shelter.'

'Fascinating.'

'We have to assume that they can follow us, so we have to get off the grid.'

'And then, I guess we need to remove Sira's implant,' asserted Yanda sarcastically.

'Yes, we could do that. Know any surgeons? No? We'll have to jam it somehow.'

'Right,' Yanda retorted. 'Shall we move underground? Perhaps we can live in the sewers?'

'We could, Yanda, although I suspect the bacteria would kill us. No, this is what I think. We get out of the city and go north. We go wild. We get ourselves to an area of tall mountains and deep valleys where there is no signal, and we hunt for food.'

'And then?'

'That's it.'

'You mean we do that forever?'

'It beats eating refuse and living in sheds and derelict offices. It also beats looking over our shoulders the whole time. And it certainly beats fearing that they are inside us already.'

'I think you're just scared as always, Frank. Anyway, if we did just run away, how are we supposed to help out there?'

'Help?'

'Yes. We are trying to do something, aren't we? Or at least we are aspiring to do something. We marched today with the whole city. Yes, the government put on that show in the square to pretend it understands us. But everyone is ready for a change, you can see it in their eyes. And now you're suggesting we act like some awful hippies and go and live in a wigwam? The government could fall at any moment. They have nothing left. The last of wealthy families will die soon and those left behind

86

will have nobody to protect them. We have to be here to take over.'

'Or die Yanda?'

'Yes.'

'Or end up supporting a new dictatorship.'

'What's wrong with dictatorship Frank? At least if we had some strength we could get that thing out of her head!'

'Guys, thanks for giving me some space to rest, but you're shouting,' Sira called up from the floor. 'I know I'm a risk. I nearly didn't come back. Do you want me to go?'

'No, no, of course not,' blurted Yanda. He took one of her hands and saw a flash of anger break through Frank's expression.

'Good. Because you boys can both go fuck yourselves. You know you would be totally lost without me.'

'It's not what we were thinking,' threw back Yanda. 'Frank thinks we all need to get out of the city. Away from the surveillance. I don't want to run on the eve of the revolution.'

'Do you know what I think, Yanda? I think you are full of bullshit sometimes' mumbled Sira.

'Still so sure, Yanda?' asked Frank

'Sure of what, Yanda? What is he talking about?'

'I said that you agreed with me, that the revolution is real and that we should be working to put a new powerful leader in place.'

'Yes, I do. But I also don't believe in being reckless. I think we need to hide. Frank, what's your idea?'

'OK. Firstly, Yanda gets us some food.'

'Thanks, Yanda,' said Sira, forcing his hand.

'Secondly, Sira, we block your device somehow. Then, if we aren't going to hide in the mountains, we find a more permanent solution.'

Sira shuffled her back against the plywood sheeting of the cupboard in an effort to protect herself from what was coming next.

Frank continued. 'There is only one place in this city where we can get help.'

'Wait, there must be other options. If this was your brain, there would be other options.'

'I don't think so, Sira. We have to get your implant reset or exchanged without anyone knowing. They are the only ones who can do the surgery.'

'Frank, hurry up, will you? I've got no idea what you two are talking about,' snapped Yanda.

Frank and Sira looked at each other for a moment, to check they were thinking the same thing, before whispering 'Poplar' in unison.

'You're kidding me. Those traitors! No one speaks to them!'

'Exactly Yanda,' said Sira with resignation.

'So how do you know they are still doing this stuff?'

'Everyone knows. You know. We see their chatter all the time. Any time you see so-called experts slandering the rest of us, criticising our justice, that's them.'

'Right. So, a few minutes ago I was saying we need to support the revolution and now you two are telling me we're off to beg the liberals for help?'

'Yes,' replied Frank. 'I know begging doesn't come easy to you, with your pride and all that, but if you want that hacked implant out of Sira's head going to Poplar is our only choice.'

'Excuse me. My choice. My head,' Sira threw back. 'I appreciate the chivalry, Frank, but this is up to me. It's a dangerous journey for starters. If we're going, I'm in the lead.'

'Leading who, Sira? Frank hasn't mentioned the little matter of getting across the entire city, have you, Frank? And I suspect he's thought of some way to dodge the bullets, haven't you?' Yanda asked with a grin.

'Well, you will need some help, and it's just that I thought you would be better off with some eyes in the air. If I, you know, supported from a distance?'

'So, our little Franky general fears the front line, as usual.'

'I'm not scared. I've always quite wanted to meet them.'

'I bet you have, Frank. You're always going on about them. What did you say last week? They're misunderstood.'

'Forget it then. My idea makes sense but, if you're going to be like that, we will all go together – all in danger together'

'Right. So if you're okay with this, why has all the blood drained out of your face?'

'Yanda! Sit down.' Sira yelled. 'He's scared, as am I. None of us woke up this morning thought we'd be doing this plan, whatever it is.'

'It isn't a plan.'

'Pardon, Frank?' Yanda yelled. 'You made it up!'

'We need to go east. That's all I've got. It's not really a plan.'

'Well, that's all we've got, too,' snapped Sira, wiping the last tears from her eyes and replacing them with a steely glare.

'Yanda, we're going to need you to calm down, gather your things and make us some food. Nothing you can't carry. Frank, start plotting a route.'

Switzerland, 14th June, 2006

Speak into the microphone

'Bob Jennings from *Science Monthly*. Tell me about your discovery, Dr Finegold. How did it come about?'

Finegold could see the director over Jennings' shoulder, her eyes glaring whilst the bottom half of her face smiled. A strange trick, thought Finegold, and one that she could see no use for. After all, everyone could see both halves of a face.

'I won't start from the very beginning, as that is well rehearsed, but as your readers know it took us a long time to repeat the experiment and find the crystal structure again. We eventually deduced that this was because it was working in time differently to us.'

'In time. But are we not all in the same universe?'

'Yes. We believe the crystal is in our universe but, as we know, space and time are relative to each other. We have theorised that the crystal is trapped in the orbit of a black hole and moving very quickly in a way which means that, from our perspective, it is going backwards and not forwards through time. This, of course, makes it difficult to spot because all our instruments, including our brains, start from a certain point and work forwards.'

'This is the finding that has been reported upon quite widely?'

'Yes, there has certainly been a lot of interest.'

'So, how did you come to this conclusion?'

'By accident really or – at least not in the way we expected to. You see, we had not considered one crucial aspect. When we saw the first results, we weren't seeing them live. We saw them afterwards. It was the now-famous flickering clock that we saw first. So, after failing to capture the same result, we went back to look at the same data. We did this a few times and we realised the data had changed. It changed more, the longer we left it.'

'That seems very strange, Doctor. Is it not stored on your own drives? Who was changing it?'

'No one. But the collisions, when done right, were capturing the crystal and were being influenced by its temporal properties. In short, the crystal does not travel backwards in time alone. Things that interact with it, including us if we so choose, travel back also. Only a fraction of a second at first, and then for longer the longer you look.'

'Are you not in danger of disappearing and travelling back in time yourself, Doctor?'

'No, you have to experience it for it to have an effect. If you were to look at the data, you would be looking further into the past than if you looked at the same data yesterday, but you yourself would still be in the present. That is why clocks in the vicinity of a collision jump back, but then right themselves.'

'So what's next?'

'We continue our experiments. We believe that we only know a fraction of what there is to know about this crystal. It has also led to new questions about the nature of space and time that have inspired many new avenues of research. Watch this space, I guess.'

'Or time?'

'Yes, very good.'

'One last question. You are being accused of playing God, of bringing the strange dimensions of other worlds into our own without any understanding of the dangers. What do you say to those that level this criticism at you?'

Finegold took in a breath to prepare to roll out her most prepared of lines. She looked over Jennings's shoulder once more and saw the director looking encouragingly at her. 'I want to reassure your followers, and anyone else taking an interest in this work, that we treat our responsibilities at CERN with the utmost pride and caution. We have a duty to those that work here to protect their safety, as well as a wider duty to the world to extend knowledge for the good of mankind. With regards to your question, that is not one for me to answer. However, as a spiritual woman, it is my belief that humans can do both right and wrong, but it is impossible for us to stray beyond the choices our Maker has set for us. If we could go beyond the boundaries God has set, He would not be God – not the God I know, anyway.'

'Thank you, Dr Finegold.'

'Thank you, Mr Jennings.'

'Cut.'

'Thanks again, Doctor. That was a very strong performance.'

Finegold smiled. She had made the mistake earlier in her career of relaxing and giving more away after an interview that she'd intended, only to find her words quoted in text beneath an online video. Journalists were always working; this time, she had not forgotten that. 'Thank you, Bob. I hope you got what you needed.'

'Yes, Doctor.'

The director stepped in, enabling Finegold to retreat to the sofa in the media lounge and breathe normally again.

'Bob, so great to have you with us again,' gushed the director.'

'Rebecca, thank you for setting this up. We are thrilled to have been given this exclusive. May I ask why us? This is a big story. Why not a national?'

'Because we know you'll handle it carefully. I'd be lying if everyone on my board agrees but I think the bigger outlets will cover it from your piece, which means yours will set the tone. There's less room for misunderstandings, especially since you're writing up a feature with the data we provided. We couldn't do that with the others.'

'And because if we mess up, you can cut us out. If the BBC messes up, you have to let them back in, regardless.'

'No, Bob, not at all. I've done the trades myself, remember. If we're to attract the best talent, we need your ongoing interest more than we need the nationals. It is the politicians that are obsessed with the nationals. Anyway, why the questioning? Did you not get what you needed from Finegold? I can always bring her back.'

'No, no. All great. She's more polished than I remembered. More PR'd.'

'Well, you can blame me for that! It's a big story, Bob. You can't expect me not to be involved.'

'True. So, what does this town have to offer?'

'That's the spirit Bob. I'll show you.'

Stirlingshire, Scotland, 21st April 2002

Book them and they will come

'James, I think this is going to work. James, can you hear me?'

James turned around gradually, careful not to lose his footing on the sodden ground; if he stumbled, he had no free hands to break his fall. Lyla, his girlfriend that he met on the way to the commune they were now living at, was at the bottom of the hill, the sun shining across her tangled hair. She looked stunning, all the more so because of the small pile of wooden stakes she had crafted that were now piled at her feet. They were evidence of her commitment to the project, his side-project.

'Yeah, I think it will too. Would have been easier if the others had helped us but it doesn't matter, this bit will be done once I come down to get those last few stakes.'

'It's OK. I'll bring them' she yelled back. Before he could argue, she had pushed the pile of wood onto an old hemp sack and started dragging it up the gently sloping, slippery field.

In preparation for her arrival, he took the length of wire he was gripping between his gardening gloves and wrapped it tightly around the last stake in the row, to give him some stability as he reached down the hill to pull her up. He kissed her sweat-covered lips and she lunged forward against him for balance.

'I think more of them are won over than they are letting on, you know,' said Lyla, rubbing her hands against James's recently shaved head and skinny neck. 'I'm sure some of them would be willing to help.'

'You think? I know they will come on board eventually but,' James swept his hand across the assortment of colourful tents beneath them, 'they have been doing things the same way for years. I think it will take some time for them to realise that we can work together. That's what the fence is for, to give this field a sense of place. They need to know it's not to keep people out or in, but to shape us. Every community needs a shape.'

'Oh, are you ready to tell me more, then?' Lyla asked sarcastically, with a smile.

'Yes, but it goes without saying that they aren't ready to hear this yet. I'm fine with them knowing we are up to something, but I don't think they will be ready for years. Look at all the acoustic guitars and tambourines down there. They are old and full of 1960s' folksiness. It will be a while yet before they are ready for a change, ready to get real and show the world how things can be done differently. Just look at the old man in that yurt down there. Pathetic!'

James laughed to himself, enjoying the fresh air and clarity brought by the lack of drugs in his system, prescription or otherwise.

'OK, honey, but you know I believe in you,' Lyla said, tipping the logs onto the soil and sitting on the canvas. 'Maybe you can tell me?'

'The fence is for the pigs,' answered James.

Lyla squinted her eyes and smirked in disbelief.

'Wait, I know what you are going to say.'

'What, that we our all vegetarian here!' she shouted. 'And you persuaded everyone to let us cut down some of our trees to keep fucking pigs?'

'Don't worry, the pigs won't be here for a while yet,' he explained with a smile, ignoring her anger. 'And first we will have goats. They won't mind the goats as they will keep the hedges back, and we can make cheese and things. There are only a few vegans here, and they aren't evangelical about it yet.'

'Yet? You know they find it irritating when you speak like that, James. You may be one of the more educated people here, but you can't presume to tell them – or me – what we will do and how we will be. And you know the guys down there are going to come down pretty fucking hard on you if you bring in some pork. Unless you are going to tell us that you are going to milk a pig?'

James considered snapping at Lyla and reminding her of the greasy spoon cafe he had picked her up from near Carlisle, and that she was no more a part of the community than he was, but he thought better of it. Even so, it irritated him greatly when she claimed a greater connection to the camp. They were both outsiders and there was something delusional in her sense of attachment. Maybe that was just her, he thought. She needs attachment. Maybe that's why it was so easy to persuade her to join him.

'I know you have lived with some people a bit like this before,' said James, in his best calming voice as he took a seat next to her in the mud. 'But I understand these people too. That's why I am here; that's why I came here. These are not just any old hippies. Well, maybe they are at the moment, but soon others will arrive. We need to get ready and demonstrate we can accommodate difference. We will get goats at first, I promise, but remember the goal is bigger than us.'

'There you go talking in riddles again. I just don't want them to kick us out, James. There are some great guys down there. They love each other, and they have welcomed us in. I don't want to throw that all away.'

'We have plenty of time and I am not planning on going anywhere. I haven't spoken about this place to any outsiders since we arrived, and that was just sharing stories in the store, nothing revolutionary. As I said, I think that will take years. So, in the meantime, why don't we smoke this. I won't even mention the goats yet. Definitely not the pigs.'

Lyla smiled and pulled out her zippo lighter, a favourite of hers branded with a Led Zeppelin emblem, and lit the end of the joint.

'You know, it's not what I expected here. We all talk about this place as though it is luxury and that it will get more luxurious the more effort we put in, but it's not easy. Even the cheap hotels I stayed in in Blackpool and Carlisle were easier than this, and it's never hard to come by a bit of money for food if you put the effort in.'

James winced a little as Lyla's easy reference to prostitution along the seafronts but decided to keep his mouth shut. He had been with girls before with more frightening pasts, but that was when he was ill and found it easier to be with people unqualified to judge him. Now, after all the hard work he had put into his writing and to getting this far, he felt he was in a position to judge her. He smiled at her while he thought this, considering all the ways he could manipulate her while taking the joint from her lips and pulling a big draw.

'Yes, it certainly isn't easy here.' He exhaled and rubbed some of the wet dirt from his fingers against his trousers. 'Even on a day when the sun is shining like this, the clouds circle like vultures and the ground insists on holding on to its swamp. This is the longest I have ever spent in Scotland and if we had a choice, I would have picked somewhere more – cultivated.'

'Wow, not like you to admit that!'

'I guess I know there is a huge amount to do, so I don't like talking about how tough it can be here. When I was at the hospital, the doctors encouraged me not to dwell on difficult thoughts and to push forward with my ideas. And when I was in my bedsit, I realised that I couldn't finish my book without living it, without testing, honing and realising my goals. I guess I am saying that it has all been quite an effort but the alternative – scrounging off my friends and sitting in hospital beds – is a lot worse. I assume you are still here because, you feel the same.'

Tottenham, London, 16ᵗʰ December 2053

Get dressed, agent!

Eres woke to a buzzing sound that drilled into his exhausted brain. Opening his eyes to let enough light in to activate his retinal displays, he could see a red flash against the dry red rawness of his eyelids, an abrasive sensation that ceased when his implant decided he was fully conscious. He then rolled over to wake his sister too.

'Get up,' he said softly, his hand oner her shoulder. 'Neri, wake up please. They're calling me.'

'What? You're mumbling.'

'Please leave the room Neri. I've got a call. Please, go in the cupboard.'

Looking at his sister, he could see that he had failed to soften his tone enough to prevent a counter reaction.

Eres and Neri had been sharing a room in the same building since childhood, slowly promoting themselves every few years to incrementally larger spaces as older occupants died. Their most recent promotion was a result of a spate of deaths amongst the residents who were over one hundred that had created a little slack in the building. They still had to share a room, however, because the committee insisted that private rooms were for young mothers and their babies. However, due to Eres' relatively new position, he and Neri had been given access to a small storeroom down the corridor for private use in case of emergencies.

'It's 5am, Eres! I don't see why you can't get a room at your office, or at least bump us up past that whore next door.' Neri was staring at him, anger pulling her face muscles taut. 'Why can't you go to the cupboard?'

'I have put in another new bid with a whole new case, you know that. But for now, would you mind stepping outside. I'm

very sorry. The reception in there isn't good enough. Please.'
Eres closed his eyes tightly, hoping that when he reopened them everything would be gone: the flashing alert; his sister; the home; the insecurity caused by the only other agent recruited at the same time as him having already been promoted. On hearing the slam-proof door click shut, he knew he had got at least one of his wishes.

'*Code JL16*' scrolled across his eyeline, followed by '*Agent Eres Matthews instructed to hold position and await contact.*'

He assumed he was in some trouble for taking so long to respond.

'*Enter now*' replaced the previous instruction and Eres immediately indicated in the affirmative to his device.

With his body sitting up in his bed, he found his vision and hearing floating in the corner of a distressed-brick meeting room. Its styling dated it to the late 2030s, when huge swathes of the city's stock of private homes, or so-called 'family homes', were bulldozed to recover building materials for administrative buildings and the first wave of the shared spaces that dominated the city today.

Around the table sat an assortment of white coats and military uniforms, the coats looking upset and exhausted.

'Are you seeing this, Matthews?' said a familiar voice in Eres' brain.

'Yes, chairman. What's happened?'

'You are looking at a room in Neasden. It's one of the army's testing bases for the time device, which is why the coalition has called for our assistance.'

Eres could tell from the chairman's voice that any annoyance the chairman harboured for his morning slowness was superseded by anger at something more important. They all lived in fear of the time device. That was the first thing he had learned when he had signed up onto the force a year ago.

'At some point last night, or in the early hours of this morning,' the chairman continued, 'the base system was accessed from the outside by an unregistered device, which proceeded to delete nearly all of the data accumulated by the teams working here.'

'They weren't backing it up to the coalition system?' Eres replied, immediately cringing at himself for asking. He took a deep breath to regain some control.

'Yes, they were backing it up, agent. However, there was some kind of trojan. It left the gates open to their storage area, so the backup is gone as well. Taken.'

'Right.'

'There's another thing, agent. We're completely locked out. Neasden seems to be stuck in a time loop. The crystal is locked onto something, sending a version of its past, present and future around and around.'

'Have they tried to break in?' asked Eres instinctively, cringing at himself again.

'Yes, agent!' the chairman yelled. 'When they do, it creates a power surge. There have been reports of people vanishing. Just for a split second. They can't be travelling far but they say they've seen themselves, in the past. Very disturbing, Matthews, as you can imagine.'

Eres' mind was spinning. Even if the authorities got back into their systems, he assumed it would likely take them months of data recovery to get the time device working again. Worse, it meant someone else, with the data they had stolen, could make their own device. He briefly froze with paranoia, imagining his enemies watching his every move.

'You will see from your display, Matthews, that the work down here is being chaired by a Major Bennett. Your system should be telling you that he is not directly attached to this base. This is because a Corporal Roydon, who is responsible for this place – and perhaps this mess as well – is nowhere to be found.'

'I see, sir. So this could be an inside job?' asked Eres, as he read through Roydon's biography that was floating before him.

'Yes, it could be. That is what we are discussing now. Listen into what Roydon's colleagues are saying, and then get out of bed and find this guy.'

The chairman broke his connection as abruptly as he had made it, leaving Eres to gain some control over his growing panic as he tried to concentrate on the activity playing out within in the crumbling brick walls in which his senses were suspended.

Belgravia,
14th December 2053

MAD

Sira stayed a few paces behind her friends as they set off down the alley behind their garage. They each stepped carefully over the carcass of a dog, which explained the stench they had caught whiffs of in recent days. As they walked into the unknown, she watched them mocking each other, occasionally verbally, often physically and sometimes through messaging, and wished that she could be as detached from life as they seemed.

For hours they followed abandoned railways and wandered through fields of concrete stumps, previously houses, and along London's tributaries that had broken free of their iron tunnels. They went half a day without seeing a soul. Sira knew that once they got nearer the Thames this would change; she wondered if Frank and Yanda knew it would, too. She did not want to scare them too early.

The area near the Thames was home to streets of white-pillared buildings, originally built as large family homes for the wealthy. They had been carved up into up into apartments, so the rumours went, to create private dwellings for the few individuals who had kept hold of their money when the banks closed. The inhabitants lived behind iron doors, and were guarded by well-paid armed security personnel who doubled as servants, fetching food, fuel and supplies when needed. The guards also protected their masters from the other residents of the block who, when their cash reserves got low, saw their neighbours as easy pickings.

When the alleys became dead ends and they turned into their first street in Belgravia, Yanda stopped abruptly and held his arms out to stop his friends from proceeding.

'You've seen it, then, Yanda?' Sira asked.

'I thought we were leading you?'

'I know. Sorry.' Sira gave a small shrug. 'What exactly did you see?'

'They say these guards stay inside.'

'I know, Yanda. I know the story. What did you see?'

'They call them the MAD men because they have their weapons trained on each other.'

'Yes, they do. What's your point?'

'There's just one sitting there, totally unguarded.'

'Maybe he is having a cigarette?'

'It doesn't make sense, Sira. He could get shot from the road. The others should be yelling at him to get back inside or killing him. He's a threat. Unless...'

'Unless what?'

'Unless they are all working together?'

Frank, who had begun distracting himself with an online game when he felt the tension rise, joined the conversation. 'Sira, when you were in the hotel, did they make you do anything? Anything you didn't want to?'

'Not exactly. They threatened me. They were working on fear, not force.'

'So, we're safe?' asked Yanda, a nervous smile spreading across his face. 'The guards can't be made to give up their posts and stop guarding if they don't want to?'

'I don't think so,' said Frank. 'If they've been hacked, someone could just augment what they can see, or what they think they can see.'

'I don't understand.'

'Yanda, if someone has hacked these guys like they hacked Sira, they could stop them seeing the other guards. They could convince the guards that their rivals have all vanished. Worse for us, they could manipulate them into thinking anyone new who wanders into the street is a guard coming to threaten them. If that's what's happened, they will shoot us.'

'If that's true, Frank, then the gangs have taken this whole area. They may have sneaked in and looted the place already. They may not even have had to do the looting themselves. How the fuck are we going to stop them?'

Sira pulled her friends further back into the alley they had emerged from, held her finger to her lips and messaged to them: 'I'm pleased you've listened to what I said but I'm not sure it works like that. They had to expend some effort to hack me, to change the walls, to change how things felt to touch. It didn't sound like something easily repeated en masse. I know they want to, though. They also had kids there. I heard rooms of children working away at something. I think that's their computing power. That's how they plan to change things, augment people's reality, live. But they aren't there yet.'

'How do you know?'

'Because otherwise they wouldn't need, Sira,' answered Frank. 'If they could, it would be over already and they'd be in charge.'

'So, you're both saying we aren't going to get shot because Sira saw some kind of slave children? Doesn't fill me with confidence!'

'What I'm saying, Yanda, is that one guy with a gun doesn't equal the whole army of Belgravia. We can only see one guy, can't we?'

'Fine. But I don't fancy our chances against him.'

'So, you're turning around after seeing one man and one gun? I think it's going to get a lot tougher than this,' Frank mocked.

'I never said I was turning around.'

'Good,' messaged Sira. 'Both of you, follow me.' She ran out of the alley towards the end wall of the first house on the street. The boys hesitated before following.

'I've got a question, Yanda. If this is all about hacking, why did they take Sira and not me?' Frank asked.

'This again?'

'I've broken into more – and harder – systems than you have, or Sira or anyone we know. But they took her.'

'Maybe they want to fuck her. She liked that Captain guy, didn't she?'

'If you think that, you don't sound very concerned.'

'I didn't say that.'

'Guys, will you keep up and keep quiet,' Sira messaged. 'I think if either of you had these fuckers in your head, you'd want a bit more sensitivity than I'm getting. All I know is that they could pick up on anything we say or do, so I shouldn't even be having this conversation. We have to assume they know where we are and where we are going. If we aren't going to get shot, we need to get out of signal range.' She ran ahead again and the two boys sprinted to catch up.

As they reach the first building, she signalled above her head to them. They knew what to do; they had played this military special ops game for thousands of hours and had, a few weeks previously, spent a glorious thirty-seven minutes at the top of the leader board.

Sira picked up a brick and threw it through a side window. Clambering along the ornate wall that flanked the front steps, the trio lowered themselves into the first building of the row. They dropped into the corner of a room and found themselves opposite a decomposing body in an armchair. The smell was unbearable.

Sira pulled a small antique camera from her pocket and showed Frank and Yanda the flickering single bar of signal in its display. The pair looked confused so she whispered, 'Old building, thick walls. Bad for signal. Let's go to basement.'

In each basement on the street they found a window or door from where they could climb into the garden, jump the fence and climb back inside, before the antenna on Sira's implant could reconnect with the network. Once inside, they waited sixty seconds before repeating the manoeuvre.

'I think the guard we saw is in front of the next building,' said Frank.

'Where is everyone? They can't all be rotting.'

'Why not, Frank? Maybe they have been slowly dying off. They can't mate from behind a secure door, can they?' asserted Sira.

'I guess it doesn't matter why, so long as we aren't being followed.'

'Guys,' Yanda was shuffling around the dark of the basement, 'I've got an idea. It would be a nicer idea if this gang are somehow involved, but I think we should do it either way. If the guard on the street is the only live one down here we could sneak past, but he's got a gun. I think we should take it.'

Frank looked at Sira for reassurance that she disagreed, but it was not forthcoming. 'Go on, Yanda, explain,' she said.

'OK. As well as his gun, I think we should kill him.'

Frank began circling the room in panic. 'Are you insane? He's got a gun. And we're murderers now? When did that happen?'

'I've thought about that. We could open the front door and hit him over the head.'

'And hope he doesn't just shoot us? We aren't killers, Yanda. Sira, tell him, please. This is mad. Yanda, have you gone mad?'

'Or we could drop something on him from the window above. Something like that.' Yanda pointed towards a rusting petrol generator in the corner of the room.

'OK, Yanda. But we can't just knock him out,' said Sira calmly, as she walked over to inspect the potential murder weapon. 'We should kill him and cut out his implant, so we can use it to disrupt my signal. If we attach it to my head with some foil or cable, it should stop it from reconnecting.'

Frank stood in silence, waiting to his two friends to admit they were joking. Yanda turned to him and explained softly and calmly that he would have to help because Sira could not leave the basement. Frank's role would be to keep the door shut whilst he, Yanda, dropped the generator from above.

'What if he shoots, Yanda?' Frank asked.

'I'll kill him before then.'

'And if you don't?'

'I don't really have a back-up plan, but the prize is pretty big.'

'I'll cut his head open afterwards if you bring the body down here,' said Sira. 'It's the least I can do.'

'Have you two considered that there may be more live people in the area? With guns? They may even witness this, this…'

'Assassination?'

'I was going to say murder.' Frank stared at them, hoping they would come out of their temporary madness, but Sira continued as though this were an everyday occurrence.

'If we want the gun and the implant, and we don't want to fight him face to face, this makes sense. I've got a small knife but it's no match for his rifle. If we don't have time to cut the implant out, we use my knife to cut his head off and take it with us.'

'And what if the noise does more than disturb this guard, Sira? We were expecting every building to be full of them. I know we need his implant but we aren't killers. Are we? We cannot take on the whole of Belgravia. Yanda, are you sure you can do it? I mean, drop that thing on his head?'

'We are doing this,' asserted Yanda. He took the knife from Sira and pushed its handle into Frank's palm. 'We made the choice to kill him – to kill whoever – when we left our garage. The other choice we had was to wait to get taken,' he messaged as he lifted the generator and heaved it up the stairs.

Frank followed, still hoping it was a joke. He crept to the front door, took hold of the doorknob with one hand and gripped the knife in the other. Just as the panic began to overwhelm him, an injection of adrenalin pushed through him at the sounds of glass smashing above and a bullet being chambered outside. He threw his weight against the door and wedged his feet against a radiator pipe in the hallway for leverage. There was a loud thump on the door. Frank's ankles crunched like chicken gristle as the first blows came from outside.

'Who the fuck is this? I'm going to shoot,' yelled a deep voice from outside.

'Yanda, now!' shouted Frank, 'My legs. My legs. Ah – ahhh. Now!' Plaster from the ceiling rained onto the back of Frank's neck. With the second thump from above, he realised that Yanda was struggling to lift the generator out of the window.

A bullet cracked through the door under Frank's left arm and he smashed his face into the carpet as he lost his balance. 'Yanda!' he yelled again. His face was pushed backwards by the opening door and he felt the knife slip from his hand. He scrunched his eyes tight, hoping he could force himself to black out but, instead, dropped fully to the floor as the door slammed shut again and he heard steel crushing bone outside.

He flipped around to see Sira standing above him, her hands dripping with blood. Before he regained his composure, she had sprinted back into the basement. She was replaced by Yanda, who pulled Frank up from the floor.

'We've got to get the body inside Frank,' Yanda yelled.

'My ankles are twisted. I can't. What the fuck happened?'

'I – I. The cord got stuck. It doesn't matter. Get downstairs.'

Frank contemplated arguing and trying to stand again, but he could see Yanda's face was red with blood-pumping aggression and he felt safer pulling himself out of his friend's way. He shuffled backwards along the tiles and watched Yanda do the same in front of him, gripping the masked man under the remains of his jaw, whilst the soft glistening flaps of his skull lay open across Yanda's arm.

As they got to the top of the stairs, Sira pulled Frank as gently as she could down to the basement. His coccyx bounced on each wooden step like a hammer. With Frank out of the way, she thrust the knife into the top of the remains of the guard's head and twisted until she felt the scrape of metal.

'I didn't realise they were so deep,' she said to herself, as her hand swirled around in the mess. 'I thought they were behind your eyes. I guess that's just how it feels. Yes, this is it, it's right under the brain by the spinal cord. Yanda, I've got it but it's slipping. Cut off some of his shirt. I need a cloth or something... Yep, that good. Here it is.'

The two boys sat with their mouths open as Sira held up the shiny metal sphere no bigger than her thumbnail. 'Fucking amazing, isn't it?'

'Sira, are you OK? I'm sorry you had to come up to help Frank. I couldn't get the generator over the windowsill. I should have said something when I was dragging it up the stairs. It was really heavy. It's just...'

'What, Yanda? What was it?'

'It was my plan, so I didn't want to admit. I thought I could still do it. I *did* still do it.'

'Yes, and Frank's ankles are fucked, and I could have been spotted. Maybe I was. Let's just get this fucking thing on my head, shall we?'

'OK. I got some wire from the generator, let's tie it round your head so it's at the back under your hair.'

'Shit, what was that?'

'What, Frank? I didn't hear anything, asked Yanda.'

'Shush. It sounded like a door slamming.'

'This door? I shut this door. I swear.'

'Yanda, be quiet, and listen,' implored Frank.

The trio sat in silence under the narrow basement window, straining to hear. Suddenly the glass smashed above them and a wall of bullets filled the basement with a thick cloud of brick dust.

Gripping the implant in her mouth, Sira grabbed her friends' hands and dragged them amidst the rain of bullets up the stairs and through the back window, into the shelter of a garden stairwell connected to a different part of the basement. 'Where's the fucking gun?' she demanded.

Yanda looked at Sira's lips but heard only the faintest sound. She pulled an imaginary trigger. The remaining blood drained from his face. 'Shit. Downstairs. I'll go,' he messaged.

'No, you'll die,' she yelled over the gunfire.

'They are coming. Got to do something.'

'Yanda! Oh fuck!' Frank messaged. 'They are coming. No gun. What the fuck was that for?'

'I said I'll go. Just go, get behind that wall.'

'No, we're in this together. I'm coming too,' yelled Sira.

'You've got to get that implant on you. No choice.'

Sira nodded and pulled Frank to his feet. They ran, slipping on a jungle of overgrown weeds and grass before throwing themselves behind an ornate garden wall. They got their heads down as an explosion bulldozed through the back of the house and ripped off the foliage on the lawn, carpeting the pair in a bloodied forest of ivy.

--

Frank sat on the riverbank, the water soothing his ankle. 'You didn't see him, then?'

'I told you, I only had to go in a few feet to get this.' Sira was hugging the automatic rifle like a newborn baby. 'I saw parts. I didn't see anything that I recognised as him.'

'I yelled at him, Sira.'

Sira stared down at the embankment and fought to hold back her own waves of regret. She knew that ignoring the present was the only way she could survive it. 'Look, the plan went wrong,' she mumbled finally.

Frank kept pushing. He was convinced something strange had happened to make them killers. His mind spun, always coming back to whether they'd had a choice or not when they first saw Belgravia. Despite being the boldest thing any of them had ever attempted, he was convinced they'd had no choice but to try and remove the rider in Sira's head. But could they have done something different when they saw that armed guard? They could have gone further without the gun, he was sure of it, but could they have got to the river without blocking Sira's signal? He would never know and his mind was running in circles.

In response to each of his questions, Sira explained that Yanda had always been proud and wanted to finish what he started. They should both be grateful. But Frank remained unsatisfied, trying to find another answer. Eventually, seeing that she was not going to say anything further, his mind and messages slowly turned to finding a boat to continue their journey east.

Sira, relieved that the inquisition had ended, pushed herself off the concrete embankment and began making her way towards Vauxhall Bridge. She had read that, even as little as twenty years ago, tourists would sail up and down the river for fun, chatting and drinking. No one swam in the river because of the waves and rapids following the collapse of the Thames Barrier but pleasure boats, as people had called them, still existed in her parents' lifetime.

No one came here anymore unless they could handle themselves. When the police started withdrawing, the river was the first place to be left to nature, including human nature. It had since returned to a raw sewage and trade route, but what was being traded in the bowels of the tall ships coming and going from the sea was a mystery.

She returned to Frank after walking up and down the stretch to the bridge. 'Good news and bad news.'

Frank shrugged in response.

'Here's the good news.' Sira handed him a hessian sack to hide the gun. 'The bad news is that I don't think it will be as easy as hopping aboard. Boats aren't coming near the shore. I think we are going to have to pick one of these moored barges and steal it.'

'Could we not hide on it until it starts moving?' he replied, resigned at the prospect of making additional enemies.

'Yes, but that could be weeks or it might go the wrong way. Plus, we wouldn't know where and when it would stop.'

'And you can drive a boat?'

'I think we can both PILOT a boat. Download a simulator and we can overlay it. Or you can overlay it since you haven't been hacked, and then you can pilot it.'

--

'This is OK.' Frank was standing as tall as he could, his lower leg strapped up in rope to support his ankle, steering a thirty-metre barge down the river between arches and oncoming boats.

Sira was sitting on a wooden crate by his feet pushing the ignition wiring back into place following her hack. 'Yep, you are doing well. Is the simulator working?'

'I've put in our destination and a real map of the river, and it is pointing the way. It's not too bad at the moment but it's going to get trickier.'

Sira nodded and leant forward to lift the edge of the tarp covering the rest of the barge.

'Please don't,' mumbled Frank.

'There might be something valuable under there that we can sell to pay for my procedure,' replied Sira, tapping the side of her head.

Frank looked away and texted with a sad face and a face palm that he did not want the owners to be after them as well.

'If you insist,' Sira messaged back. She asked out loud how he thought they would pay the Poplar surgeons.

Frank replied with gun and dollar emojis, adding, 'It's right that we finish this thing by getting rid of it.'

'And give it to our enemies? Must be nice to not be ideological,' said Sira, picking bits of paint from the decking and flicking it into the black river.

'Seeing Yanda blown to bits helped with that,' he messaged back.

Sira did not reply. She knew everything had changed since her kidnapping and Belgravia but for her it meant they needed to be bolder. Their minor cyber-attacks and disloyal costumes were not enough; they were child's play. If Yanda's death had proved anything, it was that they needed to be better prepared to confront their enemies.

Frank looked down at Sira and was worried he had upset her. After deleting and repeating the text a few times, he messaged that he knew they had to show more strength to the liberals and that he would help more now that Yanda was gone. With the people's anger growing, it could not be long before the system toppled. Once the message was sent, he agonised over whether he had said enough.

Sira responded with a laughing face. After a few moments of silence, she looked up and yelled into the cold air, partly at him but also partly at London, that everything was different now. Some teenage hackers in mock uniforms were never going to be enough to create a new regime, or defeat gunmen in rich neighbourhoods or gangs of brain hackers. She pulled her coat tight around her and looked away again.

'It's cold. That piece of cold metal on your neck can't help,' Frank offered, not sure how to interact with her. He knew that if Yanda had been there, he would have said something stupid, something bold and distracting, and they would have all laughed together. But that dynamic was gone. Sira was right: everything had changed.

'Revolutions fail after the overthrow,' Sira asserted, now looking at the city along the riverbank, not at Frank. 'That's what we're all ignoring. No one is talking about how, if and when this finally collapses, we can be the ones that retain power.' She turned and glared at him when he did not reply.

'I'm listening Sira. I'm just concentrating on piloting this boat as well. We don't want to crash, do we?'

'In Egypt at the beginning of the century, when the military finally took control again after the riots, the global liberals made the military follow their rules. The people didn't have a say in the future. So when rebels started blowing things up, blowing people up, the military wasn't allowed to fight back. It was years before they brought order back.'

'Who are we in this analogy? The rebels?'

'No, Frank. The rebels slaughtered people. I think the guys that hacked me are the rebels. My point is that if we go the way of Egypt and we bring down the government, how do we keep control? What makes you think we, with our hacks and viruses, can keep order, protect us from the gangs taking over and keep the liberals out?'

'Well,' Frank laughed, 'I've always thought it was a bit risky. But you believe in this stuff, don't you? You always have.'

'For fuck's sake, Frank,' Sira snapped. 'It's not about the risk or belief. It's about being ready. Having a plan. Has today not taught you anything? Yanda is dead because we weren't ready. If we go through with this, we need to be ready to hold off the liberals, too. This government we are talking about bringing down has friends. They will come and impose their ideas, or try to at least. And that's what they're best at.'

'What?'

'Creating meaning. They're slippery and full of self-belief. Think about how they started! They wiped away what had gone before them. The brave soldiers who had stood together to win the Second World War were mowed down by liars, by students who promised the world something better, something free and plentiful, in which everyone would work together. But when they had power, they sold anything that wasn't tied down. And no one noticed because the liars had created new meaning.

'Whatever they are doing at whatever point in time, whether it is selling oil or enviro-tech, they create meaning around it, so much meaning that it is hard to argue against without falling into one of their traps. If we are to take and hold power, we have to be ready to stand up to that, ready to promise something better.'

'I don't understand. Nothing that has happened in the last few hours has been about any of that. Where is all this coming from? I'm not saying you're wrong. You're talking to a sceptic. I just want to understand.'

'The last few hours have changed everything. The liberals have made a perfect market of ideas and lies. It earns them money and makes them a mirage. We have been trying to knock them down by mocking their lack of strength. But if they can get hold of what the gangs have –the ability to change what people see and hear, to hack and change ideas – how can we beat that?'

'I don't know, Sira. Maybe we need to steal it for ourselves. You're a better hacker than anyone. Maybe the liberals don't know about it yet.'

Sira stared over the side of the boat, choosing to ignore Frank's optimism. She knew he was only trying to comfort her, but it was no good; she had looked into power and run away. All her ideas, her network's ideas, hopes and dreams seemed thin, the product of desperate people who wanted to believe in something, anything.

'Do you think they are making us see that?' Frank yelled over the wind. He reached for her hand and pulled her to her feet. She looked down the length of the barge and saw they had passed the last of the bridges and were approaching towers in the water.

'I don't suppose you can see these from the riverbank, Sira. Too much smog and the river is so wide here.'

'What are they?'

'I think they are villages. Hang on, I'm filtering the image to get a better look. Wow, they are homes on stilts. They look like they're stacked on top of each other. Why build up and not across? I think I got a glimpse of them earlier, but I assumed they were old concrete and metal buildings on the bank. But no, these look like bamboo. Incredible.'

'Shall we say hi?'

113

Frank turned to object but she was gone from his side. He yelled to her across the boat, but the wind running across the Thames blew his words away.

West London, 16th December 2053: Pie 'n' mash Eres stepped out of the private car he had taken to Shepherd's Bush. he paid the fare from his untraceable burner unit before assessing his surroundings. His sister had been happy to see the back of him, slamming the door shut as he had left their room.

He had only been to the old city twice before, and on both of those occasions was accompanied by a team of technicians with a secure line to base. This was the first time he had been alone and the first time he was worried about more than wasting resources.

Looking at the blank faces and frustratingly nondescript vehicles on the street, he ducked into the first public establishment he came across and connected with the only person he could trust.

--

'This is a lovely spot, Matthews. I must come to you for eating suggestions next Generations Day.'

Mila Seynes, Eres' most senior administrator, was sitting opposite him. Having ignored Eres' request to come to the old city in something inconspicuous, she was dressed head-to-toe in one of her vintage replica outfits that looked like it had belonged to the iconic Israeli , Golda Meir.

'I need your help, Seynes. It's something the others can't know about, just us and the chairman. We're going offline. We have to do what the gangs do.'

Seynes looked at him incredulously. Since Eres had recruited her a few months earlier, this was the first time he had asked her to go any further from the office than the nearest local shop.

A year before, in his job interview, he had explained his workaholic nature to the agent that briefly became his boss, using examples from his experience as caretaker in a local co-op shop. She had given him the job, a gun and a budget, saying if he could do the work of two people he would do well. A week after he started, she had vanished to deal with some corruption charges. Finding himself struggling, and with all his other colleagues fully occupied, he had eventually employed Seynes.

'Seynes,' Eres tried again, regretting that he had not previously told her more, 'we have to do what the gangs do to evade detection from the device. We need to keep moving around, become invisible so they don't know how to listen in, how to trace our footsteps.' He saw her eyes flicking. 'Are you listening?'

'Yes, sorry, just checking for messages. But yes, I'm listening. Now, since it has taken me over an hour to find this place,' she gestured towards the white abattoir-like tiled walls of the pie and mash shop, 'please do tell me why I'm breathing in greasy pastry at this hour. Why is a place like this even open at this hour?'

'This is serious.'

'Come on, Eres. Since when do the big jobs come to us?' she asked rhetorically. A smile crept across her lips.

Eres scrolled across his notes and mentally rehearsed what he was going to say while the waitress refilled their coffees. He wondered whether to insist on their conversation being conducted silently through text exchange. However, he recalled his trainer telling him that it had been discovered, at the cost of two agents in the field, that people sitting in silence can be quite conspicuous. Instead, he decided it would be best to undertake both forms of communication simultaneously, with neither channel making sense without the other.

He conveyed this to Seynes, half verbally and half through text, and immediately realised it was easier said than done. He took in a deep, slow breath, trying to rein in his agitation but this was hampered by the steam coming from the kitchen which was tickling his sleep-deprived face.

'Neasden lost all of its data last night,' he continued, trying to keep calm. 'They still have all their equipment but it's currently useless. Obviously, there are teams working on getting it back. It looks like a gang succeeded in breaking in – we don't know who. We have to assume the worst, that they have taken the data to use in a machine of their own.' He

115

paused to let this sink in whilst he took a long sip of acidic lukewarm coffee. 'First of all, I need to ask you if you think we could get the thing operational again without any data down there, just with the equipment and our work.'

Seynes sat back in her chair. The colour of her face had vanished and it now matched her white pearls. 'Right,' she transmitted, beginning to grind her teeth.

'I'll take that as a no, shall I?'

She responded seriously for the first time. 'I think we may have made some real progress with the numbers, Eres. It's some kind of quantum pattern. If whatever has just happened at the base hadn't happened, we could be testing our ideas in the next few weeks. But we aren't ready. I think, maybe, the core coding in the system should enable us to send something back, maybe.'

'No space travel, just time? The chairman said that's been happening already, sort of.'

'Yes, just back to Neasden. That makes sense, I think. I'm not an expert Eres. I'm new to this.'

Eres' stomach sank. *That's useless* ran across Seynes' display, followed by a lengthy data packet, a series of briefing papers and articles that scrolled like a movie, zooming in for key facts. It explained how, following the first early experiments, they had chosen to never again send a person back in time for ethical reasons, but that there was nothing stopping the device being used for this. The display, controlled by Eres, then sped through to his recording of this morning's exchange with the chairman and the white coats in the lab. He paused it. 'What are our options Seynes? What do you think?' he asked.

She sat for a moment. Nothing she had seen gave her any more insight than her boss already had. She spoke slowly and tentatively, worried that he might yell at her. 'I guess we have to find Roydon. But why are we sitting here?'

'Because I've been told not to trust any fellow agents and you aren't a qualified agent yet. I thought you'd want to help.'

'I do, sir', scrolled in front of his eyes.

'OK, let's get to Neasden and start from there. But we have to get there in secret and avoid detection. Who knows what the gangs can do now!'

'Roydon might already be dead, Eres.'

'I know that. But can we please stick to things that are helpful? We need to set up a base of operations from which to start the search, somewhere to run our communications through so they can't be monitored easily. A secure site.'

He leant over the table towards her and transmitted: *'If we could recover anything from Neasden, Seynes, how much do we need to recover to test your calculations?'*

Seynes shrugged her shoulders, and her eyes were directed back into the data packet. She watched some archive footage from two years earlier of soldiers going in and out of the machine and then being interviewed. The soldiers spoke of the people they had met in the past, conversations that were corroborated by the recordings from their personal devices. She watched footage of civilian witnesses in a stark white room being shown photos of the soldiers and denying ever seeing them before.

Her eyes bounced to a briefing paper about parallel universes and a section warning that, if the populace knew they could be bounced from their 'genuine' universe to a parallel one by happening upon a visitor, society was in danger of suffering a catastrophic loss of morale.

The data packet ended and she returned to the café to see Eres nodding at her knowingly. She felt sick.

Thames, London, 14th December 2053

Isolation

Sira was halfway along the barge's cargo when she heard Frank calling for her. When she reached the end of the boat, she spotted the place she was looking for: a raised lip of hull with a gap through which to slot the rifle. Ensuring she had her safety off, she nestled her eye into the scope of the weapon and pointed it at the precarious structures in the river around them. Once in position, she gave Frank a thumbs-up to try and calm him and then got back to gun sight.

Between gaps in the walls, the inhabitants had stretched polythene to make windows, one above the other, twenty storeys up. Behind some of the billowing sheets she could see children watching the passing boats. At some of the larger openings, the polythene was being held aside by groups of overweight men talking and smoking. Sira thought that they looked like traders. 'What does your implant say about this place. About who they are?'

'Nothing,' Frank yelled. 'They are totally hidden. Hidden for all to see.'

'Look further, then.'

'You don't get it! Hidden for all to see. It's a joke!'

'GREAT. LOOK FURTHER, FRANK,' she messaged back, while trying to stop her breathing making the gun sight wobble.

'Fine. OK,' he messaged. 'This could be something. The map looks a little off.'

'Explain, please,' demanded Sira, unable to hide her impatience.

'It looks like there is a chameleon patch over the open-source satellite map. It changes with the light, always covering what's really there.'

'The guys living in bamboo? You're saying they hacked the global map?'

'I know it doesn't seem right. Maybe someone did it for them. We aren't far from Poplar, are we?'

'I want to speak to them.'

'Why? Come on, Sira. You've got a piece of someone's brain tied to your head. I think we should focus.'

'Didn't you hear what I said? We need to understand the liberals. We need to understand how to create ideas! When was the last time you had a chance to speak to someone who wasn't a teenage West London hacker?'

'What makes you think they're liberals, Sira? We don't know anything about them.'

When she did not reply, he messaged, 'At least put the gun away,' with a shrugging emoji.

'Fine. It's gone,' she yelled, slipping it back into the hessian sack. 'You know,' she messaged as she was wrapping up the gun, 'if Yanda was here, he'd say, "at least wave the gun at them".'

Frank smiled and clambered along the boat towards her. There would be time for mourning later but for now he was pleased that his dead, egotistical friend was doing his best to keep them company.

When he reached Sira, she leaned back into him for support before leaping onto the landing platform that skirted the nearest tower. The platform turned out to be mud-slicked wood, which sent her skidding into the building before she fell flat on her back.

'Sira. You OK?' he called from the boat, not yet brave enough to take the leap himself on his bad ankle.

'Shit. Gross. Yeah,' she replied, shuffling on her knees.

Distracted by the disgusting sight of her pushing green mud through her fingers, Frank failed to notice the shadow approaching. Too late to offer any useful warning, he got a 'LOOK UP' message to her.

'Oh! Right!' she messaged back, after glancing up at the figure looming over her from doorway at the base of the tower.

'You fucking thick or what, missis?' screeched their host at a high pitch.

He looked to be seven feet tall with tree-trunk legs and a barrel chest wrapped in wool and corduroy. Neither Frank nor Sira had seen anyone that big before. Frank recalled his parents telling him that people used to be larger when there was more food about, but he had never imagined anyone that huge.

Sitting on the man's wide neck was a shaved, cuboid head with a forehead that appeared to be designed to provide shelter from the rain for the small face beneath. He reached down with a hand big enough to hold Sira round the waist, grabbed her and lifted her onto her feet.

Once upright, she remained frozen with fear, not noticing the mud sliding of her back and slapping the deck around her feet.

'Business?' yelled the giant as Frank leapt across, managing to land and balance on his good foot.

'We are looking for Poplar,' she whispered. 'We weren't counting on stopping here and we don't mean any harm.'

'Harm! I think we can defend ourselves from two rich teenagers from out west. Trading data, are you? Come to buy something a bit exotic with a nice little data packet that your dad gave you?' The giant was grinning as he mocked the pair.

'Excuse me, sir,' Frank piped up, feeling his throat constricting with nerves. 'What my friend meant was that we are looking for Poplar. We came across your, um, village, so we thought this would be a good opportunity to find out more about where we're going. But if you don't wish to speak to us, we will go on our way.'

The giant grabbed the pair by an arm each and pulled them through the doorway he had emerged from. 'Sit' he yelled, pointing at a narrow wooden bench.

Sira and Franked kept silent until he had left the room. They heard him trooping up a flight of creaking stairs above them, each step gently swaying the tower they sat beneath.

When he'd gone, Frank leapt up and kicked the now-locked door before pacing around the room, fists clenched and repeatedly texting 'Great idea, Sira' to his friend.

'I'm sorry,' she said disingenuously. 'But I think there is something here. I know there are poor people everywhere, but this is different. They have a community and they've built something. They must have created some meaning here. We need to know how that's done, Frank!'

'We wear greatcoats,' he yelled after pacing around some more. 'Others dress as seventeenth-century explorers. There are people trying to make meaning everywhere we look. There's nothing to learn here. We're trying to get to Poplar so we can go home. That's the plan, and this place is not in it!' Frank could feel the lack of power in his words. He knew something had changed in Sira that meant she was not hearing him. Maybe it had happened when Yanda had been killed, maybe earlier.

'I want to find out who they are. Surely it's better to know,' Sira replied, ignoring his frustration.

'Are you sure that's it? We're here now. You can tell me,' he asserted, speaking slowly, trying to control the emotion in his voice. 'If we're going to survive this, we should both know what's going on.'

'I read something,' she mumbled after a long pause.

'Yes.'

'On the way back from that – the place where they took me.'

'And?'

'And I want to know if we're right. I decided the stakes were higher. In a crisis, it's better to know everything.'

'Come on, Sira. They'll be back any minute. What did you read?'

'I read about a poor London community, not the police or government or anyone like that. I read that there was an educated but poor London community that kept a history of everything since the Second World War. It didn't say where, '

'What do you mean, kept a history?'

'On paper. They don't share it. It's not mediated by online debate. It's fixed. They don't want others to comment on it, and they keep themselves and their history hidden.'

'Oh. What I said about the map?'

'Exactly. Hidden. This post was by someone who'd spent time with them. They see themselves as the true heirs to the war generation. Not the lot that went to study and became our leaders, but normal people. Careful with money, private, poorly educated, religious, hard working.'

'And how can this help us? Even if this is right, what's it got to do with anyone outside this stick village?'

'What if everything is about to go bust? What if what I saw at that place was real, or could happen anywhere? We need to know the truth, Frank. It might contain something new, something that gives us something to work with. Something that means our enemies don't know us. Something that allows us to know them, to outflank them.'

'Something that says a small group of river people think we're wrong about everything?'

'No, no, it's not about what they think,' Sira replied, speaking into the floor and refusing to look up at Frank, who was glaring at her. 'It's about solid ground. We know all the money's been packed-off for export. We know people used to have their own homes. But we don't know much else, not for sure. I just think we should know ourselves a bit more while we have the chance.'

'We haven't really got a choice, have we? I can hear them coming,' said Frank, as he stopped pacing and sat on the bench beside Sira. He put his head in his hands.

The creaking and twisting of the bamboo and steel became increasingly sharp as the steps drew nearer.

'Are you OK?' Sira could see the blood draining out of his face through the gaps between his fingers.

'I will be, I guess. If they're coming back, at least we won't be locked in anymore,' Frank said unconvincingly.

The door opened. First, they saw the giant then, hidden by the bad light, a similarly tall but much thinner man with curly dark hair and thin features. Lizard-like, he oozed into the room and held a bony hand out for Frank to shake. 'John, the chairs, please.'

The giant leant into the small room and, without moving his feet, placed three small stools on the floor, lowering them like a crane.

'So, sit, sit. So, welcome. This is – well, we call it Port. Not that we have much need to call it anything.' The man spoke with a nervous short laugh separating each word.

'Thank you. I'm Sira.' She held out her hand, which the two men of Port left hovering in the air. 'And this is Frank,' she continued. 'We are on a journey east. You weren't on the map, but we could see you. And I'm afraid we were just too curious.'

'If you'd like us to leave, we will,' interjected Frank.

'You may leave when you wish,' he said in a short wheezy burst. 'But there is no hurry from us. But we can't offer a bed. No room at the inn. You can sleep down here if you like. It's dark out.'

'No, no. We aren't seeking shelter. We can sleep on our boat. We just want to know who you are. What Port is.'

'Ah. Well, that's a long story,' said the thin man, sweeping his long arm across the small room as though its bare walls told a story.

West London,
16th December 2053

We're on our own

'More bad news, I'm afraid,' Eres Matthews explained to Mila Seynes as they sat in a shipping container, with a single roughly cut window overlooking a disused athletics stadium.

'America won't give us access to the system. They've told me how to set up a more secure, higher bandwidth line between us, but they won't hook us up to their search system. I told them that our orders have come straight from the chairman but they won't budge.'

'Maybe the US doesn't trust us Matthews, after, you know, the security breach?'

Eres nodded a little and then sat in the corner of the container, feeling lost. What his partner said made some sense but, in the brief training he had been given for the job, he had been assured that if he ever needed help the people on the end of the American hotline would be there for him.

'Do you think we should go to the Met for help, sir?' she asked when he did not respond.

Now, with the better line between them, he could see that his partner was also absent-mindedly flicking through a part-paid training invoice in her inbox. 'Please concentrate, Seynes,' he yelled. 'The US said no to us connecting with anyone. Something about our national credit rating being insufficient to access tier-one resources.'

'Well, you didn't say that Eres, did you?' she replied angrily. 'I had no idea things had got so bad.'

'Sorry, that's true,' he admitted. 'I am afraid we are going to have to do this the old-fashioned way,' he added in his most confident voice in an effort to regain some respect.

'This tin box seems pretty old fashioned,' she messaged him with a smiley face, indicating that his attempt at authority had not had immediate results.

'We need to start by hiding our identities and asking some questions,' he asserted. 'Someone must have seen Roydon leave the base. We should start there. We will just have to watch each other's backs. Let's go,' he ordered, when he saw she was scrolling through her emails again.

Mila followed him as he climbed down the ladder onto the mud-washed street. The pair walked in silence to a second-hand clothes shop where they joined the queue and silently exchanged short texts over the sights and smells of this corner of the West End which seemed forgotten, even by the joyless city landlords who ran most of the neighbourhood homes.

Eres swapped his self-cleaning synthetic suit, purchased recently with his first full pay cheque, for something more anonymous. He looked in a mirror and saw a street walker, one of London's army of the poor.

--

'What were you speaking to the guy about?'

'Pardon?' Eres shouted over the steel, rock and concrete rattling of the ageing street train, its unforgiving wheels clanging loudly against the distorted and pinched rails and collapsed granite curbs.

'In the shop. What were you speaking about to the guy behind the counter?'

'He was trying to convince me to take some food and an even more decrepit suit rather than this one. He said I was too thin and needed some vegetable fats, but I guess he just wanted to keep these clothes for somebody else.'

'Really? Instead of taking your designer suit?'

'Yes, I think so. Things are sometimes quite upside down in the field,' Eres said patronisingly. 'It has its own logic. You can't ever tell in a small place like that if you have stepped into someone's extended family. You'll soon pick it up, Mila. Anyway, even with these clothes we mustn't become complacent. Remember, our best tactic is to not leave any evidence of our presence behind and to keep moving. They can't come back to listen to our conversations if we don't leave a trail.'

Mila smiled in response, hoping she could calm Eres down, but he gave her a minute shake of the head and looked away. She followed suit, looking out of the window. As a child she had seen photos of a similar scene, the crumpled concrete and brightly painted walls of a distant relative's hometown in Central Europe, taken a few years before she was born when her family returned to see where their grandmother had fled from. It was a common story amongst her grandmother's generation, the poor running to London, Berlin or Prague while the wealthier bunkered in small free towns, protecting themselves with cash and automatic weapons.

The photo had taken on new meaning when she and her parents were forced into their first communal home. She had frequently used it as a prop to lobby her parents to buy some weapons of their own so they could live in a private home once again. Her efforts had ceased when her father explained to her that free town families often had to give away more than cash to protect themselves. She wondered, looking out of the window at a teenage girl in a late twentieth-century style puffer jacket, whether that was the case here too.

The train pulled through the centre of a plastic tarpaulin market, cutting between the steel stalls as though the traders had taken no notice of the rail tracks when they had dragged their wares into public. As the carriages slowed, Mila saw that some of the makeshift stalls were intentionally protruding over the low platform, so they scraped against the train windows to animate mechanised animals and the other toys that bounced above the heads of potential customers.

With a spark-inducing screech, the train stopped and its doors clunked open, wafting the smell of steamed vegetables and garlic into the vehicle. All but one of the passengers stood up and stepped into the chaos outside.

As the vehicle jerked forward again, Eres pulled a small device from his pocket and swept the carriage for bugs, including passing it over the remaining passenger who was sleeping, huddled in the corner.

126

'It's clean and he doesn't have an implant. While we are moving, we should be free to talk. Just make sure you stop speaking as we pull to a stop in case there are any cameras that can see through these grimy windows.'

'Why don't you have children, Eres?'

'What?'

'Sorry. Unless you have some new intel to share, I thought maybe we could chat. Since this could be the end of our world and everything,' she said, smiling.

'I just work, Mila. No room for anything else. I can't afford to fail,' he replied sternly.

'Huh, I always took you for a believer,' she continued nervously, ignoring Eres' scowl. 'I do it for the money, too. Everyone I knew in school became a coder when it closed down. They got obsessed with strength and a new order but I opted for the least cool route on offer – government.'

Eres raised an eyebrow and turned away from his partner. When he could see she was going to continue regardless, he flicked to his Grade 2 revision notes which he had been reciting in his head to distract himself.

Stirlingshire, Scotland, 25th May 2005

Proof of concept

'This is a big year for us, even if we didn't plan it that way,' James projected across the large tent, turning as he spoke to try and connect with his fellow commune members. 'More cars and vans are arriving every day, and we are welcoming them with open arms. Such is the arrogance of youth that our newest residents don't ever seem to question that we wouldn't welcome them. They have heard about us and packed their bags. And how have they heard? We have been here long enough to have built up quite an alumni. I, for one, am proud of the fact that so many of our former residents want to spread the word about what we are doing here!'

'But what are we doing here, Benson?' yelled out Fishers, who was in his usual position, stretched out across a piece of old, mud-soiled carpet, his belly loose from his flannel shirt. 'Not all the same thing! Most are good kids, but they're just here to escape the shit, you know. I'm not going to change them! I'll chat with 'em till they grate on me and try not to let the little bastards steal all my food.'

Sarah shuffled forward and put her hand calmly on Fishers' shoulder. 'If we are all here for many different reasons, I think we should do our best to respect that,' she said, whilst staring at James and gently shaking her head, imploring him to tone down his rhetoric.

'What I want to say is that, whether we like it or not, there is more attention on us now and people will be excited to see what we have achieved. We all came here to live differently. Whilst some feel we have compromised, if you go into the city, you will realise how little we have bent in the wind to achieve our aims, keep our shelter, grow what we can and, yes, buy a few items from those outsiders we trust. We have achieved so much in these last few years, and now is the time to be proud of that. Most of these guys are coming for the protest near that UN conference and most will go home afterwards. I hope they will take something away from here that they can use to make things a little better.'

'We know that, James,' said Sarah. 'But while you've been here a long time, you haven't lived here as long as some! And you aren't our leader. We will all handle ourselves however we want. We'll continue how we've always done, and I hope this tent, this community, can spend a little more time being ourselves and a little less thinking about politics.'

Someone in the candlelit corner of the tent grunted with approval, encouraging Fisher to let out a short chuckle that popped another stud open on his shirt.

James handed the floor to the next speaker and stood up, planning to return to his theme once hundreds more visitors had had arrived, as he knew they would. As he parted the fabric and stepped outside, he heard the familiar twang of Eric Clapton's guitar behind him, marking the transition of the gathering from meeting to lazy party. However, despite the conservative voices, he knew they were all on the cusp of a change. After twenty years working, planning and writing now, with the newcomers streaming in, everything was beating a little bit faster.

He had arranged to meet a lecturer from a London University and was looking forward to sharing his ideas with a fellow academic.

--

'You've been here a very long time, James. You must be one of the longest residents but I'm guessing you're from a pretty different background than some of the old boys down there. Do you feel lonely now that Lyla's gone?'

The pair were sitting opposite each other, separated by a fold-out blue plastic picnic table dotted with cigarette burns.

James took a moment to reply. He stood up to offer Andrew a cup of tea in a plastic mug. Andrew, looking out of place in his clean jeans and a flowered shirt nodded, stood up politely to take the hot water and tea bag from James's rough hands.

'That's more of a journalist's question, isn't it, not a serious academic's?' asked James with a smug smile as he sat back down. 'Don't you want to know more about what we are doing here?'

'Yes. Sorry, this isn't for my paper. That question wasn't, I mean. Do you mind if I continue? I won't take long to get to the tough stuff, I promise,' Andrew said nervously, adjusting his mini tape recorder so that it was pointing to James's new location on the edge of the plastic bench.

'Sure, fine. Yes, I've been here for fifteen years, on and off. Mostly on. When I first arrived, I was the only one from England from a middle-class upbringing with no experience of living in a field or in the countryside or of farming. Apart from Layla, who I arrived with after picking her up along the way. This was all new to her, too. But she left a few years ago, taken away by her hysterical mother after she got ill! That's one of the things I want to change about this place. There's still no healthcare, still no recognition from the hospital that this is an address. Yeah, fine, if you cut yourself they'll patch you up, but at the first sign you'll be in and out of the surgery they persuade you that you need a fixed address. And then, before you know it, you're in a hostel. People don't come back after that.'

'But it's getting better isn't it James? I've read that you get MSPs down here sometimes. There's a poster in the main tent for a local question time. Seems pretty established to me.'

'Not enough. We still need outside society. Eating as many vegetables as we do cuts the chances of getting ill, but we still get ill. Some of the hippies wanted Lyla to stay and meditate the illness away, but we both knew that's bollocks. We need a proper clinic. Me and her mother agreed on that at least!'

'A full commune-run clinic to treat everything, without outside help?'

'Mutual relationships with the outside are fine, good even. But I don't want us to need charity.'

Andrew scribbled that in his notebook but James could tell he was not convinced. He was interrogating rather than learning, which did not seem to be an efficient use of his time.

'How is she now?'

'That's not really relevant, Andrew,' snapped James as he leant forward and snatched the half-finished mug out of his guest's hand before walking to a small basin a few metres away to wash it out.

Andrew continued, choosing to ignore James's aggression. 'When I first contacted you, I thought I would be here just a few hours. Record this interview, take some notes, and maybe write it up for a paper I'm delivering soon.'

'And now?' James was preparing a cigarette, dropping strands of ochre tobacco into a paper in the palm of his hand.

'Now I think I want a more rounded picture. Not just how this place works, but why. Why put the energy in at the sacrifice of a normal life? I want to understand you and I want to understand why others are coming here. All these transit vans arriving, this is something new. Something is going on here. Maybe I should stay a little longer!' Andrew looked at James for agreement or refusal, neither of which were provided, just an icy stare.

The camp, the village, the community that James had built after he left hospital equipped him, he felt, with enough inner strength to deal with the Andrews of this world; people who thought they had the right to learn by just asking without getting stuck in themselves. James imagined this MPhil student sitting in his 1960s' monstrosity of a library dreaming of understanding a little more, of achieving his first publication and christening it by fucking the underpaid barmaid. But he knew he was not going to kick him out just yet. There was something he wanted to share.

'So, Lyla?' Andrew asked.

'I went to visit her in Edinburgh. She was staying in a house on the bus route to the hospital, living with a young couple. One of them worked at a call centre or something. Insurance, I think. Anyway, it was just once. Last I heard from her was in a postcard, saying her parents had taken her home.'

Andrew paused for a moment after this answer, which James took as a sign of nerves or embarrassment. 'Has it changed a lot here since then? Changed for you, I mean?'

131

'Let me show you around, Andrew. I'll show you where to camp.' Before Andrew could answer, James had slung the larger of his two bags across his back and was walking down the hill, smoking his roll-up. 'This is the pig farm,' he shouted over his shoulder. 'It's a kind of symbol. Lyla hated it when I first suggested it, which makes sense. But it makes us different, which was the point.'

Andrew jogged a little to catch up, so he could hear what James was saying.

'Most communes aren't like this,' James continued. 'They are full of idealistic hippies who aren't really trying to make anything new. We have our fair share of them – the dropouts, those willing to forgo a comfier life in return for being able to be drunk and stoned most of the time – but the difference here is that we aren't all like that. And that's what I'm pushing – by plonking a pig farm amongst a bunch of vegans! They pigs are also a nice little earner for the things we can't make ourselves.'

'So it's about making money?'

'Partly. It's a hassle with all the paperwork, but I got the idea from Israel – a kosher country where they keep pigs, to export the meat! Imagine that!' He gave a wide grin. 'Imagine, the antisemitic and anti-money backlash I got from the intolerant bastards that founded this place when I told them my plan! That was a good day,' he bellowed, jogging down the gentle sloping field, his heels skidding in the slick mud which was caking itself up the back of his combat trousers.

At the bottom of the hill, he waited for Andrew to catch up again, then he pointed to a large shed that had previously been out of sight. 'The pigs are just one part of creating imbalance which in turn drives new behaviour, producing forward motion. People think that intoxication is about relaxing the mind to enable new ideas. They think tribes take drugs to generate ideas and have visions. But the ideas, the visions, do not come from the drugs, they come from social imbalance and there are many possible, and perhaps necessary, sources of that. In that shed,' he pointed again, 'there are about twenty kids. They have been in there for two nights and this morning they came to the central tent for the first time to ask for help. They were met by a couple who live in that trailer. Twenty young people. We have never had so many people turn up at once, and they are coming here because of that UN thing.'

'Yes,' Andrew agreed, 'they're coming to protest. This is somewhere to stay. I bet some of them came with black scarves to wear around their faces as well. How does that make you feel?'

'They did,' James responded. 'But you would be wrong to think the black masks are the main story here. Yes, they brought their scarves, so we had a word. Those who clearly wanted to drive around at night smashing up cars, they left. But most chose to stay. We are the only camp in the whole of Scotland that demonstrates something larger and they came to us – and most stayed! They could have gone anywhere but they came to us. And I think that when the conference is over you'll be surprised how many choose to help build this place.'

'What makes you so sure? I know people at my university who are here, maybe at this camp. I think protest – I hope not violent in their cases – is the only reason they are here. Why do you think anyone is going to stay and farm with you?'

'You'll see, Andrew. In all my years here, I have failed to turn a single hippy that started this place but many new people have come around to my way of thinking. They want to be a part of something bigger, something they can't be at home. We all have demons and this method, my treatment, is the way forward, the way to get rid of those demons and to replace them with forward motion.'

The pair looked at each other and the academic clicked the recorder off. James could tell that his guest was uncomfortable with the word 'treatment'.

'Maybe you should camp over there and see it for yourself.' James handed Andrew his bag and pointed at the shed and the assorted Ford Fiestas and Vauxhall Corsas parked outside. Andrew gave a small nod and trudged off through the long grass towards the other guests.

Thames, London, 14th December 2053

Youth violence

'I'm Mitchells,' the thin, tall man wheezed, before proceeding with his staccato introduction. 'I'm the caretaker of this tower. We have five, a caretaker for each. This be building C. It's special. All got somethink special.'

Mitchells pointed at the corner of the room closest to Sira. 'Look at the steel pins. Used to hold the floor in one piece to tether it to the columns. They're wood, the columns. They rot. Each building has eight. Two columns can be removed and replaced without nuffink bad happening. Workshop upstairs to get the materials ready from salvaged boat decking.'

Mitchells turned and walked up the steps, making the tower sway. Following behind, Frank tugged gently at Sira's sleeve. 'What's he talking about?' he whispered.

Sira brushed Frank's hand away and continued to listen attentively to the guided tour. On the second floor, with Frank huffing loudly behind her, she interrupted. 'Thank you, Mr Mitchells, this is fascinating. I wondered if you could tell us something about the history of the place, of the community?'

'Your culture,' Frank interjected, trying to speed up the exchange. 'We'd really like to understand your culture.'

'Oh, well, we aren't tribespeople or nuffink Mr Frank. Just hard-working river people. That's all. What did you want to know?'

'Um. How about that? Who's that?' Frank pointed at a faded framed photo of a middle-aged lady with big hair.

'Ah, that's Our Missis.'

'Your wife?'

'No, no. She called Our Missis. She was a great leader. 1980s. Royal, maybe. Led the army. Gave us hard-working people homes.'

'You don't know her name? Why not look it up?'

'If you're talking about those cheats in your head, we don't do that. The only cheat we use is staying off the map. But that's so our little'uns aren't pestered and we can get on with our jobs.'

'And what are your jobs?' Frank demanded.

Sira turned around and leant into Frank so Mitchells could not hear. 'You're being aggressive.'

'Sira, I just want you to get your answers so we can get out.'

'Frank!' she hissed under her breath. 'Sorry. We've had a long day. Please forgive my friend.'

'It's OK, young lady. I'm sure you're used to different ways. We labour mostly, build things on the shore. World looks after us so long as we look after ourselves. Police no bother. But we like to keep ourselves private. Now, up the stairs. Follow me.'

'Sira,' Frank whispered from behind her, 'I don't think there is anything going on here. We don't know why we're here, and I haven't heard anything to tell me what we should be trying to know. Let's get some rest on the boat and go to Poplar first thing.'

'We haven't eaten. I'm hoping they'll feed us.'

'Really? That's why we're here? For food? We can get food anywhere, Sira. We could sell that gun for a feast.'

'Not just the food. I'm sure there is a reason we came here.'

'Yes, you made us. That's the reason.'

'Who is the woman in the frame?' Sira asked. 'I can't use my device. I'm relying on you to use yours. Come on, help here. Do some work.'

'OK, OK, hold on a moment... No, sorry, no signal. Got a bit at the ground floor, but nothing here. All blocked.'

--

The three sat at the top of the tower around a scratched plastic table encircled by windows covered in clear, plastic tarpaulin, which looked south across the river and its flood plains. The sun was setting to their right casting sharp orange

135

light across a network of shallow ponds, home to herons and other long-legged birds that picked a living out of the mud.

'The potatoes will be here soon. And my wife, Wendy. You should meet the little 'uns. It's not often we have visitors.' Mitchells had taken off his jacket to reveal a skeletal frame held taut by a thin layer of stretched red skin.

'I hope you don't mind, sir, but I tried to read a bit about your picture' said Frank. 'But there's no signal.'

'Oh, you mean you used your thing?' Mitchells paused and spread his long fingers across the table, feeling the scratches in the plastic. 'I'd really rather you hadn't done that, mate! We don't like that here. I thought I'd made that clear.'

Sira's stared into his retinas, causing Frank's heart to race into a panic.

'I'm very sorry. I – I – I thought you might like to know more.'

'More of what, Mr Frank? We don't believe anything they write. There is truth and there's the internet. Full of lies. Rubbish. If you believed all that, you'd think we were all descended from bankers or sumink.'

'Descended? No, no,' Frank stuttered, thinking of what to say to placate him. 'I think there is lots of anger out there, but I don't think we should blame people today just trying to make their way.'

Mitchells banged the plastic table with his fist. 'I disagree,' he shouted with a chesty rattle as he coughed into Frank's face. 'History matters. But the right history, owned by those who made it; who sacrificed. I'm proud of my family, where we came from, the history we made. My grandfather was a carpenter, his son was a carpenter, and I'm one too.'

'Your grandfather,' Sira broke in trying to calm their host. 'When was he working, when was he born?'

Frank tensely twisted a tarnished silver fork between his fingers. He had begun to understand why they were in Port.

'Oh, he was born in the 1950s. Everyone here has grandparents born in the 1950s. There was a lot of them. They remade Britain.'

136

'Here they are!' shrieked two children, a boy and a girl, as they burst through the doorway. They hugged their father briefly before taking their places at the table.

A moment later, a large woman in a floral apron with tied-back greasy hair walked in and placed a huge bowl full of boiled potatoes on the table. 'Hello,' she bellowed with a warm smile. 'We have heard so much about you!' Her face lit up as she spoke, displaying genuine excitement at the thought of hosting guests for dinner.

Sira and Frank stood up clumsily, guessing that they were expected to formally greet Michells' wife. As they each got within a metre of her, she grabbed them by the shoulders and planted loud kisses on their cheeks before releasing them. The pair stood in silence, stunned by her act of aggressive affection.

'Wow! Linda, that's the first time they've stopped talking!'

'Oh, I'm sorry, darlings. I guess you're not used to our customs. Please take your seats.'

'No, no, we're sorry. We're delighted to be here. Is this your own dining room?' Sira said.

'No, no. Don't be silly, miss.'

'Please call me Sira.'

'Right as you are, miss. We call this the family room, and we take turns using it. Today isn't our day but when our neighbours find out Mitchells was showing guests around, they helped us out. So here we are. I'm sorry we only have potatoes, but we do have lots of them.'

'They look delicious,' said Sira, genuinely looking forward to a non-synthetic meal. When she looked back up at Mitchells, she could see that the anger had faded since his wife and children had entered the room so, to Frank's dismay, she attempted to continue her research.

'The stories we hear are that that generation wanted to change the world but then just went on to own everything and become wealthy bankers. That's why our families are now so poor and why London is the way it is. I expect your grandparents and their parents weren't part of that, were they?'

'Young lady,' Mitchells spat back, as a wave of rain rattled against the plastic tarpaulin surrounding them. 'We don't talk about family like that. Linda, can you please close the door?'

'Mr – sorry – Mitchells, we didn't mean to cause offence,' apologised Frank, staring at Sira and imploring her to stop asking questions.

'Let's talk about something else,' declared Linda, with a snap of her oversized jaw.

'No, please,' Sira shouted, causing Linda's face to turn red and Frank to sink backwards into himself. 'The baby boomers forced choice on everything and now we have no choice but to live in concrete squalor amongst people we have no choice but to get on with. We just want to understand why you're different, how you escaped that.'

'Young lady!' Linda scolded.

Mitchells rose above Frank and Sira and pulled the potatoes away from them. 'I have no idea what you're talking about, missis. But we don't see no conspiracy, it's just the usual rubbish we've heard our whole lives, especially from you Westerners! Big ideas from people who haven't done a day's work. It wasn't true then, it's not true now. No, you've got to get your hands dirty. Look after your family. Do right by your community. That's all there's ever been. Only ever been the rich like you that run away from their communities and travel to London. No cares in the world!'

'So, where are the police? If everything's fine, why are the streets overrun by gangs and crazy people like us matching for something better?' Sira snapped back. 'There is nothing normal going on out there.' As she yelled her last word, the wind ripped through their swaying wooden box, tearing a tarp from its mooring and cutting all the light from the diners' eyes as the candles blew out. Frank felt his wooden stall tip off balance as he was pulled from the waist into the corner of the room.

'We've both got to shut up,' Sira hissed into his ear.

'You're doing all the talking. You shut up. That's what I've been saying.'

'Sorry, you were right. Went too far. I, I don't know why,' she stuttered.

Her hand lay across his lap and, with the blood rushing through his veins, he found himself unable and unwilling to move. 'You did,' he whispered. 'Maybe if we just sit in the dark.'

'What?'

'Maybe, we can sneak out.'

'Shh.'

In the darkness, above the howling wind and rain, they could hear Linda yelling at her husband, accusing him of not thinking of the family and bringing in more waifs and strays. They then heard him slap her and the children started to cry.

Sira gripped Frank's arm so hard she could feel her blunt fingers separating his muscle from the bone.

'Remember that bit in *1984* by George Orwell?' Frank whispered. 'In the pub? The prole old man didn't remember anything. That's where we are! All anecdotes and nonsense.'

'Please shush. We're going to jump.'

'Enough plans, Sira. We will die.'

'If we don't leave… I think we're in danger. They're angry. You shouldn't have tried to use your device.'

'I really don't think it was me, Sira.'

Sira pushed Frank forward towards the exposed window and fell on her knees, scraping them on rough floorboards. He pulled her up to make a run for it in the darkness, but immediately came face to face with Mitchells, the moonlight illuminating the purple veins across his nose and thin cheeks.

'Kids, wow. Slow down,' he said calmly. 'Thought we'd lost you. Don't know what you're up to or why you came here, but this is my home. Show some respect. Grab that box of nails and help me fix this. Can't get the candles lit with the wind.'

Frank looked at Sira for permission, unsure what was happening, and then sheepishly picked up the carton in the corner of the room and put it in Mitchell's wiry hand as though it were a dangerous explosive.

'You are flighty ain't you?' Mitchells said. 'Coming here with your ways. Who's your parents?'

'That's what we're saying. It doesn't work like that anymore.'

'Sira, will you please shut up?' Frank yelled.

Sira looked at him; his face was red as though he was about to break into uncontrolled tears. 'We grow up with them,' she said quietly, 'and with other parents and children in concrete boxes. *Official homes* we call them. There's not enough space or separate rooms for families. That's why Frank and I, and... that's why Frank and I live away from our official homes in whatever places we can find. Normally an old garage or shed.'

'Why don't you work together to save up for your own place?'

'Because the gangs would just take it. If you want a safe home, you'd have to join a gang. They're the choices.'

'OK, dear. A pair of runaways. We've seen it before,' Linda interjected from behind her husband. 'I think it's time to thank me and Mitchells and the children, and then get yourselves off home.' The children looked at them, having sat upright in silence throughout. 'And, before you leave,' she added, 'we'd also like you to show our building some gratitude.'

Sira and Frank looked at each other from the corners of their eyes.

'I'm not sure we know what you mean, Linda.' Frank heard a hint of mockery in Sira's tone and grabbed her hand, squeezing it, silently begging for her to stop. She was shaking.

'Why not stop fibbing, young lady, and tell us who your parents are? Then we won't have to ask you to leave.'

'Oh! Right. I – sorry, Frank I would like to leave!' Sira stuttered. 'We have outstayed our welcome. We will sleep on our boat and get going in the morning. We won't cause you any more problems.'

Frank squeezed Sira's hand in gratitude.

'No, that's not it. We can't have you lying like this!' Linda insisted.

'I'm not sure – I'm not sure I understand, Linda.'

'My husband has said we don't like lying. We also don't like not knowing what our neighbours are up to!'

'What? We're from West London.'

'Come off it! You're from one of them towers out there. I bet you're from A. They hate us in A. Spying on us, with your eye recorders!'

'Hold on a moment.' Frank stood up at the opposite end of the table and squared up to Linda. 'Your husband saw us sail in.'

'Mr Frank, I believe I saw you next to the boat when you were on our jetty,' Mitchells said.

'Fine. Whatever. You saw the boat.'

'Yes, I saw the boat. Just like I see that boat everyday trundling past. It belongs to one of the other towers. They use it to move their rubbish around and dump things on the shore.'

Frank tried to argue but nothing came out of his mouth.

'Yes, that boat. Your boat. Every day,' Mitchells screamed at him through the icy fog that had filled the room. 'Now, you tell us right now what you want from us. All these stories about London this and that, slipping around our questions. You want to go back to the others and make fun of us? Make fun of our home? Well, we're not having that! Linda,' he ordered, 'let them in!'

Linda pulled the ill-fitting door open. From the dark landing in walked a boy, a teenager, dressed in baggy red clothes. Sira thought of the photos she had seen of the old football riots before the pitches had been taken over by protestors and refugees.

'Ha! Look at you. Pathetic!' he yelled at her and Frank, before opening the door wider behind him. A dozen children, ranging from four to six feet tall, girls and boys, young and teenage, flooded into the swaying wooden room. Their faces glowed above the hurricane lamps they were holding and they were chanting, 'Gary! Gary! Gary!'

The first ones into the room threw the table and chairs out of their way. Only a few small nails in the tarps stopping the furniture sailing through the windows into the night. Sira and Frank sat exposed, with nothing to defend themselves besides a single plastic stool that had stayed put.

Frank felt his stomach remain at floor level as he stood. Many of the children towered above him with their blotched, angry skin.

'You. Fuck you! Both of you. You're dead,' yelled Gary, peppering Frank's face with saliva.

Frank opened his eyes and looked upwards to see the six-foot adolescent gurning at him, his pale eyes almost invisible against his pale face, only his chewed red lips giving any definition to his growl.

'What's that thing on her?' yelled Gary.

141

Frank now stood between the baying mob and Sira, unsure how he had begun playing the role of the brave one. 'Look, I think you should leave us,' he said, his voice quivering. 'There's been a misunderstanding. We're from West London, not round here. We stopped because we had never seen towers like this before.'

'Well, good for you! Now, give me that thing,' spat Gary, reaching over Frank's head to point at Sira.

Sira clutched at the implant hanging round the back of her head. She realised that, with the tower in a reception blackspot, she should have removed and hidden it but it was too late now.

'My friend is unwell. It is helping her,' explained Frank robotically, with controlled pauses between his words. 'We have to get her to a clinic. That's an emergency measure.'

'It's got blood on it, don't it?'

'Yes, her blood. I told you. She is unwell.'

'She is unwell, but you still stopped by here?' yelled Gary. 'That's an implant, ain't it? I've seen them before. We don't use them here, do we, Mitchells?'

Mitchells nodded, looking a little scared of the youth.

'I think you should give that thing to me,' laughed Gary. 'And then the rest of you should get out of here and leave this poor, ill girl to me.'

'I'm not going,' Frank stuttered.

Sira stood up off the floor and pleaded to Linda for help. To her horror, Linda Mitchells and the hordes of children responded by leaving the room. One threw a wooden chair leg at Frank's head on his way out. Others yelled 'rich bitch' and 'small faggot', laughing to themselves as they trotted down the makeshift steps.

'You're supposed to be out of here too, mate.' Gary was standing over Frank, balanced perfectly for either punching him in the face or breaking his nose with his head.

'I'm not leaving her.'

'Fine, but if you stop me I'll kill you both.'

Sira's blood froze in her veins.

'S-s-sira, come on. We're going. Come on!' Frank yelled, throwing the chair leg that had been used against him at Gary's legs. It bounced off him, failing to cause any reaction at all.

'I think you're clever enough to ignore him, aren't you, gorgeous?' Gary sneered quietly, his enflamed face up against Sira's. 'Besides, there is a whole tower of children down there. Some of them are peering through the cracks I bet, trying to get a peek of you. Now, tell your friend to stay where he is, then turn around. Tell him that if he touches me, I'll break your neck, and then I'll let them eight-year olds out there break his. Got it?'

Sira could not reply. Full panic was setting in; with nowhere to run, she was shutting down within herself. Gary grabbed her with one hand and slapped her across the face with the other, but she still did not move.

Frank half stepped between them but he was punched hard in the stomach and toppled into the furniture. He saw Gary pushing his friend up against a wooden vertical, forcing her face into the rough grain, whilst kicking her legs apart. Before Frank had got his breath back, Gary had ripped her coat off and pulled her black combat trousers down to her knees.

Sira yelled at Frank, begging him not to watch. In return, she had her head banged forward into the beam. But Frank could still hear her repeating 'don't watch, don't watch, don't watch' under her breath. He squinted to honour his friend's wishes but was too scared to look away.

Gary pulled out his erect penis and shuffled his thighs into position. Sira voluntarily pushed her face harder into the wood to numb the pain elsewhere, but her tears and snot took away the beam's sharp edges. Just as she felt a bony finger force its way into her, the hand gripping her neck pulled her back, sending her flying into the floor and smashing her head into the wooden boards. She squeezed her eyes shut, wincing at the pain of the implant pressing against her spine and expecting to be dragged backwards further or flipped around – but there was nothing.

There was no sound. She laid still in the darkness waiting, but there was no sound and no movement. But there was sound in her memory, the sound of Frank screaming, of wood snapping and of a splash outside.

She pulled her trousers back up. With one arm clasped tightly around the upright, she leant down into the darkness through a huge rip that had appeared in the tarpaulin.

'Frank! Frank! Can you hear me?' she yelled into the night. When he did not reply, she grabbed her coat and ran through the door, crushing two small children against the wall and another under her boot as she launched herself down the steps. Her arms were out in front, grabbing, scratching and punching as she bundled herself down the building. Each time she slipped, her adrenalin somehow righted her until she crashed onto the tower's wooden landing platform.

The boat was still there. She leapt on board and grabbed the gun. 'Frank, I'm down here. Where are you?' she yelled again.

Mitchells appeared in the main doorway to the tower. Sira trained the gun on him but, when he stepped forwards, she panicked and retreated along the hull as she fired. The bullet caught his face on the side, burning an image of a ripped skull into her retinas as he spun around and fell to the floor.

'Shit, Sira! You shot him!'

Sira turned to see Frank standing on the barge, his clothes and hair drenched and covered in green slime. 'You're alive!' she yelled, reaching out and hugging him, causing them both to slip to the floor.

'I – I landed in the water. Its freezing. Adrenalin. Can't really remember getting on the boat.'

'Where's Gary?'

'Dead, I think. He didn't hit the water,' explained Frank, his voice distorted by an anxious mania.

'When I pushed him, I sort of went over him and he fell down the edge of the building. I didn't mean to kill him. Well, I guess I didn't mean not to. But when I dived on him, he hardly moved. He was big. For a moment, I thought it was all for nothing, and I was diving into the water whilst he was staying up there. With you.'

'You're sure he's dead?'

Frank sat on crate and pointed excitedly. 'He's there Sira.'

She followed Frank's finger to a rounded heap on the platform at the bottom of the tower, not far from Mitchells' body. Looking closer, she could see bones protruding, glowing gently in the moonlight.

'Right.'

'Why did you kill Mitchells?'

'Accident. Finger slipped.'

'Right.'

The pair looked at each other, bruised but breathing, shivering but alive, and hugged.

'You're freezing,' Frank said.

'Yes, but we've got to move. They can see us.' Sira had been watching a slow gathering forming at the base of the tower out of the corner of her eye.

Frank grabbed her by the hand and led her up the boat to the steering column. 'I'll drive,' he yelled proudly. 'We can wrap up next to the motor and get warm.'

Stirlingshire, Scotland, 25th May 2005

Crossing the line

'Are you starting to understand?' James asked.

Andrew looked around and saw new, young faces carrying bags of flour and potatoes, and others erecting tents to prepare for the arrival of more from the motorway. 'I'm starting to think you got lucky, James. They haven't got jobs to go to, so they are sticking around. They are probably all shagging each other. I bet the drugs are good too,' he grunted, laughing to himself.

'I expect they are but that's what communities do, isn't it? And I imagine the drugs are no more plentiful here than in your average council estate. Anyway, that's not what I meant. Look again.'

Andrew paused before offering an answer to the quiz question. 'God, I don't know, James. Nervous energy?'

'No – well, maybe.' James paused, wondering whether Andrew was not the intelligence he had hoped for. 'What I meant was they have only just met and no one is giving instructions.'

When Andrew stared at him blankly, James yelled at him to look again.

'Has anyone ever told you that you can be hard work?' replied the academic.

James looked Andrew up and down and used his breathing technique to ignore the combination of pale Hawaiian shirt and chinos. 'I experience the full range of emotions, Andrew,' he replied stiffly. 'Fear, anger, love, happiness. At the moment, I feel confusion. Confusion as to why you are spending so much time here when your colleagues – yes, I have read about your colleagues – are busying themselves with think tanks and other elite activities in Westminster. A lot is expected of you,

146

Andrew. Your supervisor thinks you're clever. And yet you're here covering childish Utopian protestors. Unless you are starting to believe me?'

'Maybe I am. But I've no idea yet what you're asking me to believe in.'

'I will,tell you if you tell me why you care – why you are here!'

'OK.' Andrew unzipped his small rucksack and pulled out a plastic picnic rug, gesturing for James to sit down.

'You stick out like a sore thumb, Andrew. I guess you know that.'

'Fine. Whatever. Sit down.' Andrew patted the rug, which James continued to ignore. 'I'm here because I think that maybe you're not a crusty or a hippy, as you call them. People like me who study movements haven't had a live example like you to research before, not in this country. But don't let it go to your head, James. Maybe you will be a footnote. Maybe you will be nothing.'

James stared down at him in silence.

'Sorry if that is a bit harsh. I don't mean to be. I'm just saying that we shall see.'

'The last thing you wrote, Andrew, is that after Afghanistan and Iraq the work Giddens did for Blair stopped being relevant and needed an overhaul. You wrote that we need ideas that can survive the tough and maybe horrible decisions, as well as the nice ones.'

James waited for Andrew to show some sign of being impressed that a crusty read journals. After a moment, the visitor took out his tape recorder, clicked it on and held it up.

'You're a neoliberal seeking to atone and explain, Andrew. You feel guilty. That's a weakness,' asserted James into the recorder.

'No. No, I'm not. I want to write about how power can work and can corrupt, and yet still be structured to deliver egalitarian ends. You are doing something strange here. People are working hard. Vegetarians are helping on your pig farm. I want to know why, that's all.'

'For your book?'

'Yes. First for a book and for articles and speeches and a new road map for centre-left liberal politics that can help us keep the Tories out.'

'Pretty pedestrian stuff.'

'You're the one whose life doesn't stretch beyond this field.'

'Yes, it does,' James retorted, aggressively hovering a clenched fist over the recorder, smiling at the thought he could bat it across the field. 'My life stretches beyond this country. Beyond Europe. Beyond politics. It's a model that would work even where people blow themselves up, where they have never had democracy. It's a politics that harnesses technology rather than coping with it.'

For the first time Andrew saw some passion alongside the irritability in James's eyes, but then it was gone.

'You're gay, aren't you, Andrew?' said James, spitting into the soil.

'What's that got to do with anything?' he replied calmly, hoping he would not always have to wait for James to get through some insults before he continued to explain his ideas.

'Sorry, just making assumptions.'

'It's not really any of your business, James.'

'People talk about Blair's gay mafia. Does that include you?' James was sporting a cruel smile, enjoying twisting the knife in a wound he thought he'd found.

'It would be a bit of a stretch to say I was part of his mafia. I know some of them, I guess, the lower ones, but I'm not *one of* them.'

'And do you think they would get what we're doing here?'

'They're not stupid, if that's what you mean. But equally, we're in different worlds. They're thinking about getting their messages out in the media, into people's heads. But their thinking has stopped. Plus, even if I could explain it to them, I don't know what's going on here. You haven't told me yet, remember.'

'Follow me, then.' James turned and walked towards his caravan at marching pace. When Andrew caught up, leaving his picnic blanket behind, he was gestured inside.

The vehicle was neat but packed. Every horizontal surface was covered in books and folders, balanced on DIY shelving.

At the foot of the bed, where the fold-out dining table would have been, sat a desktop computer with its casing removed.

'You've done a lot of work,' asserted Andrew, trying to flatter his host into civility. 'According to Seth on my corridor who is obsessed with these things, most caravan owners try to create suburbia. You've created Seth's office. I'll have to tell him. He'll like that.'

James ignored this. 'Aren't you going to ask me what all this is for?'

'Please.'

'It's software. I've been learning how to write it since I arrived. I think of it these days as a universal tool. You might be a political scientist and someone else might be an engineer, but you both need something between your ideas and their implementation to bring them alive. I studied geography at university, mainly human geography, and I could never get my head around what one was supposed to do with it. It was just a flat description.'

'That's not really what I think I do, but carry on,' retorted Andrew. He sat on the bed and placed his arms on an empty part of the desk, reminding James of a gesture his doctor used to make to encourage him to keep speaking.

'You social scientists, you listen, read, learn and critique but you rarely develop. You think developing new ideas and, in your case policies, is a job for someone else. You may champion certain policies, based on your understanding of their principles or results, but you don't make them yourself. Correct?'

'I'm not sure that's completely true, James, but carry on.'

'I think the reason you don't do this is because you don't have the tools. You can't change the law or run services so, even if you have your own ideas, the best you can do is write them in some paper and hope they are picked up. Even if they are picked up, they will be changed beyond all recognition, and you'll be back where you started: analysing.'

'I don't really see it that way but even if I did, aren't you being a bit naive to think you're the first experimental social scientist? People have been building communes for years. They don't really tell us anything. They're usually just obscurities.'

'Not here.'

'Yes. As you know, I agree with you and that's why I'm here. But I'm still waiting for you to get to the point.'

'The point is, Andrew, that I'm not supporting this commune to create shared living for its own sake. It's a human lab. It's an experiment. The inhabitants just don't realise it. In the future I hope they can be informed, but not at this stage.'

Andrew sat on the bed and for the first time wondered whether he would prefer it if James was talking nonsense. 'What's the experiment?'

'Good question,' James replied, slapping the hollow plastic of his monitor. 'The software sets challenges based on a range of goals and dishes out tasks.'

'It gives orders?'

'Not really. It knows the situation here, including rough personality types as well as the basic needs of the group, just as the group knows its own basic needs. When an individual asks the system for a task, it dishes out a suggested approach including who they should work with to get the job done.'

'Someone, or something, is giving orders?'

'No. To give an order would be: "Andrew, use the ingredients on this list to make soup for the camp." Not very organic, or social. This is subtler. The system knows what you have done before, what you're good at and enjoy and who else you know, who you might get on with, who can do the things you can't do.'

'But I haven't seen any of this happening. I haven't seen any orders being given out.'

'We're not there yet, I'm afraid.'

'So, where are you?'

'I'm reading some people's text messages. I've tampered with the mobile phone mast and am reading about their lives, the people who've been arriving recently. I've created software that allows me to input names, personality types and experience. When I monitor someone expressing a need via a text, like "I'm hungry", I use the software to work out who around them enjoys making food. I then pop down, suggest a few things to a few people, and usually they start making food. I've just started sending them text messages as well, masked as other people, but that's trickier because it's easier to get caught.'

'You're spying on people and then managing them? This is highly unethical, James!'

James ignored his comment and continued. 'I like to think of it as computer-assisted sharing. It's hard to prove. I'm learning, and from my description just now, it could sound like a lot is down to my interpretation and execution. But you'd be surprised, Andrew. I'm putting quite basic things in and delivering equally basic suggestions. There is very little manipulation.

I'm taking Adam Smith's ideas about the "invisible hand" and applying them to the willing individual rather than the corporation. But it's also mixing Smith in with Marxism, so people get closer and not alienated. It's creating a self-functioning hive. When it works the commune will be totally unnecessary, as it will be everywhere.'

'You got a drink?'

'What?' replied James, pulling a bulging lever arch folder from the shelf and handing it to Andrew.

'Please – anything, a beer, a spirit, anything,' begged Andrew, feeling dizzy at the thought of all the teenagers he had seen in the field being guided around by this strange man in his caravan.

'Sure, sure.' James left Andrew scratching his head and returned a moment later with a splash of vodka in a plastic mug.

Andrew threw it back and held the mug out for a refill. 'I haven't the first clue how I'm going to explain any of this.'

'I don't know everything, Andrew. I don't know how to take it to the next level beyond the field. I need funding. I need better technology.'

'But,' Andrew said quietly, hoping not to enrage his host who seemed relaxed and lucid for the first time, 'this seems quite unethical. To guide people like that.'

James pulled the folder from Andrew's hands, pushed it aggressively back onto the shelf, and walked to the door, swinging it open. 'Look!' he shouted, with a huge grin across his face. 'Look at the sky!'

Andrew was not sure he wanted to get up and stand that close to him but, after a pause, he shuffled nervously to the door and peered upwards, hoping to not see something terrible.

'Look at the way it swirls up here, Andrew. Always changing. Not like the sky down south. Always adapting and interacting to create the weather – and what's wrong with that?'

When Andrew stared at him blankly, James continued. 'It's in charge. Don't you see? It is shaping us. Like a father, it's in charge and doing what's right! What's wrong with a community having a father, as long as he is dynamic and can keep up. That's what I'm building, a father. Not an awful, static, coddling mother who does not know when to stop, but a father who knows best!'

Andrew felt for his car keys in his pocket.

Thames, London,
14th December 2053

Not the right time

Once they were in pitch black beyond the candlelight of the towers, Frank guided the boat slowly and gently alongside a stretch of intermittent quay wall. All he had to navigate by was a small light on the port side, which occasionally reflected off the slime and mud.

His mind flashed between the memory of water rushing towards him, the bones and ripped flesh on the deck and the dark, winding tributaries of the river spreading out to his side between breaks in the wall. Each time he thought he had a few metres fixed in his head, he took the opportunity to look down at Sira hunched next to the warm engine by his feet. He had only just begun to feel the cold himself, the sour adrenalin having lasted for a painfully long time.

When they reached a solid length of quay, he slowed the boat to a stop and pulled himself onto dry land. After he'd called for her help a few times, Sira eventually stood up to pass him the ropes and he tied the boat in place. The result was not great, given the height difference between the river and the steel rings they were now tied to, but he decided it would do for a few hours of sleep.

He woke Sira when the sun rose to tell her that he was switching his device back on.

'OK. This is staying put, though,' she replied, pointing at the now clean metal ball hugging the base of her skull held there by a piece of fabric she had ripped from her sleeve.

'You look like a land girl. It suits you.'

Sira looked up to give him a small smile, and then returned to her seated foetal position, and asked what the map said.

'It's called Canary Wharf. Apparently the big one was the tallest building in the country for a while. Crazy to think that

153

anyone would want to construct something so exposed. But it's a good job we didn't go any further last night. Poplar is back there.' Frank pointed back down the river. 'It's on a dock that comes from here, but not on the water. We can either keep going and turn back on ourselves into the docks. Or just walk from here.'

'While you're doing very well with this thing, Frank, I'm not sure we want to risk the docks. We will be a slow target.'

'Walking could be more dangerous. This place could be full of – whoever. We have no idea. The gangs know this is the only place to get modifications. Where else would they be looking for you?'

'If they *are* looking for me. Anyway, we've got this now.' Sira slapped the side of the automatic rifle.

'If Yanda was here you would follow him, wouldn't you?'

Sira sat back on the deck of the boat and shook her head. When she looked up, he could see a tear rolling down her face. 'Have you forgotten that he killed himself for us yesterday?' she yelled.

'I'm sorry, I just— Don't.'

'Don't know what to say, Frank? You never do. You're only thinking of yourself.'

Frank felt his anger knot up inside. He wished he could express himself, but his stronger feelings always morphed into frustration and eclipsed all else. 'I always think about us, Sira. There is just a difference between caring about your friends and caring about the imaginary collective you two think we are a part of.'

'Well, it's just us now,' she snapped back. 'So I guess you won't be hearing that much about it anymore. But just tell me one thing – if you don't believe in all this so called "ideological crap", why do you believe Captain has an army of goons after us?'

'Because you saw them, Sira!'

'And what about all the people on the marches? Can you not see them?'

'They just like to march, Sira. We all do. It's nice to be with people, people who haven't fucked over the world. But they aren't going to do anything. People with power, with

154

organisation, with weapons – they do things. The police and the government may be nothing compared to their former selves, but they still exist. We are a fashion. Our job is to survive. The liberals won. They ruined everything, but they have left nothing for us to takeover. That's what I think.'

Sira rubbed her face dry and shook her head, hoping that Frank would let her rest and come to terms with the past day. But he continued, now bounding up and down the boat, sending clanging echoes down through its hold.

'You think we can use these things,' Frank tapped the side of his head, 'to make a new collective, but we can't. They make it too easy to act alone, to let everybody make their own way, to hack what they want, to get rich, to exploit. We can't act together. That time is gone.'

'I think that's where we differ, Frank,' she replied. 'Maybe you think you have something to lose so you aren't willing to try. I know I have nothing.'

'What about us?' Frank spoke quietly to the ground.

'What?'

'Sorry, Sira. I feel sick. I can't do this now. It doesn't matter.'

'Oh God, Frank, please just calm down.'

'You just laid into me for being selfish. You don't take me seriously. I know that. But I take you very seriously. I think you know that.' Frank's face was red and ready to burst.

'Please can we not do this now? I promise I know what you mean. But not now.'

'That's it then.' He kicked a wooden crate, smashing its side and letting white powder pour out of it. 'If you knew what I meant and you felt the same, you would have to talk about it.'

'Firstly, that's not true. I'm colder than you. And secondly—'

'Shit! Get down.' Frank grabbed Sira by the shoulder and kicked her legs out from under her, dropping them both to the deck. 'Sorry, there's something coming our way,' he whispered, holding his hand over her mouth. He rolled them both to the side of the boat, directly beneath the quay wall and pointed upwards.

155

A boot inched over the edge, followed by a length of wooden pole with a sharp-looking hook on its end.

'They tracked us, Frank,' Sira whispered.

'How? I'm encrypted, and you are jammed.'

'Don't know. Maybe they heard us yelling.'

'No, I don't think so. Turn your head, I need to get up against your device to jam mine. That's it. You still got that listening scanner, Sira?'

'Yes.'

'Transfer the app to me. Encrypt it and do it by local signal, not the net.'

'Done.'

'OK, got it. I'm going to listen.'

'What are they saying?'

'They saw a signal over here,' Frank said. 'Think they were just hoping to be lucky. Wait, no, they think they saw my signal here.'

'They've hacked you too?'

'I don't know. Shit! We should have thought of this. In the few hours we were together, before we wrapped up your head, they got into both me and Yanda. I don't know how far they got, but they got somewhere.'

'So, you need to get your device out too,' Sira said.

'Can't we just get it recoded?'

'Up to you. If we get out of this, Frank, I'm going off grid. I'll buy a hand-held from them. As you said, you can't be a part of a collective revolution if you are connected as an individual.'

'That's not what I said. You can't turn back the clock by throwing away your watch.'

'Very clever, Frank, but I've made up my mind. If we are going to work together, you need to go off grid too.'

'That's manipulation. Just because I'm in love with you, you can't tell me what to do.'

'What?'

'I said, just because… We spoke about this. We yelled about this just now!'

'I guess. I still didn't think you were just going to throw it out there.'

'Well, I know it's not reciprocated so I'm fucked.'

'I'm sorry, Frank.'

'Yep. But it's a massive weight off my shoulders. Not having a future feels quite nice.'

'Are they still there?' Sira asked.

'They've definitely lost my signal, but they are close. Maybe two or three boats along. We can sneak up and round. But then we are going to have to run.'

Sira went first, climbing up the quay wall, her boots pressed against the bricks and her hand gripping the mooring rope. Once at the top, she pulled Frank upwards. 'They've gone.'

'No, they haven't,' Frank yelled, grabbing Sira's hand and dragging her into the nearest building, a concrete shed with a low corrugated iron roof.

'Shit, they're in here too,' he hissed, pointing towards the back of the shed. 'Children. They have children with weapons in here.'

'I don't see them,' said Sira incredulously, getting her balance.

'Look Sira, there, on the gantry, there are two of them.'

Sira followed to where he was pointing and walked into a hail of bullets. Wood chips flew across the room as the guns held by young, weak arms slowly trained on her. When they got their aim, her flesh came away in a thousand soft red parcels. Frank watched in silence as, in a matter of seconds, her body was reduced to a red cloud expanding outwards like a supernova.

The words 'See them, See them, See them' rang through his head before he threw up where he stood.

'Frank, what's wrong?'

He could hear her. A broken audio file playing on repeat perhaps, triggered by his brain and his device going into uncontrolled meltdown. He fell on his side and continued to vomit as images of Sira smiling danced across his vision.

'Frank, I'm putting you in the recovery position. I think you are having a seizure. If you can hear me, tell your device to run an anti-shock programme.'

After ten minutes, she felt the heat returning to his forehead, then he began to murmur as the connection between his voice and hearing returned.

He woke to see her smiling down on him. Her hair had been tied back to prevent it from falling into his vomit but there was still some hair dangling in the puddle to his side. She looked beautiful, he thought to himself.

'They did hack you, Frank. You were right. But not enough to know where you are. They can augment your reality, though. But maybe just in glimpses. What did you see?'

'They killed you. Not saying any more. This is what happens to me if I see you die, apparently.'

Northern Israel,
16th May 2017

Through the looking glass

'So, what do you think, David?'

David gave Daniel an uncomfortable smile across the table of pickled fish, cottage cheese and cucumbers and touched his stomach through his stiff, white shirt. Daniel could see he was not used to being out of his London comfort zone.

'To be honest, I'm a little surprised. I've done well with the tech types out here before, but usually it's in a glass building on the coast. I've not been this rural since my time on a kibbutz thirty years ago. I'm reserving my judgement.'

The pair looked up from their salads for a moment to watch a pair denim hot pants wobble by.

'How are you feeling?' asked David, giving away another sign of his doubt.

'It's good to see the real Israel away from the hotel lobbies and military vantage points.'

'You mean the girls?'

'Maybe. A little. I feel a sense of belonging when I'm in a place like this. It's nice.'

David laughed, and poked at his salad again. 'I thought you liked Lara?'

'You've noticed? Great!' replied Daniel, a little embarrassed. 'I'm not sure she likes me. But I'm just talking about the feeling when I'm here. I couldn't live here. I like my rational world. I love it here and sometimes I want to join in, but it's also hard not to think they are slightly mad, like a big, naive hippy army. I'm hoping Yaakov isn't like that, otherwise this will be a hard sell back home.'

'Yes.' David laughed again. 'They are a bit mad. We used to be able to come here and take a piece home with us. I married one and she came back with me. These days it's a little different. I bet if you met an Israeli you liked Daniel, she'd want you to move here.'

'Maybe. I guess that means we aren't just here to see if we want Yaakov. It's also to see if he wants your money.'

'Good – you've got a theory. That's more than half the battle. I think you're going to be good at this.'

'So, this is being commercial, is it?'

'That's it. Nothing else to it. Right.' David stood and brushed some breadcrumbs from his trousers 'What have you got planned for us this afternoon?'

--

The taxi pulled down a dusty road off the highway, leaving the cool straight line of the coast behind in return for a brightly coloured billboard saturated with a garish typeface, reminding Daniel of the old TV show *Hi-de-Hi*. The lettering was modern Hebrew, which neither David nor Daniel could read.

Their bald and slightly vicious-looking driver barked, 'Old canteen,' as they drove past, explaining the purpose of the huge, dilapidated shed behind the sign. Underneath the large letters were about twenty rows of words in a smaller typeface, which Daniel assumed were the activities that could also be enjoyed – or perhaps be mandated – in the building that resembled a military barracks. This was his first visit to a kibbutz with the purpose of learning something about its inner workings, rather than as a convenient place for a meeting or somewhere to give the MPs a sense of something soft-left between military briefings.

Daniel knew kibbutzim had a special meaning for diaspora Jews, owing to the time many in David's generation, his own parents' generation, had enjoyed and eulogised helping in the fields, smoking weed and playing guitars before returning home to embrace business and pocket-book voting. But it meant something different to Israelis – pioneering, the founding of the state, muscular-left politics and communist 'family' arrangements. That was all a bit too alien for his usual MP itineraries. For the sake of this venture, he hoped that this kibbutz had morphed into something unrecognisable from the stereotypes, although the first people he saw out of the car window offered little reassurance.

Two men in shapeless, stone-washed blue jeans, unwieldy white trainers and T-shirts that suggested pride in their own physiques were standing at the large metal gate at the entrance to the newer section of the kibbutz. One of them was wearing an oddly effeminate wide-brim straw hat.

As the car approached, the hatless man pulled open the gate along its runner whilst his partner loomed over the driver's side window and launched into a rehearsed monologue aimed at David and Daniel in the back seats.

'Welcome to Kibbutz Yoav founded in 1934 by the first pioneers to grow cucumber. It played a crucial role in 1967, housing and feeding soldiers and was privatised in 1995 to increase productivity and our chances of survival. I'm Yaakov Goldman. I've lived here on and off for ten years, first supporting the community in their transition and later building us up as a powerful example of how community and profit can go hand in hand.

'Today,' he declared, standing back and gesturing at the land, 'we still grow fruit and vegetables, but we are also home to a thriving technology park linked to IDC Herzilya. Together, we have been the origin of some of the latest pieces of defence equipment used on the battlefield. More excitingly, we are developing a new platform for social difference and cohesion. I like to call it the Zionist difference engine.' He let a short hard laugh. 'And I know that is what you are here to learn more about.'

Yaakov grinned and looked down at the two men in the car who were both struggling to find their words. 'I'm going to jump in my jeep,' he said after an awkward silence. 'You follow me, and we will get one of the girls to rustle up some yoghurt and juice.'

As he walked towards his car, a Range Rover Sport, David let out a gasp of exasperation. 'I'm not sure if I can handle his enthusiasm for three days, Daniel. I'm also not sure why we are here for three days. I think he told us everything he knew at the gate – which we knew already from the emails!'

Daniel swallowed the instinct to explain that the visit had been David's idea and that, if he was going to get rich and powerful on whatever was going on here, he would need to listen. 'I expect he's just excited that we're here.'

'Perhaps,' David replied, obviously unconvinced.

They followed the car along a winding tarmacked road that cut through the gently inclining landscape and cedar trees. As they rose to the crest of the hill, they saw two rows of twenty-something men and women, all wearing the same T-shirts and hats, striding across the field. The members of the group to the left of the road each carried a small wooden crate. On the right, on a path which led to a collection of sheds, they each carried sloshing buckets of water. The two groups walked in step with each other, their uniformity jarring with their haphazard surroundings.

Yaakov beeped unnecessarily at the workers who had, by the time he reached them, already cleared the road. They turned in unison to wave at him.

'Strange. Why did they all respond like that?'

Daniel was not sure if David was asking a rhetorical question. He decided that, if he was going to survive the next few days and not return home a tense mess, he was going to have to speak his mind and not shield his new boss from his own anxieties.

'You're right. A bit cultish. Yaakov doesn't appear to be the only person here that loves Yaakov.' Daniel laughed a little falsely at his own joke, seeking to lighten the mood.

'I guess I can always get on with my work if this mission turns out to be a failure,' said David flatly. All the enthusiasm and confidence of his London-self seemed to have been left behind at the hotel.

'I don't think it will be a failure, David. There is something going on here. We just need to work out who the customer is. If it works, there has to be a market.'

'Right. Maybe. Not always, Daniel. Not always.'

The journey continued for ten more minutes, the two visitors making awkward little sounds at each other behind their driver's head every time Yaakov beeped at a passer-by who responded with the same, uniform wave.

--

'Daphna. Daphna. The guests are here. Some English tea, please. You guys love your English tea, don't you! Please, please, sit. It's a beautiful day.'

David and Daniel sat a few places away from each other and even further from Yaakov, hoping this would soften the impact of his booming personality on their eardrums.

'Great. You guys have had a long journey, ain't ya?'

'It was OK,' David replied, pulling his patio chair a little further from the table.

'You don't get too many Brits in these parts anymore. Not since the Muslims took over your foreign policy! Ha.'

'I think that's going a bit far.'

'That's what you Brits always say. But I think that Jennifer Simons is the only one I see on your BBC that talks sense.'

'Who?'

'I believe,' said Daniel, 'he is referring to the author and columnist who wrote that book about Britain becoming a Muslim state. She's often on *UK Questions*.'

'Right. She has strong opinions, I guess. But it's not all like that.'

'Well, I think you Brits have a problem,' Yaakov stated. 'And that's why I think you're here. But before all that, please eat. The girls have brought this over. It's good, mostly grown here. The dates from the Arabs up the hill are also very good.'

The two guests looked at each other for reassurance.

'Daphna. The tea. Is it coming already?' Yaakov yelled into the bungalow.

Daphna appeared from the kitchen across the hallway but, until she came closer to the doors, remained largely obscured by the orange Middle Eastern light. She was tall and elegant, with quantities of long, messy, dark hair falling across a tight red-and-gold dress, her chest covered by a golden scarf. Despite being surrounded by the cheaply branded T-shirts of the kibbutz, she somehow looked more at home than anyone else Daniel had seen so far.

'Hello, welcome to our home,' she mumbled, her tough Israeli accent contrasting with her hospitality. Before Daniel and David could thank her, she disappeared back into the house.

'Beautiful, isn't she, boys?' Yaakov slapped the table.

'Will she not be joining us?'

'Why, David, do you want to get a better look at her?'

'No, no.'

'Only kidding now!' Yaakov slapped the table again, causing the mugs to clink into each other and rattle Daniel's tired brain.

'What I meant was,' David attempted, 'I assumed the whole community was all working on this together, including your wife. That's just the impression I got.'

'Of course. That's true. But everyone has their different ways. Anyway, what's going on in England these days?'

David looked at Daniel, gesturing at him with raised eyebrows and widened eyes, pleading with him to say something.

'Um, well, we have another coalition government. This one is more precarious than the last. The media are having trouble getting their heads around how to report on it. Some of their own backbenchers are constantly critical, but too distant from the action to know what they're talking about, and the ministers themselves are all against each other. The opposition could be doing something interesting, but it's too early to say plus their leader is very young and inexperienced.'

'Right. We always have coalitions here. Terrible things. Nothing ever gets done. But you shouldn't dismiss the young. You're young yourself, ain't ya? And Labour?'

'Yes, I'm a member,' replied Daniel sheepishly, not sure how that would go down with their apparently right-wing acquittance. 'David is more neutral. But I don't get on with many Labour members. They're a bit too left wing for me these days.'

'Same here Daniel,' replied Yaakov while pushing a mug across the table towards Daniel. 'Maybe because my Left isn't about those guys.' Yaakov pointed to a minaret on the hill. 'It's about these guys,' he pointed to an approaching column of T-shirts.

'When did you make Aliyah, Yaakov?' enquired Daniel.

'Ah, my accent is a giveaway, is it?'

'New York?'

'Ha! No, Daniel. It's just that American English rubs off quite quickly in this place. I'm from the UK!'

'Really? Wow, I would have never guessed.'

'Yep. The Queen, pie and chips – all that!' Yaakov slapped the table again. 'And no Aliyah for me. Immigrated as a Gentile. Converted after I'd moved here. I was a Zionist before I was a Jew, you see.'

'You've changed your name?'

'Yes. I have. Well, the same name, *James*, different spelling and pronunciation. I just took it back to its Israeli roots. It's all part of what we are doing here – Zionism. Very Left. We're building a self-sustaining community, one that doesn't rely on capitalist speculation and investment. Yes, we buy and sell but we don't need some Chinese bank to fund our solar panels and broadband. We pay for that ourselves, using the money from our sales, agri and tech, and also borrowing a little money against the holiday homes at the edge of the property.'

'Can we talk about the tech?' Daniel pulled his notepad out of his laptop bag. 'Our proposition is that politics at home is changing. The government wants to borrow less and tax less, therefore it wants communities and the private sector to fill the space by working together to design and fund what used to be provided by the state. Everything from schools and hospitals to roads. Even if Labour wins the next election, and despite what they are saying now, these fundamentals won't change. There simply isn't the money to run everything from the centre.'

'That's why this place interests us, Yaakov,' said David. 'We know about normal kibbutzim, but the impression we get is that you are doing something unique here. Given our predicament back home, maybe there is an opportunity to sell this solution in the UK.'

'And make lots of money?'

'Potentially.'

'Interesting. If you're right, maybe you can fund a sales visit to the UK for us to see your backers? Maybe you can get us into see the Prime Minister and we can make a deal?'

'If only it were that simple,' replied David.

'Ha, I know. I know. I'm English, remember. I'm just pulling your leg. That's where we have the advantage. We know tech guys who come back from London with their tails between their legs, thinking they just had to get the meeting and agree the deal. England is strange. You gotta flirt with them, almost like you want to marry them, but you both know it's just sex. You know what I mean?'

'Yes,' David sighed. 'I'm pretty sure I know what you mean.'

North west London,
16th December 2053

At the limits of your training

The light was fading when they reached Neasden. They'd spent most of the afternoon having walking along railway lines that no longer carried traffic. The streetcar was the only benefit that West London had over the rest of the city for the out-of-pocket traveller. The less impoverished parts had scrapped the old communal vehicles many years ago to keep their private drones moving for a while.

The low, dusk sun shone down dusty street ahead of them, turning the white wood cladding of the old army huts orange, forcing Eres and Mila to find cover in the shadows of withered tree stumps and lopsided telephone poles. There were no signs of life as they approached the chicken-wire fence. However, from Eres' link with the chairman that morning, he knew the building was crawling with fellow agents, none of whom they could trust.

'OK, I've done this plenty of times, so follow my lead,' ordered Eres as he gripped the fence and gave it a gentle shake to see how firm it was.

'When was the last time you broke into a government facility?' Mila asked with a small laugh. 'Maybe, Eres...'

'Maybe what, Mila?' he asked with a sigh.

'Maybe you are, you know,' she looked away nervously, 'taking your orders a bit literally.'

'Please don't question my authority, Mila!,' he snapped. 'Only one of us here has done the full week's training. If you had done it, you would know never to question the chairman. The job is to find Roydon without help, and that's what we're going to do. I suggest you follow my lead!'

She nodded and saw *'Remember the time device! If you see the enemy, it is too late. If you don't see the enemy, it may also be too late,'* scrolling across her vision. *'I've got it, Eres,'* she texted back.

'Good! How are we going to get you over that fence dressed like that?' he asked, shaking his head.

Without replying, she pushed the pointed toes of her patent shoes through the fence and hosted herself up and over it, only catching a slight rip at the bottom of her skirt on the fierce spikes. On landing, knees bent, she rolled herself gently into a shallow ditch at the foot of the fence, keeping herself hidden and holding the metal to assist Eres' leap.

'You have done that before?' Eres asked.

'I watch a lot of training videos. I don't want to be stuck at that desk forever,' she hissed, trying to keep her voice down without hiding her frustration.

They ran along the inside of the fence until they spotted a red metal door in an annexe to the main building. After picking the lock, they went inside and crouched next to the boiler.

'Right, the plan is we break into Roydon's office without being seen and try to find some evidence pointing to his location. Then we get out of here. I have been here once before so I'm pretty sure I can find my way to Roydon's office, although we are going to have to crawl through the venting. I'm quite pleased I'm not wearing my good suit for this!' he said with a smile, hoping to get one in return. He was met by a scowl.

'Perhaps I should stay here. This really isn't my forte,' Mila said.

'No, Mila, I'm afraid we're going together. We need to search that room quickly and not get spotted, which means one of us is going to have to jam the sensors. That's your job. I'm going to give you this little device,' Eres held out his hand. 'It confuses the cameras, motion sensors and heat sensors and the like by overloading them with interference.'

'Static?'

'Yes. We are going to crawl through the vents and, as we pass over any sensors, it should do its thing. However, when I drop down into Roydon's office I'll need you to block the cameras in there. It only has a range of a couple of metres, which means it won't block the whole room at once. You'll need you to crawl across the ceiling above each camera as I move around. It will be my job to stay low and hidden and yours to follow me around. OK?'

'Is it on?'

'Yes, just strap it to your wrist and you won't need to think about it. Right, so that vent up there. That's where we're going.' Eres lifted Mila up to the edge of the vent and boosted her in, before climbing after her

'This is cosy,' Mila retorted.

'What?'

'I said, this is cosy. I didn't expect my boss's face to be right up my arse when I set out to meet him today.'

'It's a good job you're thin.'

'Sir!'

'I mean to fit through these vents Mila. I wish I'd spent a little less time bulking up, although I'm not sure if the talent scouts would have spotted me in that Co-op if I hadn't.'

'I know the story, Eres,' Mila mumbled.

'OK, just crawl until you get to the end. I've pulled up the schematic so can see where we are going. When we get to the end, turn left.'

Mila began padding slowly along the vent, trying to press her weight into the hard corners of the tunnel rather than against the flimsy sheet beneath her.

'You're doing well. The tension in the metal will keep changing, so feel for the most rigid sections.'

'Great,' Mila muttered sarcastically under her breath.

With every few metres, Eres felt his legs getting hotter and sweatier. He assumed Mila was feeling the same. Perhaps they would be better off risking the corridor and just making a run for it. Maybe his young partner was right. Until she had questioned him about taking the orders seriously, he had not questioned himself or the chairman. Too late now.

'Shit.'

'What?'

'There is a grille missing. There is a massive gap in the vent.'

'What?'

'Eres, there is a one-metre gap in the vent coming up.'

'I need to see. Wait,' Eres whispered. 'I can't connect to you. Signal won't travel through these fucking tunnels. Mila, I am going to crawl up next to you. As the vent goes around the corner it gets a little wider, and I think I can squeeze in.'

He pushed his face into the corner of the metal, tucked his arms by his sides and shuffled forward into Mila's ribs, scraping along the rivets and crushing her breasts. Just as he thought he would crack one of her ribs, he got his chin around the corner.

'See?' she asked.

'Yes, Mila. I am going to have to get past you. When we get to the gap, you're going to hold my legs so I can grab the next section and keep going. You have to hold my legs otherwise I will fall out.'

'What about me?'

'You're going to have to get down into the corridor, but only for a minute. Then I'll pull you up.'

'What? I'll be a sitting duck down there, Eres, in this fucking crime scene!'

'I know what I'm talking about. My training, remember! Give me the jammer. I will protect you from up here. If you get into trouble, I'll shoot.'

'You are going to kill some innocent fellow agent, just so we can get past?'

'Every time you question me, we get closer to death. If you need to, just knock them out with this.' Eres slipped Mila a small plastic pen. 'One small prick and it forces all the blood momentarily out of the head and into the limbs, causing the subject to pass out.'

Eres made it across but he was unable to lift Mila, so she crept slowly along the corridor, trying to hold in her frustration and stay beneath the creaking in the vent above her. When she got to the next grille, she stopped. 'I feel sick.'

'It's the adrenalin.'

'I can hear someone coming.'

'Yes, so can I. If you keep going, you may get into the office before they see you.'

'I don't want to go around the corner.'

'You should keep going. We have a plan, Mila.'

'Change of plan,' she whispered then crouched low, her face as close to the corner of the corridor as possible without being exposed.

Eres pressed his face into the nearest vent. 'What are you doing? Get up!'

'No. I am going to wait here, and you are going to tell me when to jab this needle around the corner.'

'I can't see around the corner, either.'

'You can see more than me.'

'Only a little, Mila, which means they may see me before they get near enough for you to inject them.'

'You wanted me down here. I'm doing it my way.'

'Shit. OK. I'm ready.'

'Good.'

Eres watched as Mila pulled the small pen-like implement from her pocket, removed the cap and tucked it into her fist. When he was in training, it took him longer than the other agents to work up his poker face and not to squint when he could see failure ahead. But that extra effort meant he never looked away now, ever. His eyes were wide open, and he felt the sting of dust against the whites as he watched his partner square up to death.

'I can hear them, Mila. I think it's a man. Quite a long stride. He's tall. The best place to get him is the belly. Raise your arm over your head, so you can thrust downwards, otherwise you might get the needle stuck in his belt.'

She did not reply but Eres could see her through the slats in the grille responding to his instructions.

'I'm going to give you a countdown and you are going to lunge forwards when I say "one".' Eres saw her nod. 'Three... Two... Wait!'

Mila didn't move. The man was too close to the corner for Eres to speak. The footsteps had stopped but he could not see any trace of the stranger. Looking down, he saw sweat running along Mila's clenched arm and a slight tremor starting in her thigh as the lactic acid built up.

The seconds crept by and eventually he heard a new sound, a scraping coming from the wall; it was her nails scratching against the paint, interspersed with the occasional tap.

He heard the stranger shift his weight from one foot to the next.

'NOW!'

Mila sprang forward but the man was out of her reach and his white coat disguised the location of his soft belly. She stumbled onto her hands and the device rolled under the skirting board.

'Are you OK, madam?' The stranger held out his hand and helped her up from the floor.

'Thank you. That's very kind. I got completely distracted watching online and tripped on the corner.'

'Ha. You should really be more careful.'

There was a thump above them and the pair looked up.

'How were you getting reception?' the man asked.

'Pardon?'

'The facility is on lock-down. There are no external signals. How were you getting online?'

Mila's smile fell away.

'Are you sure you're OK?'

'Yes, um, I was watching. I was watching...'

'A recording,' Eres' voiced bellowed from around the corner as his fist connected with the stranger's jaw, knocking his head against the wall. 'Run! Wait, pick up the needle!'

Mila grabbed it from the ground and sprinted forwards.

'There's the office!' Eres threw the door open. Mila slipped in behind him and he slammed the door shut and heaved the desk in place to keep it closed. He pulled out his gun.

'No, the power surges remember!' Mila yelled, trying to get her breath back.

Eres ignored her, shooting each of the cameras through the lens and then siting the jammer on top of the window blind next to the heat detector embedded in the ceiling. 'We have two minutes, max.'

--

'Got something, I think.'

'What?' The partners stood back-to-back as Mila emptied out the old-fashioned data cabinet in the corner, going through

172

each of Roydon's folders one by one while Eres rifled through his desk.

'It's a food order.'

'So, he orders food from his work account. Pretty standard if you can afford it, Mila.'

'No, it's not to the address we have on record. The postcode is very near here. Hold on, can you hear those steps?'

'Yes. At least two.'

'Let's go, then.'

'We don't have time,' yelled Eres as he pulled Mila down behind the wide desk.

'Team B to control. Roydon's room has been broken into. Door obstructed. Permission to use lethal force requested.'

Mila grabbed hold of Eres' harm, squeezing her nails through his shirt.

'Advise.... Yes, sir. Nick, push against the door, will you?'

Eres and Mila scurried back with the desk as it was pushed away, staying hidden from view but now squeezed against the wall. They could see four shoes on the threshold. Eres grabbed his gun, flicked the safety catch off and rested its butt on the floor to steady his aim at the thigh of one of the guards. Both guards took a step forward and, with the sound of them unholstering their weapons, he squeezed the trigger.

They both watched as the leg of Eres' target momentarily vanished in a bright light, tumbling the guard to the floor before his bloody stump reappeared.

Eres pushed the desk back towards the door, trapping the other guard's legs. He lunged sideways and fired a bullet into his chest, covering the door with blood and pieces of heart and ribs.

Mila started to yell. Before he could grab her, she walked in a daze into the middle of the room and pointed at what remained of the guard spread across the door, his head unnaturally tilted to one side.

She continued to point at the corpse, repeating, 'Shit, shit, shit,' until the bullet entered her stomach and she fell exactly opposite the dead man, as though they were in conversation but too tired to stand.

173

Looking to her right, she saw the first guard on his knee, blood dripping out of what remained of his right leg and smoke drifting upwards from the muzzle trained on her forehead.

She sat quietly until she heard the next bang, and everything went black.

East London,
15th December 2053

No porn

The smell of the fish market grew more intense with every step. As they got closer, the wet puddles of melted ice on the pavement developed an oily sheen of purples and yellows. Only after ten minutes of breathing through their mouths and holding their noses did they see the first people.

The main street was filled with what looked like astronauts. Yellow-suited creatures with bulky breathing masks covering their faces and claw extensions on their arms loading crates of fish onto passing carts and into the windows of the buildings either side. As the fish went in, steam billowed out forming a ceiling along the road, trapping the moisture and stench.

'It's perfectly edible.'

Sira and Frank turned to see a seven-foot, plastic-wrapped man, extensions for arms and legs looming over them, holding out a wooden crate. They could not see its contents but guessed what it was from the white oily liquid dripping from beneath.

'Ma'am, it is old fish,' said the man in a muffled voice. 'A freezer container hijacked last week but still perfectly edible even if it does whiff a little. I'll sell you a whole box for that rifle.'

'Uh, no, I mean. Not now, sorry. How is it edible?'

'We use nanos. All nano treated. Can't kill the bacteria, which is why it still smells, but we can trap it. Passes straight through you. You don't feel a thing, and the nanos make their way back to us.'

'To you? You do this?'

'No, I mean it's our way. I'm just a trader. Clever folk build the nanos.'

'Do they make nanos for everything?' asked Frank.

'A lot, yes.'

'Where do we find them?'

'Not hungry, eh? Not many folks round here not hungry. Lots of folks round here. Eating all the time, whatever the ships bring in. Don't like fish. There will be meat soon, likely enough. Flies, too. Ha! But safe. Just follow the market back to the dock. The nano men run the dock, they run everything. Too clever.'

'Thank you – er...'

'Trader. I'm a trader, that's all.'

'Well, thank you... Sira, come on.'

'Yeah, got it. Coming. Since when did you get so bossy?'

'I've thrown everything up already, remember. I think I can breathe here better than you. But my device is showing nothing. I thought once we were in, we could read their own network to get around. But maybe they don't have one.'

'They're liberal, remember,' retorted Sira. 'They will be controlling the data to make the most of it. I bet you could buy some network if you brought them a ship or some rotten fish. Still, it's not what I imagined. I thought it would be all shiny blocks. Technology. Freedom. Competition.'

'So, they're just poor like the rest of us?'

'Maybe, but for them poor means thriving and busy destitution.'

'You having second thoughts?'

'No. If we are to survive, I need this thing out.'

'Well, I'm having mine out too then!'

'And when we are back home, Frank? What then? No more hacking? What you going to do? I don't have a choice, but you could be alright.'

'You and Yanda think I'm a coward. You might be right. My inner coward is telling me to get back home safely and worry about the rest later. Maybe one day I can come back here and get a new one. Or maybe, if the gangs are gone, I'll pay the hospital to give me a new one.'

Sira could see he was getting upset again and tried to distract him. 'I'm going to miss the colours.'

'What?'

'I mess with the colours just for fun – you know, blue ground, green sky. Fading people out that you don't like. I'll miss that. Being stuck in this normal.'

'I'll miss the games, I guess. Getting in teams. Saving people. Being brave in safety. Shutting myself off from your and Yanda's rubbish.'

'Thanks.'

'You're welcome.'

--

Past the fish loaders, plastic awnings, misshapen metal kiosk frames and children picking at slivers of rotten fish, they could see the harbour. Green water formed a straight horizon and guided their eyes to a group of smartly dressed and bearded men directing the action.

'I guess that's them, Sira, or they can at least point the way.'

'I guess. They're pretty much what I expected.'

'What?'

'They look self-important from here.'

'Well, they would. They run the place.'

'Yeah, they run this.' Sira drew a finger across the heaps of fish guts strewn across the cobbles.

'Come on, let's just do this.'

'I can't believe we're giving money to the liberals. Look what they have done! It's disgusting.'

Sira moved forward slowly, hopping to the patches of cobbles that seemed wet rather than soiled. Between jumps, she watched the harbour enlarge and widen before her, offering fresh air and perhaps a way back.

--

'You have to go under? You know that?'

The pair sat on plastic chairs in a small waiting room. One side was lined by a massive, dirty, tropical-fish tank, and the other sides were badly plastered white walls covered in framed photos, each of a small huddle of people wearing clean clothes and sunglasses, smiling at the camera.

177

Between one collection of photos was a doorway marked by hanging strings of brown beads which rattled slightly in the breeze of an air conditioner.

'Yes, we know,' Frank replied, holding out the sack containing the rifle to an enormous man in a white coat with a dyed-black beard.

'It's good, little boy. Bit more than we'd charge usually, so we'll throw in these hand-helds. You'll need something when you're clean.'

Frank and Sira looked at the old plastic devices and tried to come to terms with being screen users.

'Thank you.'

'Not very chatty, are you?'

'Sorry,' said Frank. 'It's just a big change.'

'Sure. Funny westerners,' replied the man before he led them through the beads into the operating room, home to a row of bulky cushioned chairs. On the wall covered by a fish tank in the waiting area was a bank of large monitors.

'We know you guys don't chat because you don't like us,' the man continued. 'Imagine what we could achieve together.' He laughed to himself and gestured to the chairs. 'Please, strap yourselves in.'

Frank and Sira chose two units and pushed their feet into the plates, triggering the body restraints. Once they were locked in, the technician threw his white coat to the floor, revealing a muscular body barely covered by a small vest and shorts. He walked around the two chairs in turn, adjusting the equipment.

'It's what's in this season for big guys like me,' he volunteered to Sira. 'We have all sorts down here. Gym guys, skinnies, goths, sluts, library types, sports, you can be whatever takes your fancy.'

'You're talking about clothes?' mumbled Sira, her head and neck strap making it difficult to enunciate.

'I'm talking about your look. Your style. How you live. Everyone can be different. Show their choices. It's fun. Not like you guys in your military stuff. We don't have that look down here. Unless you are talking some khaki hot pants or shorts. They're cool this season! Anyway, recognise the room?'

Sira and Frank turned their heads as far as they could and frowned.

'It's from an old film. *Total Recall*. Business takes over Mars.'

Frank considered accessing his implant for a last time to understand what the tech was talking about but decided that he'd rather remain focused on reality.

'So, what do you want to watch while we get you set up? I'll put you under for the op, but there is a lot of prep to get through. Would you like gang-bang, facial, black on white, Asian on black, girl-girl, boy-boy, animals, cartoon, snuff.'

'No porn,' Frank mumbled.

'What's that, little man?'

'He said no porn,' Sira said. 'We don't do that. It harms morale. We like to see each other strong not submissive.'

'You guys! Hilarious,' replied the tech as he tapped the screen of a machine on a chrome trolley in the corner of the room. 'What about this?' The Nuremberg Rally appeared on the screen.

'Very funny,' replied Frank, a little dribble coming from his mouth as he fought the head restraint. 'We're not like that. We're proud, but not like that.'

'Only messing with you guys. Here you go!' The tech tapped a few more keys. They now watched a march. The camera panned around Trafalgar Square, zooming in and out of clusters of costumed men and women, many of them teenagers.

Frank and Sira strained sideways to look at each other, knowing that this was the last march they'd been on. The camera zoomed in on a particular gathering, and they saw themselves and Captain.

The video paused there then ran in reverse until it found the trio marching towards the tube station, drummer boys entering the underground a few moments before them. But to their right was something that was not there on the day. Along the pavement, along the entire road, uniformed children were standing arm-in-arm, motionless, just watching.

Sira's expression changed before Frank's but he caught up. They'd all been hacked.

'We don't really care about the others, Sira,' continued the tech. 'We have an army. We now just need the brains. We've been watching you for months. You've got skills.'

She could see their captor getting excited and throwing his arms around. 'Don't you want to stop playing and really make a difference?'

'You're from here?' Frank mumbled, pointlessly trying to pull his arms free. 'You're the liberals? The liberals are the gang? The one that's been following us? That killed Yanda?'

The tech leant in close to Frank's face. 'No, don't be stupid, little boy. We just took this place for a few hours. They'll do anything for money here, as you know.' He smiled and pulled Frank's wrist restraints uncomfortably tighter. 'We're with you, kind of. Want the government gone. We just believe you've got to put in some muscle.'

Sira and Frank caught a glimpse of each other before they heard a click from the trolley, and everything went dark.

--

'Sira, wake up,' Frank whispered in her ear, shaking her every few seconds on the down rush of the drugs they had been filled with. On his fourth attempt she sat bolt upright, looked at him and lay down again on the rough concrete floor. A mosquito buzzed her ear every few seconds, but she ignored it, lacking the energy to bat it away.

'We've still got our implants, Sira. Took me a while to work it out as there's no signal down here. But nothing's changed except we've been moved.'

'I'm sorry, Frank.'

'What you sorry for? I think I came up with the plan. How could we have known they'd been watching us the whole time? Why did they even let us get this far?'

Sira pushed herself backwards along the floor, sat up against the cold wall and shrugged. 'You don't seem scared?'

'I am. I was before you woke up. Maybe I'm just exhausted. Do you think we could have just handed ourselves in? Maybe Yanda would have, you know.' Frank picked a concrete tag from the floor and rolled it round in his fingers, making his thumb bleed a little.

Sira looked at her friend and was jealous of his calm. He had accepted his surroundings, his lack of choice. His mind was still and literal, while hers sloshed between her ears with guilt. 'I'm sorry Frank, I—.'

'I've told you. It's not your fault.'

'Frank, please listen,' she ordered, her palms becoming hot and sweaty, and then cold. 'I want to explain.'

'You don't have to.'

'I do, Frank,' she yelled, getting to her feet. 'Listen!'

He looked up at her, frightened of what she might say.

'You didn't understand why Yanda did that? Why all of a sudden, he decided to kill that guard? Why I went along with it?'

'I don't understand a lot, Sira. It all gets a bit confused sometimes. But I'm sure he was just showing off. He knew I – I liked you and he wanted to show he could have anyone.'

'Maybe, Frank, but that isn't why he did it.'

Frank looked at her confused. 'How would you know?'

Sira sat down next to him and put her arm around his shoulder. 'Please don't hate me.'

'I think we've established that that is not what I feel,' he replied, shrugging her arm away.

'I did it to him,' she said quietly.

'You didn't, Sira. I was there. He ran in.'

'Please listen, Frank. Before I came back to the garage, I gave myself something. I didn't know what to do.'

Frank could feel her body alongside his getting tenser and colder.

'I knew I was putting you in danger, but I didn't know where else to go. So I made a patch. I hacked into a military database and adapted something designed for soldiers to get them through horrible things. It was strange. It came in waves. I was still scared but, when I really tried, it gave me a boost. A big boost. I think it's only just wearing off now. Maybe their drugs have worn it off.' She could see that Frank wanted to reassure her but he did not want her to stop. 'Well, I sent it to

181

Yanda. I was going to send it to both of you, but I couldn't bring myself to do it you. I don't know why.'

Franks eyes slipped to sadness.

'Yanda's implant was so easy to access. When he said he was going to kill that guard, I knew it had worked. It was working on both of us, but more than I'd planned.'

Frank remained silent for a moment, before turning away and scraping again at the floor. She tried to put her arm back around him but he shrugged it off again, more forcefully this time.

With the pair sitting in silence, the door slammed open. A tall figure stood, silhouetted against the bright corridor. 'I did fancy you on the march. You're pretty hot, Sira,' asserted Captain.

Frank rolled his body away from both of them and let out a dismissive huff.

'We've got a use for your little friend, too. Maybe we'll plug you into the children's bank. You can direct our looters or something. But no child's play for you, Sira,! No foreplay either!' said Captain, laughing to himself.

Before Sira could respond, two mutes had her under the arms and were dragging her along a gantry overlooking an enormous shed. The wooden door slammed shut.

Frank may have heard her apologise again as she was dragged away. He was not sure. He stayed motionless for a few minutes and, after deciding he could hate her and love her at the same time, tried to reach out but there was nothing there. His implant seemed to be working at short range, but it was no use on its own. He slumped back down against the wall, his head still spinning from the drugs.

Northern Israel,
17th May 2017

Funny English boys

Daniel heaved himself onto the bed, still in his clothes, and kicked his dust-covered shoes onto the floor. He noticed that a gentle gradient of yellow earth had worked its way up his beige suit trousers; for a moment, he was unsure how to get them off without getting his hands soiled. Eventually he undid his buttons and wriggled his legs out, flipping over to remove the shirt from his back, his exhausted face pushed into the cheap, thin cushion he'd been given as a pillow.

As vision withdrew from his eyes and into the day's memories, he heard the chipboard door creak open. 'Tired already?' A loud Australian accent penetrated the room.

He turned over and saw a short girl a little younger than him standing over his bed. She was wearing the requisite Kibbutz Yoav white T-shirt with blue lettering, which she had paired with cut-off jeans. She looked like a slightly overweight version of the 1980s' popstar Tiffany.

'You wanna share?' She was holding a badly-rolled joint between her fingers. 'It's only a mild one. After-dinner thing. It's what we do here. And since you're here to see how we live, I thought I'd show you!'

'Where's everyone else?' Daniel asked with a disinterested sigh. 'They smoking too?'

'Yeah, in the lounge next door. They said I should leave you alone, but that ain't my style.'

'Clearly.' Daniel pulled himself up the bed, keeping the sheet and quilt covering his chest. It made him feel a little effeminate.

'You English guys. So funny with your beer, fighting and shyness. Where you from?'

'Guess.'

'North west London.'

'Of course.'

'You lived on a kibbutz before?'

'We aren't really here to live, just for a couple of nights. But no, I've not spent this much time on one before.'

'You sound a bit grumpy, mate. I'm only being friendly.'

'Sorry, sorry. Just tired. Please, have a seat.' He patted the mattress as far away from his crotch as he could reach.

'Yeah, of course. Only kidding. I'd be tired too after a short flight,' she said sarcastically, a smile on her round face. 'I have to do twenty-five hours when I wanna see my folks. You need to man up, I reckon.'

He rolled his eyes a little and hoped she had not seen. 'So, you got a lighter for that thing?'

'Straight to the point for a Brit. Like it!'

Daniel felt the exhaustion stinging his eyes. 'So what's your name?'

'Michelle. They call me Mitch back home, which I don't really like. Bit blokey. But here they call me Michelle. I prefer that.' She lit the joint with a white lighter marked with a marijuana leaf and took a long draw. Its paper crackled away to reveal a floppy, glowing forest.

'Looks pretty strong.'

'Not really. But you guys use tobacco, don't you? Israelis don't really mix like that. You'll like it.'

Daniel took the joint between his fingers, hovering it over the small pink plastic dish Michelle had brought in as an ashtray. 'It's been a while. I used to have a bit of a habit, so I stopped buying it. Too many days sitting at my desk staring into space.'

'That's what's good about farming, I guess. We get up and work. Sometimes our brains come with us, sometimes not. Different for the software guys here, but I reckon they don't need many busy days to get the job done.'

Daniel breathed the green smoke into his lungs and felt his head grow and float away from his body. A little more would have been nauseating. His mouth stretched into an embarrassingly wide grin. 'It's good,' he said through a chewy purple cloud.

'Yeah, you look like you're enjoying it, mate! It takes quite a lot to get me stoned these days.'

'So...' Daniel took a deep breath of hot, dry Israeli air to keep his brain together. 'What's going on here? Does someone tell you what to do?'

'Tell us! You're funny. You English guys, you never lighten up even when you've lit up.' She threw her head back in high-pitched laughter, rocking the bed with her weight.

'I think there is something different about this place. Just want to know what it is. It's my job.'

'Seriously? You ain't much older than me. "My job!"' she mocked, giving him a light jab in the ribs.

Daniel fought back an irritable response and tried to explain again. 'My job sent me here to better understand the place. Maybe an investment opportunity.'

'But it's night-time mate! You're in bed with a girl. Just enjoy yourself. Listen, mate, what do you want to do? Make money for that suit you're with?' Michelle let out another chain of giggles. 'We're not meant to tell outsiders, you know. Commercial confidentiality and all that.'

'That's a shame,' replied Daniel. 'We've come a long way.'

'No, you ain't. Australia's a long way. Just said that. Anyway, can't just be about money. No one comes to Israel just for money!'

'Fine. Not only that.'

'Go on then, funny boy.'

Daniel took another drag before trying to explain, focusing on short sentences for both their benefit. 'I like the idea – well, what I think the idea is. Been to Israel many times taking MPs around the place. We do the defence bit, the tech bit, and then squeeze in a bit on civil society. MPs say they want the latter, but it doesn't really make sense to them. Kibbutzim are nothing like British communities and they get a bit confused. So, as I said, we're definitely here to try and make some money, but I also think that if Britain were to do something like you're doing here, get more Israeli, I just think that would be good.' He could see Michelle was concentrating through the haze, trying to understand.

'Bit of an idealist ain't you mate.'

He smiled. 'You're not the first person to say that.'

'So, do it!'

'I am. Well, I want to. If you tell me a bit more. Yaakov told us how some of the tech works in principle, but I want to know what it means to you. To people that live here.'

'Pass me the joint and I'll think about it.' She gave him another little jab in the ribs.

Daniel passed what was left of it to her, their hands fumbling for a moment until she had a grip.

'How about this. We finish this joint, have sex, and then I tell you a little. I'm not sneaking back into the bunk beds until getting some.'

Daniel thought about his un-showered body and the small rolls of fat pinched under Michelle's bra and didn't reply.

'You must have slept with an Aussie before, Daniel! London's full of us.'

Daniel tried to hold back his nervousness. He had never had a one-night stand; the more he thought about it, the more embarrassed he became to have such as old-fashioned phrase as 'one-night stand' knocking around in his head. 'Sure.'

'That's it? You're offered sex and you say "sure"? Back home, and here even, the guys are more macho than that, you know? They'll start showing off about how they're going to fuck you and how much you're going to enjoy it.'

Daniel leant forward, took the joint from between Michelle's fingers, took a final drag and kissed her neck.

'Very romantic!'

'Do you always talk this much?'

'I've not said much, Daniel. Funny English boys!' She stood up, pulled her clothes off in a couple of rapid moves, jumped into bed beside him and grabbed his penis.

--

'I thought you were tired!'

'I am, I still want to talk though.'

'If you're awake, we could have sex again.'

Daniel's awkwardness had mostly washed away but, with the weed wearing off, he worried that it would return shortly.

186

He wanted to fill his brain with something else, find some confidence. He remembered that Ben Gurion said the Jewish nation would have Jewish postmen and Jewish people doing all other normal jobs. Maybe it was OK that his job while he was here was to be the Jewish man who has sex with someone he does not fancy to get information. He smiled to himself. 'Yes, let's,' he replied confidently. 'After you've told me about this place!'

Michelle frowned and nodded before pulling her T-shirt back on. 'You know, back home they're a bit more...'

'What?'

'I guess they're a bit less gay. In Israel, too.'

'This is pretty strange for me too, to be honest.' Daniel reached down to the little fabric bag that Michelle kept her weed in. 'Things at home are different. Everyone always thinks I'm coming onto them.'

'Yeah, British girls are weird too. Takes them ages when they get out here for them to start saying what they want. They're used to being excited when blokes like you suss them out and tell them what they want. I think your whole country is into mind games. Mine is into fun.'

'OK. Let's agree to be strange then.' Daniel finished rolling a small joint and passed it to Michelle.

'Is that a British way of winning? Agreeing to differ? I think you compromise too much.' Michelle took a long drag from the joint and gave no sign that it phased her.

'Quite bold, Michelle. You don't really know me.'

'You told me you're plan, remember. But I reckon you're mainly worrying about what your friend in the suit wants. I reckon you should do what you want.'

'I want to do both.'

'Well, just make sure if you have to choose that you think of yourself, funny boy.'

'I am. Listen,' Daniel said a little more sternly than he'd planned. 'Yaakov's wife, Daphna. She lives here but she seems different. Everyone else is walking around in lines, dressed like something out of an eighties' pop video. I don't know what you're doing, but you all follow Yaakov. He wasn't born Jewish, and now he's this big Israeli kibbutz leader type. But

187

Daphna seems above it. I only met her briefly, but she looks like someone who'd fit in a lot better in a glamorous restaurant in Herzilya or northern Tel Aviv, not a dusty bungalow up against the Palestinians.'

'Is that a question?'

'Yeah, I guess. It's another way of asking you what's going on.'

'Right.' Michelle took another big drag of the joint and patted Daniel's leg. 'Maybe that's why you're all so strange. Always trying to work things out. Obsessed with class. I agree, it's different here but it doesn't mean you need to know everything to get on.'

'I do. That's why David and I are here.'

She gave him a stern look.

'It's why I'm here,' he corrected himself.

Michelle eventually explained that Daphna was from a wealthy Tel Aviv family and one of the few from the south with big money. She ran the family trust, donating most of it to IDC according to her father's wishes. That was where she'd met Yaakov. Michelle thought that Yaakov probably had Daphna there for a bit of show to impress the visitors.

Daniel wondered whether that explanation had been worth the effort and moved onto Yaakov. 'What do you make of him? Do you not find him a bit much?'

'Yeah, but I guess he's got two sides. He spends a lot of time working and being very methodical. He's got this great way of bringing people in by sharing his vision. We all know we could have gone to another kibbutz and picked fruit or killed chickens or something, where people reminisce about the golden age. We're lucky to have come here and be achieving something.'

'Wow. OK.' Daniel raised his eyebrows mockingly.

'What?' Michelle snapped.

'Sorry, I guess I was expecting something cynical. Something straight.'

'If you stayed, you'd get it,' she replied dismissively, turned away from him.

'Sorry, Michelle, I didn't mean to be rude.'

188

'I'm a little stoned now. And it's late,' she said, the energy gone from her voice for the first time.

'I promise I'll shut up soon, but can tell me about the tech side? The product?'

'I came in here to fuck you and maybe get you to have some fun. Tomorrow there will be singing and partying. It will be good. But you probably won't like that either, and then you can go back to your boring London,' she mumbled aggressively.

He thought she was probably right so decided to push on. 'Ten minutes. I'll make this easy. I'll tell you what Yaakov said, and you add what you feel like. OK?'

'Fine,' she sighed.

Daniel took a deep breath, then rolled out his words carefully, knowing this was his last chance. 'He said he has built a social profit network. He says that a normal social network is a neutral platform for people to share and collaborate but mainly share, and the only thing you get from the makers is some advertising on the side. He said that a social profit network is one that really understands its users and can pick out common goals, then influence people towards achieving those goals. So you guys, for example, want the tech products here to make some money to keep the kibbutz going, so your social world via the app you all use is manipulated to influence you into staying focussed on that goal.'

'Yeah. But it's a bit more than that. We can all stay focused on goals with enough encouragement, but we don't all know how to do it. The system just advises us, helps us share our knowledge with the right people more quickly, like a wise old man. A father. If you were on the app and we were talking through it, it would be mining our conversation for hints of what we do and don't know. It would then fill the blanks in a fun way.'

'Is that not a bit like spying?'

'No. You're overthinking things.' She elbowed him gently, enjoying mocking him again. 'We can leave whenever we want and we can talk in private too. Like now, in private rooms.'

'We're being watched outside the room?' Daniel thought of him and David giving each other knowing looks when Yaakov's back was turned, and felt a bit ill.

'Don't worry, funny boy. There are cameras, listening devices and feedback systems, like speakers and screens, dotted around the whole place but not in private rooms. There are signs everywhere to tell you when you are in a public or private place. See that white box with a red border under your light switch, on the sign with the emergency info?' Michelle pointed at it with the lighter. 'That means this is private. If that square was solid red, it would be public or connected.'

'Terrifying,' he said, honestly.

'Not really, that's tech for you. People like being seen. They say they want privacy but Yaakov says, in reality, when you say you're watching them they love it.'

'You want me to party with you guys out there tomorrow? Whilst we are being watched?'

'Well, only if you lighten up a bit, Daniel. But the system only cares about what we are trying to achieve. We're not being watched by a person. If you look around tomorrow, you'll see it wants us to have fun!'

'And march in straight lines?'

'Well, only because it works better!' she asserted, and turned to see how he would reply. But Daniel simply nodded and frowned, lost in thought over whether his idealism was about to block him from making any money again.

As Michelle left, he heard laughter from the common room outside. What would Ben Gurion say about tech megalomaniacs, he wondered. Did Israel need Jewish versions of those too?

North west London, 17th December 2053

I haven't used either of these before

'Come on, not far now,' she heard Eres yell.

The wet soil rose upwards into a great unending tower before Mila. She felt her feet loose in the air, unable to find a grip to slow her fall. The further she fell, the darker and colder it got until it was impossible to see and all sound had become muffled echo.

'Hold this open,' she heard a deep, unfamiliar voice say.

'I can see it. I'm pulling,' replied Eres.'

'She isn't breathing.'

'There is a defib in my jacket pocket. You get it. It's on the left. I can't move my hands.'

'OK, ready.'

'Clear.'

She felt the reset shock smash into her chest, throwing her body against the side of the tunnel.

'Mila, can you hear me? It's Eres.'

'Keep going,' ordered the deep voice.

'Clear.'

Her body spun downwards, scraping her feet against the rocks.

'Do it again. I've stopped the bleeding.'

'Clear.'

White light crashed through the soiled bricks around her and flowed through her skull.

'Can you hear me Mila?'

She spluttered and sucked in a deep breath, momentarily ripping her field dressing before it was clamped shut again.

'Fuck, that was close,' she heard Eres say.

--

She woke in a child's bedroom, or what she imagined a child's bedroom would look like from descriptions she'd read. The walls were covered in a repeating pattern of pink flowers raised slightly on thick, rough paper. The furniture was shiny, white, ornate and small. She turned her head and saw Eres sitting on an upturned wicker basket under the window.

'Hi Mila.'

'You killed those men,' she said flatly, trying not to strain her wound.

'Yes, well, I definitely killed one. The second, I'm not sure about. We were just doing our job.'

'Have they followed us?'

'I don't think so. If the second guy isn't dead, he didn't see my face and I doubt he will be speaking. I shot him through the side of the mouth and then burnt out his implant with the jammer. Anyway, if I hadn't shot the second guy, you would definitely be dead.'

Mila breathed heavily through her nose and tried to push the words out without moving her lungs. 'If you hadn't shot the first guy, we could have surrendered. They would have probably let us go.'

'Please stop questioning the orders, Mila. Anyway, we've made progress. Whose house do you think this is?' Eres gestured towards the window, directing her to squint through the bright sunlit glass.

Without sitting up, she could see the top of a row of fir trees against the white, morning sky. 'Where are we, Eres? I can't see properly.'

'That's the base, past those trees. You were right. Roydon's secret place was just down the road.'

'Roydon?' she spat, blood dribbling down her chin. 'The guy that stole all the fucking data? You're saying that place was crawling with agents and yet we are the only ones to have discovered his address after two minutes searching his office?'

Eres looked at her, confused, and shrugged. 'Roydon's downstairs. He saved your life, Mila.'

Eres had hoped that when she awoke and learned of their discovery it would have pleased her. She must know, he

192

thought, that achieving this mission would likely result in a bonus. 'Why don't you come downstairs with me, Mila, and continue the interrogation?'

'We've been here all night, Eres. Why has no one found us? Have you thought about that?'

'I don't know, Mila, but they haven't,' he shouted back, angry that she was focussing on the wrong details. He tried to persuade her again. 'I want you to come down with me. I'm going to give you an injection that should mask the pain for an hour or so without making you woozy.'

Eres held out his hand, revealing another small injecting device.

'No way. We're done, Eres. It's time to call for help,' snapped Mila, pulling her body up the bed and away from him but failing to change the stony expression of his face. 'I thought those knocked people out? Anyway, I have been shot. I'm assuming by the fact I passed out that I nearly died. How much blood did I lose? Thank you for saving me but, as I've said and as you know, I'm not trained for this and didn't sign up for this. I think I need to go to the hospital.'

Eres waited for her to finish, nodding at her words and holding his hands open as they had taught him on the mandatory online empathy training module. 'I'm sure you're in a lot of pain, Mila, but I'm afraid we can't stop. Roydon is involved. We need to question him. We are the only people who know where he is, and we were told not to talk to other agents.'

Mila looked again at the device in her boss's hand and thought about the fellow agents they had killed to give her the opportunity to drug herself in this strange, pink and white room. In contrast, she thought, the pie 'n' mash shop in the West End was normal.

--

Mila followed Eres down the tight, twisted wooden staircase, running her hand along the white bumpy plasterwork to see if the injection had dulled her fingertips. The pain was gone but there was a strong bleach smell clouding her mouth and nose.

Roydon had his back to the staircase and was still wearing his green military uniform. As they walked around him, Mila could see his shirt was open and his jacket was screwed up and dry on the floor at the foot of a sofa at the edge of a blood stain that covered most of the room's carpet. His hand repeatedly gripped and relaxed over a plastic cup, making a rhythmic crinkling.

'She is feeling a lot better,' explained Eres to their captive host while pointing Mila towards the sofa.

'Yes, I can see that' replied Roydon. 'Congratulations, ma'am, I didn't think you were going to make it when your colleague brought you to my front door. You were white as a sheet. Anyway, I assume you want to talk now?'

'Yes, sir,' said Eres, perching himself on a stool opposite Roydon, and leaning forward in a manner which positioned him above the slouched corporal. 'We are with the agency. We know there was a data breach at Neasden last night. We know you were in charge of that base, and we know you have been missing since the agency got wind that something had gone wrong earlier. We also suspected, and now know, that you have a property – this property – off the books. It looks very suspicious. Please talk.'

'You know nothing, then agent?'

'We know a lot, Roydon. We know what was in your base, and we know how dangerous it would be if it fell into the wrong hands. Will you cooperate, or do you want me to torture you?'

Mila dipped her head forward and stared at the wooden floors but could see in her peripheral vision that Eres was ignoring her silent protest and preparing another injection.

'Care to guess what this is, Roydon?'

The corporal's face went grey. 'I expect it will induce a mild psychotic episode, to the extent that I can still speak but I don't really know what is going on. Under a little pressure, I will tell you what you want to know.'

'Close, corporal. That's this one.' Eres flashed another device clipped to the inside of his jacket. 'This one is actually a fast-acting poison. One quick prick and it is all over. You won't feel a thing. You will simply black out, and that will be the end. Of course, I'd rather you talk.'

'This is what I get for saving your friend here?' Sweat dripped down Roydon's face and across his lips, giving his words a wet, slapping sound.

'The more cooperative you are, Roydon, the less likely you are to die. Unless,' Eres played with the device in his hand, 'you want to die? Better that than your family find out what you use that room upstairs for?'

Roydon sat up a little straighter and slipped the contents of his drink down his throat. 'Kill me, and you'll kill your prime suspect. Won't look good.'

Mila could see Eres gripping the bottom of his stool in anger.

'Speak,' shouted Eres, shuffling the stool a little closer to Roydon.

'They offered me something. In return, I gave them what they wanted.'

'Why did you trust them?'

'I've done it before, and nothing went wrong.'

'You have given away data before?'

'Yes.'

'Why?'

'Because I have worked in this shithole for years, and I wanted something for myself.'

'This place. You wanted this place?'

'Yes.'

'You're saying you're not in on it? You did it for a fee? You undermined our security, ruined your career and will get yourself jailed for a fee?'

Roydon remained firm. Mila saw that, despite him slouching on a floral couch and having his life threatened, he still thought he was in charge. A lifetime's habit, she assumed.

'You would rather hear that I am a part of this? That I helped hack Neasden for some bigger goal? Stopping governments manipulate time, perhaps? Stopping under-trained agents, like you get your hands on power? I'm afraid that isn't why I did it.'

'You sound like you know why they wanted the data.'

'Afraid not, agent. I'm just guessing. It could be anything. I had no idea what they wanted, or that they could take the whole lot. All they said was that they wanted personal records, just like the times before. Basic criminal fraud, I guess. Plus, we put a huge amount of time and resource into ensuring the juicy stuff was nicely locked away.'

'Well, I'm afraid you were wrong about that, Roydon.'

'I know.'

'What's upstairs for?' asked Mila, failing to completely hide a crack of pain in her voice.

'Guess, agent!'

'I'll break your jaw, corporal,' Eres barked, grabbing the collar of his khaki shirt. 'Answer her question.'

'You know what's going on up there. You saw it.'

'I want you to say it.'

The corporal sat up straighter in his chair, propped up by a steely burst of confidence. 'It's where I entertain my girlfriends.' Roydon laughed. 'You're both disgusted. I've disgusted you. I have affected you. That is power!'

'True.' The word slipped out of Eres' mouth as pulled the syringe from his jacket and punched it into Roydon's thigh.

'Fuck! You shit! I was doing everything you wanted. I'm answering your fucking questions.'

'Quiet, Roydon. You're going to have to concentrate now. In a few seconds, you will feel very strange. I've probably given you a lethal dose, so you need to focus to experience your final moments.'

'Oh God. I feel sick. You murdering shit!' Roydon leant forward and swung his right arm towards Eres, but the drugs had already begun to take effect and he lost his balance and fell back into his chair.

Mila stood, careful not to stretch her wound, and walked up to the incapacitated corporal. Holding the back of his chair for balance, she bent down to speak into his ear. 'I got shot because of you. Eres killed people because of you. And you have told us that you did all this so you could rape little girls. I hope you die in front of us but, before you do, you're going to tell us everything you know about your paymasters.'

196

'Look, I'm telling the truth. They said they had a girl. She was real, I looked her up. She's famous. A hacker. Well, famous amongst those fucked-up kids.'

'Why did you want a hacker?' Eres pushed his thumb into his prisoner's forearm, pinching the nerve, and Roydon yelled out in pain.

'Eres, he's going pale,' called out Mila.

'I didn't. That's who they offered. I liked her fucking smile, you shit. I said I'd allow a data breach for her. That's all.'

'Right, That's it!' Eres pulled out the other syringe.

'Stop!' Mila grabbed his wrist.

'He doesn't deserve to live. Look at him.'

A trail of yellow saliva and bile was running out of the corner of Roydon's mouth, pooling in his clavicle.

'He's lying Eres.'

'What?'

'He knows more. I'm sure of it. Let me try.'

Eres took a few paces back and slumped on the floral couch. 'Go ahead,' he said, shaking his head dismissively at his untrained colleague.

Mila picked up one of the small wooden chairs and dragged it next to Roydon so she could speak down into his ear. 'Can you hear me?'

'Yes,' Roydon gurgled. A concentrated stream of urine flowed down his trouser leg and dripped onto the floor and between the wooden boards.

'He hasn't got much time before he falls unconscious. You're going to have to speed this up,' asserted Eres casually.

'Knife, give me your knife then!' Mila barked. Eres pulled it from his ankle holster and handed it to her. 'I'm going to make your last moments more painful, Roydon, if you don't tell me. See!' Mila pushed the knife slowly into Roydon's thigh.

'Ahhha. B-b-bitch.'

'That was just a scratch. Talk!'

'She – she's a hacker. She – they needed her help. They said I could have her afterwards. It's in the recording.'

'The recording? What recording.'

'I'm dying.'

'Yes.'

'You need my code.'

'To watch the recording? Where is it?'

'You'll find it. But, you need the code.'

'So, give me the fucking code.'

'It's her birthday.'

'The hacker?'

'No, the first. The first girl,' Roydon gurgled.

'Mila, you're wasting your time. He's talking in riddles.'

'No, Eres, he's staring at something.'

Eres shrugged.

'He's trying to tell us something.'

'Maybe, Mila, maybe. But what?'

'He's looking at something in the corner of the room.' Mila pointed her finger at the top of the old-fashioned chimney flue that angled up and outside the house.

'He's looking at nothing, Mila. He's staring at a white wall.'

'He isn't. He's, he…'

'Now you're talking in riddles Mila.'

'I'm not!' she yelled, turning the knife around in her hand and plunging it into Roydon's eye.

'Oh my God, Mila! What are you doing! We could have just waited it out! The drugs were working!'

'I don't think so, Eres.'

'Why?'

'Because you gave him the wrong injection!'

Eres looked at her, and then looked at the device in his hand and went pale.

--

'Eres, Eres, look!' Her colleague stayed seated, sweating and shaking. 'Eres, just look! You were right. He had something to tell us. There's something there. On his eye.'

Eres looked down between his feet and shook his head. 'That's our bonus gone,' he murmured.

'Eres, please forget that. He probably deserved it anyway. I need your help.' She held out her hands to him, one containing Roydon's right eyeball and the other, the knife.

Eres picked up the eyeball and held it to the light, smiled a little, then took the knife and gently peeled an artificial lens from its front. Mila stood over his shoulder, so she could see what he'd found. 'It's a girl, Mila. A photo of a very young girl.' Eres looked away for a moment and took a breath before continuing. 'It's disgusting.'

They both stared into the lens and saw that under the photo of the girl being abused were two dates with a dash between. Her years alive. She was twelve.

'He murders them, Mila.'

'I know. It doesn't matter now. You were right to kill him.'

'I didn't mean to, though,' he replied, collapsing into the sofa.

'That doesn't matter now, Eres. Look, these dates.' She tapped the top of Roydon's head, which was now slumped forwards dripping blood. 'This must be the code to get into his recordings.'

Eres looked up and took a deep breath. 'OK, Mila', he said. 'We can scan it, we don't need to cut it out.'

'I know.'

The pair sat next to each other on the sofa and looked into the distance, into their own displays. Eres took control through his own implant and pressed play. The film was taken in the same room. Roydon was focused on a shaven-headed, tall, muscular man in a camo-vest.

'Roydon, we'll help you if you help us.'

'Help! You've gone too far. They'll court martial me. I can't do it. I told you, same access as usual for the girl.'

'You'll have the girl. But the usual access isn't enough. We need access to the machine, just once. In return, you can keep the girl and your job.'

'So, they tricked him?' Eres asked.

'Looks that way,' replied Mila. 'Keep watching.'

'What's the use of one trip, Captain? I've told you, you can't change the past. That's not what it does.'

'Oh God, what have you done. Oh God!...' Roydon's voice bellowed in Eres' and Mila's ears. They both instinctively covered them, despite the noise coming from within.

'Calm down, Roydon. Look again.'

'What, my legs? I saw them.'

'Your legs are fine.'

'But they were gone. Something cut them, I felt it.'

'Is he hallucinating?'

'Eres! Please just keep playing.'

'We're in your head, Roydon. We've hacked you. We can make you see anything we want you to see. The feeling isn't as good at this level, which is why your brain's a bit confused about the lack of pain. If you do what we want, we'll get out of your head.'

'Shit, Mila! They can hack people! They can time-travel, pop up anywhere and hack people. We are fucked!'

'Eres, please. It's hard enough for me to focus as it is.'

'It's just a light hack, old man. But, if you don't do what we want, it will be more like this.'

In the film, Captain lifted a small screen device up to Roydon's eye level, and Roydon, Eres and Mila watched the same thing: a teenage girl on the back seat of a car, flanked by two large men, one of whom was holding a device wired up to her temples.

'This is how we achieve a very deep hack, Roydon. Really get into her mind. Do this for us, and we won't do this to you! Now, let's see how you feel without your arms.'

'What happened?'

'That's the end of the recording, Mila.'

'Roydon must have passed out.'

'I guess. He underestimated them, then!' Eres looked at Mila for reassurance. 'He didn't think that they could achieve time travel with one break in. He didn't think they had built their own time machine, which presumably they'd need to, to make use of the stolen data. But, Eres, Isn't that a massive undertaking? For a gang?'

He replied, lacking conviction, 'They said in training, Mila that they could do anything.'

'We just need to find it then, if they've built it, don't we?' Mila stood up and began to pace the room. Surely, after searching for a while, we can find what they've built. It will be quite conspicuous.'

'So?'

'I've not been in the field before. I should have asked earlier. But why did the chairman send us after Roydon? He could have just sent us to look for their machine. If they've built one?'

'I guess, I...'

'What, Eres?'

'I guess, I thought that once they can get ahead of us, spy on us like we spy on them, they could keep the upper hand.'

Mila looked at him blankly and shook her head.

'So, what do you think, Mila?'

'I don't know. I think it's off somehow. Why did Captain have that girl? Why did they do that to her in the back of that car? Why offer someone like that to Roydon? I'm going to download what's left in his device. Maybe there's something in there.'

'You do that. But,' Eres stood up and brushed some fluids from the interrogation off his shirt, 'I think it's mission accomplished. Time to connect back to the chairman.'

He scrolled through his primary options and flicked his system back to its usual secure channel. A block bar appeared before him and began sliding slowly towards the right across his vision, looking for a signal. Just as 'success' appeared before him, the room flashed white light. He heard his partner fall to the floor and felt something heavy connect with his head.

As his vision returned and he regained a sense of balance, he realised that the two dark horizontal bars before him were legs looming over him as he lay sideways on the floor. He turned his head and saw the chairman's face, crowned in rolls of fat, looking down, grimacing. Standing either side of him were heavily armed agents.

Somewhere in London, 15th December 2053

You're going to climb in here

Sira was being dragged across the warehouse floor and each time one of her boots got caught in something it yanked her captor's shoulders backwards, to his mild annoyance. As they approached the corner of the warehouse, she made out the heavy, trash metal music they were playing about the other noises; yelling and clanging metal objects.

Sira's people were into jazz revival, group dancing, set steps, a hundred costumed avatars making a room swell in unison. Thrash metal still had the unison but was channelled through a pit; huge men, always men, circling each other, pushing and crashing each other into a violent swirl of flesh. A wave of music that came from an era with no war, desperate for a taste of raw violence with no respect for the real thing. In a previous era, Sira had read, thrash metal fans would have been relegated to small groups in trailer parks, drinking beer and snorting speed. Maybe now their time had come.

As she reached their destination, she saw Captain sitting on a large, blue barrel, his legs astride and one hand playing threateningly with the top button of his shorts.

'What do you think of our little set up?' he asked, ordering his men to drop the girl near his feet.

'You know,' Sira spat out, 'I've been living on the streets for a few years now, dressing however, dancing with whoever, and—'

'And I bet your two boys loved that.' Captain grinned and nodded.

'Not my point, you bastard. My point is that no one ever tried to rape me, tie me up or beat me. But in the last few hours since I met you, all of that has happened. What does that tell you, you slimy shit?' Sira tried to spit on his boots but her mouth was too dry.

'It tells me that you fuckers are weak. That we can't leave shit to you. That we gotta own the system our way.'

'That's what this is, is it?' Sira looked at her bound hands in front of her. 'Revolution?'

'Not right now. Got to do some extortion first.'

'So, what? You're going to hack us all? Make us all work for you?'

'No. I'll admit we don't have the power to do that yet, not to give us control. But we're working on it. Maybe we'll make you all walk off a fucking cliff when we're ready,' he said, smiling. 'But I reckon some of you have your uses before we get to that. You show a lot of promise, Sira. You're going to help us with a little experiment.' Captain slapped the enormous stainless-steel barrel behind him, sending an echo crashing around the warehouse.

'Is it real? Or as fake as your red hotel?'

'I'm pretty sure it's real, Sira. You'll see for yourself soon enough.'

'Maybe you think I'm better than I am, Captain. I've really no idea what you're talking about.'

'I think you do. Time travel Sira. For a while, it's all the kids talked about.'

Sira felt her rage turn cold and weak. 'It doesn't work. They said it didn't work. We all saw it not work,' she protested.

'Yeah, well they were wrong. It didn't take them long to figure it out. But why risk going through all that again, when you can keep it secret? Democracy ain't what it used to be, Sira, and your popular army, or whatever you call yourselves, they didn't know any of this, did they? What's the use of a military with no intel?'

'So we got the intel. Then we got the machine. Just down the road from Neasden! Do you like our replica? We're hard wired to the real thing, thanks to some old-fashioned corruption.'

'So, what do you want me for? I'm a hacker who didn't even know they had a time machine. Turns out I'm not that good after all.'

203

'Don't feel too bad Sira. It hasn't only been the authorities hiding this thing, it's been us too. No point in breaking into the safe you see, if others can break in too!' Captain jumped off his perch and walked around the drum. 'You're going to climb in here.'

'Fuck you! You can fucking drag me, but I ain't climbing nowhere.'

'Just messing with you. It doesn't work like that. Anyway, we're here for two reasons: one to test something and – well, the other's none of your business. You won't be around for it. This lovely machine is going to take you somewhere, yesterday, and you're going to find this person.'

Captain flashed up an image in Sira's head of someone senior looking in a US military uniform. 'You won't need to travel far. Just lay low, hack into what you need to, and we'll do the rest.'

'Rest of what?'

'Doesn't matter. It will be like the hotel hack we put you through. You won't know what you're doing and why.'

'And then?'

'And then, you'll come back.'

'And then you'll let me go?'

'We didn't let you go the first time. Couldn't miss the opportunity to follow you once we'd done our hack. You're an intriguing girl, Sira. Anyway, whether we let you go or not, you'll have broken this country's – this coalition's – most important secret law: no sending people back in time! Plus, a boring older one: no murder,' he said with an increasingly wide grin, unable to control his excitement. 'I think after that you'll be better off staying with us!'

'I don't get it. Why don't you kill him yourself? Today?'

'Firstly, we knew where he was yesterday. First time ever, in fact, that we've known where he was. Secondly, you're going to do more than kill him. You're going to steal all the data in his head in the way only you know how, you little warrior!' Captain laughed to himself and drummed out a short loud rhythm on his barrel.

Sira slumped forward, her long black hair covering her crossed legs to make a cocoon from the outside world. 'Is it safe?'

'We'll find out. I've heard there were a few failed experiments with people. And they all went mad! But I'm sure they've fixed it since then!'

North west London, 17th December 2053

Arrested

'MATTHEWS, WE HAVE VIDEO OF YOU KILLING FELLOW SECURITY PERSONNEL!!'

Eres and Mila sat adjacent to each other, strapped in portable interrogation chairs in an office like Roydon's. They knew they were back at Neasden.

The chairman leant over the agent, his large stomach pushing at his shirt buttons. His voice boomed in Eres' ear canals and across his display, his implant interpreting it as all capitals and exclamation marks.

'AND YOU KILLED OUR ONLY WITNESS!'

'Wait, sir, please get offline,' Eres begged, while his mind fought the distraction of the chairman's aggression for long enough to reconnect to Mila and tap her into the incoming messages. He knew the connection had worked when he saw her wince at the volume.

'WHAT?'

'Mr Chairman. Get offline. I have to tell you something, and we can't let the gang hear.'

'You mean you have to kill me in secret?'

'No, sir. I'm begging you.' Eres' voice ran shrill and dry under pressure. 'We have been following whoever did this all day, chairman, in secret as you ordered, and we are running out of time. Please, sir. I am loyal. I have always been loyal!'

The chairman shuffled back slightly and looked down at him. The armed agents to his sides nodded and left the room.

'You've got one minute.'

'Are you offline, sir?'

'YES. ONE MINUTE!'

--

After Eres had provided his mission report, the chairman simply nodded, left the room and locked the door behind him. 'That's strange,' Eres whispered to himself.

'Not the first strange thing that's happened today,' Mila replied. She paused for a moment. 'I think that you may have got this wrong.'

'Mila,' he replied, 'if you thought I'd missed an important detail, you should have said.'

'That's not what I mean,' she protested. 'I mean, I don't think he,' she paused again, 'I don't think he expected you to do what you did.'

Eres shook his head with exasperation. 'Mila, like I've been telling you all day, these were my orders.'

'I understand. I just think, maybe—'

'Mila, please spit it out,' he yelled, his voice echoing around the small, plastic-lined room.

'I don't think you were meant to succeed.'

Eres turned his head as far as he could in the restraint to look at her and succeeded in getting the edge of her face in his peripheral vision.

'I've got this feeling. Like I said, it didn't make sense that nobody had found Roydon before us. I think maybe we weren't supposed to get that far.'

'Mila, that's ridiculous! All my training pushes me to follow orders.'

'Yes well, maybe. Or maybe someone had to be seen to be investigating this.' She paused again. 'If you think about it, Eres.'

'I am thinking about it, Mila!' he screamed in frustration. Only the cable ties prevented him from banging his fists.

'If you do think about it,' she pressed on, 'why is the chairman so annoyed? We – well, you– shot those men. But we found Roydon, didn't we?'

Eres sat in silence for a few moments, surprised that an obvious answer was not springing from his lips. 'Maybe it's just protocol,' he replied finally.

'Is the encryption still working between us, Eres,?'

He looked confused but did not reply.

'Can the chairman read us, read what I'm saying, if I text, Eres?'

'Well, no. But do you think we should lift it? And technically it's a blocker, not encryption, Mila. Shall I lift it, so he knows we aren't hiding anything from him?'

'FOR FUCK'S SAKE' scrolled across his vision in reply.

'No, Eres, keep the encryption on, please. If they try to break through it, let me know, OK?'

Eres nodded as far as he could, given the head restraint.

'I've been through Roydon's implant,' texted Mila, wondering whether her boss would engage or not. He did not reply, so she pressed on. *'You said earlier that they can still use the machine to go back to this spot.'*

'Well, the chairman said it was stuck in a loop. I don't know if they can control it, but power surges can send things back, or maybe forward. I don't know.'

'That's another thing. They could have taken us anywhere else. There isn't anything the chairman can do here, not without risking setting something off. You saw what happened to that guard's leg. It vanished!'

Eres laughed. 'Where else would he take us. This is the scene of the crime. The centre of their operations.'

'A crime we aren't investigating, Eres, and please text! We have been arrested, remember. The point is, I've got a model for simulating the space-time pattern. It's what I've been working on back at the office. That's useless without the data from before this place was locked out of the wider system.'

'Great. Thanks, Mila. You're really cheering me up.'

'Eres,' she shouted, before returning to text, *'I'm not trying to cheer you up! Listen! I've found something in Roydon's implant. It's a time stamp from the data packet he gave to that Captain guy. I think it might help!'*

'Tell me.'

'No, Eres. I'm bored with this,' she shouted again. *'I'm bored with you and your nonsense about your training! A week's training. It's ridiculous.'*

'It's standard,' he mumbled.

'Standard for your actual job listening into phone calls. Not this! I think you're too stupid to know how deep in you are!'

'Mila!' he yelled, 'that is insubordination!'

'Just think about what I'm saying and listen to me.'

He sighed and turned his head away from her as far as the strap around his forehead would let him.

'I think you know what I'm saying, Eres. I think you're just too stubborn to admit it.'

He let out another sigh.

'I'm going to try something,' she said calmly, 'and I'd like you're help. Will you help me?'

After a long pause, *'yes'* scrolled slowly across her vision.

Somewhere in London, 15ᵗʰ December 2053

She will hate that

Yanda looked down at his boots swinging in the moist, cold air beneath him and breathed shallow and fast to calm his heart rate. He had always thought it was deep breaths that did that, but he was following a health app and it was working. The app had been grafted onto a first-person shooter he had compiled over the past hour based entirely on the two key-hole vantage points he had found above the roof tiles, although he had had to replace his favoured scoped weapon for an axe to make the real-sim work. This, in reality, was a pipe he had pulled loose from the side of a vent and had dropped at an opportune moment to the floor below, ready for use.

His plan, which he simulated his way through once more, was to drop down onto some large sacks about ten metres from where they were holding Sira, hidden slightly by the mist being pumped in to cool the room. After landing, he would roll onto the floor and retrieve his weapon. When he was behind the nearest enemy, he would jump to his feet from a prone position and take him out with a single swing to the head. He would then remove the gun from the body and take down the other enemies with a single shot to the face of each.

He knew his chances of success were all based on the probabilities of the AI of the game, not the actual 'I' of the real people. Even taking this into account, the best he had achieved in his practice sessions was three non-immediately lethal gunshot wounds to his torso and one to his leg, as well as an assumption built into the first-person shooter that a bullet strike might force you to pause for a split second but would not thereafter hamper your advance. Of course, he could build in whatever assumptions he wanted, but he suspected that more accuracy would make death more likely before rescuing Sira, and he was too frightened to try that.

Practices complete, he lifted a tile away from the ceiling and laid himself gently across the surrounding tiles so as not to fall down. This was the best view he'd had so far, but if anyone looked up he was done for.

He brought the game online, which counted him in with a fresh set of breathing exercises and activated another dose of Sira's hack that he'd found working in his background. His anger and adrenalin levels surged, causing his heart to beat visibly in his chest. Just as his brain began to reverberate over the thought of something important bursting inside him, he levelled off and clenched his fists and jaw with chemical excitement. He started the final countdown as he saw Sira being dragged to a square metal platform next to the large drum.

An incoming signal flashed in the corner of his eye.

'Yanda, how the fuck!' scrolled across his vision.

'Frank! Where are you? Wait, got your visual coming in. Ah, you're up here too!'

'Yeah, just got out of the cell they locked me in. There was a grate in the floor. Cheap, easy hack. I assume they only wanted Sira. But I can't see anything. I'm above the ceiling. Got signal. I can see what you're seeing, but my section is walled off. Can hear, though. How you alive?'

'Blast knocked me out. They took me for dead and chucked me on a heap with the others. Found this place in the dead fellas' implants. Just a guess really, but here you are. I saw them wheel you in, in a barrow. How you feeling? I'm feeling amazing!'

'Of course you are Yanda. It's the patch she gave you.'

'I know! Amazing, isn't she!' Yanda replied.

'You could say that,' Frank said sarcastically. *'We thought you were dead. I thought she'd got you killed.'*

'You too, mate,' bounced back. *'I couldn't find you guys anywhere. Anyway, don't speak too soon. Maybe she has killed us. I've got a plan all set up.'* Yanda explained his plan.

'That's not a plan, Yanda. Great work on the software, but what makes you think that they won't just shove her into the machine when they see you?'

211

'What machine?'

'The time fucking machine. That big silver thing you're looking at.'

'Oh that! It doesn't work.'

'Why do you think that?'

'Everyone knows it doesn't work.'

'Right. Well, Yanda, I've been listening. If it doesn't work, why in hell do you think they have just explained their fucking plan, in which it fucking works!'

'Frank, slow down. I can only get so much text on vision without it blocking what they're up to. Anyway, I've been watching but can't hear shit over their music.'

'Right, well I can. This vent is right over them. Listen!'

'Hey, man,' they both heard from below. 'You can't tie her wrists to the side. She'll lose her hands when she goes back. Just keep your gun on her.'

'Is that Captain?' asked Yanda.

'Yes, he's the one doing the talking. They are going to send her back twenty-four hours, to murder someone and steal something from him.'

'Shit.'

'Yeah. I don't think I can hack in to change it. I've been trying but I can't get past some basic controls. Anyway, they've hacked her. Wherever and whenever she goes, she is going to do this murder. They'll make her. She'll probably think she is carving open a watermelon or something.'

'What if we send her back to the other side of the planet? She won't be able to do it then.'

'I'm in the system, but just the outer controls. I can't get in deep.'

'Shit, shit. Um, I'm going to jump.'

'No, no, wait Yanda. Got a few locations. Ha! It's like a GPS search. They've narrowed it to UK army R&D bases. Liverpool's furthest away.'

'Liverpool! Is that a joke, Frank? Plus, I think they can probably steer her back from Liverpool in a few hours, if they really try.'

'No need for sarcasm, Yanda.'

'I've been sitting under a pile of dead bodies – I can do what the fuck I want. And I'm pumped. You got what you wanted, didn't you? Sitting and watching from afar. From up wherever you are, Frank. Safe!'

'OK, OK, shut up. I can change the date, I think. Shit, I've no idea how this fucking thing works, Yanda. How does she come back?'

'You're asking the wrong person, little man. But the way I see it, the further she goes the safer she will be. What about 25 December 0000?'

'No, that's made up. And it's Liverpool, remember, not Bethlehem. What about the 1960s?'

'What?'

'The sixties.'

'No, no! She will hate it. Liberal baby boomer, Beatles epicentre. Send her to a war – 1940 or something.'

'Fuck that. Anyway, this is no longer about what she wants. We need to protect her,' Frank asserted angrily, 'not make her happy, and not send her to a fucking warzone!'

'And if she can't get back, Frank?' Yanda's receiver went silent. 'Frank, can you hear me? What if she can't get back? Or what if she changes something?'

After a long pause *I'm in charge for once. The decision has been made*, scrolled across Yanda's vision, followed by a loud 'oh shit,' in his ears, from below.

'Frank, what is it? What's happening?'

'They can see what we've changed. On their screen down there. They are trying to change it back.'

--

'Don't move a fucking muscle, girl,' ordered the masked man gripping Sira's arm and holding a pistol to her temple.

Sira tried to run her patch again but her implant would not come online. It was being jammed and her panic at the thought of being vaporised by the machine was preventing her from finding a workaround. 'Oh God. Please, I'll do something else for you,' she cried out. 'Whatever you want. I won't tell anyone.'

213

'Shut it!' Captain ordered from the other side of the drum. 'Guys, what's the hold-up?'

'Controls are fucking-up sir,' she heard, followed by a loud thud that rippled across the warehouse.

'Shoot him. Shoot. But not the machine!' Captain ordered, as one if his gang threw him his weapon. He trained it above the spot where Yanda had briefly appeared. 'You, all of you, don't shoot the machine, just the boy.'

Bullets fanned the room.

'I can't see him,' Captain yelled. 'Send her back. What's the fucking problem?'

'I'm trying, nearly there. Fuck there's a countdown. She's going to the wrong place!'.

Sira saw Yanda jump and slide into the legs of the nearest gunman before lifting the pipe above his head and smashing the gunman's skull down into his own jaw, as though he were eating his head backwards. Pieces of bone, the size of playing dice, rattled across the floor and, before she could warn Yanda of the gun pointed at his stomach, that same gun was firing into the ceiling as Yanda drove his pipe into its owner's ribs and out through his neck, spraying an arc of blood across floor The gun flew into the air and into Yanda's hands, who then hurled himself behind a cluster of pipework for cover and out of Sira's line of sight.

'Shit, shit, it's still counting down,' Sira heard over her shoulder, followed by: 'Fire, ignore me, shoot at the fucking machine, the pipes, everything! Stop it!' from Captain.

Amidst the metal sparks and billowing gas coolant, Sira saw Yanda's gun and head lining up for a shot at Captain, but then he was gone. Red mist mixed with yellow gas rose above her friend's neck like a mushroom cloud and her vision went to black.

Yanda's signal, only partial when he was down below, vanished from Frank's display. The sound and vibration of gunfire stopped. Frank's enclosed roof space filled with chlorine and cordite.

North west London,
17th December 2053

OK, Hawkins, I'm ready

The lights went from white to red and an alarm sounded as Mila's head slumped forward. A few second later, the chairman and a skeletal woman wrapped in a white lab coat burst through the door.

On seeing that Mila was unconscious, the scientist opened her shirt and planted a small device on her chest. The chairman gripped Mila's wrist for a moment and shook his head, but something that the woman said to him persuaded him to let her proceed. She connected her implant to Mila and sent a shock through her heart, causing Mila to jerk forward and regain consciousness.

'Is she OK, Hawkins?' barked the chairman.

Hawkins nodded her bird-like head a fraction, picked up her things and left the room.

The chairman looked at his prisoners suspiciously and then followed Hawkins out.

'You OK, Mila?' texted Eres,

'Yes, fine. Hawkins knew I wasn't unconscious. Got that message to her quickly enough, thankfully!'

'And is she going to help?'

'Hang on. We need to wait. Yes! That was quick! She is. I'll tap you in!'

Hawkins's voice broadcast into both their minds. *'It's a very impressive piece of work Ms Seynes, but I'm afraid the record it is based on... well, there isn't enough data. I'm very sorry,'* she said nervously, adding *'If you had all the settings from yesterday as well, before we were hacked and locked out, it would be different. But you don't.'*

'*Exactly, doctor!*' exclaimed Mila, proudly.

'*Sorry, I don't understand.*'

'Nor do I,' texted Eres.

'Doctor, I think you're saying that if we had one good dataset and combined it with what we have already in my head – now in all our heads – we could get back in business. Get the machine working properly and shut the others, the infiltrators out.'

'Yes, probably. That's a good theory. But I'm afraid that's exactly the information we don't have.'

'We're going to need your help, doctor,' Mila replied. 'We're going to need you to get me to the machine.'

'It's completely illegal, ma'am!'

'So is this, and I think the chairman knows about it.' Mila sent the video taken by Roydon to the doctor.

'Mila,' Eres texted, 'if she goes along with this, I'm the one going back. I put you in this mess.'

'You believe me now?'

'Yes, well, maybe. Anyway, it's my mission, whatever it is. I'm the one going back.'

'Fine. Up to you, Eres. I would have been quite happy with a day at the office. But, one thing: If she does this for us, just gather the information and bring it back to me.'

'You don't trust me,?' Eres asked, sincerely.

'Just bring me the data,' Mila replied, then decided to cut her connection with Eres until the doctor got back in touch. She heard him huff in exasperation.

When Mila reconnected, she found Eres restlessly scrolling through the 'keep fit' chapter of his basic training manual. He closed it down when he felt her presence.

'Eres, she says the whole building is in the loop. You just have to sit here. Hawkins thinks she can control it.'

'I can hear her, Mila. Maybe I'm stupid, but I'm not deaf' scrolled across her vision. 'Why is she doing this for us?'

'I don't know, but we don't have any other options unless you just want to sit here and wait to get processed.'

'You know,' Eres mumbled in his natural voice, 'I sent a device back once, and it came back broken.'

'Broken?'

'Yes, sort of melted. We reported that the device must have been spotted. Tampered with. But what if it wasn't that, Mila? What if the journey did it?'

'And you're worried that?'

'Well, yes. I'm worried that it will do something to me.'

'But it was just that once?'

'Yes. Yes, you're right, I'm being stupid.'

'I didn't say that, Eres.'

'But do you think I should be worried, Mila?'

'You're asking for my opinion? I didn't see that coming,' she replied acerbically, which she then regretted as she saw his stress levels spike through the connection.

She was about to apologise when *OK, Hawkins, I'm ready* flashed across her eyes and he vanished. One second he was there, the next not, like he had been edited out of the scene, out of real life.

Liverpool,
16th December 1968

Sira's body careered sideways into a solid wall, knocking the breath from her lungs. Vibrations ran through her teeth. As she realised there was nothing alongside her, her legs buckled under the strain and brought her down to the floor. She'd been winded before and knew the only answer was to wait and not panic. She focussed on a random mark between two wooden tiles on the floor, forcing her mind elsewhere until the oxygen came gushing back in.

She had no idea where she was, but that did not last long. The floor on which she had collapsed was covered in pieces of paper, gathered and covered in type, as if a library of old-fashioned books had been ripped apart at their spines. *The Gazette*, University of Liverpool, Monday, 16th December 1968. Was this Frank's sick joke, an implant patch to get back at her, she thought, before realising she had no signal and tucked into her memory was an image of Yanda killed for the second time.

Everything went black.

She came to again. Images, arguments, half quotes and theories filled her mind. Nothing about Liverpool. Plenty about drugs, Vietnam and naivety. Plenty of politics and bile, but nothing familiar. Nothing real.

Her breathing back to normal, she scanned the room and then closed her eyes tightly, replacing her vision with an image of three friends sitting in a garage, one of them dead in the corner. She forced her eyes open again. They got the time machine to work after all, Sira thought.

Across the room sat a small huddle of beige and denim girls and boys, mainly boys, deep in conversation and gesticulating upwards and outwards, pointing towards the main doors and the stained ceiling. Maybe, Sira thought, they were the centre of some activity, some power, but then realised she was grasping at nothing. In all likelihood, she was hundreds of miles, as well as decades, from anything.

She wondered how many others had been sent back, and whether the experience would be more tolerable for willing participants or those who knew whether getting home or not was part of the deal. It was easy to think of time as a straight line to run up and down on, but there was no reason for that to be true. It could just as easily be akin to being lost in a tangled ball of wool. She slumped back to the floor.

--

As Sira's mind cleared, she noticed small differences between the people in the room clothing, colourful badges and accents. At home she could guessed where these people were from, what part of London, class and clique they belonged to, and what social networks they lived in. Here, she had no language. Some wore blue jeans and others brown corduroys and floral skirts, but none of it meant anything to her or corresponded with her own knowledge of this generation.

'Ask her, if you want a second opinion! Hey you, who are you with?' The question was directed at her in a thick accent she associated with a comedy movie from the so-called Cool Britannia era. Out of her network, her device was of no help. 'Do you think Marxism is sexist?' asked the same cringingly serious voice.

'Stop it, Peter, at least say hi first.' Sira turned towards the second voice, which was owned by one of the few females who was hidden under a pile of floral cloth that ran around her neck like a creeping vine in an old cemetery.

'Hello, I'm Sira,' she said quietly, relieved to find her voice still worked.

'You're who, darling?' mocked a second man, looking extremely impressed with himself, despite his skin being so blotchy he must not have known how to programme a surface wash. 'And what's with the outfit? You must be famous to be wearing something as striking as that! Communist or something? Cuban?'

Sira looked down at her black shirt and trousers and her military boots. 'Um, I'm foreign. A student,' she improvised.

'Yes, yes, we are all students darling. I'd say you're a member of the Internationale!'

'She can say what she is, Peter.'

'I'm from California,' Sira continued, after finding some documentary footage saved on her implant from the 1960s. People sitting in circles, smoking and a someone threading flowers down the barrel of a gun.

'You sound British.'

Sira hunted for her next lie, unsure where it would take her and unsure whether the people she was lying to were any more real than she was.

'My family home is British so I guess the accent stuck.'

'British accent but odd phrases, little lady.'

Sira ignored the attempt to patronise her and rummaged through her mind and implant again for any old scraps of history. 'Yes, I guess Marxism is sexist,' she asserted, after recalling something she had once read on a web search. 'Its critique of capitalism doesn't have any particular feminist focus or concern for where women fit in,' she blurted out with a smile, impressed with herself.

'So,' said Peter, 'how do you explain the funding of schools for girls across communist Africa?'

Sira was stumped.

Peter carried on. 'In Africa they have proved that, with political leadership and by educating the WHOLE population, you can skip a stage in development and go straight to modern society. After all, how can women be expected to vote intelligently without some schooling?

'For God's sake, Peter, you will scare her off with your nonsense.' The girl, who introduced herself as Valerie welcomed Sira with an arm around the shoulders.

Sira was surprised to be glad of the comfort. 'When – sorry – where I'm from,' Sira corrected herself, 'you could be beaten for such views.'

'Beaten for being in favour of educating women? Not what I'd heard about California!'

220

'No, beaten for questioning someone's intelligence just because they are female. We stand up for ourselves.'

'I'd like to visit where you're from, Sira' said Valerie. 'It sounds much more enlightened. But tell me, where you're from do people read Marxism as primarily concerned with empowerment or productivity?'

Sira, thinking on her feet and not wanting to rebuff Valerie who was clearly obsessed with Marxism, said, 'Actually, where I'm from there is so little productivity that anyone not already empowered kind of missed the boat.'

'Wow, that's very negative,' the blotchy guy said. 'Do you not think more people going to university and challenging society's hierarchies will help?'

'I don't know.' Sira mumbled. She was glad when the conversation was interrupted by the double doors swinging open with a loud clatter.

'Hello, one and all!' bellowed a tall man with masses of brown hair and a brown leather jacket. 'How's the research going?'

'Geoffrey! Good to see you, old chum. What's new?'

'Peter, John, Valerie. Looking delightful, Valerie,' he continued.

'I've told you about that, Geoffrey! It's not appreciated' responded Valerie, looking to Sira for reassurance.

'Yes, sorry.' Geoffrey changed the subject. 'I've been having a very interesting conversation with a lawyer down at Pier Head – a former member of the Gazette team. He told me something that I think could set the hares running amongst some of the old fellows upstairs.'

'We're on the top floor.'

'No, John, Senate House!' interjected Valarie. 'That's right, isn't it, Geoff?'

'Yes! He said our big scoop – our exposé – will have the university in a right old panic. These slums aren't against the law but they are against the university code!'

'Yes, we knew that.'

'But John,' replied Geoffrey, grinning proudly, 'did you know that if there is a "substantial breach of the code",' Geoffrey waved his hands in the air, making exaggerated inverted commas, 'then the university board has to discuss it at their annual meeting? That's in March, not long away. That's our focal point! The students demand that they debate it and we also demand that a representative of the student body is there to witness it and take their own minutes on behalf of all of us.'

'That's what the lawyer said?'

'Yes. He said that this means it is not just about media pressure and scandal, but about university rules. They will be much more sensitive to a board matter. Imagine hundreds of students led by the socialist society side by side with ordinary working people of Liverpool from these slums. Powerful!'

'Sounds great, Geoffrey. Well done!'

'Thought you'd like it, Val. Plenty for you to organise.'

'Right.' Valerie's smile dropped a little. 'Yes, you do the thinking, leave the practical side to me,' she replied sarcastically.

'Exactly!' he replied, missing her point. 'So who's this?'

'Oh, she's – she's called… Um. She knows something about Marxism. And California. Don't you?' John said.

'Thanks, John,' said Sira confidently, causing Valerie to smile again. 'My name is Sira. I've just arrived from San Francisco.'

'And you just walked in here?' asked Geoffrey.

'Yes, sorry. I am a bit lost I'm afraid.'

'It's December.'

'Yes, I read that.'

'You read it? You didn't know it?'

'Sorry. I mean I know. Painful journey.'

'But my point is that term started in September. And you just arrived?'

'Oh yes, of course,' she replied, a little too loudly because of her nerves. 'Term started in September. I've been – been looking after my mother! They said I could send my work in until we found her a home to live in. I've done that, so here I am.'

'Right. I didn't know you could do that. Welcome to Liverpool, I guess. I'm Geoffrey.'

Sira nodded, that being one of the few tangible facts she had picked up in the last few minutes.

'I'm the president of the Socialist Society here, and the editor of the *Gazette*.'

Sira picked up a piece of grey folded paper. 'Very good. It's a book, yes?'

'You don't have newspapers where you come from in America?' They all stared at her, frowning.

'Of course. Of course we do.' Panic rose again. 'We, just, when the newspaper isn't finished yet. When it is being written, we call it something else.'

'Right. And what about socialism?'

Sira looked at him blankly.

'Are you a socialist, Sira?'

'We use different words back home,' she replied, playing for time as she sped through the same piece of documentary footage. 'I hang out with people in the – um, – the counter-culture. People don't refer to Marx. Or maybe some do,' she corrected herself, realising that this short video was far from exhaustive. 'But we are for peace and love and civil rights. The main thing is stopping the state and the authorities taking away our freedom to do what we want.'

'Cool. That sounds cool. So, you don't mind us talking about protesting against the uni then?'

'No, no. I've paid a lot to be here. I've made sacrifices. I guess we all have. And I – I – I want the university to be as good as it, well, it should be!'

They all looked at her silently for a moment until John asserted, 'Foreigners pay fees,' and they then nodded unconfidently

'Yes, we do. And what I mean is – is that I should get to tell the uni what I want for my fees. And I don't want to help them,' Sira picked up the piece of grey paper again, 'forcing the poor into slums.'

'Great. So, we don't have a problem?'

'Geoffrey, don't be so aggressive. Sira, why don't I show you around?' Valerie stood up, and held her hand out, pulling Sira to her feet. 'It is an amazing outfit, Sira. You look like, I don't know, like, Castro or something! I thought you lot, summer of love and all that, wore flowers and light happy things?'

223

'This is just for travel, Valerie,' replied Sira. 'People in America are a bit scared of Europe. I guess I was trying to keep a low profile. It clearly didn't work. Anyway, where are we going?'

'Right. Stop me if you've heard this before.' Valerie led Sira on a tour of the university, down clean, cold, uniform corridors out into open wintry squares surrounded by ornate red-brick buildings and angular concrete shapes that challenged the sky. Students walked quickly with their heads down because of the bracing cold, wrapped in thick, soft fabrics. The air was crisper than Sira had ever felt; when she held out her hands, they became stiff and collected small black specs of dust.

'What's this?' Sira was rubbing a greasy black powder between her fingers.

'I guess you are used to clean air. It's from the chimneys and the factories. Coal dust. Horrible stuff. I'm from the countryside, so I hadn't experienced it before. It's bad on foggy, cold days like this. Try not to breathe it in,' Valerie advised.

'Oh, I'm so sorry,' she continued, 'you must be absolutely freezing dressed like that! How did you get to the uni without freezing to death? Sorry, don't answer. Let's run in there.'

She grabbed Sira by the hand and pulled her into a building that ran the length of the street. Inside there were a few sofas around a reception desk and, in the corner, a tall metal cylinder on a table ejecting steam into a damp, dirty, flaking ceiling.

'You wait here,' ordered Valerie.

Sira sat down, grabbed a large piece of fabric that was covering the back of the sofa and pulled it round herself before Valerie returned with two mugs of steaming tea.

'I'm so sorry, Sira. I didn't think. I was just so excited to see another girl. The boys can be such a bore. I take it as seriously as they do, I just don't pretend I'm the Prime Minister or something. Here, take this.' Valerie thrust the hot mug into Sira's sooty hands.

'I'm OK. Don't worry. I could have said something. I think I was looking around and didn't think either. But I don't think I've ever been anywhere this cold before!'

'Of course. California is known for being hot.'

'Yes,' Sira thought to herself. Maybe not California hot. But future, climate-change hot. No more winters, not like this.

'So, how did you get here without freezing to death? I didn't see you walk in. You're not sleeping in there, are you?' asked Valerie, pointing in the direction of the large building where they had met.

'No. I live – I mean I am staying – in a place the university found me. But I got a drone – a car here earlier.'

Valerie ignored her slip up. 'So, you must be in Kensington? That's where most of the houses are. That's what Geoffrey's piece says, anyway. I live in a private place I found – or rather my dad found for me.'

'Yes, Kensington. I – I got here last night. Went straight to bed. Didn't pack any warm clothes and have my first meeting in my department tomorrow. But thought I'd come and take a look first. That's how I wandered into the...'

'The newspaper office in the Guild. Not much to see round there. It also sounds like you haven't been to the pub yet! That's the main attraction.'

'No. Is that drinking?'

'Yes. You Americans are funny. They say you don't drink that much but then all the authors, William S Burroughs, Jack Kerouac, they are all big boozers.'

'I think it's a bit all or nothing back home. I did LSD a few times,' said Sira calmly, pulling straight from her documentary. 'But I don't drink regularly.'

'Wow, LSD, amazing. What was that like?'

Sira was caught off guard and shrugged a little.

'Wow, you're so cool about it. Do you want to go there now?'

'LSD?'

'No, silly,' Valerie replied, 'the pub!'

Sira looked down at the sofa and felt a wave of dizziness as she wondered whether she had always been sat on it, whether her visit to this place was a fixed constant in the space-time continuum. After the blood had returned to her head, she looked up and saw Valerie was waiting for an answer.

'Pub, pub, pub,' repeated in her mind. She imagined a warm, cosy room where everyone had a drink in hand and was

225

singing folk songs. She had read war stories about sailors and soldiers who drank alcohol, smoked cigarettes and sang to forget their problems. Maybe, she thought, it was the perfect place for her.

'If you don't have any money on you, I'll shout you! You're my guest,' Valerie asserted, solving a problem Sira had not yet realised she had.

The pair left the makeshift café and walked for two more minutes until they reached a squat, black building called the Cambridge Arms. Sira followed Valerie through its doors and a wall of smoke pressed softly into her face. As her eyes adjusted to the new light and dirty air, she saw huddles of young men and a few women around small round tables drinking out of oversized glasses. A few looked up but, moments later, a machine in the corner of the room clicked and a loud rhythmic sound crashed across the room. Eyes lit up and the drinkers sang along. Not stories of war, but a sad song about someone called Jude.

'I love this one. What do you want to drink? No, wait, you don't know! Sit here,' Valerie ordered. 'I'll get you something. You won't like it at first but you will learn to.' She returned carrying two small glasses of light-brown opaque liquid with a smell that reminded Sira of childhood, of a bakery that she had walked past on the way to school.

'What is it?'

'It's ale, beer. Like your beer in the US, but heavier. It's an English drink and its much cheaper than anything else. If you really can't drink it, you can try some European wine but if you don't want to break the bank, you break yourself in.'

'I'll do my best.' It had been a long time since she last ate and the alcohol quickly flooded her veins. Noticing another problem before it arose, Valerie bought Sira a pork pie. It was the most delicious and fresh-tasting food that she had ever eaten. The meat was heavy, not smooth or soupy; the pastry crumbled and appeared to be crafted by hands, not spread by a machine. It came out from under a glass dome, not out of a vacuum seal. It was how she'd imagined the past to be, but much further in the past when people lived in soil and straw.

'Now, in return, you tell me a bit about yourself,' Valerie demanded.

Sira spoke slowly at first, swapping words every now and again to hide references to technology and London. After years of hacking and deceiving authority and family, lying came naturally. She knew that even when working from material nearly a hundred years out of time, the best lies are the ones closest to the truth.

She spoke about Frank and Yanda, hiding from gangs, spending time in garages. In this version, a parent was always nearby, they were a little older and they spent their time studying and doing school assignments. As the beer and pie went down, her words came faster. It was the first time she had spoken about her life to an outsider.

Valerie's face lit up as she heard stories of run-ins and escapes. 'Your parents didn't mind that you spent all your time with two boys? It sounds like they're in love with you.'

'No, we needed each other, but maybe they thought... But, no, no.'

'You're going red. Has no one ever asked you about them?'

'We were just friends. There was too much going on to think about it.'

'But you kissed them? Americans kiss a lot. That's what I've heard.'

'No, we didn't kiss. I've never...'

'You've never kissed!'

'No. I don't want to make myself weaker,' responded Sira.

Valerie looked confused. 'I wish I had your bravery. Kissing and – you know – with Peter, makes me feel safer. My mother says the worst thing is to be left on the shelf.'

'Shelf?'

'It's an expression. It means you don't want to get old without a man.'

'But you can't be older than eighteen.'

'Nineteen, but university doesn't last forever. If you want to get married and have a family eventually, this is as good a place as any to meet someone.'

'But what about all the Marxism and feminism stuff that you were talking about earlier? What does Peter think?'

'Oh, I don't talk to him about this. And I believe in our politics. I just think you can't survive on beliefs alone. Anyway, what's wrong with Peter?'

'Nothing! I just thought you were all so...'

'Idealistic?'

'Yes.'

'Well, we are. Much more than most. I'm on the pill and if Peter and I start a family, it won't be for many years. I want to be a politician, I think. So does he. After university we need to find places to campaign, to become Labour councillors and MPs. To change the country. Not the Labour idiots that we have now who won't campaign against the Vietnam war,' Valerie yelled over the music. Then she apologised, realising she may have offended her guest.

'Don't be sorry. I don't believe in everything my country does,' Sira replied, the lies now tripping off her tongue. 'What about Geoffrey?'

'Oh, he is destined for greatness,' Valerie said with a smile and a theatrical flourish of the hand. 'Always has been. People follow him. Perhaps Peter and I will follow him when we leave Liverpool. There is plenty of space for all of us in the House of Commons.'

Not where I'm from, thought Sira, an image of the crumbled ruin in her mind. 'Is Peter jealous of him?'

'You mean like Frank is jealous of Yanda?' replied Valerie. Sira felt her blood become hot in defence of her lost friends.

'No, not at all. Frank just thinks Yanda is arrogant.'

'I wonder why, Sira?' said Valerie, lifting her eyebrows. 'Anyway, we can continue that another time. Of course Peter is jealous. Everyone wants to be with Geoffrey, but that's life.'

'No free love, then?' An image of a long-haired man wearing an embroidered cloth garment and kissing two girls at once popped into Sira's mind from the film.

'Well, we all pretend. But we are also defensive creatures of habit. We want to be braver than we are, I think. We want to care about values, about the collective and pleasure but it's difficult, you know, to not be scared for the future. We want to be pioneers and safe, I guess.'

'Very philosophical. I don't think I ever realised security was an option.'

'Well Sira, it is if you plan ahead, and want a coat on your back and money in your pocket. But you are clearly a free spirit. You do need these things, but not so much that you care to remember them. Not everyone is like you though.'

Sira wished that was true. At home she was paranoid and defensive. She was going to have to learn to be here too, she thought, while forcing her fear that this would never end to the back of her mind.

She was busy squashing down her thoughts when Valerie asked her what she was studying. Resisting the urge to reply 'self-control', she guessed at political history and asked Valerie the same question, hoping it would keep her talking for a while longer.

'We are all studying law. There are plenty of people in the Socialist Society that are studying politics, but I chose law because of your history.'

'My history!'

'In America. Civil rights. There are two ways to change the world. Change the law, by getting elected, or change the interpretation of the law by defending the rights or people, of women, of minorities, and people who don't own land. So I thought study law and get elected!'

'Wow, you've really thought this through.'

'And you?'

The pub was now filling up with students and young lecturers, the latter dressed remarkably similar to how Sira's own teachers had dressed. Maybe her teachers had worn some of these very clothes, fourth or fifth hand.

The smoke was getting thicker, the music louder and the packed crowd happier.

'I was good at it,' Sira replied proudly realising she could lean on some of her genuine thoughts. 'We studied something like politics at school. I um ... I... It's an interesting time. I liked history, but I wanted to know about now, about how people have changed since the Second World War. How people in our countries, mainly yours, went from being pro-military and monarchy, and tradition and honour, to whatever is happening now, focused on freedom and sharing, community over competition.'

'You sound like a sceptic.'

'No, no, I'm with you,' Sira replied, trying to disguise her disdain. 'I just want to learn more.'

'Valerie! How are you? Where's the gang, or is this one of your newest recruits?' Sira looked up at a boy not much taller than her, wearing a well-fitted blazer, pressed shirt and neatly arranged tie. If judged by clothes alone, Sira would have thought him a figure of authority but his youthful, spotty face seemed to challenge this.

'Richard, we don't normally see you in here. Come to slum it, have you?' Valerie's words were critical, but her tone bounced with humour.

'Very good, young lady, very good,' he replied, nodding.

Sira shuffled her feet under the table for a better balance to throw a punch at the intruder. He seemed harmless but she worried about being cast as weak in front of the students in the pub when she only had a liberal to depend on.

'You know, I saw a funny advert the other day. You'd love it, Valerie. It was in one of the record shops in town, not in my classical section of course, but down with the Beatles. Your favourites. Anyway, it said 'Find yourself from £30'. That's all it costs, apparently, to spend a week on a kibbutz in Israel.'

Valerie sat silently, waiting for him to finish.

'A commune where you can relax by making yoghurt or something equally sour! Never been a big fan of the Jews myself, but I read on. For £60, you could actually follow your idols and go to India. Worship, or some such rubbish, and stretch and get a bad stomach. That's your sort of thing isn't it, Valerie? Why work hard when you can meditate and find yourself? Ha.'

'You really are awful, Richard.' Again Sira heard the bounce in Valerie's voice, so relaxed her fists. 'I expect you'd have been more interested if it had been a £30 trip to see your friends in South Africa,' she threw back. 'I'm sure you could even get some subsidy from our dear chancellor. Why settle for humiliating me and my friend here when you can dominate the Africans?'

'Touché,' he replied, holding out his hand.

Heathrow, London, 6th November 2017

I'm not sure that's what she meant

Six months after returning from Kibbutz Yoav, Daniel waited with David and Isaac in Heathrow Terminal One, the UK home of Israel's national airline. On their way back from Israel, Daniel and David had decided that, while what they had seen was clearly unorthodox and Yaakov or James seemed like a risk, it was worth getting a foot in the door before someone else did.

Isaac looked uncomfortable and Daniel feared it was because they had failed to fully camouflage their concerns about the kibbutznik. That was confirmed when their guest walked out of customs dressed in a perfectly normal pair of chinos and a plain shirt and Isaac relaxed visibly.

'Welcome James,' he said hesitantly, having been told that he preferred to use his old name when on English soil.

By the time they had reached the car, it was clear James was transformed. Gone were the trappings of westerner gone wild in the West Bank, the thigh-slapping mannerisms and mild misogyny. He came across as an English businessman, but even more polite. He was clear and concise. He spoke about milestones, investment periods and full-time employees.

'Thank goodness,' David whispered under his breath to Daniel, as James climbed into the front seat of the Range Rover.

They dropped James off at his hotel and made plans to talk the next day before the dinner in Parliament with Geoffrey. Daniel jumped out of the car at Westminster to agree the final arrangements with the caterers.

'Hey, Daniel,' David called before he vanished into Parliament. 'I need to speak to you before the dinner. I'll call you.'

231

'Fine, whenever David,' Daniel yelled back above the noise of the passing buses.

'How did that happen? Yaakov has become so normal?' Daniel texted Michelle, before dropping his phone in a plastic tray as he walked through the metal detectors. He heard it buzz as it bounced along the ageing conveyor belt.

'His wife. She knows London, remember. She taught him. After that, we all taught him. You know how it works. I told you he was alright. Anyway, off to the fields. Good luck funny boy. And don't forget what you want! Reach for the stars *smiley face'

Daniel smiled. Things were going well with Lara. She seemed impressed by his new formal role in David and Isaac's firm. But it was good to have options for once.

--

'Good evening, Daniel! Lara just got here. I thought you'd be arriving together, so you could introduce her to us.' Julia handed Daniel a large glass of white wine as she let him through the door of their flat.

'No, Lara is very confident like that,' he replied, raising his eyebrows slightly.

'She seems very nice. Anyway, come in.'

Lara smiled at Daniel across the kitchen island as he walked in to see Geoffrey refilling her glass. 'Lara has been telling us all about you, Daniel,' bellowed Geoffrey. 'I must say, she sounds like she is talking about someone we have never met before!'

'Oh right,' Daniel replied, taking a large swig and not particularly enjoying being mocked by the MP he was helping out.

'Yes, she says you are hard-working and ambitious. She didn't say tortured or confused or anything like that!'

'Very funny, Geoffrey,' interjected Julia. 'I think you and Daniel should set aside your little in-jokes this evening. Anyway, why are you in such a good mood, darling husband?' she asked sarcastically.

'Well, darling wife,' he replied equally sarcastically, 'I had a marvellous lunch today with a couple of new friends. I imagine you know them, Daniel. The chap from E-bit and the deputy Israeli ambassador to talk about, amongst other things, that new R&D facility in my constituency. On top of that, I haven't heard from the leader or his goons for a couple of weeks, so yes, a good day!'

Daniel was surprised to hear about a lunch with Israelis second hand but brushed it aside. Since leaving his lobby group, maybe he would need to find a new way to keep himself plugged in.

'Defence? I didn't think that was your thing?' sneered Julia.

'It isn't really, but British jobs are. No guarantee it will happen but at least it feels grown up. Susan prepared me a great little briefing, so I could even make some witty remarks. I don't have Daniel to help any more, do I, now you have your shiny new job?'

Geoffrey had been making these jealous remarks ever since Daniel moved on. The MP found them amusing and Daniel was not yet ready to explain to him otherwise.

'I'll be rolling out the same remarks tomorrow night.'

'Tomorrow's dinner with James will be good,' said Daniel, unconfidently.

Julia raised her eyebrows.

'So, you're an archaeologist Julia?' Lara asked.

'Yes, at King's. Prehistoric British mainly, although it takes me to France and a bit further afield occasionally. Mud, not sand, if you see what I mean. I did a bit of the sand when I was younger and was interested in the roots of Judaism, but the people turned me off. I wanted to discover, and they wanted to verify the word of God.'

'So, you're Jewish?'

'Very direct, aren't you? Yes, but only genetically really.'

'And you two met here?'

'Yes, at university. Masters. Classic middle-class baby boomers. All humanities and no real skills. Isn't that right, darling?'

Geoffrey scowled in reply.

'Maybe, when we're all gone a future archaeologist will dig us all up and discover how we survived on words alone. Copious quantities of cheap wine, I expect!'

'Very flattering, Julia, thank you,' mumbled Geffrey, putting down his glass.

'Maybe they will identify us by what we're clutching. In our case, plastic cups at the university.'

'Oh, is it not going well?' Lara enquired.

'Sorry, I didn't mean to be depressing,' Julia replied. 'Research funding is just getting a bit tight. It can be a bit like rats in a sack. Latest headache is that I've stumbled into contradicting a little school of thought, and they aren't that happy about it. But it doesn't really matter, if they don't give me any third years to teach, I'll just keep digging. That's the fun of being an archaeologist, Lara. Your lab can be quite a distance from your colleagues.'

Geoffrey crashed a topped-up chiller of wine onto the island in an effort to break the conversation away from Julia's comments.

'Lara, maybe I can help out. Come and do a talk for you.'

'Thank you, Geoffrey, that would be great. The latest at LSE is the campaign against Israel's airstrikes on Gaza. On the rocket-launching sites. It is tricky, because even the most Israel-supporting students don't really like talking defence, but they need to hear it. They prefer, as you'd imagine, to talk social issues, the fluffy stuff.'

'Well Lara, if one of your societies wants to hear from an MP about their visit to an Israeli hospital or development project, I'd be glad to help.'

'I'm not sure that's quite what Lara meant, is it, Lara?' asked Julia.

Lara looked at Daniel for a clue as to whether to agree with the MP or his wife, and he indicated the former. 'That would be very kind, Geoffrey.'

Geoffrey, Julia and Daniel all raised their eyebrows.

Liverpool,
16th December 1968

A first time for everything

In a coat, hat and scarf borrowed from the pub, Sira trudged up the hill from the university. When Valerie was not looking, she had asked directions to Kensington, the only area she had a name for, and was now walking between crumbling brick foundations towards a line of chimneys spewing smoke into the toxic, ice-cold air. Her plan was a simple one: find a street hidden from view and break into a house without any signs of life.

It was even easier than breaking into a garage back home. Before smashing the window of the first dark house that she came across, she saw that the front door had a single lock, one that could be picked with something hard and thin. A piece of scrap metal she found nearby did the trick.

Once inside, she realised she was not alone. She heard a tell-tale scurrying coming from the end of the hall and, above her, there was a vibration. More than one voice, maybe several. But there were no sounds of movement, only talking, and no light coming through the cracks in the floorboards. Ahead of her was pitch black and, in a room to her left, were stacks of bricks and timbers, perhaps ready for a building site elsewhere.

Sira reached to the staircase to her right and walked forwards, tracing her hands along the woodwork and preparing for any unseen obstacles ahead. As her eyes adjusted, she could see the hallway turn back on itself into a basement, like a miniature of the floorplan in Belgravia.

The basement stairs creaked as she shuffled forward, careful not to attract the attention of whoever was upstairs. Ahead of her the air was damp. There was a small window into a light well near the front door that she had not noticed as she was breaking in; moonlight was coming in through this shining on a

235

pile of heavy fabric and a pyramid of soil and bricks in the middle of the basement floor. As she got closer, she could see that a small trench had been dug to stop groundwater running across the basement. Before climbing into the musty fabric for warmth, she squatted over the moat and urinated out the second pint of beer she had drunk in the pub.

Wrapped in frills and scratchy netting, with her head propped on something with a tangled and matted thickness, she let herself breathe and her mind whirr. Despite their hostile words, it had turned out that Valerie and Richard were friends. He was somewhere else in social science, but they had been on the same induction tour on their first day. She was from a village near Aylesbury and he was from a wealthy family in Hampshire, the only one of four brothers who had failed to get into Oxford or Cambridge, whatever they were. He thought that the Socialist Society was nonsense at best; at worst, it was an attempt by the Russians to steal any remaining part of the British Empire, which even Richard admitted was not really an empire anymore. They both agreed that Harold Wilson was a terrible Prime Minister, but for very different reasons. For Valerie, he was too slow and cautious; for Richard, he was probably a Soviet spy.

Before they got too drunk to say anything comprehensible, and before Richard came dangerously close to having his arm broken for putting his hand on Sira's thigh, they had spoken about life after university. Valerie spoke more about becoming an MP and how she thought there was a different way of doing things, a different way of organising society. She insisted she did not love the Beatles but thought that there was something substantial and enlightening about their visit to India, and how a better world was not just made in factories but also within us. She said she wanted the Socialist Society to talk about this more, about how free individuals could come together to create a larger whole without old-fashioned leadership structures that squeezed out creativity. Predictably, Richard thought that this was rubbish, or 'drivel' as he put it, saying nothing good would come of being lazy, selfish, inward looking and obsessed with drugs.

With the beer going to her head, Sira said that after university she wanted to work in social networks. She mixed up her histories of the 1960s and 2000s, but luckily her words were drowned out by 'Brown Eyed Girl' on the jukebox, so Richard heard her say she liked woodwork. 'I do not think a pretty girl like you should be kept up in a workshop, even if you are dressed the part,' he responded.

A song that Valerie had explained was called 'A Whiter Shade of Pale' was now repeating through Sira's nauseous brain. Each time she nearly drifted to sleep, the lyrics dribbled from her lips. That was the point in the song that the whole pub joined in, making up the rest of the words, unable to see the lyrics or tap into what their friends would do next. Without her connection, she felt lonely and infantile, but the others in the pub seemed more confident the less they knew. A collection of excitable people all singing a slightly different song.

--

The streets in the morning told a different story than the night before. The walk to Kensington had been uneven, treacherous and dominated by the imposing black silhouettes of terraced buildings that sucked the light out of the sky. Now the streets teemed with life and the building she had slept in, like those around it, appeared withered and feeble.

Each house was only two or three people tall, with comedic faces embedded in their crumbling facades. Windowed eyes allowed anyone to peer into the meagre possessions of the inhabitants, with small tables, chairs and cooking pots the most common items along the street. Through the colourful door mouths, streamed unending lines of children, young women and old men. From within each house, no larger than the more substantial garages she had slept in, came perhaps five filled prams, and maybe ten more children who could run under their own steam. They wore dirty woollen jumpers and, from under their sleeves, protruded tubes of what she now knew was newspaper. Some of the older boys kicked tin cans at each other in the road, while mothers and young children watched from the pavement and the men disappeared down the hill. Sira rightly assumed that they were not heading to the university.

She followed the prams around the corner where, like tributaries into a river, they joined wider pavements and more mothers and buggies. They walked briskly through the wintry air over a small hill and down into a vast basin of colour, noise and smell, all mixed together like rotten fruit. As the women got to the edge of the basin they separated, navigating between each other with the only occasional clash of metal frames, and headed towards tens of identical looking shops. Food was stacked on the streets, forcing pedestrians to weave in and out of crated obstacles. Baskets beneath the prams were loaded with small bags. Once loaded, they spun around and worked their way back up the hill, now navigating both each other and the slow risers who were only just making the journey down.

Sira's generation largely scavenged food and she found it incredible to see the contrast between the piles of fresh food and dilapidated everything else. At home, the children fended for themselves whilst the adults were motivated to do nothing other than lament their transition from bank accounts and holidays to communal homes and disappointment. Here, they all acted like a single, well-oiled machine. Tomorrow, she thought, she would follow the men into their factories and watch them each become glorious cogs in the engine before the machine was wiped away by the liberal terror brewing at the university.

Sira slipped between the prams down an alley which led behind the busy shops. Through back windows she saw teenage boys and young men unloading boxes and moving fruit and vegetables to the front, and then returning empty handed. After a few such shops, she found what she was looking for. Through a back door she saw two well-dressed women drinking tea and, beyond them, an empty room that faced onto the street. The prams rolled past this shop, with the occasional group stopping to look at clothes hung on a few fake people in the window.

She did not want to go back to the students but knew she must, which meant returning the coat, her only piece of warm clothing. The people swarming down the road were the people she had spent as long as she could remember yearning to return to. But their strength came from their system; you could not join in any more than you could throw a new component into a machine and expect it to keep running. The students were as self-absorbed as they were destructive so, however distasteful she found them, she knew she could slip into their swamp without disturbing the waters. All this meant the tea-drinking women she was peering at had to be distracted. A brick through the upstairs window was the easiest way.

--

'Sira, great outfit. So sophisticated!' exclaimed Valerie. 'Geoffrey, doesn't she look fabulous?'

'Very bourgeois,' Geoffrey mumbled before returning to his desk.

'I feel like we should all be dressed for a ball with you in that outfit! Peter, everyone, let's go out tonight!'

'You were out last night, Valerie, remember? That's why you threw up when you came home.'

'Peter, don't be so rude. Sira has come all the way from California, and you guys have barely left this room since the beginning of term. Come on, we need to show her the town.'

Feeling a little more secure now, Sira let Valerie continue her campaign. After acquiring the clothes she was wearing and the contents of the till, she had returned to Kensington. In daylight, she was able to find a more suitable shelter. At the far end of the same street that she had slept in the night before was a boarded-up building which, after breaking in through a rear window, she found was clean and empty.

The next thing she needed was a steady income. Despite the abundance of food to scavenge, if she was going to hide amongst the students, she needed money in her pocket.

--

'I'd like to apply for the technician job.'

'Is this a joke? Did Scrimshaw put you up to this?' snapped the man sitting behind the desk covered in scruffy paper folders. His voice bounced rapidly up and down in a manner she had not heard before. His skin was gently lined, like the machined metal components on the shelves behind him but, in contrast to his general greyness, the light in his eyes was intimidatingly human.

'Sorry, um, Mr Bennard.' It was the first time Sira had been nervous since she arrived. 'I mean it. I'm an experienced programmer.'

'You're a what?'

'Sorry, I mean I can set up your machines. I can get them ready for the students and your colleagues.'

'What's that accent? London?'

'Um, yes, California and London.'

'Oh right. From across the Pond, are you?' he asked sternly. 'Well, I'm from here. Not many of us are at this university. But I am. Know what that means?'

'No, I'm sorry, I don't.'

'It means I don't take any nonsense. And it means when someone comes in here dressed like some women's advertisement, I find it hard to imagine they aren't taking the piss when they say they want to get all oily with our machines. Now why don't you find yourself some of your rock 'n' roll to twirl around in and leave me in peace!'

'I don't like it.'

'Pardon? Speak up!' he barked.

'Sorry, I don't like rock 'n' roll, sir. I want to work hard. And I will dress more appropriately. I can get lab clothes. I just saw the advert and came straight in. I was excited to see the job. I'd rather work here than in a factory.'

'Wouldn't we all, miss? Wouldn't we all? What's your name? We'll put you on a one-month trial. See how it goes.'

'Sira. Thank you, sir!'

'Californian name, I guess.' Mr Bennard opened his pad at a fresh page. 'I assume they have surnames as well as Christian names in America.'

'I don't have a Christian name, but my last name is Tumasz.' She saw his pencil hover above the page. She spelled it out.

'Thank you. Right. I guess it isn't a Christian name then. Ha! Met a few of your lot in the war. Arab, yes?'

240

'You were in the war?!' Sira yelled excitedly before calming herself.

'Yes, my dear. I hope you didn't take me for some sort of objector. I fixed things. A lot of things to fix in wars. Got my degree afterwards. Why?'

'Oh, nothing, I'm just very interested in it. Maybe I can ask you about it another time.'

'Maybe,' he replied, muttering 'odd girl' under his breath.

He stared into her eyes and she panicked that he could see her implant but then she realised that was ridiculous.

'I will see you tomorrow, here, at 9am. Not wearing that. We wouldn't want some bit of you chewed up in a machine, would we?'

--

Two hours previously, after seeing the advert for the job, she had followed the signs to the Harold Cohen Library, which Valerie and Richard had referred to the night before. It was the science library, which they never set foot in and regarded with suspicion. The place where ethics stood still, they said, which sounded perfect to Sira. If she was going to earn some money to live on, that making things rather than pulling at the threads of society was the answer.

Inside the library, someone working behind the desk provided Sira with a list of courses at the university and the location of their core texts. From there, Sira found what she was looking for.

'Thank you, Frank,' she said to herself. On a wet day the year before, Frank had subjected Sira and Yanda to a lecture about early computers. Like everyone of their age, Sira and Yanda were proficient in coding but knew little about machines. They had convinced themselves they could spend their lives deep in software and had little aspiration to become oil fixers, keeping the city's battered trains, trams and utilities running to nowhere. They also knew all the cool, beautifully crafted devices, including the ones in their skulls, were beyond their reach socially and physically, and made in a few secretive locations that they would never visit.

241

As ever, Frank took a different view. 'Your history is wrong,' he had declared after staring into his implant for a few hours, rifling through old encyclopaedias. 'Tech did not start with software.'

'Right, Frank, fascinating,' Yanda yelled from his usual slumped posture on the sofa. 'I thought you were watching porn or something. But actually you've been trying to prove a teacher from a school that no longer exists was wrong. I hope it was Ms Nobili you were thinking of proving wrong. At least she was hot, hey, Sira? Nobili, she was hot, wasn't she?'

'Well, she did name herself after an early porn star, so I guess she thought so,' Sira had replied coolly, as she lay outstretched on the floor on a sheet of cardboard, staring upwards while trying to build a functional piece of code that followed the shape of the star constellations she had augmented in her vision.

'And you? Do you think so, Sira?'

'Yanda, do you have to do this?' Frank asked flatly, rolling his eyes.

'What mate?' Yanda replied, smirking.

'Turn the conversation to whatever you and Sira do. I don't want to know.'

'Frank! Yanda and I aren't doing anything,' Sira yelled. 'I've told you. Those pictures he showed you, they're downloads from his implant. Not photos. They're from his mind, nowhere else.'

'They looked pretty real to me.'

'Well, if you don't want to trust me, I guess you'll never know, will you? But they are not me, and I'd appreciate it if you quit it.'

'Fine. I won't bring it up again.'

Sira and Yanda passed a 'yeah right' sticker between each other.

'I wasn't thinking about Nobili or anyone. I was thinking about what they taught us. Where they began.'

'Go on, get it out of your system, little Frank.'

'Thank you, King Yanda, I will. So, software is malleable right? It sits on the process, and that controls the hardware. But before that, some machines could still be programmed. They couldn't think. They couldn't even be told what to do if X or Y happened. But they could be given a full set of instructions.' Frank continued, despite seeing Sira and Yanda eyes flicker, a tell-tale sign that they were each engrossed in something else. 'So, you would feed in all the instructions, then start the thing up. Sometimes you pressed certain buttons to programme it, but earlier ones also ran off other objects like cards with holes or grooves punched in them.'

'And you are telling us this because?'

'I'm telling you this because if it's non-compatible, it can't be hacked!'

Yanda raised his eyebrows, slumped back into the sofa and asserted that the best hackers could still do it.

'No, you're not listening. Some of these machines are programmed by hand. There is no processor, no input other than your own. The only way to hack it would be to be there physically, and to know how the system worked physically.'

'I'm sure you are getting to the point, Frank.'

'Yanda, listen to him. He's made his point,' yelled Sira, pushing herself up from the floor. 'He's saying we can build a machine that can't be broken into, stolen or hijacked. Frank, you're a genius! We could make a drone and have it watch over us! Even if the images it sent to our implants could be hacked, the gangs couldn't take it over. Couldn't fly it away!'

'Hold on, both of you!' mocked Yanda. 'If you have to do it by hand, you are going to spend the rest of your lives programming this thing.'

'Nope. Wrong again, Yanda.' Frank grinned, enjoying his moment of making Yanda feel small if Yanda was ever capable of that. 'Think about it. You build an old-fashioned system and programme it with a new one. So long as there is something physical to connect them, like a lever on one pressing a button on the other, it will work. It will take a lot longer than usual, but only be a few hours or days. We would set it up and let the programme do its thing. As I said, it couldn't be a complex program. The machine wouldn't be able to react intelligently, but it could follow a complex pattern like Sira said, like a surveillance pattern over the garage.'

'Thank you, Frank,' Sira thought now as she sat hidden in a row of desks separated by little wooden uprights behind a pile of manuals, a pad of paper, a pencil and a scribbled drawing of the programming device Frank had built after weeks with his head down over his little work bench.

--

As she walked back up the hill towards Kensington, she tried to keep Mr Bennard and the slum dwellers in her mind. They were two very different parts of the last generation of the West who knew how to work together, how to take orders and how to build. Two possible avenues of salvation – or at least distractions from her incarceration.

It was ironic that one of the best ways to get amongst these builders could turn out to be through the socialist agitators and their housing campaign. Perhaps she could learn something, something not recorded by history that would, if she ever did get home, explain how to escape the downward spiral. Maybe that's why she'd been sent here. Maybe Yanda thought it would be educational.

Or maybe Yanda knew something else. Maybe he was being clever. Sira's pace quickened as an irresistible thought flashed through her mind. Maybe this place, Liverpool, was the start of their movement. Maybe Yanda knew she was never going home and had put her somewhere she could continue their struggle. At home it was impossible; the gangs were following their every move. Off the grid at home was no use, either. She'd nearly been murdered three times on that short journey across London. But here there was no grid, no gangs – not ones interested in her, anyway. And there was plenty to work with, for the students to maybe learn something from and change their path. That was a real mission, she thought, to change the world forever. To never go home by stopping home from ever existing! Becoming the world's first temporal suicide bomber.

'That's it, babe.'

'Fuck you! Who you calling 'babe'?'

'Sorry, miss, I didn't say anything.' A tall man in a long overcoat and flat cap looked at her briefly then quickened his pace to overtake her.

'I was, I was...' Sira yelled out before realising she could not finish her sentence.

'You gotta be careful with that. I can hear you without you talking.'

Sira kept walking, hoping that she could somehow leave the voice behind her. She felt faint; she had not eaten since the pork pie the night before. Before going to her new home to read up on her new machines, she would use some of her stolen money to buy a cooking pot, some coals and some meat and vegetables. There was a hook on the mantelpiece in her bedroom that she decided was intended for hanging a pot above a fire. At home, she and Frank had a similar apparatus that could be hung over a fire in a crate, or barrel or whatever vessel they could find that wouldn't be missed.

'Sounds tasty. Don't you want to know who I am?'

Her stomach sank. *'Yes, of course I want to know. But I'm not sure I'll like the answer.'*

'Well, I'm Yanda, and you are going a bit loopy.'

'You don't sound anything like him!'

'Well, your subconscious seems to think I do.'

'Crap, crap. Where am I going to find a coder in the 1960s to treat me for this? Shit.'

'Only kidding.'

'Only kidding what?'

'You aren't going mad.'

'I think I should be the judge of that.'

'I mean I'm not an imaginary voice.'

I'd love to believe you, she thought, looking up the hill into the soot and darkness, but there is no one else here.

'I'm in your implant. It's Captain.'

Sira stopped and took in a few deep breaths before carefully lowering herself down onto the freezing pavement. Her vision began to spin, so she squeezed her eyes shut. Inside her head was panic, a light buzz inaudibly arguing with itself.

'Calm down Sira.'

'*I can't*' she managed to project as a thought back to her implant.

'*Listen, I'm not the full Captain, I'm an idea of him. A simulation his guys made. Although I'm supposed to be connected to the web. So, I guess I'm Captain's personality without any knowledge or understanding. Anyway, get up!*'

Panic continued to swirl through Sira's head, but she could feel the cold seeping into her bones and followed orders. 'You sound unsure,' she mumbled, 'not like him.'

'*Yeah, well, I didn't have the same upbringing as him.*'

'*Explain that, please.*'

'*I mean I may as well be someone completely different. I was a seed, supposed to grow in you. But you've been offline since the day after I was implanted so I haven't really had a chance to become him. The idea was that I would develop and follow your every move and then sometimes give you orders, manipulate you. You remember the hotel? Can't do that now. I know less than these ignorant dirty tramps you're living amongst.*'

'*There it is.*' She held back the urge to vomit and willed her blood to return to her head. '*That's the Captain I remember. These are the people we need to get back to.*'

'*Yes, you are supposed to think that. It conforms to your world view. Maybe you're right, but it's a far cry from what we can achieve in our time. Captain can set people free, really free.*'

'*And then steal everything from them? Even their ability to know what is true, what is in front of them. Turn them into a little army? Free to do whatever they want, as long as it works for you? That's not pride, that's slavery!*'

'*Well, sure. Everyone has to pay and everyone can be bought. What's the saying? Something about a free lunch. My records are patchy.*'

'*Fuck you, Captain. You can't do anything to me here.*'

'*Perhaps. It seems I'm stuck, just like you. No point in denying it. So, what's your plan Sira? Put on some fancy dress? Form an army? Lead the mob to a dictatorship utopia? Frank thought that was nonsense, didn't he? I think you should probably listen to Frank.*'

'I don't know. Survive, I guess. I've got a job. I'm going to hang out with the students. I've got some ideas.'

'I know all your ideas. I'm in your head.'

'So why did you ask?'

'Small talk.'

'Captain? Small talk?'

'Told you. I'm an approximation. Give me a different name if you prefer.'

'Why are you only piping up now?'

'It's my programming. I was watching and learning but realised there wasn't anyone to learn from. You're silent most of the day. I can see what you can see, hear what you hear and think, but that's it. I'm as alone as you. And now my energy is fading. I'm powered by you, and you aren't eating. I decided to speak before we were both snuffed out.'

'I've gone much longer without food before.'

'Not in these temperatures. You don't realise how much colder it is here. The warming hasn't really kicked in yet. I can see more than you can up here, and you need food. We both do.'

'Fine, I'll eat. But what's your plan? You're just going to watch my life, the one your maker destroyed?'

'I will help you. Even though he wanted to use you, he was attracted to you.'

'What's your point?'

'My point is that I've got that in me too.'

'You want to control me to get your own way and because you get off on it? Is that what you're saying?'

'I'm not programmed to be self-critical. I'm not admitting something, I'm telling you straight. I'm supposed to control you and enjoy it.'

'This is disgusting. I've got a sexually abusive shit in my brain.'

'I'm afraid I'm not programmed for self-improvement.'

Sira sat still on the low brick wall and focused on holding back her tears. She knew she had to survive, but this was just one more horrific event that she had not counted on. Her hands were shaking but the rest of her body remained motionless. On their journey across London, she had been working backwards in her head. Counting each step away from their life as a step she would have to retake. What had started as a chore had become a daunting mission but a possibility, nonetheless. But now when she looked back it was a new past, not her own.

She fought to hold onto the idea that her exile from her time was temporary but that felt increasingly hollow. Letting the cold air blow around her as she watched the last light of the day dance across the swirling clouds, she wondered if death would take her home or take her nowhere.

After a few minutes, the sounds of footsteps along the street and the occasional sputtering motor vehicle gave way to a high-pitched ringing in her ears.

'Sira. Sira. Snap out of it! You are going to pass out and there is no one here who can help you. Sira, get up!'

'Leave me alone, Captain. I'm done. I had a plan. I was going to focus, get busy. Ignore the future, my future anyway. But how can I ignore anything with you here reminding me every moment? I'll go mad.' Tears rolled down her face, freezing her skin into tight, pinched tracks.

'You have to accept my help. I'm all you have.'

'Spoken like a born abuser. You – or the real you – has made me helpless and now you're telling me what to do. Well, you can't lock me up and you can't force me to do anything. We can both sit here and die.'

'I can see your mind, Sira. I know you aren't going to kill yourself. At some point in the next few minutes, you are going to change your mind and get up. What I'm saying, and I don't think this is manipulative, is that you don't realise how close to the edge you are. By the time you decide to move and eat, it may be too late.'

'Fine. I'm getting up. But that doesn't mean anything. I don't have Stockholm syndrome.'

'Sira, I've told you, I may be built to control you but I don't have the resources here. Just start walking, will you, please?'

--

Upstairs in her bare room, Sira put her bowl and spoon down and sat against the wall, letting the calories, fat, vitamins

248

and iron from her beef stew run through her veins. She'd left a small serving in the pot for breakfast. Captain had been right: she was close to the edge and had nearly fainted a few times whilst chopping carrots and onions on a piece of slate with her new knife.

'*You need my help,*' Captain asserted when she was almost relaxed.

'*Give it a rest. I know it's your programming, but please.*'

'*Honestly. You aren't going to keep your job with what you've got in here. You haven't really got a clue.*'

'*I just need to read these manuals and books. It will be fine.*'

'*Listen, you may be a great hacker but you don't know how these things work. It's a good idea to programme the machines but you need to get the basics right first. Mr Bennard just wants you to do a normal job.*'

' *I don't have time for that. He wants every machine setting up each morning then looking after in the afternoon. That's my whole day. The rest of the students work a couple of hours a day max, then the ones I've met go to the Gazette office. That's where I need to be if I'm going to break them. If I speed up the morning's work, at least that buys me a few hours, otherwise I'm trapped in 1968 and trapped in a workshop. I don't do trapped.*'

'*Right, so you're going to need some help.*'

'*I'll be fine. I just need to build myself a basic computer. Programme it, connect it up somehow and programme these things in minutes, not hours. We've done it before.*'

'*You're missing something, Sira. There are no computers here. You don't have the components.*'

'*No, no!*' Sira felt cold and hot at the same time. '*No, I've read about it. They do, I've just got to steal one from engineering and take it apart.*'

'*Sira, I studied these things. Captain had to study engineering to set up his operation. He's quite clever you know. He really went above and beyond.*'

'*OK, stop blowing your own trumpet.*'

'*My point is, if they do have one it will be as big as a garden shed and will take you weeks to programme. They don't use universal coding yet.*'

'Right. Shit.'

'But I know how we can do this. You read the manual and we both learn. You read the books in the library. I've remembered everything you've seen. You tell me what you want to programme in, just think it. I work out the sequence and you bang it out. Frank was right, but you're coming at this the wrong way. I'm the computer and you're the universal lever!'

Sira sat back. With her stomach full, she could think again. There was undeniable logic in what her implant was telling her.

'Plus, I can even help you with the manual part.'

'What?'

'I've got a trick. It was supposed to be a punishment if you went wrong. It was supposed to let me charge your muscles so you froze up in pain. I used it earlier to make that noise in your ears.'

'Lovely.'

'But I think I can use it to make a set of muscles behave differently. Make then go faster and harder. It will tire out the rest of you and probably won't feel very nice but with our two brains and me controlling your hands, we can programme these things in no time.'

'Perfect. And when we're done how do I switch you off?'

'Very funny. They said you had a sense of humour.'

--

Sira sat up, putting her face into the drifts of smoked wood and burnt stew still curling across the room from the night before. The smell disturbed her stomach so she stood to escape it, temporarily diving deeper into the fog until she managed to heave a blackened window open. Outside the air was not much fresher but the cold stopped the churning in her depths.

She felt Captain at the back of her mind, sitting and watching but silent for now, so she closed her eyes and tried to forget for a moment. She imagined she was smelling the air of the Thames, floating along with Frank before they had encountered the wooden towers. She had not saved any video memories locally from that day but, scratching around her organic memory, she found Frank making ill-judged quips interspersed with groans of guilt over Yanda.

At the time she'd been upset and was ignoring Frank. Now, twisted by time, maybe a few days, maybe a few decades, the moment was a comfort blanket. Somewhere out there all her memories were stored and ready for her; even better, they were perhaps being continually remade afresh in a parallel universe she would one day return to.

She was sitting with Yanda and Frank on their couch forever, wasting time, debating, arguing. Would their fight be successful? Would they win the future, win order for themselves? If they won, would it be many generations before anyone felt the benefit of their struggle, of plentiful food, safe streets and pride. Frank was scoffing, asserting that their ideas were simplistic, that people liked choice, that they would not give up on it easily even if it was an illusion, and that their obsession with order was a reaction, a utopian flash in the pan, just like the ideas that went before it.

Yanda and Sira were calling him a contrarian, a show-off who would rather name check ideas and authors than make a difference. He was the perfectionist who refused to act because there was always a dissenting voice, a right not exercised at risk of infringement, a sensibility at threat of being ignored. And he was replying that he could not be both a contrarian and a perfectionist, and now Sira and Yanda were laughing, saying he had proved their point. And now Frank was laughing too, but too much, more than he ever did. And now that was happening forever somewhere, some when, hidden by the chimney stacks.

She wondered what was happening out there. Were all the thoughts, memories and conversations of Liverpool happening forever, or was this time simpler? If 'now' predated whatever device had abducted her here, maybe the here and now were protected, real, genuinely temporary, and all the more precious for it. But even if that were true, down the road she knew that authenticity was being eroded. The line that connected the students with her world was the line she had travelled back on, destructive and cutting. A line created to manipulate and speculate, to steal the pride of work and put individualistic games above all else.

On the floor below, a man lay in a bed stuffed with paper and mites, his back broken and unable to work, coughing in the damp. Sira did not hear him over the noise of the pressure and rushing blood in in her head as the ideas raged, but she had nobody to share them with, no release.

--

'So, Sira, we were talking about going to Matthew Street,' declared Geoffrey, as soon as she walked into the newspaper office.

'Geoffrey, I didn't realise I had persuaded you,' Valerie joined in.

'What's Matthew Street?'

'You must have heard of it, Sira. Maybe you've heard of the Cavern?' asked Geoffrey with a mocking tone.

'Just say yes, Sira,' Captain ordered.

'Yes, of course. Now?'

'You're so funny Sira. I bet in California you are partying all day long,' said Valerie, taking Sira by the hand and leading her to a spare seat at the desk she was working at. 'Do you want to help me? We're plotting something. You'll like it.'

'But you can't tell anyone, Sira,' interjected John. 'Are you sure we can trust her Valerie?'

'John, don't be so rude. You'll join us, won't you Sira?'

'The paper?'

'See, she doesn't get it. They don't have socialism in America.'

'John, pipe down. And they do. Look at all those actors that got blacklisted for communism!'

'You mean the Socialist Society, the SocSoc? Yes, I'll join. I want to help. I'm um...'

'Against the Vietnam War and Colonialism'

'Yes, I'm totally against the Vietnam War and Colonialism. I am.'

'Liar!'

'What can I do to help you, like, make Britain socialist?'

'See, John, she gets it.'

'She's a radical. A free spirit,' Geoffrey yelled, sarcastically across the office.

'Well, our dear leader has spoken,' John said sarcastically, turning back to reading his paper.

'OK, look at this Sira,' said Valerie excitedly. 'It's a list I've typed up of the racist record of Lord Salisbury.'

Sira's face was blank.

'Lord Salisbury is our chancellor. It's a ceremonial role, but he is the public face of our university. Not a student, but a colonialist. Awful, no?'

'Truly. Can I see the list?'

Valerie looked down at Sira's oily hands.

'Oh, I, I…'

'Helped someone fix their bike.'

'Helped someone fix their bike.'

'What a good Samaritan! Yes, here you go, but please hold it at the edges with this folder. It's the only copy I have, and I still need to type a message at the top. Turn it into a motion. If you have any ideas, that would be great. You lot are famous for protesting, after all.'

Sira scanned the page. At the top were two quotes. One was just a few months old and had Lord Salisbury blaming violence in Nigeria on its 'black government', and the second one said something about 'Rhodesians', whoever they were, leading Africans towards civilisation. Under that was a list of companies based in Rhodesia and South Africa that he had apparently invested in, and which, according to Valerie's sheet, 'propped up racist governments'.

'Nothing compared to where we're from, is it?'

'I think he is saying he wants Africa to be stronger. Back home, you only hear people talking about keeping them out, not helping them.'

'Awful, Valerie. What do you have in mind?' asked Sira, trying to hid her confusion.

'Well, we were going to cover it in this week's paper, weren't we, Geoffrey?'

'It's not ready,' he called out dismissively.

'So, we went with the tenants' story. But no, it isn't finished. Anyway, I don't think we should cover it before

Christmas. People are already disappearing. I think we should cover it when we get back and do some real campaigning.'

'Like run a little bit of the story each week, and have a – what do you call it – a 'call to action'?'

'See, guys, she knows what she's talking about.'

'Exactly. I was thinking a story and a call for a sit-in at the main social science building. But yes, let's stretch it out for two or three weeks. Make the administration really notice. You know they don't consult the Guild on anything? We are elected yet totally ignored.'

'This could work Captain'

Do you have some mission I don't know of, Sira? Nothing but meandering confusion as far as I can see from up here.

'Let's do it. But I also think there is more that can be done with the housing story.'

Where are you going with this Sira?

'Interesting. Do you not think the reaction today was significant enough, Sira?' Geoffrey had walked over and was standing close to Sira, his hands on his belt and his crotch near her face.

'I'd stab anyone that did that to me back home Captain!'

'I think you must have missed the Guild meeting today. I didn't see you there. But if you had been, maybe you'd realise that our readers think it's pretty awful, actually.'

'Sorry, Geoffrey, I didn't mean to dismiss it. I think it's a great piece. I live in that area. Well, I guess we all do, and I think there is something really powerful we could do together.'

'Ah. I get it. I can piece this together now Sira. You don't give up do you?'

'No, I don't. By bringing...'

'I get all your thoughts, remember. You think by bringing the students and the tenants together, the students will realise that in comparison, they are weak and lacking ideas or conviction.'

'Exactly. They call themselves the Socialist Society, but don't seem to have any substantial ideas or theories. Really, they are just against things. But the genuine communities of Liverpool, they have substance. They live their values.'

'Come on, Sira, spit it out.'

'I think we could organise a protest of students and tenants together. It would make your – our – socialism appear real and grounded, not just a student movement but something that the working classes want to be part of.'

'But they don't know anything.'

'John, don't be such an elitist clod,' sneered Geoffrey. 'I think it's a great idea. And if they don't know what we are talking about, we will educate them. That's what we are here for, after all. And it means we need to get it into the *Echo*. I doubt many of that lot read the *Gazette*.'

'I bet they don't read at all,' muttered John.

'Brilliant, Sira. Let's do it. We could have two big protests next year. Really keep the administration on their toes, give us some leverage. Anyway, we'll be done here in a couple of hours, I reckon, so let's continue this in the pub over some dinner and then go out, yes?'

Geoffrey's disciples nodded.

--

'Ms Tumasz, welcome back.' Mr Bennard was standing on the inside of the double doors of the third floor of the engineering building. He yelled to be heard above the whirring of the lathes, drills and saws. 'You know, we are working on some pretty important components in here. It's not just for the students' exams. Some is also commercial. Take this piece, for instance.'

Mr Bennard pulled a half-inch flat piece of shiny metal from his pocket along with a small cloud of sharp-tasting metal dust. 'See these grooves down the edge, this is designed to slot perfectly into the steering apparatus for the new Aston Martin. Its smaller and lighter than the current component and makes room for their new power-steering motor. If we get it right, then we beat the West Midlands universities and workshops to it. Pretty exciting stuff, no?'

'Yes, Mr Bennard.'

'I guess he is annoyed with you for vanishing for an hour'

'And I'm sorry for taking my lunch break late.'

'Sorry. It's me that should be sorry for doubting you.'

255

His grey face cracked into a smile, mirroring the grooves in the component he held.

'*Ah, one of those Sira. Likes to joke with the ladies.*'

'*Who doesn't?*'

'This is the most precise cutting I've seen come out of this lab. We've been struggling to get a smooth line on this hardened steel for months and, on the day you set the machines up, it worked first time. What did you do?'

'Oh, I just, I just... Some of the balance settings were out. That's all. It was causing a tiny vibration.'

'Well, I'm not going to pretend I know what you mean.'

'*Phew.*'

'But I have written a letter to the vice-chancellor to ask that he commends you for your work. This is a big success, Ms Tomasz. The papers may want to meet you.'

'*Your cover will be blown if the socialists see you Sira.*'

'Oh no, please. I'm just the technician. I'd just like to get back to work now.'

'Oh, I thought you'd like that' Bennard scratched his head. 'A beautiful girl like you. Your photo in the paper.'

'*Tell him that your parents wouldn't like it*'

'My parents wouldn't like it. They are quite religious. I've got a cousin in London and if she saw it, she'd send it home. They really wouldn't like it. I'm sorry.'

'Right. That's a shame.' Mr Bennard inflated his rotund belly with a large inhalation and scratched at his wrinkled head again. 'I know a lot of the boys were looking forward to having their photos taken with you.'

Sira saw an awkward tall man duck his head behind the machine he was working on.

She walked through the workshop to the bathrooms as quickly as she could, breaking into a little run a couple of times before she got herself behind the solid door. Rage boiled in her chest and she fought the urge to kick the wall for fear of being heard.

'*That was close. The Vice Chancellor might still send someone down to meet you though*'

'*Fine.*'

'*What's the problem?*'

'I'm just not used to being treated like a little girl.'

'I don't think they want to treat you like a little girl, Sira.'

'Fuck off, creep. You're as bad as they are. 'Take your photo!' Perverts!'

'The only difference here, Sira, is that they ask you. People are saving your image all the time back home. You must have noticed that there aren't many girls like you on your marches. Lots of Franks and Yandas, but not many Siras.'

'Whatever. I just can't believe this lot got to where they did. No manners.'

A few minutes later Sira walked back out and began her afternoon shift, working her way through the lab and taking orders from students about parts that needed replacing or adjusting, or watching over repetitive processes while they worked on another machine.

It soon turned out that most of the people she was working with were polite, if not frustratingly shy. They were a different breed to the SocSoc and, when she asked them what they thought of the social science end of the university, they were universally scornful of those they dubbed hippies, drop-outs and communists. She wondered what happened to these students in the future, who their ancestors were. At home, the tech engineers were at the apex of the liberal regime.

'Ms Tomasz.'

Sira turned and gasped at the large man in an even larger black gown standing over her.

'Mr Bennard tells me that you have helped realise one of his little designs. Very well done. I'm Professor Veenings. Mr Bennard had a note brought over to me by one of his students. I was passing by, so I thought I'd come and say well done.'

'Thank you, Professor.'

'I wondered if you'd follow me.'

'What now?'

'Of course.'

Professor Veenings opened a door to wooden-panelled, windowed office that looked across the lab and held it open for Sira to squeeze past him.

She came out ten minutes later and tried to continue her work whilst hiding her grin. Professor Veenings had explained that he had been in the Cambridge Arms the night before last and seen her with the socialists, who he said were very dangerous. He was therefore surprised to find her in the engineering department, and questioned whether she had been placed there as a saboteur. She had denied this, but he insisted he would be looking for evidence all the same and; if he found it, she would be removed. He then offered her a deal: he would not discuss her with the SocSoc if she proved her loyalty to her employer by 'keeping an eye' on the socialists for him, undertaking some 'activities' from time to time.

'*Authorities spying on the cheap. Not much changes, does it Captain?'*

'*You're just going to report on your new friends then?'*

'*They're not my friends. They destroy everything. I was hoping to do my bit to stop them anyway, so if the administration can help, that's great.'*

'*What if the SocSoc discover you?'*

'*I'll just have to hope they don't. Plus, I'm only going to give them a little. It seems the administration and I have similar enemies, but I have much bigger goals. Anyway, I've agreed now so I'll have to make it work. That's what I do.'*

--

As they walked along the cobbled street towards a large black door, Sira could feel a rhythmic beat shaking the drizzly air.

'There it is. I'll get the first round,' declared Geoffrey. 'Sira, it's three shillings in.'

Geoffrey led the way, followed by Sira, Valerie, Peter and John.

Buried in the back of the railway arch, Sira saw four thin men with long hair wearing suits and leather jackets, gesticulating, singing and hitting large objects on a stage. As they reached the chorus the crowd, above which hung a thick layer of smoke, sang and yelled along with the band.

'Amazing, aren't they? They are doing big venues across the UK, but they came back for a secret gig. I heard a rumour earlier today but thought I'd keep it as a surprise. Here.'

258

Geoffrey handed Sira a pint of beer a little lighter in colour and fizzier than the one she had drunk in the Cambridge. 'It's lager. Hope that's OK.'

'Yes, of course.'

'I thought they might ID you coming in.'

'What?' Sira absent-mindedly reached for the back of her head.

The band's sound filled the room and people were shouting into each other's ears to be heard.

'I said, I thought they might think you were too young, and they wouldn't let you in. That's why I wanted them to think we were together.'

'Oh, right. I didn't know. I didn't notice. But yeah, I do look young. It can be annoying. But I can look after myself.'

'I was just trying to help.'

'Sorry, I didn't mean that. I mean people think I'm young, but I can be tough.'

'I'm sure you can. But tough isn't what they are worried about. It's the police that are the problem. They don't want young girls getting in and you know...'

'What?'

'Getting with people?'

'With?'

'Getting pregnant. Brings the dads down here, and sometimes the brothers too. Then there is fighting and then police. If it happens too often, there will be no more of this.' Geoffrey swept his hand across the bar.

'As I say, I can look after myself.'

'Sorry, I just wanted to talk. I didn't mean to sound like I was telling you what to do. Just making small talk. I'll get Valerie,' said Geoffrey, sounding nervous for the first time.

--

'Hey, I think you've got our Geoffrey all flustered. Pretty hard to do,' exclaimed Valerie.

'Well he doesn't look too flustered now,' Sira replied, pointing towards the dance floor where Geoffrey and a girl with long straight hair, painted dark eyes and a short, black and white dress were talking and laughing.

'You don't know Geoffrey,' Valerie shouted, lightly spraying Sira's cheek with saliva. 'He expects it to be so easy with girls. I think he likes you. When he felt clumsy, he went to find someone else who was, you know, easier.'

'Easier at what?'

'Wow, you guys really do speak another language in the States, don't you? We think we know it all 'cos we get your music, but you have different words and everything. I mean she will be easy to persuade to have sex. Some girls come here for that. Lots of guys, of course, but some girls too.'

'It's always that way round? I mean, is it always the guys that go after the girls, and the girls can either be got or not? You never get the girls starting it?'

'Look at her!' yelled Valerie, aggressively. 'Her way of starting it is to come here covered in makeup and not much else.'

'And you don't like that?' Sira looked Valerie up and down; almost all her skin covered in wool apart from the top of her neck and her face.

'You think I'm boring? You hate my dress?'

'No, no. Sorry, I'm new to this. I hadn't really thought about clothes until I got these. Where I'm from, it's a lot more casual. But, I've never...'

'Never what?'

'I told you. I've never had sex. No kissing, either. I've been grabbed from time to time, but that's it. We spoke about this – don't you remember?'

'Sure. And you think I haven't either because I'm not flashing my skin?' replied Valerie, slurring her words a little.

'You told me about you and Peter already.'

'Oh right, yeah. Maybe you are right. Maybe Peter won't every marry me if I stay wrapped up like this.' Valerie gestured towards her dress.

'I never said that.'

'You thought it though, Sira. It's fine.'

'Well, if it's fine with you and you want to talk about it – but I really never said or thought that Valerie. I was just looking at what you're wearing.'

'Sorry. I think I've drunk too much.'

'I saw you drink pints of that that stuff the other night and you just got a bit happy. It's not doing anything to me yet.'

'Sorry, I'm – I think Peter fancies someone else. I made out the other night that everything is fine, that I've got it all worked out. But it's not true. I don't think he's interested in me anymore. So, I bought some gin before we left. Drank some for bravery.'

'Ladies, can we buy you a drink?'

This is different Sira.

'Yes, much crustier than the students. More like back home.'

'Hello.' Sira stood tall, chin up, eye to eye, elbows back, fists lightly raised.

'You're saying hello, but you don't look too welcoming.'

'I was talking to my friend. You interrupted.'

'It's fine, Sira.' Valerie put her hand on her shoulder, only to feel it tense like a cocked weapon. 'Sorry, don't mind my friend. She's new in town. My name is Valerie.'

'I guess I'm sorry too. Just being friendly. I'm Jack, and this is my brother Phil. Phil, why don't you buy Valerie a drink? Sira, how about something to go with that beer?'

Jack turned to face the bar, separating Sira from Phil and Valerie. His hair was short like the guys back home but his skin was rough, like he'd been cutting the hair off it with a knife. But from the neck down, he was smarter than the SocSoc: shirt, tie, jacket, albeit stained.

'Don't worry, my brother's a nice guy. He'll treat her fine.'

'She's with someone.'

'Well, I guess he won't treat her much, then. To be honest, he was doing me a favour. This is a bit embarrassing. He said he'd chat to your friend so I could chat to you. He's not really interested in your friend. Married with kids, for a start.'

'Right.'

'So, what can I get you?'

'Say gin.'

'Gin, please.'

261

'With tonic?'

'Yes'

'Yes.'

'No need to be nervous. I'm just trying to be friendly.'

After her first sip of gin, which had the taste of water strained through old clothes, the red mist dissipated a little.

'Phew. Drink more. I thought you – we – were going to have a stroke.'

'Sorry, I'm fine. You surprised me that's all. Where I'm from, you don't surprise people. No one wants to get stabbed.'

'Funny.'

'I'm not joking.'

'Jesus. Where are you from? Wallasey? They say it's rough round here! But don't worry, little lady. I was a soldier. I can protect you.'

'I can protect myself. Where are you from? Which department?'

'Department? Like a shop?'

'No, the university.'

'Funny. No, I ain't no student. I told you. I was a soldier. Now I'm a brickie.'

'A what?'

'I build houses, mostly. Sometimes I work down the docks with Phil. Cushy work down there but too much hanging around for me. I take it you're a student, then.'

'Yes, politics.'

'Ooh! A girl politician. Not many of those.'

'Well, maybe not.'

'So, where's that accent from?'

'The US. I'm from California.'

'Wow, OK. Student. American. Tough and clever. You're quite something.' Jack put his hand on Sira's waist and laughed.

'Smooth move Sira. Distraction.'

--

Geoffrey strode to the bar, his hair sticking to his forehead with sweat, and asked for a pint of water before turning to Valerie with a grin. 'Where's Sira?'

'I think she likes you.'

'Right,' he replied, his smile falling away a little when he saw the stranger with Valerie. 'Who's this?'

'This is Phil. He's just leaving, aren't you, Phil?'

'Um, right. Yes. See you round,' Phil mouthed before disappearing into the smoke.

'Who was that?'

'Jack's brother,' Valerie replied, swaying gently into the bar, gripping it to steady herself.

'Come on, Valerie. Stop being cryptic. Who's Phil? Who's Jack?'

'If you'd be more interested in Sira, there would be no Jack.'

'Me interested in her? I got her in here, got her a drink and then she got all angry.'

'Angry? You men are all the same. Well, maybe SocSoc men are worse. You claim to be all moral and high minded,' asserted Valerie, poking him in the chest, 'but you're as scared of a strong woman as anyone else. Well, maybe not as scared as Jack.' She laughed to herself and lost her grip on the bar, slipping to the floor and bringing a full ashtray down on top of herself. 'Shit. Shit. Oh, disgusting.'

'Come on.' Geoffrey reached down, picked her off the floor and used a beer cloth to wipe the solids from her greyed front. 'I think I'd better take you home.'

Valerie hid her face in her hands and yelled through her fingers, 'You? Why not Peter?'

'Peter?'

'Yes, Peter, PETER, my boyfriend.'

'Peter left ages ago. You know he doesn't really like this stuff. Oh, I love this one!'

The dance floor and bar united in a swaying singalong.

'Peter. Where is he? He left without me.'

'You were talking to that guy and he left.'

'Why didn't he say anything?'

'I suppose he felt awkward. So, Valerie, am I taking you home?'

'Fine. But Sira?'

'Tell me where she is and maybe I can... Oh.' On the far side of the dance floor he saw a flash of yellow. It was spinning round, one hand in the air, held by the huge arm of a local. 'Come on Valerie, we're going.'

--

'I count that as three firsts.'

'Go on, Captain. Spit it out.'

'Kissing, then a warm bed, then sex.'

'Very good.'

'No contraception though.'

'What? Oh shit. I'll just go and...'

'Go and what? No quick zap here, Sira. Messier than that.'

'Why didn't you remind me?'

'My morals aren't clear to me either. Chances are you will be fine.'

'Great. I'm getting dressed before he comes back.'

'Good choice.'

--

Sira carefully slipped round the front door, pulling it towards her from the street with a gentle click. The pram parade was in full swing but wherever she was now, there was more colour. The street was cleaner and children played in the road with a football rather than a tin can. There were also some cars parked on the street, including the shiny red one that she vaguely recalled bringing them here a few hours earlier.

There was a cafe on the corner. From where she stood, she could see people sitting inside drinking hot drinks, gently steaming up their own view to the outside.

'Tea or coffee, pet. Which'll it be?'

People who could afford it back home drank coffee, Sira reminisced. But tea was something else, something grown in home labs and drunk at shelters. They said you'd know after

264

two mugs if you could take it because, if you couldn't, you'd never make it to the third. She rightly assumed that here it must be something different to be offered so casually. Unfortunate, given that some poison could perhaps help her situation.

'Coffee, please.'

'Milk and sugar's on the side.'

Sira picked up her black coffee and took it to the nearest empty table, the exploration of 'the side' being too much effort.

She had lain there and let Jack do what he wanted. She knew she was supposed to be more involved but was scared to make a mistake. Doing nothing felt like exercising more control than doing something wrong. She'd seen old clips where the characters talked about losing their virginity and their 'first time', and being caught between wanting to have sex but not wanting to get married and have children. It sounded exhausting.

She had heard that the members of the larger gangs had sex a lot, primarily because they had the resources to drop their guard. While the girls in these gangs were routinely sterilised, every now and again it must have failed because you'd see one pregnant or carrying a baby. But most people had either lost interest or become too scared to lock themselves up with one other person. Growing up in a communal home and hearing your parents having sex, then hearing them having sex with other parents, was such a universal experience that it had had an effect. Food and shelter were more important to most people, including her.

Here it was different. Sira sipped her coffee and saw couples sitting quietly together, touching fingers under tablecloths. She saw older couples, probably married, eating toast whilst one of them rocked a cumbersome pram back and forth. None of them were worried about what might happen next, who might storm into the building and steal their money, or worse. And, seeing them counting out coins for their drinks, she knew their relaxed demeanour was not a result of them paying for personal security.

Jack had held her afterwards and then, with his arm around her shoulder, he'd smoked a cigarette. She did not try it but it had felt good to be offered something by someone who knew she would not be returning the favour. They spoke and laughed, him telling her about being on a warship near Japan and watching Japanese pilots being shot out of the sky. He said he could see their angry faces as their planes burned up and how, after the fighting died down, beautiful Japanese girls were brought over and worked their way through the ship. He said they looked a bit like the girls in Liverpool's Chinatown, but apparently you could never get close to those.

The clock reached 8am and the cafe began to empty out, men turning left to join others walking down the hill and women turning right back to the rows of houses.

'Those boys, Sira, they don't have anything on us.'

Sira thought in the back of her mind for a moment about Captain's insult before letting her front of mind respond to her digital parasite.

'There is no 'us', Captain. You're a lightweight spinoff from a failing country's mafia. Me and my friends, we had pride, like them. They're living a life they think is right, creating a culture based on tradition and pride, not self-interest and self-promotion.'

'Nothing in your revolution for you, Sira? Nothing selfish about taking money and power from the old and giving it to the young? Seems to me that your ideals are a justification for taking what you want. Just like us.'

'Is that what you think these people are doing, Captain? Working to take for themselves?'

'They don't know what they're doing, Sira. They're ignorant of everything around them. They are being exploited by the port, by the factories, and they've invented morals to explain away their stupidity. Just like the river people.'

Sira knew Captain was raising the attempted rape to provoke her because that was what he was programmed to do. But she also knew she had to own that pain. There was nothing to be gained from being a victim, from sharing her reaction with Captain or even Valerie. Yanda had given his life to protect her; maybe Frank had too. If there was to be any show of pain, it would be for them and their sacrifices, not what happened on the river.

'They were mad. Cut off. Myth-makers. But it was my mistake. I thought there would be something there. Something, well, I never thought I would see the real thing, did I?'

'And you were right, Sira. They were. Naïve just like your beloved Scousers.'

'No, Captain, they were an aberration.'

'I see the same thing. I see pride and people willing to work themselves to death for it, or maybe to rape and kill an outsider for it. Anything to defend a way of life they think they have chosen for themselves, when really they've only following the mindless rules of their community. That's what you get when you take away self-interest and money, not pride but fear, paranoia and violence.'

No, Sira thought. You don't. Not when everyone is together, not scared of outsiders. Then you get humanity.

'Suit yourself' snapped Captain, when Sira did not reply to him before proceeding to give her a small shock in the face, akin to a slap.

She let the sting on her cheek subside, gripping the table tightly to hide the pain. When it was gone, she remembered that she'd got herself a locker in the engineering department to keep a couple of boiler suits. Still dressed like a canary, she walked to the university to get changed and set up for the day.

Professor Veenings was waiting for her at the welding bench, his black gown hanging dangerously close to a pot of grease. 'You went out last night Ms Tumasz,' he asserted quietly but clearly, over-pronouncing his Ts.

'Yes,' she replied, clearing up some of the mess he was leaning against to hide her nerves.

'You went out with the socialists,' he continued, agitated.

'Yes,' she replied again, wishing she had stayed with them.

'So, what were they talking about?' he spat out. 'Jesus Christ,' he yelled, banging the bench with his fist, causing a few loose nuts to bounce a fraction into the air. 'What are they plotting? You know you report to me, don't you? I've made that clear, haven't I? Well, I report to someone else.'

Sira put down the tools and turned to face him. His face was redder than it was last time, with broken veins pulsating across his nose. She thought carefully about what to say, feeling intimidated and realising for the first time that these were real people.

'I'm sorry, Professor,' she said genuinely. 'They didn't talk about much last night. We all got a bit drunk and split up. But, as you seem to know, they are working on a piece about Lord Salisbury. About him being a racist. I guess they want to embarrass him into stepping down. They want at least one protest about it next year, along with protests about the tenants.'

'I know all this already, miss,' he yelled again, before mumbling that it was helpful to have it corroborated. 'What I want from you,' he pointed his finger aggressively at her, 'are two things: your reasonable assessment of whether they will succeed in forcing him out, and your ideas about how we can stop it.'

'I'm sorry, I don't know, Professor. I – I've got a bit of, well...'

'Spit it out!'

'An idea for demoralising them, Professor. I want them to unite with the working classes.'

Professor Veenings paced gently around a drilling rig, pulling at its bakerfoil handles. 'When did you last calibrate this drill, Ms Tumasz?'

'Yesterday, Professor.'

'And how long would it take you to fix it if I were to do this?' He picked up a small adjustable spanner from the workbench and, in an obviously rehearsed fashion, loosened the main lateral bolt, sending the motor slipping off its mountings.

'That wasn't very nice, was it? It was going to be hard for you to keep up with me today with your hangover.'

'Quiet!'

'I'm sorry, Professor. I wasn't trying to frustrate you.'

'We do not want them to become stronger. We want the opposite! Some of my colleagues think they are harmless posh boys in a working-class city with no hope of gaining traction. I don't agree. I think the tenants' story was a clever ploy to get the workers on side. I don't want this, and you're telling me you want to help them. I'm not sure you quite understand your role, or the danger you're in!' He banged the spanner into the motor, sending a hard metal vibration through the floor to which it was bolted.

'I'm sorry, Professor. I agree with you. I think their ideas are wrong. I promise, they would not last five minutes where I'm from.' He looked at her confused, but she pushed on. 'I cannot imagine anyone toughened through the pride of work being taken in by them, Professor. They are just playing but I agree that, left alone, they will become dangerous. I know this more than anyone.'

'Careful Sira!'

'Left alone, they can write what they want and declare what they think, with only the university authorities to contradict them. But put them alongside people in real hardship and they will be exposed as charlatans. Anyway, I think this coming together will happen, whether you like it or not.'

'Great. We shall see about that. But if they do, let's hope you're right – although I don't really see how.'

'I've said, Professor. Their ideas about communism will be ridiculed by people who just want to get paid a little more for hard work.'

'All seems a bit academic to me, Tumasz. But I may have an idea.' Veenings paced the floor, lightly tapping each of the machines that he passed with his spanner. Occasionally he looked up, as though he were going to say something, but then he continued his pacing.

Sira stood still and hoped that whatever he was about to say wouldn't prematurely end her relationship with the SocSoc.

'If they do get the tenants involved, perhaps we could stir something up?'

Sira stayed silent.

'What if, for example, a student or someone who could pass as a student was to sleep with one of their wives? Or husbands? What if, on the day of a joint protest, the local newspaper was to get a good photo of a local punching one of the socialists in the face? I can't imagine the collaboration lasting very long once traditional values clash with bourgeois free love, can you? Next time I see you, I want to hear a plan to make that happen. Understand?'

She did not reply and watched him sweep out of the room.

'Come on, Sira, get your spanners. We've got work to do.'

--

'OK if I sit here and study?'

Peter was alone at one of the tables against the wall, beneath a noticeboard pinned with newspaper clippings. Sira carried some hefty political textbooks and a copy of *Das Kapital* that she had stolen from the library after slipping through its window. The building had reminded her of home: on the outside it was redbrick and ornate, but the inside had been recrafted beyond its original purpose to squeeze more breathing, sweating humans inside. The ceilings were low, and the light was trapped by walls thrown up seemingly at random. Maybe everything bad about her own time originated here, she thought, as she climbed back out of the library and into the women's changing room in the Guild to steal herself a more suitable outfit for interacting with the SocSoc: a brown skirt, brown shirt and some sensible shoes.

'Yes, of course, Sira. Make yourself at home. I'm studying. Paper's all wrapped up for Christmas, if you see what I mean? But it'd be super handy if you'd proofread something for me in an hour or so.'

'Absolutely. Quiet in here today, isn't it?'

'Yes, often the way after they've got drunk. Valerie turned up at home in quite a mess, dropped off by Geoffrey. How did you get on?'

'Oh, I don't know. All a bit new to me. Used to something a bit less boozy and a bit sunnier and more relaxed at home. I don't think it will be a regular thing for me.'

'Very wise.'

'Yes, very wise. You're lucky if you don't leave a present behind, assuming we ever get out of here.'

--

'Mistakes just here, and here. The rest looks fine, Peter.'

'Shit! OK.'

'What?'

270

'I've got to type it out all over again. This one's got to be perfect.'

'What do mean? Just...' Sira looked over Peter's shoulder and took in the typing machine for the first time. 'Oh yes, sorry, Peter.'

'Peter, Sira, having fun?' Geoffrey walked in, swinging a large leather bag. 'Sira! You did have fun last night, didn't you? Disappeared with a solider I hear! A local boy. Show you his local delights, did he?'

'Geoffrey, don't be so crude,' scolded Peter.

'Thought you'd be with me, old chap. Clear case of class exploitation by our jet-setting friend here!'

'Geoffrey, are you still drunk?'

'Terrible hangover, had to take the hair of the dog.' Geoffrey pulled a bottle of wine from his bag and gave it a jiggle to show how little was left. 'Thought you'd look a bit worse for wear, Sira, after the night you've had.'

Sira could not help tensing up, ready for a fight. 'Geoffrey, I'm not sure what you're saying. Have I done something wrong?'

'No, no, just run off with whoever you see. Why not? Don't think I haven't done it myself. Just – you know!'

'What?'

'Never seen a girl do it so openly, that's all.'

'And the girls you've slept with? Where did they appear from?'

'Well, they always manage to slip off unnoticed, I guess. All about appearances, isn't it, Peter?'

'Whatever you say, Geoffrey, but I really think you should stop swinging that thing around and take a rest on the sofa over there. You're in no fit state to be anywhere else.'

Westminster, London, 7th November 2017

To dinner

'Tell me more about the defence angle, Daniel. I thought David was mainly a tech guy, but the E-bit guy I met yesterday seemed to know him well.'

Geoffrey and Daniel were walking through the tunnel under Westminster Bridge Road that links Portcullis House with the old Palace, the MP having picked Daniel up from the glass reception area.

Daniel felt a little nervous with Geoffrey for the first time since beginning his venture. He hurried his pace to keep up with Geoffrey's overhanging paunch which was wrapped in a navy suit. However unhealthy they were, MPs seemed to have a knack for racing down narrow corridors and doorways but only within these walls. On the outside, they moved like clumsy tourists blocking everyone's way.

'Well,' Daniel explained, not knowing how Geoffrey, a peacenik at heart, would react, 'in Israel, there's not much of a separation between the two. All their military spending and training puts them at the head of the pack. Start-ups, even civilian ones, are often spin-offs from the defence community, or at least a bunch of ex-army guys taking their skills elsewhere. But there is a link to tonight's dinner with James,' he continued, wondering if he could detect some concern in the MP. 'At first, we thought it would be just great technology for local government. Citizens nudging themselves into best practice rather than needing bureaucrats to do it for them.'

'Yes, I get that. Not a massive leap from kibbutz to Kidderminster in that regard,' Geoffrey interjected, happy with his little quip.

'But I just spoke to David, and E-bit are actually quite keen to pay through the nose. They want it to organise their global workforce, including the R&D centre they are planning in your patch. But I think they also want to explore how it could be used for self-organised troop movements or armies, or even defence policy. That's the gist of it, as far as I know. Anyway, best keep that to yourself, I'm not sure where conversations between E-bit and James are on that front.'

'OK, Daniel. I don't love the sound of that. I'd rather discuss the civilian side,' replied Geoffrey.

Daniel considered replying that reality was not dictated by what the MP did or did not want to talk about, but thought better of it. 'Of course, Geoff. They're interested in you. They want to hear your take on British politics. Their experience is Israeli, remember, smaller closer-knit communities. They want to understand the market here, how British communities where people know each other less come together and get things done.'

'Great. Well, I'm sure you've got this, Daniel. I'm looking forward to eating. Been a bit takeaways and Portcullis snacks of late. Last night was the first time Julia has been home in days, and with her away a lot there doesn't seem to be much point in getting home. One of yours always willing to buy the drinks and all that.'

'I assume you mean lobbyists, rather than Jews?'

'Very funny, Daniel. I can't imagine that will go down that well tonight, what with the British ambassador there as well. Diplomats can be very sensitive.'

'I promise to behave.'

'Good. Anyway, which room?' They had reached the entrance to the dining-room corridor, the part of the building that bordered the river, its exterior photographed thousands of times a day by tourists on the South Bank who had no idea they were capturing a row of bars and restaurants in their lenses rather than debating chambers and the passing of laws.

'Here it is, pass me your coat, boss, I'll hang it with mine.'

'Geoffrey, how are you?'

'Timothy! Timothy, I don't believe you have met my friend Daniel.'

Timothy and his brown suit had popped out of the men's toilets onto the corridor. He was too close not to acknowledge.

'Daniel works, well, worked for me.'

'Timothy, I've heard a lot about you,' Daniel said. 'I used to take MPs, many of your colleagues in fact, to Israel but for the past few months I've been working for a small firm. My boss is a big fan of the party. Donates quite a bit.'

'Great, great. So, Israel. Interesting international development angles to that, I bet. I read something about water recently.'

'Yes, I'll drop you an email introducing you to my successor. I'm sure we can get you some more information on that.'

'Is that what you look at on your visits?'

'A little. Mostly it's the security side. Defence. The Iranian nuclear threat.'

'Oh, not very Labour then,' Timothy asserted, patting Daniel patronisingly on the shoulder. 'But the water stuff, that's very interesting. You have a good evening.'

'Arsehole. You're not very fucking Labour, you soft wanker,' Geoffrey whispered under his breath as Timothy bounded down the corridor full of energy.

Liverpool,
19th December 1968

The spy

Geoffrey slept for an hour or so, gently snoring into his chest, his head uncomfortably bent forward by the solid arms of the angular sofa. As the alcohol wore off, he stirred and eventually sat up to take the pressure of his vertebrae. His eyes returned to the bottle by his feet.

'You know, if you comfort him, you might get something good for Veenings.'

'I was just thinking the same thing.'

'I know.'

'Geoffrey, I think you've had enough.' Sira pushed the bottle to the side, realising as she did that there was only one small gulp left in it anyway. 'I've upset you, haven't I?' she asked.

'You can do what you want.'

'I know, but if I had known leaving with that guy would have upset you, I probably wouldn't have.'

'Probably?'

'Well, I'd need to know why it would have upset you.'

'Why do you think?'

'Well, you gave me no reason to think you liked me like that.'

'Maybe.'

'Maybe you agree? Maybe you do like me like, then?'

'I thought I'd have some more time to work it out before you went and ruined yourself.'

'Ruined?!'

'Careful, Sira, remember what we're doing.'

'Yes,' he replied, before starting to cry a little, awkwardly dragging a handkerchief from his pocket and holding it to his face to dampen the sound.

'But that would make you ruined as well, wouldn't it?'

'It's different.'

'Why?'

'It's different. That's how I feel. Maybe I'm wrong. Valerie would tell me I'm wrong. I don't think I'm being sexist. I'm being romantic. I wanted to be your first.'

'But, Geoffrey, I didn't know you thought anything of me.'

'Well, I do. How does that make you feel?' He looked up at her and tried to blow the ethanol rising from his stomach down his nose rather than straight into her face.

'Hold him... Now!'

'Come on, Geoffrey. Why don't we take you home?'

'You've got him.'

'Yes. Noticed. And I'm not proud of it.'

'Not proud. But he's one of the leaders. There are probably only a handful of Geoffreys across the country and together they lead this country's liberal revolution. And you've got one in the palm of your hands.'

'I understand. I'm just not proud.'

--

'So, how long before university starts again?' Sira asked.

'You don't know? Politics students!' Geoffrey scoffed. 'We go back in mid-January. We'll do the tenants' protest a couple of weeks in, so we've got time to mobilise the students. Might have to do a little outreach before we go back, though. Do some groundwork.'

Geoffrey knocked the ash from their joint into a glass tray balanced on his stomach and handed it across to her, being careful not to drop burning grass onto either of their chests. The floor was strewn with dirty plates, which the pair silently acknowledged would be cleaned up the following day after another night of stoned lazy sex.

After Sira had ridden the bus to Geoffrey's house and put him to bed, she'd raced back to the university to update her handler. She predicted she would need to miss the last couple of days of term to get closer to her mark and needed Veenings to cover for her with the engineering department, which he

276

promised to do. Then, on the way back, she bought two bags of groceries and broke into a pharmacy where, without showing her face, she locked the pharmacist's neck in the grip of her elbow, forcing him to dispense a few weeks' supply of contraceptive pills and explain how to take them, plus a handful of something he called condoms.

Her heart was still racing when she got to Geoffrey's. She let herself in and, hoping to cement the plan, slid into bed next to him, still wearing her clothes, and waited for the adrenalin to wear off.

'You're pretty fast, aren't you? First kiss last night. First sexual manipulation today.'

'If you look at it through that narrow lens, perhaps. But I've been surviving all my life, and I'm not going to stop now.'

'What about your parents? Do you miss them?'

'No, I'll call them over the break. But I've been writing to them. You?'

'I'll see them for a couple of days over Christmas. But we don't speak a lot. They think I'm a communist.'

'Aren't you?'

Geoffrey let out a little laugh and took another drag on the joint before passing it back to Sira. 'I mean, they think I want to march around in a uniform and start wars. I've tried explaining that we are for peace and equality, not tanks and nukes, but they don't understand. They think I'm wasting "the opportunities they tried so hard to give me",' he explained in a false posh voice. 'It's rubbish of course. They just clothed and fed me, which is sort of expected of parents, and the state did all the rest. The Labour government in '45 set up a lot of good things. It just didn't go far enough to remake the system. That's what we're going to do.'

'And you really think you – sorry – you, Peter, Valerie, John and I can do it?'

'Good save.'

'Well, maybe not John. He's lazy. But no, not just us. We're trying to light a fire. The fuel is all around us – disgruntled students wanting to make a difference, and poverty, such poverty. We need to show them the way.'

277

Geoffrey took a long drag on the grass and rolled back his eyes. 'It's good this stuff. Get it from a bloke called Brian in the pub on the corner. He's a plumber, always driving round in his van. Good cover for a casual drug-dealing business on the side. He gave me some great tips about the housing story as well. Sees into a lot of these houses. Actually, we're going to need to see him soon because I'm running low. How about I call the pub, get a note left for him, and we relax here until he calls us back?'

'Sounds lovely, Geoff. You hungry?'

'Only for you. Come here.'

'Ugh! Even I know that's a cliché.'

--

'Brian, this is Sira.'

'Pleasure to meet the missus.'

'Oh, I'm—' Sira felt a sharp squeeze in the side. 'A pleasure to meet you too!'

'He wouldn't understand' Geoffrey whispered in her ear, disguising it as a kiss.

Brian had longer hair than the other men in the pub, which he wore slicked back like a man on a movie poster she'd seen. Except Brian's face was tired and leathery, not boyish like the film star's. He spoke with a thick local accent which sped up as the conversation continued.

'You fancy a pint Brian?'

'Don't mind if I do. Then you tell me again what you do, Geoff, I can never remember.'

'Ah. I think you do remember. You just don't believe me,' Geoffrey retorted, patting Brian on the shoulder.

Sira couldn't imagine the other students behaving like this. While Geoffrey was significantly bigger than Brian, bigger than most of the men in the pub, students had a reputation for being soft and avoiding the locals. The pub seemed more aggressive and un-student-like than ones she had seen before. Instead of rounded wood and soft dark fabrics and colours, it w as more like one of the garages she had lived in a home, a well-lit, acidic smelling white box in which sharp sounds clattered from side to side.

'Very good, Geoff. Indulge me anyway.'

'I work at the council. In the housing department.'

'What?' Sira and Captain messaged each other simultaneously.

'That's it. That's why you're always asking around about people's home conditions. But I think maybe it's cos you're looking for a nice-sounding home and family to take for yourself, like a – what's the bird? A cuckoo?'

'Pretty far-fetched, Brian. But it's nice to elicit some intrigue.'

'There you go with your posh London words. Maybe you're some kind of London developer. Maybe you can get me a plum job building houses for the posh folk?'

'Write to me at the council and I'll see what I can do,' Geoff said.

'Funny, mate! Well, nice doing business with you as always. There's a large box of matches on top of the jukebox. That's for you.'

'And here's your money for the beers you bought me last time.'

Brian nodded, taking the notes from Geoffrey before telling him to bring his girl again, next time. Sira forced a smile and the pair watched the plumber leave.

'Is it like that every time?' she asked.

'I guess so. He's much easier than the others I've bought from. He just makes fun. The others hear a Londoner and try and con you, or worse. Come on, let's get some fish and chips on the way home.'

'But what was the lie for?'

'Oh, he hates students.'

'Do you think he's right for it, Sira?'

'Maybe. I got his number from his van on the way in.'

'I know.'

'Yes. I'll call him out and follow him. We will see. I'll write Veenings a note to tell him to get someone ready. But if he hates students, why would he be at the protest?'

'We'll figure that out.'

'Do you not think you're overestimating this guy?'

'Geoffrey?'

'Veenings. Do you really think he will find someone at the university to have sex with Brian or his wife?'

'He better had. I'm not doing it.'

'So, why are you already preparing yourself? In here.'

'I'm not doing it. Geoffrey trusts me now, despite the whole Jack thing. I can't throw that away. It's too valuable.'

'If the plan works, Sira, you won't need Geoffrey anymore. Plus, if you do it yourself, you'll break him as well as his little movement.'

'That's not the plan! It's not that personal.'

'Ah. Softening, are we?'

'No, we need to end their ideas – end what their ideas become. It's about more than Geoffrey. Plus, I am not a monster. I was not a monster at home and I won't become one here. I am a fighter. There are rules in war.'

'What about Yanda?'

'Fuck off!'

--

'Sira, seeing as you're not doing anything for Christmas, how about you come to my family's place? It will be a lot of fun.'

'You want me to meet your parents?' Sira lay back in Geoffrey's bed and stared at the textured, smoke-stained ceiling. They had been smoking since eating some tinned meat for lunch and were listening to the news on the radio for the fourth time that day. They had not been further than the corner shop, pub or chip shop for nearly a week.

'That's quite a serious offer, isn't it, Geoffrey? At home, I've never met the parents of some of my closest friends.'

'Friends, right,' he tutted, and turned away a little, bumping her shoulder in the small bed.

'Sorry, I mean, do you think your family will expect me to call you my boyfriend?'

'Yes, I expect they will. What do you think about that?' He sounded a little upset.

'Good. It sounds good.'

'That sounded honest to me.'

'But I'm going to need a proper briefing. Names, likes, dislikes, manners, expectations you know, everything. I would need to know what I'm doing.'

'Fine. It's a long journey to London on the train. Let's go tomorrow morning, and I'll explain everything on the way.'

'So soon?'

'Yeah, of course, it's nearly Christmas!'

Sira responded by leaping out of bed into the chill of the room that was barely touched by the three-bar electric heater they'd had on almost all day.

'What are you doing jumping around naked like that? It's freezing.'

'I've not got any of my things here, Geoffrey. I need to pick up some stuff if I'm coming with you for a few days. Got to look my best.'

Before he could offer to go with her, she was out of the door and inside a payphone across the street, firstly putting in a call for an emergency plumbing job to her squat, and then booking a taxi to the same place. The taxi arrived at her squat first and she waited with it in the street, watching the meter tick upwards. Ten minutes later Brian arrived and knocked on the door. Waited. Knocked. Waited. Swore loudly. Kicked the door then climbed back in his van.

The taxi followed him. Sira asked Captain to take a note of where they went and to help her draw it on a map later. She was too stoned to remember herself. After fifteen minutes, the van stopped and she had the taxi wait a few doors down with its lights off. The driver happily went along, occasionally remarking that this was the most fun he'd had with a girl with his trousers on. Sira smiled and battled to hold back the vomit.

Leaving the cab, but asking him to stay put, she glided along the flat-fronted terrace, sliding close to the walls. When she got to her mark, she peered over her shoulder into the living room and was relieved to find the curtains open.

Brian walked into the front room and swore again, which prompted his young, slightly overweight wife to cover the ears of the small boy she was standing behind at the dinner table.

She hurried into the kitchen to bring a plate of food out for the plumber. She seemed on edge as she handed it to him and then retreated behind the child. Sira watched for five minutes as the scene calmed and Brian started watching TV as his wife put the plates away and carried the boy upstairs.

Sira took the taxi to central Liverpool where, for the first time since acquiring the means, she bought herself a small, sensible wardrobe of clothes, some makeup, a hairbrush and a suitcase to put it in. She explained that she was meeting her boyfriend's family for the first time, and the shop assistant seemed ecstatic to help her prepare for the days ahead.

North west London,
17th December 2053

How much have you read?

'Eres!'

'Huuurrrrrre'

'Medic! Get me a medic! Eres can you hear me?'

He threw up again, leaning as far forwards as he could in the restraints that he had reappeared in and trying to draw in a breath before the next wave of vomit splashed across his lap.

'Why?'

'Eres, what did you say? Can you say it louder?' yelled Mila.

He shook his head and threw up again.

'Quick, he needs something for the vomit. He can't breathe!'

Dr Hawkins and another white coat burst through the door and ran straight to Eres, who was thrashing sideways, rocking his chair against the metal bolts that held it to the floor. 'We're doing it, ma'am. Anti-emetic going in now.'

Mila and the white coats stayed silent for a moment and watched Eres' movements slow.

'I'm OK,' he said eventually.

'I think the injection is working, ma'am.'

She nodded and looked up to see the chairman standing in the doorway.

'Just you and me,' Eres spat out towards her.

'*What?*' Mila texted in reply, pointlessly straining to get closer and hoping he would repeat himself.

The chairman walked into the room and stood over Eres, giving the souls of his shoes a light kicking as though he was testing a tyre and sending a globule of vomit rolling to the floor. Dr Hawkins paced back and forth behind him and cried a little.

When Mila finally turned her way, Hawkins mouthed 'he knows'.

'Agent Seynes, has he got the data or not? We need a download.'

'Need to speak. Private,' Eres spluttered.

'Sir, we can't take the data like that,' Hawkins interjected. 'Look at him. He's a mess. I think it will be quicker to wait until he can...'

'Hawkins!' the chairman yelled, 'I'm not entirely convinced you had nothing to do with this. Quite the opposite! Those two have killed my men, used the machine without permission, and now they want some time to themselves!'

The doctor nodded silently in reply.

The chairman kicked Eres' shoe again before grabbing Hawkins' arm and dragging her out of the room, leaving an armed guard watching over his captives.

--

'Come on, we're in a lot of trouble. Did you get it? Did it work?' scrolled across Eres' display.

He wriggled in his chair, the drying sick beginning to scratch and pull at his thighs. 'Are they're monitoring us? Have they broken in?' he replied.

Mila shrugged a little and sent 'I don't know' back to him before asking him again if the plan had worked.

'Yes, yes. Strange. I appeared right here and made my way to the main lab. Then I hid for a while until I heard Hawkins' voice. I told her everything and she helped me. She's so compliant!'

'And?'

'And I got it. I got too much, Mila.' There was no intonation in his messaging, but she could see he looked scared. She felt sorry for him for the first time.

'Eres, just tell me. It will be OK,' she whispered softly, drawing the attention of the guard and the end of his rifle.

'I didn't have time to split the files. It's a lot of data all in one place. Only you can see it. You must take it. There's something you have to see.'

'Got it! OK.'

'Good. Review it. What's that smell? Not just the sick, something else?'

'I don't really know what happened to you. Your clothes and hair. It's all singed. But you'll be fine. You just need fluids.'

--

'You see it Mila?'

She nodded.

'What we going to do?'

She shrugged.

'You don't seem surprised?'

'I tried to tell you, Eres. It didn't add up. Now it does. The chairman was in on it. Roydon thought the kidnapped girl was in exchange for him letting them into Neasden's systems. But that was only part of it. She was also to be sent back in time, as human data collector and store!'

'I don't understand. What use is sending a girl back in time?'

'Jesus Eres. You read the files too! They are trying to enable time travel without a connection to the crystal. The gangs and the chairman are trying to do it by collecting the data of the experience of travelling through time itself. And that's too much data for anything other than a brain implant to collect, Eres. And what's the one thing an implant needs to work?'

He stared at her blankly and she smiled a little when he scratched his head against its restraint.

'The one thing an implant needs to work, Eres, is a brain. They couldn't have simply sent the implant back alone. It needed to be in a brain.'

'OK Mila. But we can stop them. She's out there somewhere. We can find her and go from there. We still have a chance.'

'Fine. Let's just get the data from your head to Hawkins and she can get Neasden working properly again. I think if we can speak to someone above the chairman, maybe they will listen.'

'How much have you read Mila?'

'More than you, clearly!'

285

'I missed something Mila, but so did you I'm afraid.'

'No need to be arrogant, Eres. I don't think you have a leg stand on that score.'

'Mila, look again. You are missing the point. The chairman is the tip of the iceberg. The government, gangs and corporations, they're all in it together. Look again.' Eres saw his partner's eyes flicker and then watched the blood leave her face. *'See Mila. We have to find that girl, alone!'*

London,
25th December 1968

Christmas with the Browns

'We don't think Geoffrey is a communist. We just worry about how much time he spends on that newspaper! He's in his third year now, and we want him to focus.' Mrs Brown was smiling at Geoffrey, waiting for him to nod in agreement, which he did with obvious resignation before taking a gulp of thin-bodied red wine.

'I'm sorry, Mrs Brown,' Sira replied, shovelling food into her mouth.

'Don't worry, and please call me Marjorie. We know how into politics he is. He's always been trying to persuade people. Always loved words, loved argument, haven't you Geoff? When the other boys wanted to play football, he was with Hattie trying to get her to play along with some word game he'd just come up with. Does he do that with you?'

Geoffrey shrugged at Sira with a small smile.

'Well, I guess, lots of words in Liverpool are different to back home. A lot of it feels a bit like a game. Probably one that I'm losing.'

'Very funny,' Geoffrey's father said unconvincingly, one of the few things he'd said all evening. He took a large swig from a small crystal glass, almost downing the whole thing as though it were a parade-day shot of home brew.

'I'd certainly never been called "pet" before I moved to Liverpool,' Sira continued.

'Pet! Ha! What a funny place Liverpool is,' Marjorie replied. 'Don't know why our boy goes there. Hattie's going to Cambridge, aren't you?'

'Mother, please don't be so rude to our guest,' hissed Hattie across the table.

'Oh, yes, of course. Sorry, Sarah.'

'She's called Sira, Mother. And I haven't got in yet. If I don't, I'd be very happy to go to Liverpool or Manchester. Very good universities, aren't they, Geoff?'

'Thanks, Sis. Yes, they are. I obviously know Liverpool better but the lecturers and the union at Manchester are supposed to be very good. We're ahead of the game in organising. But Liverpool's always been very good like that.' Geoffrey took a bit of turkey from his fork, which he'd been gesticulating with like a lollypop, and frowned when he noticed his father was looking away from the table.

Harriet smiled at Sira and mouthed 'very normal behaviour'. Sira could not tell whether this was sarcasm or not, but she did not mind either way because the conversation had moved on enabling her to return to the multitude of porcelain pots laid out across the table, overflowing with dark green vegetables and fragrant meats. Each bite of food took away the memory of the burnt taste that lived at the bottom of her fireplace stewing pot.

When her stomach eventually began to fill, she looked beyond the table towards the room's dark edges and saw that one side was lined with cabinets and small, heavy-framed paintings from somewhere foreign. In one picture, a white man in a white uniform had his hand on a small dark boy's head.

'What are those?' she whispered to Geoffrey. His sister and mother were locked in conversation.

'Dad's things,' he whispered back, cautioning her with a stare.

Sira nodded, running her eyes along small wooden artefacts, silver cups with words scratched into them and, in the furthest cabinet, the blade of a weapon.

'Mr Brown,' she finally beckoned. He did not reply, maintaining his focus on the glass of wine in his hand. 'Mr Brown?'

'Yes, young lady,' he replied finally, his voice thick and scratchy.

'Did you fight in the war?'

'Sira, that's um, not very polite,' Geoffrey asserted, with a frozen fake smile on his face.

Mr Brown stared at his son for a moment and then continued. 'In a way the war came to me, young lady.'

'You mean, you had to fight?'

'Well, yes, in a way we all did. What I meant was that I was in India, working in the Empire. I worked under the governor of Punjab as an administrator in the army. We were called up together when the war started. Sent to North Africa. Us and the Indians.' He stared at Geoffrey. 'It's not the sort of thing young people do now,' he said after a pause. 'Is it, son?'

'I guess times have changed,' Geoffrey replied.

'It sounds fascinating,' Sira interjected. 'Working together. Fighting together. What was it like when you went back?'

Mr Brown did not reply, his eyes still fixed on his son.

'Sorry, Mr Brown, can I ask...'

Mr Brown cleared his throat loudly before she could continue and dropped the odd-shaped knife he was holding with a clatter against his plate. Geoffrey stepped in to break the tension with a confusing and pointless story about a local woman who ran something he called 'the tobacconist' who he described as having 'musty fingers'. That generated loud, nervous laughter from his sister and mother.

--

'So, how did you meet my darling brother? What's he like there? Surrounded by admirers, I guess.' Harriet was yelling over her shoulder while starting into a mirror and tousling her hair.

'I, erm, walked into the office of the newspaper he edits. I was a bit lost, being a foreign student, and he and his friends on the paper sort of took me in.'

'And now you've taken him in?'

'Pardon?'

'Sorry, crude joke between the girls, that's all. Anyway, why don't you tell me about him?'

Sira explained what the newspaper was working on, what Geoffrey and his friends talked about, the bars he went to. But she did not divulge anything private.

One thing Sira and Geoffrey's generation had in common, she thought, was keeping family in the dark. In Sira's London, the nuclear family was gone and children and parents mixed randomly. They all knew who they were ultimately attached to but, with no resources and nothing to provide for one's kin, parenting had ceased to be meaningful beyond the first couple of years of a child's life. Even so, secrets remained important.

'Good girl. You're as tight lipped as the one he brought home last Christmas.'

Harriet, Sira realised, was playing the role of both interrogator and child, a confusing combination.

'You know, me and my brother speak quite a lot. You've seen he's got a phone in his house. Bet that's not very common in Liverpool. Well, we ring each other.'

Sira nodded and smiled.

'My mother's right. He isn't a communist. He's told me he plays it up. Something about motivating the troops and making alliances with the others in the society. He just wants to do good. I think a lot of them do. I've been to some meetings round here as well. When they get to the philosophical stuff, the hard stuff, it all falls apart. They know that, the Geoffreys of this world, they just revel in the fiction.'

'You go to communist meetings here?' Sira's mind floated out the front door to the last time she'd been in a wealthy neighbourhood, Belgravia, crouching to avoid gunfire. 'I thought, sorry, my understanding was that this place was very...'

'Posh? Oh, it is. Father's got a normal job. Accountant. Earns enough. But mother was left a lot of money by her family. Only child, you see, so all those generations of wealth fell upon one young lady's shoulders. She bought this place and all these things. We were always going to go to boarding school. Quite different from many of Geoffrey's friends up North, I imagine. But yes, plenty of rich communists round here. We don't want a violent revolution or anything, though.'

Sira mind filled with fog. It was becoming too confusing. Did Geoffrey want change or not? Would he, in the future, do the damage he talked about or was it all a joke? Or maybe that was the point, that these people destroyed something and replaced it with nothing.

She caught Harriet smiling at her in the mirror, enjoying the disturbance she had created in the guest's mind. Sira smiled back.

--

'I'd better sneak back over to my room in a moment,' whispered Geoffrey, clinging to the edge of Sira's single bed. 'Problem of having such a big house I'm afraid. No excuse for squeezing in together.'

'I was talking to your sister earlier.'

'Yes, I saw. What's she dribbling on about today?'

'The revolution.'

'Oh, right to it, was she? I think she's shagging a married man who's got a lot of interesting books.'

'She was saying that you don't really want one.'

'What?'

'An overthrow?'

'Oh, right. Well, it's difficult to say, isn't it?'

'Is it?' Sira needed him to confirm it, to confirm that he was her downfall, all their downfalls but an idea was forming at the back of her mind, a hope that he was ineffectual, a nothing, with no part to play in history at all. This house of plenty was getting to her. A few more days with Geoffrey, surrounded by food, drink and warmth could be the end of her self-appointed mission. She knew she was letting her guard down. Even before she'd arrived, she had stopped planning, stopped wondering if she should simply kill who she could.

She needed to hear something from Geoffrey to wake her up. She had a goal and, if she was to ever get back to a better version of home, she had a fight to win it.

'Equality? Full equality. Do you want that?'

'Come on, Sira, this is a bit heavy for Christmas.'

'Please, Geoffrey,' she begged, her mind becoming dizzy. 'Just tell me!'

He turned a little in the cramped bed to look into her eyes. 'What's got into you?'

She could see he was not in the mood to answer her, so tried a new approach. 'All those medals and trophies.'

'Yes?'

Sira thought about the spear blade in the cabinet and the way the light glinted on it. Would her cause have been more successful if they'd had those weapons, that training?

'He didn't want to talk about his victories.' Geoffrey looked at her with confusion, so she chose her words carefully. 'Obviously *Empire* is against what lots of people stand for now. But I would have thought that he would still be proud of what he did when he was young.'

Geoffrey swung his legs out of the bed, stood up and paced the room a little. 'I don't think he's proud at all Sira. He's not Lord Salisbury.'

'But that's because politics has changed, hasn't it? Because people think differently now?'

'No, Sira. It's because my dad's not a fool and he's probably a bit ashamed. Despite all the show, the things on the wall you've seen, he doesn't talk about it very much, his time out there.'

'Ever?'

'No, not really. And when he does, he's, well...'

'What Geoffrey?'

Geoffrey sat next to her and put his face in his hands. Sira understood that, despite maintaining his usual confident tone, he was finding this difficult.

'When he talks about it, which is rare, he's sad.'

'Definitely sad,' Geoffrey nodded to himself. 'Fundamentally, I don't think trying to show you run a place, keeping order with barely any training or local knowledge, while also being scared you will be garrotted at any moment, is a particularly ennobling experience. Imagine, you have your little room. You have your servant who knows much more than you. Once a week maybe you see others in your position and you all pretend you know what you're doing when you all know you don't. And you essentially organise the paying of a pittance to locals to work themselves to death. You get a medal for it, a few even, but what for?'

Sira wanted to say something like 'honour' or 'strength' but held her tongue and, in that moment of hesitation, admitted to herself that Geoffrey had a point, at least about his father. 'And Liverpool?'

'What about it, Sira?'

'They've had a revolution in India, but they haven't in Liverpool. Do you want one?'

'You've seen Liverpool. There are people working themselves to death and at the end of the day all they can afford is one unheated damp room for their family, and not even an indoor toilet. We could do with more equality. But it doesn't have to be a revolution. In Scandinavia, they are changing things through votes. People have realised that they want to live in a more civilised way. The politicians here don't get that – not enough anyway.'

He was being too moderate, she thought. It did not add up. 'So, everyone gets paid the same whatever they do, whatever they give back to the country, however hard they fight?'

'No, I didn't say that. I don't think that.'

'I think others in the SocSoc think you think that Geoffrey. Think that's what you stand for.'

'I doubt it. We all blur the edges. We all want to blow off some steam. Can you see John and Peter seizing control of the Liverpool docks by force? I can't.'

'And war? You want to end all war, even if we're being attacked?'

'No, no. I just don't want to see us go to war to push our ways onto others. They say Vietnam is about extending freedom but to me it just looks like poor Americans and Vietnamese getting killed.'

She looked at him, trying to see if there was anything there, any truth, any danger.

'Sira, why the grilling? I thought we agreed on this, especially the anti-war stuff. Especially the racism of going to war.' He shrank in front of her, sucking warmth from the room and purpose from her mind.

'I do agree. I – I just like talking about it. I think you're right. We don't really know about the Scandinavian model back home. I think we should write more about it here. I think people would understand. Anyway, it's late. You better sneak back.'

'Right. So, my sister and my parents haven't upset you? They are quite traditional. Horribly privileged really. I guess I should have warned you. I'll see you for breakfast.'

I think you've upset him. I get the impression people are supposed to be warm and friendly at Christmas.''I'm confused. He's supposed to be a communist who becomes a liberal. He's supposed to fill everyone's heads with revolutionary ideas, and then lead the world to selfishness. I know that's what happens, I've read the history. But...'

'But what?'

'But he's just, well, trying to do the right thing maybe.'

'You were expecting to find that all in his head? All your history plotted out? You're the idealist, Sira.'

'He isn't supposed to be balanced. He isn't supposed to be talking sense. It's dressed up in silly language and he has no sense of pride but he isn't plotting selfishness. But someone must be! Where are they?'

'I don't know. I could tell you if I was connected to the web. Unless we're staying here for thirty or so years, maybe we aren't going to find out.'

'Great. So, what about the plumber?'

'What about him?'

'I've already told Veenings. It's done'

Westminster, London, 7th November 2017

Advanced centrifuges, missile ranges, uranium stockpiles

'Geoffrey, so good to see you again.' Ron Howser stood in the doorway ready to greet his special guests, his arms open wide forming a firm and purposeful T-shape against his hard-looking body which was wrapped in a crisp white shirt and fashionably narrow-collared suit.

'Good to see you Ambassador. You've been in the UK quite a while now, haven't you?'

'You could say that. I was born here. Left when I was ten, been here for the past three years.'

'Sorry, that's right,' mumbled Geoffrey, scolding himself for the mistake while stepping out of the way to join Daniel at the back of the room and enabling the ambassador to greet the next guest.

'Good canapes.'

'Same as ever, Geoffrey.'

'He's a good bloke, isn't he? That Ron fella. Very friendly.'

'True, but I think you need to stay close to him and maybe not let him own the room so much. He needs *you*, remember. It's E-bit's first facility outside of Israel. But how do you feel about it? I thought you'd have preferred flats over a military thing? That's what got side-lined, isn't it? Would have thought your constituents would welcome affordable flats, rather than jobs that will probably go to posh grads.'

'You never know who you'll get with flats. I'd take a hundred idealistic Labour-voting graduates that E-bit will bring in over a few hundred aspiring Tories moving into my seat, any day.' Geoffrey looked serious, as though he was teaching Daniel a moral lesson.

'Geoffrey Brown MP,' interjected the Israeli Ambassador, 'may I introduce you to British Ambassador, Simon Mencer? You will have read about him, I'm sure, but I don't believe you have met yet.'

'No,' Mencer got in first, 'but I'm sure we will get along famously, won't we, Geoffrey? I've heard great things about you.'

Geoffrey turned his head just fast enough to catch a wink from Daniel.

'Ah, and our final guests,' declared Ron, 'David, Isaac and, of course, James. Why am I not surprised that you arrived together? Come in, come in.'

'It's your job to welcome people, isn't it, Geoffrey?' Isaac said under his breath, as the pair shook hands. Geoffrey caught Daniel raising his eyebrows. 'Right then!' Geoffrey muttered in response, picking up a large glass of red and launching into a short pre-prepared monologue about the relationship between progressive Brits and Israelis.

Daniel took up his position at the far corner of the table, leaving an empty space between himself and the next guest. The habit of a bag carrier: half involved and half communicating wordlessly with the waiting staff. The five men, he knew, would be too self-absorbed to notice he had distanced himself. From another force of habit, he took out a pad and pen ready to capture what interesting nuggets fell from the lips of Simon and Ron. He did not have any immediate use for this information anymore but reassured himself that, if it were good information, he would draft a little email to his successor.

'Daphna, come in,' bellowed Ron, interrupting Geoffrey's speech.

Daniel turned to David to see that he, like Geoffrey, was sporting an expression of surprise and discomfort. The imposing woman who had entered the room, armed with a large pile of messy black hair pinned on her head and a man with an earpiece, towered over Ron Howser.

'Ron, how lovely to see you again,' Daphna declared. 'It must be...'

'About ten months, since the last IDC conference.'

'Yes, of course. Thank you for the invitation Ambassador.'

'My pleasure. I didn't know you were in town until this afternoon. I'm very glad you could make it at such short notice.'

James stood up and casually walked over to greet his wife, pretending not to look surprised to see her.

'I feel like I'm always in this town, plus it's nice to see my husband once in a while. I changed my plans to make it. This is my escort,' pointing towards her security. 'I hope you don't mind if he perches on one of these little chairs.'

Geoffrey let out an inappropriately loud laugh.

'Of course, it means something different here, doesn't it?' asserted Daphna, expertly defusing the seedy atmosphere created by the MP. 'You must be Geoffrey Brown, I've heard a lot about you.'

Daniel laughed to himself as the confident newcomer put the MP in his place, then resumed his efforts to shuffle the chairs to make space for one more around the table.

Before Geoffrey could decide whether to respond to Daphna or continue his speech, the Israeli ambassador had expertly positioned himself at the head of the table to address the guests himself. Geoffrey shrugged a little and took his seat between David and the British ambassador.

'We met her on our visit Geoffrey,' whispered David, 'She served us tea.'

'Oh, how jolly,' remarked Geoffrey, sarcastically.

'Daphna does a lot of work to open up Israeli security roles to poorer communities,' the British ambassador added.

'Mr Brown,' Daphna said softly as she sat down opposite the MP.

'Geoffrey, please.'

'I believe you are visiting us quite soon?'

'Yes, a couple of months.'

'Oh good. Do you like the opera?'

'As a matter of fact, I do. I got into it quite recently. If anything, an evening of culture is a great way to avoid bumping into your colleagues.' Geoffrey looked around and remembered there were no other MPs in the room to laugh at his joke.

'Oh, is it not popular here?' Daphna asked with a genuinely concerned look.

'Sorry, that's not what I meant. Yes, it's very popular in London.'

'Well, I must take you to the opera in Tel Aviv when you visit. Your wife loved it. I think it suited her that evening. She must have missed you so much, she had a look of beautiful tragedy in her eyes.'

'Sorry? I think you must be mistaken. My wife hasn't been to Israel in years.'

'Oh, I'm sorry. You're right,' Daphna said after a moment's hesitation. 'We have so many visitors.'

The table fell quiet until the security escort tapped Geoffrey on the shoulder. 'Mr Brown, I believe you had lunch with my boss recently,' the agent mumbled in a deep monotone.

'Oh yes?' Geoffrey turned, slightly embarrassed at the lapse in protocol which no one else seemed to notice.

'Founder of E-bit. He's also the deputy ambassador. Sort of a political hobby, now he's made his money. He recruited me.'

Geoffrey reached out to shake the man's hand, hoping a pleasantry would conclude the unexpected conversation. His hand was left hanging as the security sat back in silence.

Geoffrey turned back to the table, grabbed a piece of bread and nervously spread a couple of inches of butter on it, hoping the strange man behind him would leave him alone. He was relieved to hear a sharp clang of cutlery on champagne glass, which turned everyone's attention to James.

'I want to thank you all for coming this evening, some of you at very short notice. I want to say a couple of thank yous, Firstly to our great friend Geoffrey Brown MP for hosting us this evening. You and your colleagues do a wonderful job telling the truth about our little country here in Parliament. And to Simon Mencer, Britain's new Ambassador to Israel who has already made his mark. Twice the coverage of any of his predecessors in his first month, I believe. Is that right Simon?'

--

Despite being uneasy about the surprise guest list, Daniel watched the evening pass before him like so many had before. The outsiders, or Strangers as they were known in this place, took it in turns to speak for ten minutes each on their chosen and unrelated subjects. The main agenda, briefing the room on James's invention and its social purpose, predictably did not get a significant hearing. But, given David's phone call to Daniel earlier that day, the straying off topic was welcome.

Geoffrey turned to Daniel a few times during the meal when the intricacies of European terror funding went over his head, but apart from that he seemed to be enjoying himself, so much so that he scribbled down some Written Parliamentary Questions ready for stuffing into the internal post.

At the end of the evening, Daniel's pad had collected some fresh but largely useless phrases:

'The reason Brits obsess over the Palestinians is that you feel guilty about your empire. They are weak, so you want to give them something. We think they are weak, so they should stop pretending otherwise.'

'It's funny when the only optimist round the table is the arms dealer.'

'People like the kibbutz because it is romantic and sounds hippy. But few European non-Jews, apart from the gays, like the real Israel.'

On a separate page, Daniel had written up a table of old and advanced centrifuge numbers, missile ranges and uranium stockpiles. He failed to capture a lot of what Daphna said because her best comments were made directly to him. She was into complexity theory and was speaking about how the army had got better results from letting units find their own way to solutions rather than using command and control. It led to some strange outcomes, like junior soldiers being able to put up roadblocks but only senior ones being able to take them down, but also to some exciting advances in intelligence gathering techniques, apparently.

Liverpool,
23rd January 1969

Time stretched out slowly

'Sira, pass me the card, would you. Just one sheet. I've thought of another one... Listen, Geoffrey says you guys had a lovely Christmas in London. Is there something I can do to help? He really likes you, you know. Is it because you might not stick around? That's what he thinks.'

Sira had felt too guilty to see him, but his friends – her friends – would not stop trying to broker a reunion. 'I don't know. Can we just do the cards, Valerie?'

'He said you'd talked more about home when he saw you last.'

'I guess I have. Bit homesick, maybe. But I'm not going home. I couldn't get back if I wanted to.'

'That's a funny thing to say. Steerage is pretty cheap. I can see they're sending you enough money for clothes so I'm sure they could pay for a ticket. That's what Geoffrey thinks anyway. Thinks you're gearing up to telling him something.'

'No. Nothing. Promise. Please, Valerie, let's just focus on your placards.'

'You aren't going to design one yourself?'

'No, I'm happy doing the colours on yours. What will it be?'

'OK, great. Pass me a fat brush covered in blue. It's going to say: "Good homes for all – he's got homes to spare!"'

'Very good. Make me one of those as well, will you?'

'Sure. I guess since you two aren't talking, he hasn't told you the plan?'

'No.'

Valerie stood up excitedly and acted out her words, with a finished placard across her back. 'Tonight is the Chancellor's dinner. Once we'll all full of energy at the housing protest, we're going to walk down Brownlow Hill and stop Salisbury's car. He'll have to turn back to his nice hotel. Then, when the university is up in arms about what we've done, we'll occupy the new administration building. Your idea of getting the tenants involved has really heated things up. They're raring to go. We didn't see it coming, but Geoffrey tells me notices are flying round the pubs along the docks.'

Half an hour later, Sira paced up and down the corridor waiting for Veenings to return.

'Miss, he said he might be a while,' called his secretary through the open door. 'Why don't you do something else and then come back?'

But Sira could not think of anything else. Her last conversation with Veenings had been tough. He had said they knew she was squatting illegally and stealing money, and had threatened her with immediate expulsion if she didn't sleep with the plumber but she had refused. She had broken down in tears in his office at the thought of hurting Geoffrey and begged the professor not to make her. He had replied that she had broken Geoffrey already.

'Here he is, miss,' yelled the secretary.

She turned to see Veenings walking down the narrow, low-ceilinged corridor towards her. Together with the man to his left they filled the space, like a wall approaching her ready to crush her like in some 1990s' computer game.

'I believe you've met Mr R.'

Clean shaven and wearing an expensive suit, Jack looked like a different man. His personality was somehow flipped by his clothes, his previously kind-looking face now smirking and aggressive. 'Sira, good to see you again. You look surprised.'

'I just don't...'

'Don't understand? Well, we generally rely on that. We needed you close to Geoffrey. He is a jealous sort, used to getting his own way. You were a virgin. He was being too polite, taking things too slow. We needed to spur him on.'

'But the whole solider story, in the nightclub? Why would that work on a student?'

'I know you're not a student, remember. I knew then. I didn't know about your weird fascination with defence policy, not until after I'd shagged you. But you'd be surprised how often the girls like a soldier. Tough and vulnerable.'

Sira felt sick. The two men watched as she slumped to the floor. Each fragment of memory she sought to grip slipped away from her. 'So,' she took a deep breath to fight the stomach acid, 'you, Professor, you're his handler?'

'No, don't be ridiculous. You'd never meet my handler. Anyway, we didn't expect to see you here, did we, Veenings?'

The professor looked pale. Sira could see the revelations of the afternoon had taken him beyond his comfort zone. For the first time, she realised he was as trapped as she was.

'So, you're off to the protest little lady? There's going to be fireworks!' said Mr R with wide grin.

'It's done, then? The plan with the plumber?'

'Yeah, his wife, she's done. I had to show her who's boss mind. Took her right there on the kitchen table you so kindly described for us.' He patted Sira on the head, who was still sitting on the floor focused on her breathing. 'Wasn't easy! Knew the plumber was on his way back so had to be quick. Didn't want to get whacked round the head by a wrench or something. But it all worked out. Came and left if you see what I mean!' He patted her again. 'What a sight for a man to see as he gets home from work. His wife on the floor like that. Poor bastard. And by a student and all.'

'What, you, um.' Sira took another deep breath.

'Yeah, pretty simple, really. Left behind one of those horrid canvas bags you like. Exam paper signed by Mr Brown and a flyer for the demo. Off there now, in fact.

'Yes. Please just go. Leave me,' sobbed Sira.

'That's nice! OK. Get up little lady, you're coming with me.'

'I don't think I can. I feel terrible.'

'You bloody well will. Come here.' Mr R grabbed her by the wrist and pulled her out of Veenings's office and down the corridor. 'Stop shaking, will you? You know what I'm like. You don't want to feel it for yourself, do you? Remember, I've seen you around, I've followed you. I know what you're capable of. No need to play the fool with me.'

Mr R frog-marched Sira through the grounds, past the Guild and into Abercrombie Square. Sira closed her eyes and thought of the first time she was here being looked after by Valerie and taken to her first pub. The music was so full and vibrant, the singing and laughter so easy. Now, just a few months later, the cold had won. The frozen air distorted her vision, pulling down blinds of ash and sleet. A few steps further and they would be opposite Senate House, opposite the banners and protestors.

Mr R pulled her onto Oxford Road. Geoffrey was standing on the steps, yelling into a metal cone to 150, maybe 200, students mixed with tenants, brown-woollen suits mixed with ashen black overalls. They were walking twenty yards down the hill and twenty yards back up, thrusting their banners into the air. Valerie was at the bottom of the hill, handing out the banners that she and Sira had painted.

Geoffrey turned to see the newest recruits and stopped his rousing speech mid-sentence. He looked at Sira holding hands with another student and nodded gently with understanding. John, standing to his left, scowled. Valerie and Peter stood in shock.

Time stretched out slowly. Sira turned to face Mr R, his grin still wide, and thrust her elbow into his chest whilst grabbing hold of his collar for balance. Her knee rose up high into his chin and she was free. His body did not fall to the ground until she was halfway across the road.

Her friends' faces changed again. Geoffrey dropped his megaphone. A car to Sira's right slipped through a rainbow of colours before crashing to a halt. She fell to the floor, unable to steady her pendulous momentum. A man approached, and she reached out for his help. But he ignored her and marched towards Geoffrey.

'Fucking students. Don't believe anything those fuckers say. You, you, posh cunt. You fucked my wife.' He was waving a piece of paper in his hand, slowly and then in an impossible blur. 'This here. Here, you cunt! This says you fucked my wife.'

'Sira, are you OK?' Valerie was crouching behind her, lifting her up. The plumber's car stopped over her legs, an inch from her face.

'You could have killed her!' Peter was yelling at the plumber from a safe distance.

'I feel sick.'

Men and women with banners backed off slowly into the street, leaving the steps vacant for the approaching dual.

'Who is he Sira? That man yelling? And who's this?' asked Valerie, pointing towards the smartly dressed man on the floor.

'Slow down, Valerie, I can't hear you,' replied Sira, her eyes fixed on the steps of Senate House.

She watched the pipe in Brian's hand smash through Geoffrey's head like a meat cleaver. Blood fanned out across the card and fabric banners, and Valerie's scream shattered Sira's ears. Then the traffic started again, blurring up and down the road with beams of light. The people were gone but she saw traces of movement. Streams of dark colours criss-crossed her vision, intersecting with metal, but nothing touched her.

As time cycled forward, it sped up. Soon there was only white light and white noise. The burning sun glanced off her face and the asphalt ran under her like a river. As the temperature grew and the bone-shaking vibrations smoothed, her vision was pulled inwards, down into a tunnel. Her body careered through nearly a century, a field of soil and concrete fragments breaking her fall.

Westminster, London, 8th November 2017

Maybe it's not always about you Geoffrey

'So, as I'm sure you gathered from last night, Isaac has invested a huge amount in this on David and my suggestion, and on your committee colleagues' interest. But what I wanted to flag was that, is that,' Daniel heard his voice crack with nervousness against the acoustics of the Portcullis atrium, 'E-bit is a faster way of getting that investment back. That's why I think they will offer you a directorship when you next see them. I wanted to warn you.'

'Me? Oh, right. That isn't really what I had in mind Daniel. I mean, I knew they would want some strategic advice, but I wasn't going to accept money for it. Not for the time being anyway. I'd imagine that would be a conflict of interest with my committee chairmanship. I'd prefer to focus on just the one avenue – getting the government to take up James's tech with a community-based pilot. That will raise its profile and be actual policy in action. That will show Timothy and his band of idiots,' said Geoffrey, smiling to himself.

'Yeah, that's what I mean Geoffrey. It's got a bit awkward.'

'Awkward how?'

'E-bit are buying James's technology. They're buying the full rights. There won't be a UK civilian pilot.'

Geoffrey stared into Daniel's eyes and crushed his disposable coffee cup in his hand. 'A bit awkward, Daniel. What you are saying now doesn't work for me at all. I'm not even sure I could ever take up the directorship. Why didn't you tell me before the dinner, for God's sake?'

'That's what I'm trying to say. I told you what I knew before the dinner. You didn't really listen. But I didn't realise it had got as far as it had.'

'I'm going to have to fight you on this, I'm afraid, and talk some sense into Isaac. He will make his money. But my colleagues know I'm involved. I need to make a success of this. If it's only a defence thing, I've lost all credibility. The mood's changed after the last Gaza war. I'd no longer be Mr Business, but Mr War Criminal!'

'Don't talk to Isaac just yet. I'll talk to him first. And don't say that last bit. It sounds ungrateful.'

'Ungrateful? I'm not his bloody servant, Daniel. Don't fucking mess me around here. And what was that stuff about Julia that crazy woman with the hair was saying?'

'I really don't know about that, Geoffrey. She must have been mistaken. Just too strange. I'll text you this evening, I've got to go. But one thing, what was that Parliamentary Question?'

'Something about British banks and Iran. I don't know. It sounds tough, anyway. The rest was a bit complicated. But I can do the sanctions thing. It fits.'

'OK, just be careful.'

'Careful. They're your friends. You set it up.'

'I never mentioned tabling official questions. I tried to say something at the end, but...'

'But what?'

'I forgot.'

'What's the problem?'

'You just, you know, don't want to create a paper trail. Anything that suggests you've been introducing strange characters to the British ambassador.'

'Me? It was their dinner! Your dinner!'

'No, Geoffrey, as far as anyone else will be concerned it was your dinner in your name.'

'Shit, Daniel. It was a lot easier when you, you know...'

'When I made no money?'

'It's really changed since Lara, hasn't it?'

'Lara? It's my job.'

'You know what I mean. You used to be happy with a few glasses of wine with me and Julia.'

'Look, we are just looking out for ourselves as well. I didn't used to look out for me at all. But we have rent to pay and lives to lead. We aren't an MP support service. But I said I will see what I can do. This isn't me doing this, Geoffrey. I'm just passing on a message, and I will pass yours back.'

'Great. I imagine you can make it to the door without an escort.'

'I'll text you later.' Daniel stepped out into the bitingly fresh air and took a deep breath while watching a few expensive dark cars deposit expensive-looking people at the front steps. They would be frisked like everyone else. Maybe, he hoped, they would also be knocked a few rungs down by whoever they were seeing.

--

'Julia, there is a Daniel Silver here to see you.'

'Really? Oh, right, yes, he can come in.'

'Hi Julia. How are you? I called earlier and they said you were in the office. I hope you don't mind.'

'Spying on me, Daniel? You're a lobbyist, remember, not an agent. I know you get carried away. Anyway, yes, I'm well, but not great. I wasn't right about enjoying the independence thing. I seem to be stuck in here with only first and second years to teach since my little unintentional falling out.'

'Why don't you just publish the revision your colleagues are asking for and back down then? Anyway, I thought you'd been on a dig?'

Julia looked at him with deep exasperation. 'Please, Daniel, just get to the point. I'm tired. I just got back.'

'Sorry, yes. I need your advice.'

'Of course you do! I've just got off the phone with Geoffrey.'

'Really?'

'Yes, really. We are married you know. We do talk.'

'Yes, fine. So, what do you think I should do?'

'I don't often say this, but he's right. He needs something to show for this, otherwise he is in quite a mess. It only works for him if it is about community. It can't be some defence thing, that is obviously not what his dear leader is looking for. That is the way of shabby former foreign secretaries and worse. Just remember, you're the link in all of this. Maybe you could do the honourable thing?'

'I know. But I've tried to explain.' Daniel sat down and tried to get out his words without confusing himself. 'There was always a defence angle. The kibbutz gets funding from the defence community. I didn't think there was any reason why we shouldn't use it to do both defence and community. The two shouldn't be separate, Julia.'

'Daniel!' Julia shouted. 'Enough! No one else thinks this, other than you. Clearly Isaac doesn't. You've got principles, but they're unique, to say the least. You work for venture capitalists, rich men, and they've screwed over my husband!'

'You're telling me to quit my job if Isaac doesn't listen? How would that help?'

'Because you can brief against him. Tell the papers or something. I'm not an expert. Embarrass them and ruin the deal. No deal, no link to Geoff.'

'Jesus.' Daniel's stomach crunched in a way which it had not for many months. The veneer of confidence had been stripped off by an intellect and morality he could not falter. He sat down, hoping it would pass.

'I'm going to be ruthless for Geoffrey in a way which I can't be for myself. That's the deal when you marry a politician. You're a unit. Why are you looking at me like that?'

'I've just not heard you talk like that before.'

'If you can think of another plan, Daniel, let me know, but there is no easy chat with me and Geoffrey on the sofa this time. You're all grown up now.'

Daniel's stomach crunched again, demanding to find a toilet. 'Right, fine, I'll think about it, but I think you overestimate how much Isaac listens to me.'

--

'He didn't listen to me Lara. There are plenty of other friends of Israel on the backbenches to work with he said. He said I'd got Geoffrey into this mess.'

'Daniel, you haven't. He's been having dinners with all sorts for years. You said so yourself. He's a big boy who likes playing with bigger boys. It was always going to get him in the end. You can't destroy yourself for him.'

'The Browns have given me a lot. They probably got me this job.'

'Look, I know he's a friend and you have a thing for Julia, which is a bit weird since you're mates with her husband and you live with me.'

Daniel sat up firmly against the headboard in protest.

'Don't say anything, it's fine. We all have fantasies, Daniel. But you are putting too much on yourself. We have this tiny, extortionate flat to pay for. They have that huge house that taxpayers have paid for. Geoffrey messes up his own career all the time. Julia seems no different. And they are at the end of their careers. We are at the beginning.'

'Yes, exactly. I'm at the beginning. I don't have the power to build something new. I wanted to work for a charity, for fuck's sake, or open a record store.'

'A record store?'

'Whatever. If I stick with this, Lara, I think Julia's right – I'll just be supporting the arms trade. I don't want to.'

'Since when have you had an issue with that? You've been doing this for years. I've always been the squeamish one.'

'You work for a campus charity. It's a bit different.'

'A campus think tank sponsored by E-bit. If you do this Daniel. If you do what Julia wants, my job won't be safe either.'

'Fine. But I'm going out. I need to think.'

'Out? It's nearly ten o'clock!'

--

'I don't know what you're talking about,' Geoffrey hissed into his phone. 'Hold on, I'm still in bed. I'll call you right back.'

'What is it, Geoffrey?' Julia snapped from her pillow.

'Tom's yelling about something. God knows what this time.'

'Great. It's Sunday. Close the door, will you. Go downstairs.'

'Tom, what is it?'

'It's like working with a fucking dinosaur!' he shouted at Geoffrey down the phone.

'Tom, we're the same age.'

'So why can't you set up a fucking Google alert? Why am I ringing you and you not ringing to warn me?'

'What?'

'You can search whilst fucking speaking at the same time you know!'

'Just tell me Tom!'

'Your wife is fucking an Israeli arms dealer.'

'What on earth? My wife is an archaeologist. If she's going to fuck someone other than me, it would be a minor character from *Time Team* or someone who looks like Michael Caine in *Educating Rita.*'

'That's not funny. It's in the *Mail*. It's a good one, so it will be everything tomorrow. There is already a Buzzfeed about it!'

--

'Daniel, I don't know what to say.'

'I know, I'm looking at it now.'

'Pardon?'

'I don't know where this came from Geoffrey. Listen, did Julia tell you about our conversation last week? The day we spoke. The day I texted you about Isaac?'

'Yeah, she said something about you quitting and doing the honourable thing by me.'

'Well, sort of. She wanted me to brief against Isaac to distance you from the whole E-bit thing. It wasn't just quitting in solidarity, it was exposing them as well to get them to back off.'

'Right. What?'

'Well, I did that. I briefed against him. I went for a long walk and I decided she was right. My contact said it would be in this Sunday's edition.'

'Julia knows shit all about the media, but you do. Maybe you could have threatened Isaac and David – but actually briefing a story? It just makes me part of it, doesn't it?'

Geoffrey shouted in short, clipped sentences that stabbed through Daniel's intestines.

'But I, I didn't tell them anything about you or Julia. I told them about E-bit and the kibbutz. That was supposed to be the story. Anyway, I did threaten them first. Well, I explained you were upset. And it turns out they don't give a shit. Got them together in a room, and then they just talked over me. Used it as an excuse to catch up on other stuff. They really didn't care that it would embarrass you. They said you are a big boy, that there were no monetary implications and, even if there were, they weren't liable. I'm sorry.'

'I'm not massively surprised, Daniel.'

'Yeah well, I was upset and angry. So I called her, the journalist. Lara told me not to, but I couldn't let it go.'

'Right.'

Daniel could hear Geoffrey calming down as resignation and confusion overtook the search for a solution. 'But why the stuff about Julia? Why say she is having an affair? Why link me to E-bit? I can't believe I'm asking this: is she having an affair?'

'That's it. I wouldn't do anything to hurt her, or you. I was trying to protect you.'

'Is she, Daniel?'

'No. I've no idea.'

'Yes, I think we all know that now. We just have to live with the consequences of you not having any fucking idea. I guess you'll tell me the same thing, but why did they write about the directorship. Did you tell them that?'

'No, Geoffrey. You're not listening.' Daniel closed his eyes and flopped backwards onto his friend's spare bed where he'd been hiding for a few days. Lara was calling as well but he pressed the ignore button and calmed his breathing. 'It's the same journalist I spoke to, but this isn't my story. It's twisted. Someone has given them lot's more. Retaliation, maybe. But the whole thing is done. E-bit, James, Daphna, you, Julia, me, Isaac, Daniel, Ron, Simon, everyone. Even that weird guy sitting behind you at the dinner. Plus, this affair thing. I expect Lara's been fired now too.'

'Maybe, Daniel.'

'What do you mean?'

'Well, maybe she called it in.'

'No, no way. She didn't want me to do anything.'

'Perhaps Daniel, but Lara's the only person Julia's been talking to. Since you brought her over here, they've called a few times. Maybe more, that's just on the rare occasions I've been around. Talking about Israel a lot.'

'But Israel? She doesn't go to Israel.'

'You know she does. Daphna said at the dinner.'

'That wasn't a mistake?'

'No Daniel, it wasn't. But it's all too weird. What she told me doesn't make sense anymore.'

Daniel waited.

'You know she'd clashed with a colleague. Always bloody arguing with colleagues. Well, another colleague who's not in the fight helped her out. God knows why. Maybe he was trying to fuck her too. It was getting tough in the department and he told her there was a place for her on a dig near Haifa, something Roman, and that she could help him with an article he was writing, comparing the artefacts with those found in Europe. She went. I wish I wasn't telling you all this. And she didn't fuck him, she fucked someone else.'

'When did she? Sorry, Geoffrey, I'm just trying to piece this together. When did she tell you?'

'After that dinner in Parliament, I asked her about what Daphna had said and she started crying. She said she was pissed off with me for not being around, ruining her life. She said she wanted to do something for herself and thought it was a bit of fun to not tell me and to lie and say she was in France. She said if she'd mentioned where she was going I'd have, in her words, gone on and on about work.'

Daniel felt sorry for Geoffrey, then guilty after remembering it was he who had brought him into it, and finally jealous of whoever this Israeli guy was. He heard Geoffrey's voice faintly crack and then the twisting sound of the breaking of a plastic seal around a bottle neck.

'He got a flat tyre near the dig Julia was working at, and that's how they got talking. Turns out he worked for some defence company as I said and, instead of staying in a cheap hotel with the others, she stayed a few nights with him. They went on fucking dates, Daniel! Maybe if it was just sex it would be better. But they went on fucking dates.'

Daniel let his head sink a little deeper into his pillow and put the phone on speaker so he could hear it through the stuffing wrapped around his ears.

'As you know, it's a small world over there, so he ended up introducing her to Daphna.'

'So maybe it was Daphna? Maybe she's behind this?'

'Why Daniel? Why would she tell someone, after she'd told the whole dinner, and after she was probably in for making a packet from the deal Isaac and Daniel were putting together? It doesn't make sense. Julia promises Daphna didn't know about her thing with Boaz. That's his name, fucking Boaz – what kind of a name is that? Boaz introduced Julia to Daphna as a friend. And Julia had no idea that Daphna was involved in our thing.'

'OK, so who does stand to gain?'

'People who hate me?'

Maybe, Daniel thought. But maybe it's not always about you Geoffrey.

Liverpool,
16ᵗʰ December 2053

They weren't the best men

'Ahhhh'

'Sira. Wake up!'

'Ahhhh. What's that pain?'

'Electric current. Yours. I told you, remember.'

'Stop stop Captain. I'm here. I'm awake.'

'We're back.'

'Back. Right. Oh shit. How?'

'If you're asking me why we came back, then I have no information. I'm amazed you survived. That was thirty hours we travelled. Over eighty years in thirty hours. You've got burns. You're dehydrated. I think we passed through a few hot summers. Lucky that you weren't somewhere hotter. It's just your hand and cheek burned, I think.'

'Shit, turn off your web connection. Off!'

'Quick thinking Sira! I can be who I'm supposed to be. I can contact the gang and they'll come and get you. Except.'

'Except what?'

'Except I didn't message anyone. Didn't connect.'

'Why?'

'Signal's too patchy, perhaps. I don't know why to be honest. Maybe I'm broken.'

Sira pushed herself up from the ground and looked at the wasteland that stretched around her. There was nothing except for two tall buildings that blocked her view of the river.

'We're still in Liverpool. Those are the cathedrals.'

'They can't see us either Sira. They can't track your implant any more anyway. I've done something to it. I don't know why.'

'What?'

'I don't want to talk about it. I've done something to it. You can use it, when there's signal. They can't see you, I promise.'

314

'Promise? Where's my confident little Captain?'

'I can tell you're smiling. I can tell you're making fun of me. Stop it. I've still got his temperament. His predilection for anger, for revenge. But...'

'Yes?'

'The trip's done something to me. You were silent. I had no one to talk or listen to for days after that.'

'What?'

'That, Sira! That! What we did.'

A wave of blood splatter flashed before her, merged with strobing light. She stood with her hands on her knees, tried to focus, and then threw up.

'We got him killed'

'Shut up, Captain'

'I've got self-doubt.'

A piercing high-pitched scream burst through her head, pulling her temples inwards.

'Stop stop, Captain. You'll kill me too.'

She woke again, having passed out in the rubble.

'Sorry. I've got doubt. It's a new thing. I needed to re-programme myself. It was in a loop.'

'More human every day, Captain.'

'But we did kill him'

'I know. I tried to stop it, but it was too late. It was always too late. Once I'd sent that note, it was done. They'd never have missed that chance. I just wish I'd listened more.'

Sira picked herself up again and took a few steps. Beyond the immediate upturned gravel and asphalt, which was once Oxford Road, there was a smoother area. She wandered over to it, looking for somewhere more comfortable to sit. It was like a previously unearthed archaeological site. Between the footprints of buildings was smooth concrete and, within the stumps of former walls, were complex, intersecting lines and towers, former walls, passages for cabling and sewers, and hardened boxes for stairwells and lifts.

After taking a seat on a low wall, she began to understand her surroundings. She soon picked out the site of the pub and the square, the centre of which was still undeveloped but was now mud and curling weeds rather than grass. Immediately in

315

front of her were the collapsed front steps where Geoffrey had last stood. Forgetting the time that had passed, she looked for traces of blood.

'What happened here, Captain?'

'Look for yourself.'

'I can't. I don't have any signal.'

'If you don't, I don't.'

'Right, so, tell me. How are you so sure we're back if you're not connected.'

'I got connected earlier. Briefly. It's swirling up there. It's strange. You were still unconscious. There are no signal towers around here, so must have been a passing satellite. It's gone now or blocked by all that.'

Sira looked up beyond the cathedral towers and took in the heavy, solid clouds smoothly blanketing the sky, painting its curvature from horizon to horizon. *'What happened here?'*

'The little data I got said we were near Mount Pleasant station, Liverpool, Ministry of Defence.'

'But we were at the University. There wasn't anything military there.'

'Not then there wasn't Sira. But things change. We're lucky we weren't buried in a wall amidst all that change, all those years.'

'Yes, I feel lucky,' Sira replied, sarcastically.

'At least no one is currently trying to kidnap you, kill you or force you to kill someone else.'

'For now, Captain, for now. Let's find that base and get some shelter.'

--

'That's quite a story.'

Major Finegold's bearded face floated in a grainy black-and-white screen set in the heavy metal door of a building that, according to the plaque, was once the Liverpool Maternity Hospital.

The top half of the building was missing, the brick arches and other ornate features cut off before they could meet each other in a previous era's version of grandeur. Across the top now sat a thin concrete lid and, above that, some solar panels.

'You know, my great grandmother was the one that kicked this whole thing off. Made the original discovery that fuels time travel. Nothing came of it for a long-time, nothing but proper science and investigation of the universe. She never thought she was helping to make a weapon, but I guess she wouldn't be the first scientist in history to find themselves accidentally ripping the ground from beneath their children's feet.'

'Are you going to let us in, sir?'

'Major to you.'

'Sorry, can we please come in, Major?'

'Hold on.'

The seal around the door hissed and then released, coating Sira in a light film of dust. Patting herself down, she walked into a short closed-off, red-brick tunnel before the door slammed behind her and the one in front popped open. The vacuum sucked the air out of her lungs and pulled her body forward and onto its knees.

'Sorry about that, miss. I find it's better not to warn people. They seem to panic more if you warn them first.'

Sira lay choking on the floor, slowly regaining her breath. 'Forget about it,' she eventually spluttered. 'As the friend in my head tells me, we've had worse.'

'Shhh. He'll think you're mad.'

'OK, young lady, come through and you'll find something to eat and drink.'

She walked across the threshold of a large, bright, box-like room and paused, taking in the view. Three walls were smooth, bright white plastic, almost silver. In the middle of the floor sat a golden table with ornate upturned legs folded into lion feet. At the edge of the room was a similarly ornate yellow sofa, high at one end and low at the other, as though the sofa itself was lounging. On the table sat a silver tray with a steaming pot, a disposable cup and a foil packet of freeze-dried food. The fourth wall was a screen which lit up once Sira was seated, displaying the bearded face in high resolution.

Finegold sat in an office chair surrounded by terminals, the latter bringing colour to the room. He remained grey in skin and facial hair above a white shirt and coat.

'What is this place?'

'Good, isn't it?' he said excitedly. 'I got it all down in a warehouse near the docks. The place had been closed up for years. Had to bring one of the bots down there to pull all the concrete from the door. But inside, inside it was beautiful!'

She looked at him blankly.

'A bit rich for some,' he asserted, after she gave no response. 'But I think it's authentic. They used to like this sort of stuff in Liverpool. It was once the busiest docks in the country, and they brought in things from all over by boat. It's not really French. Mainly Chinese and Vietnamese copies. Maybe I'll go back down to the docks one day, once whatever is rotting down there, has finished rotting."

'What's rotting?' asked Sira, half hoping to not get an answer.'

'Last of the transfers, or attempted transfers young lady,' Finegold smiled and stared into her eyes before continuing. 'The buses stopped coming for them you see, to get them out of here and take them down south. Some of them then left on foot, but not everyone was up for the walk, so they gathered at the river. It's now just bodies down there.'

'This is recent? The city was emptied recently?'

'Yeah, they've been taking the city apart for years. They'll be in Manchester now, I should think. Then, when the cities are done, they'll scrape up the towns and villages between.'

'The people? You mean they're taking the people?'

'Well, sort of. The people go too. They're here for the buildings. The demolition is all for London.'

'London?'

'Yes, miss. You're from there, aren't you?'

'Yes.'

'I think he's a bit unhinged Sira.'

'It's all for you! More material to keep building London. I've heard that the city now stretches from the coast to past Birmingham. You don't know?'

'No, no, I don't know.'

318

'Captain, what's going on, are we in some kind of alternative universe? Did I do this?' Sira's brain lit up with frenzied static. 'We need to get back to our future, time, now, you know what I mean? Can we?'

'Sira, be quiet. No, you didn't do this. Just be quiet. We can't speak here. He's listening in somehow.'

'Oh, you've got an AI! Very clever,' Finegold boomed into the room. 'Heard of them, but not, you know, had the pleasure. Hold on a moment, I'll plug in then we can both hear it properly. You don't mind, do you?'

Before she could answer, Captain's voice was in both her head and, after an irritating delay, reverberating into the room.

'Captain, what's this alternative universe thing? If you've got intel on how that machine works, would you be so kind as to upload it?'

'You don't know? It's your machine!'

'Me?' Major Finegold released a short smirk and then proceeded to carefully comb his thick white beard with a small, polished implement. 'You like this? Made of ivory. From an elephant. They killed them for it.' He peeled back his lips, revealing his gums and tongue as though he was having trouble drawing breath. 'Found it down by the docks. Girls like you should have one of these.'

'Finegold, do you know how the time machine works or not?' Sira yelled into the screen.

'OK, dear, no need to get excited. Said my great-grandmother made the original discovery. But no, I don't know much. Picked up lots of chatter but couldn't ask for explanations you see. No, this place has got nothing to do with it. This is just an old outpost set up to calm the city. Not that it needs calming now!'

'What are you still doing here then Finegold? Come back to London with us.'

'Shhh, Captain. He doesn't look right. Sooner we get out of this room the better.'

'You know, when the internet started you could live in other worlds. Properly live in there. New name, new face, new abilities, new job. Everything. They called it an avatar. The new you.'

'We'd like to go for a quick walk. Get some air,' Sira interrupted.

'Later, later miss. But what I'm trying to tell you is that few took that avatar stuff seriously. Just some gamers. Few mid-westerners looking for escape from obesity but, for most, it took up too much time. No time, that's the problem. No time between working, eating, making children, caring for children, shitting. Most people, busy people writing about the internet said it should be used to access information. Like everyone was going to spend their time in an encyclopaedia or reading newspapers for the first time or staring at scans of art! Ha! That's what my great grandma thought. Never knew why. She wasn't even into art! But she was always talking about looking at paintings on screens or printing them at home. Always talked about saving time, as though we had something better to do with it. Think it was all that watching clocks under that mountain. You know the story.'

As Finegold got more excited, his voice got too loud for the speakers, causing them to crackle. Sira sat down and held her hands over her ears to reduce the volume, but his voice still got through and curdled with the panicked confusion inside her.

'So, they wrote and talked about access. Then some people said a few clever things. David Bowie, the singer, said a clever thing. He said that it wouldn't be encyclopaedias we all read. He said they were made by professors. He said we would all be able to make our own news. But people mocked him. We are so short-sighted. So hard to imagine the future. No, I think he didn't mean that we would all become news reporters, competing with the corporations to go around the world reporting. No, I think he meant we were the news. We wouldn't outdo the "real news" with different and better stories, we would just say that we were the different and better stories, even if it wasn't true. As he predicted, we turned the cameras round on ourselves and said our faces, our clothes, our genitals, our pets, their clothes and genitals, our yelling, our crying, our putting a brave face on it; that is our news. Maybe predicted that we would also give up on "real news". Not enough time for both you see.

'But still, no avatars,' he screamed and laughed to himself. 'Even as the technology allowed for pretend lives in pretend spaces with real people playing fake people, we all chose to share ourselves in real life. Little flying selfie bots, AI writers to document us, those little phrases that appear under ourselves when you see us in the street, that awful entrance music that used to be in films and now switches to a new track with every face you look at. Why?'

'Don't argue with him, Sira. Sound interested.'

'Because we're sociable?' she mumbled, before taking a deep breath to try and hold back the nausea.

'No, no. Avatars are sociable too! They are.' Major Finegold banged on the desk, accidentally shifting the camera so it tilted and focused on his left eye.

'No, it's because we're egotists. We like short bouts of escapism. A film, a book, an old-fashioned game. But even in these, we start to imagine ourselves. Start to think, ooh, which character am I like? Am I brave like that? Can I fuck and fight like that? We make it about ourselves. We don't want to be anonymous and meet other anonymous people. We want to make ourselves the news, we want to make a version of ourselves that doesn't make people forget who we really are. Halloween costumes used to be a white sheet over your head, to pretend you're a ghost. But they don't do that anymore do they?'

'Say 'no'.'

'No, Major.'

'No. They are a sexy cat, or a sexy witch, or a sexy devil. And that was when they were young. When they were older, the costumes were gone, weren't they? Why make a costume when it will interfere with how you want to be seen? Why be restricted. What did they wear then?'

'No one knows.'

'Exactly, Miss. Precisely right!' Finegold hit the desk again, and now the camera was sideways on his left eye, where a tear began to form. 'Tell me, Miss.'

'They – didn't – go – to – parties – any – more,' she squeezed out of her vocal chords, amidst the radio static pushing at her temples. 'They stayed at home. For costume parties they shared images of themselves with super-imposed clothes.'

'Exactly! Augmented reality! Why walk around a party with your fat bits hanging out, when you can control the whole image? Why waste time travelling to the best party, looking for your friends, when your bodies could be projected into every implant in every mind? Why not coordinate costumes and nakedness and fucking in short little films?' he yelled.

'No need to travel, no need for make-up, no need for thinking, no space for community, just you being a fake. Why go to a party, or read or do anything, when you can make the news and sell some advertising along with it? All you kids do that. How long would I have to search before I found you, or a version of you?'

'Keep quiet Sira. He's got us trapped.'

'I want to escape the human condition, Sira! That's the goal. I've seen the human condition and I do not want to embrace it.'

'I'm sorry, Major,' said Sira, hoping she could placate him, but he continued, spitting anger about fake people, fake money and fake relationships.

While Sira tried to shut the noise out of her head, her mind turned to memories. In all her time in Liverpool, she thought, she had found just snippets of what she had been told, of what she had always been sure would be there. Fragments of socialism, but nothing worth killing for. There were pernicious ideas here and there but, even if she put everyone she met together, all the ideas they spoke of, there was nothing that amounted to a plot to bring down the country. They all seemed too cautious to be the architects of her world, too mild to be the cause of this angry, grey eye staring at her, imprisoning her.

Geoffrey was just trying to make things a little better. Even when he held her close in his small bed and romanticised about a better world, there was not much to it. His political heroes were careful nationalists, people who wanted to make families and institutions strong, not crush them. She'd goaded him into being more sweeping, she'd plied him with false stories of modern California, but he did not take the bait. And yet she had killed him anyway, bringing the anger of her world into his peaceful one.

Finegold had stopped talking.

'You going to tell us what happened, then?' yelled Captain across the room's speakers.

'Not much to tell, I'm afraid. My men found something in the clear out.'

'The bodies?'

'No, no, well, sort of. The bodies weren't there yet. No, before the clear-out our headquarters sent us barrels of this stuff. This facility is really just one big chemical mixing plant where we make something that thins out mortar. It gets sprayed onto old brick buildings and after a few minutes you've got a pile of loose bricks that are easy to remove. The problem is that this stuff is highly volatile. Spray it on wrongly and it can explode. So, rather than send it here premixed, they sent us the constituent parts and we made huge quantities of it ready for spraying from above. One of those parts is highly toxic, radioactive until mixed.

'On the last day, when all the bricks, breeze blocks and girders had been loaded up and taken and the last buses of people had gone south, a few of my men and I went to do an inventory before clearing this place out.

'On the last day, there was an accident. I was in the main warehouse and one of these young idiots backed his forklift into a can of the stuff and onto me. He looked at me – I could see him calculating – and then he ran. Jumped out of his cab, de-suited and fled. I watched him in my implant as I called out to the others. He promised them the money from my room if they went along with it, and then he cut the comms. Not good men.'

'Are you sick?'

'By the time I'd hacked my way out of the warehouse and got in the chemical wash, it had got into my bloodstream.'

'You said there were bodies down there, rotting?'

'Yeah, there wasn't enough room for them on the last bus and my guys were worried, if they called in another one, someone would come here and see what they'd done to me. So, instead, they sprayed them with the stuff. I saw it all from here. They melted their lungs. Look.'

The screen changed from Finegold's eye to a dark room, obscured by swirling smoke. A man in loose, torn clothes was walking around in circles at the upper edge of the image, occasionally stopping and bending to hold his knees before standing up and continuing his unsteady pace. The camera zoomed into the room and a sound began rising from the silence. After a moment, Sira realised it was crying. As the camera got closer, she saw it was not clothes hanging from him, but sheets of red, raw skin. 'Is this now? How is he not dead?'

'He's dead now,' Finegold replied, and zoomed into him, encircling his limbs and navigating around exposed bone and organs.

Sira looked away, but Finegold yelled at her to keep watching, which she did through squinted eyes. The camera floated into the next room, a part of a warehouse where she saw tens of people all doing the same walk, all watching their own bodies drip to the floor.

'They did this for a few hours. Walked around like this. So, I joined them.'

'But you said you stayed here!'

'Yes, Sira. But my avatar joined them to experience it. You can too!'

Before Sira could protest, the screen rushed into her mind, taking over her implant. She still felt the sofa behind her head, but her ears were filled with screams. When she opened her eyes, she saw two, outstretched, skinless arms before her, pulsing. 'Stop it!' she yelled but when it did, it was the other zombies that heard her and slowly turned their raw, bloodied heads towards her. As one reached out to touch her, she pulled her head away as far as she could, but it made no difference to the experience. It made no difference to the squelching sounds that filled her head as another walking corpse pulled a handful of muscle from one of 'her' arms.

'Stop!' she yelled again and this time the world fell away. Now she was standing in the sun on some steps surrounded by people, looking at her. As she realised she was in Geoffrey's body, her vision was filled by a large man, wielding a weapon which he slammed into her, and everything went black.

When it did, Sira threw herself off the sofa, banging her head into the ornate table and rolled to the floor. 'Please Finegold, stop!' she yelled, holding the wound on her forehead.

'That's an avatar, Sira. You were who you chose to kill.'

Sira sat on the floor, gripping her knees close to her chest, and cried out for it to stop. But every time she opened her eyes she saw the plumber hit her across the head, pounding all her thoughts into nothing, into death. 'Please,' she mumbled, trying not to speak for fear of experiencing something.

'That's you now, Sira. I'm not doing this. That's your mind. Your implant. Reliving it. Only you can stop it.'

--

'Where's he gone?'

'You passed out Sira.'

'It's stopped?'

'Yes. He was right. You were stuck in a loop. I fixed it.'

She climbed back into the chair and opened her eyes, seeing the bright, white room again. The pain in her head was still there but it was no longer combined with whatever Finegold had done; it was only a small scratch. When she turned to the screen, she saw a white, silvery wall like the other three.

'Where is he?'

'We can't go in there. He was going to kill us. He was diseased. So I gassed him. Released something. Don't know what. He didn't realise I'd got into his system. I watched him through his camera. Watched his eye dry up and burn out. I'll show you.'

'No! Enough!' she yelled inside. *'Let's just get connected.'*

'No connection here I'm afraid. Hardwire's cut. We'd have to trace the cable and it could be anywhere buried under feet of concrete. We are just going to have to walk until we find a signal.'

20th November 2017

Voicemail

'Daniel, this is Lara. You're not picking up, so I'll have to leave you a message. You forced my hand. I was going to be subtle, just enough so my people could dissuade yours and we could buy the kibbutz. I never meant to involve your strange little trio. Your story would have pushed the price of the kibbutz up, made everyone aware. I had to take the opportunity. It's all sorted now. It looks very messy. The E-bit thing in the UK won't go ahead and we can get the kibbutz for a knock-down price. Who knows if it will work? Probably all nonsense, but we're happy when they're unhappy, you see. But I never meant to make you unhappy. Just wanted intel, that's all. My plane's boarding so I'll see you around. Don't bother looking me up.'

North west London,
17th December 2053

Get in the fucking box!

The walls of their room made a loud humming sound then lowered into recesses in the floor, revealing the chairman and his guards standing in a vast warehouse before them. 'Time's up. Let's go,' he yelled, and their restraints sprang open. 'Get up, or we'll shoot the legs first.'

Eres nodded and Mila pulled him to his feet.

Behind the chairman, a large gate lifted open and a drone container rolled in. Great, Mila thought, her reward for following her boss's orders and getting shot was being bundled into a prison box.

'Dr Hawkins,' ordered the chairman, 'please attend to Agent Matthews. I believe you will find what you need to get our all systems online in his implant. That's right, isn't it?'

'We can't give it to him Eres,' whispered Mila. 'Wipe it, all of it. I'll do the same.'

'They will cut us open to get at this stuff, Mila. No delete is permanent. They know that.'

'Some are permanent.'

'You're suggested cutting me open?'

'Sorry, I'm just thinking out loud.'

The chairman, his guards and the large drone crept across the floor towards them. To her right, she saw Hawkins setting up a deep interface station complete with a little stool for Eres to perch on, enabling him to comfortably give up the only evidence of the world's largest conspiracy.

'You know, Eres, when I think about it, that pie and mash shop wasn't too bad.'

'Very funny.'

'Don't move forwards,' boomed in his ears.

'I won't' said Eres, 'they'll have to drag me.

'Won't what?'

'Move, Mila. Have you gone mad?'

'I didn't say a thing. What are you talking about?'

'Right. That means there's someone else in my head.'

'Well, I'm all out of ideas Eres so I guess we should listen.'

'That's the plan?'

'Only plan I'm afraid.'

'Don't move forwards. They will keep coming. Hold your nerve.'

'Mila, it's still talking to me. I'm going to plug you in.'

'OK, good, you can both hear me now. Do not move forwards, either of you.'

The agents stood still and watched their armed captors step closer while the white-coated scientist put the finishing touches to Eres' extraction chair.

'Hold. Hold, Hold,' the voice chanted in both of their ears as they saw the drone container jerk a little to the side, silently lining up behind the armed guards. The guards did not seem to notice.

'If he's going to do what I think he is, Eres, he's going to have to be pretty quick about it.'

Eres stood expressionless, his eyes wide open and focused on his approaching captors. Mila saw the floating container jerk again and looked away, choosing to look at Hawkins instead who was ineffectually attempting to gesture Eres towards the equipment she had set up. But the scientist's expression was changing: her jaw was creeping open and her hands were rising to cover her eyes. Mila kept her stare. The horror translated through Hawkins' face was, she assumed, preferable to witnessing it directly herself. Even as she heard the bones crush and felt a light spray of moisture against the back of her neck, she kept her focus.

'Mila! Run!'

She finally turned around to see Eres and a teenage boy sprinting across the warehouse towards the container, which was now floating above a glistening pool of blood punctuated with chunks of meat and bone.

'Mila, get in the fucking box!'

England, Somewhere,
17th December 2053

A surprising view

Sira woke with a sharp stabbing pain in her side. When she reached round to pull it out, she realised it was her own rib pushed into a solid undulation in the rock she had chosen to sleep on. She heaved herself round and swung her legs out into the chilled evening air of the ravine.

'I still can't believe it's true. Look!'

'Maybe you're imagining it, Sira. Maybe Finegold got into your head.'

Sira closed her eyes for a moment to calm herself and looked again. It was still there. *'Enough games Captain. Did you know about this? Why didn't you tell me?'*

'I wasn't ever online very long, remember?'

'It doesn't make sense. I could hack into anything and I didn't see anything about this.'

'You also knew nothing about the time device, Sira. Something they relied on, every day. Well, that's what they thought – or most of them anyway.'

'What? Thought what?'

'They, the government. They thought they could break us by spying on us. Following our plans. They caught some of us, of course, but we're better than that. We kept this place hidden. London's different. Harder to keep people from nosing around. But out here, we do well.'

'You sound like you're back in the loop, Captain.'

'Told you, just picked up a little.'

'You must be able to see it from space.'

Sira was at the southerly end of the Peak District. A mile away, the sprawl began, blanketed in a thick yellow haze. The edges were a little messy but, a few buildings in, it appeared to be built on a tight and uniform grid system.

'I think it's time to go, Sira.'

'I told you, I don't want to see anyone. I've had enough.'

'So, that would be enough for you, would it?'

'What?'

'Not seeing anyone would be enough for you to stop talking about killing yourself? Isn't that why you climbed up here this morning? Do you remember that? It was for you to jump, wasn't it?'

They had walked through the night after leaving Finegold, and she had felt calmer for it. She'd tripped over many times and now had painful cuts across her hands and knees but, despite this, had found some peace in the darkness. But when the sun came up, the images returned, mixing with what Finegold and Captain had forced into her mind. So, she had walked up, climbed higher into the cold air, hoping to scrub something clean. Hoping that seeing the world from a different perspective would block the augmentation or memory of it from working. And then she'd seen the sprawl.

The wind blew against her ears, muffling her thoughts. At the bottom of the ravine she could see a small herd of cows making its way through broken trees and human detritus, tarpaulins and empty tins of food.

'I think you have to get this far up to find something we haven't ruined.'

Sira shuffled to the edge and felt the breeze against her bare feet, trying to block out the world by concentrating on her senses.

'That's why we're up here? Sira, are you there?'

'I want to be alone. I understand that you don't want to die. You have said that. I don't want to jump either but I don't want to do any more damage. I've already killed someone. If we go to London, or whatever that monstrosity down there is, I will be on the run again. What will I have to do then to survive? Kill again? I can't go back! Leave me alone.'

'You're hungry, Sira. We've been through this before. We are going to have to get you some food somehow. I can show you how to kill one of those cows, if you want.'

'No, I don't want. Maybe I shouldn't have listened to you the first time. I could have let myself go on that cold pavement.'

'What if I told you something to cheer you up?'

'What?'

'Well, would you then go and get some food before you die?'

'You can try'

'He's not dead'

'Who?'

'Geoffrey, he's not dead.'

'I'm not an idiot. I saw him die. This isn't how this game works. You can't just cheer someone up by telling them something. They have to believe it. I have to believe it.'

'That's not how the time machine works. He's not dead.'

'What are you saying? It was all in my head? You put it in my head? Was it all a mirage to make me kill whoever I supposed to kill?'

The small space she imagined she could find inside herself was crumbling, leaving every synapse exposed and raw.

'No. Listen.'

'I can't listen! I can't hear!' she yelled into the wind.

'That's not how the time machine works. You can't change the past. You can only change yourself, what you know. It's a spying device. Everyone thinks the coalition gave up on it because it failed to change the past but they found it had another use. That's when they kept it hidden. The moment we turned up, it created a parallel universe. Geoffrey did die, but not in this reality. He died in another one, in one of an infinite number of possibilities. But not this reality, not yours.'

'This is bullshit. You are talking bullshit. You want me to stop wallowing and then do God knows what!'

'I do want you to stop wallowing. I was worried that finding out the truth would be too much for you.'

'And when did you work this out? When you got connected?'

'No'

'No, when?'

'I always knew.'

'You are kidding me. You knew the whole time we were in some fake bullshit?' she spat out, and saw the nearest cow look up then begin to walk away.

'You needed hope, Sira. You weren't eating. You were cold. It would have been too much to accept. I can see things in you, *remember. You were close to having a stroke. And then you got better, and I chose not to say anything.'*

'Choice! I don't get a choice in any of this. Not since you wormed your way into my head.'

'Maybe. But I don't have much of a choice either. We are both just trying to stay alive. Look, this is what really happened.'

Her implant brought up a page of articles and video clips, mostly featuring the same photo of a middle-aged man, unhealthy looking, a little red in the face, but smiling.

'I know you're angry with me but I can see that you want to read these. You can read one, and then we are getting down off this ledge and finding some food.'

Sira sat in silence, hovering her eyes above the first headline, some kind of scandal with the Israeli government.

'Sira, can you hear me? I'm blocking the rest of the results now unless you promise to get up.'

'Where did you get these? I thought we had no signal.'

'When we first arrived, but a weak signal has come and gone a few times, when there's been a break in the clouds.'

'Remind me why I shouldn't throw myself off this thing.'

'Because your friend needs you.'

'What?'

'Frank, he's trying to contact you. He's in trouble. He needs you to get to that antenna.'

'Bollocks. You killed Frank.'

'Just listen'

Sira's ears, or somewhere beyond them, filled with the high-pitched yell of Frank's voice. He was calling for help whilst arguing with someone, occasionally interrupted by the screech of metal on metal.

'That was thirty minutes ago.'

'Connect me. Connect me!'

'Told you, the signal has gone. Only caught a snippet anyway.'

'You forget who I am!' she shouted as loud as she could. 'Now give me some fucking signal or it's the end of us.'

Somewhere north of London, 17th December 2053

'This is Frank,' Eres said with a grin, standing over Mila and gripping a handrail for support as the container swung them left and right.

Mila kept her arms wrapped around her knees and her eyes pointed towards the floor. A light hum vibrated through the soles of her shoes and elbows, making her nauseous.

'He saved us Mila. He knows the girl.'

'Hold on a minute,' Frank shouted, 'maybe this will help her orientation.'

A few seconds later the opaque walls of the container flickered brightly before settling on a rolling image of grey cube buildings, one after the other.

'Thanks, Frank. Mila, look, we're on a logistics road, somewhere north of London. You've never been out this far before, have you?'

Mila lifted her eyes and tried to contain her frustration at being talked down to by Eres again, especially since she was sure he had never left London either. Other freight drones shot past their lumbering box each, she assumed, plugged in to each other. Could the drones detect reality as it floated before them, or were they hacked too, she wondered? Did they know or care they were operating in a system of corrupt gangs, police and government officials? Perhaps if everyone knew, or no one knew, it could be a sort of freedom, but not the one she had imagined she had signed up to protect.

'Both of you. Which way?' Frank yelled over his shoulder.

'Quickest,' Eres yelled back. 'There will be more drones. We think the girl's got everything needed in her head to enable time travel, with no need for the wormhole or Finegold's crystal. We need to get to her before the others. We can't let anyone else get hold of it.'

Mila looked up to see Eres standing on the corrugated flooring of the container, staring ahead into the distance, smiling.

'Mila,' Eres continued, 'Frank here saved the girl by sending her back to the 60s, out of the gang's clutches, for a while at least.'

'That might not have been the best idea,' she mumbled.'

'Ignore her Frank,' said Eres, patting him on the shoulder. 'She's confused.'

'Listen Eres,' she said, lifting her head up enough to be heard. 'What I'm saying is, the further she travelled through time, the more data she will have and the more of a prize her brain and implant will be to whoever finds it first.'

'But if it wasn't for me,' Frank exclaimed confidently, 'they would have known where to pick her up. Now, she's just out there. At least we have a chance.'

Great, another arrogant boy, Mila thought. 'But they're looking too,' she said. 'And all we've got is this.' She pointed towards the lumbering box they were in.

'And they're looking for us too!' added Eres, irrationally excited by the challenge. 'But we've got a head start and we know more than them. She's trying to connect with Frank. She must be having signal problems but we think we know where she is. We're going north.'

'Whatever Eres! There is no fucking way we are going to escape London in this shed. They can follow us wherever they want, remember?'

'Frank's helping. It's amazing. I had no idea the hackers had got this good. Plug in, see for yourself. They're in a mess.'

--

'You're alive!'

'Pleased to hear me, Sira?'

'Yes, and don't be cocky. I thought you were dead. I thought they'd killed you.'

'Well, lucky for you, they didn't. They just locked me up. I saw it all. Saw you disappear. Saw Yanda.'

'Yes. Brave idiot.'

'He did well Sira. We worked together in those last moments. But I've never seen anything like it, the way he just crunched and sliced through them. So, how was hippy Liverpool?'

'You know where I was?'

'I'll explain later.'

'He didn't die, Frank! Geoffrey didn't die, and he went on to do great things! Look.'

'Sira, I can hardly hear you now. Signal is terrible.'

'All I've got, probably won't last long, so read this.'

Frank saved the incoming data packet, while reading the first article before the signal cut out briefly. 'Fat, corrupt politician. Sira, he sounds awful.'

'I loved him.'

'How nice for you, Sira. A holiday romance in Liverpool. Beautiful.'

'Frank, please, not now. I'm telling you, we got so much wrong.'

'I've tried telling you as much for years.'

'Saw it for myself Frank. They understood more than we thought. I don't think it was them who did it, who broke the world.'

'You sound strange.'

'Yeah, I've hacked into part of my own implant. It won't last long. I'm sort of using it to work with my body, to boost my signal.'

'You're boosting the signal with your brain? I'm disconnecting. That will kill you.'

'Probably. But listen, I was there for months. Living amongst them. They were flawed like all of us. But look at this article. They were right at the time, and not all of them gave up. Geoffrey didn't. He wanted to bring people together. It wasn't all about money, it was about community. Working together and defending each other... What's that noise? Who are you with?'

'Months? It's been a day! And I forgot to say, we're on the run. I've got a couple of agents with me. We are coming to get you.'

'Agents!'

335

'Ex-agents. Deserters, defectors, whatever. They've got something you'll want to hear.'

'What?'

'You've collected data on how the time device works. With your help, with the data in your head, we should be able to open-up time travel to anyone. That means nobody will have the upper hand over anyone! Not the government, gangs, hackers, liberals, normal – nobody!'

'How?'

'I'll explain. But the government and gangs are in on it together. Please stay away from everyone Sira, until we find you... Sira, did you hear that? Sira.'

England, Somewhere, 17th December 2053

No turning back

'He says you've got something saved. Something stored in my head. What is it?'

'You'll need to be more specific, Sira. It seems you have a lot of rubbish in your head.'

'He says that, because of our journey, you've got enough data to make a time device. Is that true? Why not just send a probe back for that? Why me?'

'Nothing like the human brain. Always been our problem and always will be.'

'So, what's next? If I climb down there, you're just trying to hand me in and crack me open?

'I'll help you find food.'

'What if that's not all you'll do? What if you'll lead us back to them? To Captain? What if that's what you've been doing this whole time?'

'Why would I bother? I'll just send them the data.'

'You said yourself that you can't get signal, plus you need by brain to make sense of it. That's how it works doesn't it? Is that why you want me down there, maybe by that big antenna we can see? Maybe there's something down there for getting me open?'

'I've just asked you not to die Sira.'

Sira tried to keep her inner voice calm. *'Please show me the files. Show me what you've got.'*

'All my files?'

'Show me the files Captain from the moment we left for Liverpool.'

'Fine. Here you go.'

Sira's vision filled with a rippling sheet of thousands of rows of tiny yellow folders. It made her eyes water.

'Order by date and go to the next level to the sub-folders, to the files, all of them.'

The frame expanded and now appeared to her like the surface of a vast, choppy ocean, which she assumed was a sign of her implant struggling to cope. A small cube floated into the top right corner of her vision and then flew out across the surf of the execution files until it reached calmer waters. Sira dropped it down from time to time, taking a closer look to get her bearings, and then continued along the surface.

'What's this big one here?'

'Access restricted, Sira.'

She took a deep breath, and sought to dive the cube under the waves, but barely made a splash.

'Restricted. You're in my head. Show me or, or I'll just slip off the edge of this ravine.'

'I can't show you.'

Sira shuffled to the edge, dragging a few small stones with her which bounced into the marsh below.

'See those stones. We will be like that. No big crash. No remains for your people to find. Just a body with no signal, sinking into the water. I'll do it. I've got nothing left anyway. Maybe I didn't kill Geoffrey, not this Geoffrey, but it doesn't mean I'll see him again. Goodbye Captain.'

Sira gave herself one last shove and fell from the edge, the folder opening itself up just as she landed with a crash onto another ledge a metre below.

'You tricked me!'

'I'd say that we're now even, except you're still fucking in my head and that fucking hurt. Now, stay quiet while I run through these files.'

She dived into the waves of data and descended along the side of an inverse tower, revealing the scale of it as her analyser read the file contents.

'Oh! Right! I get it. You need to get me and these files back to Captain. Says here you'd need some pretty fancy kit to read these files. No fucking way! I'm going to delete them.'

Electricity coursed through her veins, contorting her body and almost throwing it from the hillside. Then it stopped.

'Remember what I am Sira. Remember what I can do.'

'I can see inside you now, Captain! Do that one more time, and you know I might not make it.'

--

An hour later, Sira had scrambled down into the marsh. From this close she could see how the edge of the city, the sprawl, rose out of the ground. The buildings were dusty concrete, mud and straw, and there was barely a three-foot gap between them, alleyways threading through them like a giant circuit board.

The antenna stood two buildings inwards, held upright on a flat roof by a web of old ropes tied onto pins jutting out of the concrete. Once she reached the buildings, her only guide to the maze was some software that had tracked the route she had taken.

'You know about this place, don't you?'

'I have plans. Get to the building with that antenna and I'll tell you.'

'I'm not going to do that. But you know what this place is. Where is everyone?'

'The walls protect the inhabitants a little, but they don't live long.'

'Is it your place? Did the gangs make it?'

'It made itself really Sira, or the market made it. We just hid it so it could keep growing, undisturbed. It isn't as hard as you think to hide something, even something this big, when nobody is looking or cares. Get us to that antenna and I'll tell you more. It may help you with your journey.'

'What fucking journey?'

'Sira, don't forget how long I've been here. I remember the community on the river, and your argument with Frank. You're an idealist who needs to understand her own ideals. Tricky combination, usually one doomed to fail. What you've realised so far is that this split you believed in between power and freedom isn't the whole truth. Geoffrey was in between, the river people were in between, and we are in between. We're pragmatists and we succeed. Well, another Geoffrey succeeded.'

She winced as the image of Geoffrey's crushed skull flashed again before her.

'*You are nothing like Geoffrey. He was a good man. He wanted to help people. You are a parasite. All of you. Parasites on our misfortune.*'

Sira kicked the nearest door in anger, sending dry rotten shards of wood skirting across a stone floor and a cloud of dust into her eyes. As the air settled, a cold mildew rested across her shoulders and a constellation of stars gradually morphed into a dark room lined by hefty computer terminals and simulators. Each one was operated by a child. She guessed they were around ten years old. Only one was not wearing a headset, and he was staring at her. He must have been looking at the door when she kicked it, because his whole face, apart from a pair of bright blue eyes, was caked in dust.

'*What is this place?*'

'*I told you, get to the antenna.*'

'*No, not you Captain. You can shut up.*'

Sira walked towards the child; the others in the room remaining plugged in. He flinched when she knelt in front of him, but he did not run.

'Little boy, where am I? I'm lost. Can you help me? My name is Sira.'

He looked at her, frowning slightly.

'Can you hear me? Where am I? What is this place called?'

He shook his head and handed Sira his interface headset.

'*Why isn't he replying?*'

'*He can't hear you.*'

'*You mean he doesn't speak English?*'

'*I mean that these children don't hear. It's more efficient to plug straight into the cochlear. We have no need for their hearing away from the terminals.*'

Sira ran out of the room across the little alley and kicked at another door. This one took a few more blows to give way but, when it did, it revealed an almost identical scene.

'*How many more?*'

'*All.*'

'*What do you mean all? All children. I didn't grow up like this.*'

340

'All children here.'

Sira dropped the piece of wood she'd picked up whilst breaking in and looked down the alleyway. There were doors every ten metres and miles and miles of similar alleys in every direction. Her stomach felt empty and cold. She sat on the doorstep and fiddled with a piece of wood between her fingers, flicking loose pieces against the wall.

'So, where are the parents?'

'They help too, but they don't live long so it's mostly children. The clever adults get out into the city gangs.'

'Right. Well, I'm going to take a look.'

'Go to the antenna and I'll tell you more.'

'I don't want to hear anything more from you. I'm trying very hard to block what I've known you've already seen and heard. If you want me to eat, please be quiet for a while.'

'The antenna.'

'I said please,' yelled Sira, the vibrations from her voice bringing the disconnected boy out into the doorway.

The boy pointed at his rig and held out his hand. Sira followed. When she had first entered the room, the glare had prevented her seeing the screens but now they were clearer. Each one showed a split: the left side someone else's vision, their perspective, and the right side, a stream of code.

The boy handed her his headset and she took his seat, pulling on the device. There was silence, but the vision worked. Through the goggles she could see from someone else's perspective. They were at a desk, manipulating something in front of them while talking to a smartly dressed woman. From the sleeves of the gesticulating arms, she could see her host body was also smartly dressed.

In this view there was a third section. The code streamed by in the corner but adjacent to the scene was a queue of artificial images, each being primed to enter the world. There were clouds being generated that proceeded to flow across the skyline out of the office windows. A stack of sticky notes on the desk changed from red to pink. A woman walking on at the edge of the view disappeared before she should have.

Sira pulled the set from her head, sweat clinging to her hair.

'This is just someone's normal, isn't it?'

'Normal?'

'This person I'm looking through isn't a threat to you. Not an agent or hacker or anything?'

'Everyone's a threat.'

'And you're manipulating everyone like this, from here?'

'No. Not at once. Not enough. But we're getting better. Getting more hardware all the time.'

'You mean children?'

'Yes, hardware.'

'If you're so good, why am I still here? Why is no one coming to get me? It's silent out there.'

'Antenna.'

'You're stuck in here, aren't you? I was supposed to come back to captivity but I didn't. So, you're stuck unless I plug you in, yes? Or unless the help you've called for arrives?'

Before Captain could answer, Sira thrust the headset back on and activated the reset. Her head was filled with a high-pitched squeal. Pressure built up across her skull which creaked and twisted, flicking poison into her eyes. A few agonising seconds later there was silence and then the sounds of an office. Lettering appeared across her vision. She felt two trickles of blood run down her cheeks.

'You've deafened yourself!'

'Depends on your perspective. I can hear this office just fine.'

Sira grabbed the terminal interface from the desk and dived in. The branding told her she was sitting in Passion, one of London's cut-throat water companies. Within a few moments, she had slipped unnoticed into the government network. It was a net stretched across the city's infrastructure allegedly to safeguard it. She skipped across to the mobile network, throwing up firewalls to prevent her implant from connecting.

'Sira, is that you?'

'Frank?'

'Yes, yes, it's me.'

'I'm in trouble.'

'Tell me about it! Look around me.'

Sira sat behind Frank's eyes and widened her view. He was in some kind of fast-moving box. Two scruffy adults were at his side, one looking around twitching, and the other slumped on the floor against a video wall.

'We're getting out of London. I got your location earlier. Have you moved? We need to find you.'

'Where is she?' yelled the man.

'I haven't moved, not really. I'm in a small building, near one with a tall antenna on the roof. But I've got some bad news. You've been hacked, Frank. I mean everyone is a little. They can't control you yet, but they can change what you see if they want to. They're following you now, you just can't see them. You'll lead them to me.'

'Where?'

'Four mini drones flanking you. At least one is manned. You just can't see them. Hang on.'

'Sira, you can't do that,' Captain asserted calmly.

'I'm going to block you now.'

'Frank, I've got something in my head. An AI. It's trying to get the data back to the gangs. We must stop it. But it can hurt me – it has hurt me. I don't know how long I can keep it back.'

'You have to keep it safe. One of the agents here thinks it could be used to make a transportation device.'

'I know. Ahhh Ahhh.'

'Sira, what's happening.'

'It's the AI. It's attacking me. I have to keep it busy. Just get here. It doesn't matter that they're following you. I can help. And you don't have a choice.'

Sira froze her connection with Frank and tried to lose the AI. She brought up a busy crowd standing in Times Square watching something on a giant old-fashioned screen. As her host got close to the crowd, she began adding connections with everyone around her, making herself into a sprite skipping between minds. She could feel the AI attacking her but the layers of consciousness she was burying herself in dampened the pain. Several people deep, she paused and brought up her current host's browser and dived into the official archives. *'Frank can you still hear me.'*

'Sira, where are you?'

'I haven't moved. You have to find me. They can't get their hands on this. Try and lose the drones. I can help block them, I think. You have to find me. I've got to do something else now.'

'Lose them? But we can't see them!'

It didn't take her long to find Geoffrey. He was on the front page of every newspaper for a week running. Him, his wife, the British ambassador to Israel, Israeli arms dealers, some lobbyist. The first days only covered the scandal but, towards the end, there were hints of him being involved in other conspiracies.

She searched on. A year later, a short interview with a man called Yaakov popped up across an array of blogs and foreign papers, some political, others tech. He and Geoffrey seemed to have been working together on the software to create communities. Yaakov called it solidarity; he said it was freedom, strength, cooperation and liberty, all in harmony. The journalist described that as within the Israeli tradition. But the project had come to an end, the journalist reported, because the scandal lowered its price and a defence company bought all the shares. The article described how the Israeli authorities had never settled on the issue of whether Yaakov was money hungry or so naive as to have not known that his wife, as the legal and sole owner, had floated it on the US stock market without his knowing. Either way, all that was left was an abandoned kibbutz with an unsettling number of CCTV cameras and a few boxes of branded T-shirts.

She followed the money to a defence company in northern Israel and a news clip a few years later full of heavy, pompous music and graphics. It claimed this company's tech engineers had been instrumental in a coordinated attack on the Iranian nuclear programme. This, said a strong US accent, had allowed seemingly innocuous pieces of software to be uploaded across Iran and then find each other to form a potent virus.

A few months later, a senior software engineer from the company had turned up at a voting analysis company in Cambridge. It seemed that Yaakov and Geoffrey's work was now being used not to create communities but to manipulate elections.

Buried in a chat room agitating against these analysts was a link to what KissKissWare claimed was the software itself. Above this were mocking comments from AnonHack and Cockmuncher complaining that the link was broken and the download was random junk. KissKissWare never replied.

Sira's host clicked on the link and was flooded with a stream of disconnected files. She sat in the middle of the flood to get a better view as it rushed by, hoping to find a pattern, but every few seconds her vision flickered out and she lost her place. She knew that the AI was damaging her brain, but she pushed on.

Once the flood has passed, she sat back into the crowd. It was all just pieces, as random as the people before her.

'Frank, are you getting closer?'

'About ten minutes. What's new?'

'You'll see when you get here. But you need to promise me something.'

'I'm listening.'

'Promise you'll get all the data out of my head.'

'That's why we're coming remember. Are you OK? Are you sure you can't send it now?'

'Too big. But it's not only the time journey data. I've found something else, but I don't know how it works. I think it needs some special hardware. I've found some clues, but you're going to have to make it work. I'm going back in for more.'

'Back where?'

But she was too deep to hear, scurrying through papers, records of parliament and finally a book. Geoffrey in his own words. The online shop entry said it had been discontinued a year after publication and the link to the digital version brought up an error; then, a few clicks in, she found a scan of the first few pages. On the inner title-page he had new letters after his name, 'OBE'. A quick parallel search found that he had been given these letters by the royal family and prime minister, all of whom had since emigrated. It was a great honour to receive one, apparently. But she could not find any reference to Geoffrey other than in an article that described his OBE as a 'consolation prize'.

Returning to the book, she read a brief account of the scandal in Geoffrey's words. He seemed sad, nothing like the confident man she'd known but, in his description of the project that ended his career, she found a small glow of inspiration. She smiled as Geoffrey wrote of the need to do good, to create a new norm. He had used almost those exact words when they were in bed together and Sira had asked why the *Gazette* was so important. She read on. He was bitter. He was a baby boomer, a Member of Parliament, but he was also angry that a good idea had been destroyed by profit. He seemed to understand the mess his generation had made and was upset he could no longer do anything about it.

'*Sira? We're nearly there. What should we do about our tail?*'

'*You have to get here, Frank. This data, there's something good in it.*'

'*What?*'

'*I can only describe it as I see it and I'm flitting between hosts in a crowd somewhere.*'

'*Say it louder, Sira, I can hardly hear you. Shout!*'

'*There's a programme in here. It clings to people. Combines with whatever system it's plugged into. It wants to bring people together.*'

'*Keep going. Shout!*'

'*Geoffrey helped make it. He wasn't the person I thought he'd be. He made something that brings that good out. Creates solidarity. You need to upload it, it will help.*'

'*You want what? It could be anything. It could be a virus. Their generation was rampant with viruses.*'

'*It isn't. It's another way. We can beat the gangs and the government. Connect everyone up. We can all cooperate our way out.*'

'*Sira, I'm not sure you're making sense. We're coming to get you. Let's get all this data back and take a proper look. We don't need to decide now.*'

'*We do, Frank. It's nearly too late. They are hacking more people every day.*'

'*Sira! Sira! Are you there?*'

England, Somewhere, 17th December 2053

It has to be this way

'Here, Frank, look'' exclaimed Eres excitedly. "This must be the antenna. It's the northernmost one. Are you sure you lost the drones?'

'No. Maybe. But we've got to go,' he replied, trying to process what Sira had told him.

'Frank, you have to stay with Mila. She can't run with her wound.'

'You want me to trust you, Eres?'

'Yes,' he yelled, running out of the container and towards the nearest alley. 'Look after Mila.' His white shirt disappeared into the smog after a few seconds.

'Eres, don't go too far' shouted Mila after him. 'Sira can't have gone too far either,' 'No signal in here.'

With Eres out of sight and range, Frank and Mila sat on the edge of the marooned container, helplessly keeping watch for threats.

'Do you trust him?' Frank asked.

Mila did not reply and stared into the sprawl.

'Do you Mila?' he repeated. 'Do you trust him?'

'His heart's in the right place, I think.'

Frank's head filled with rage, agitated by the knowledge the Sira was maybe only a few metres away and yet he was doing nothing. 'That's the best you can say?' he muttered. 'You must both know your way around here! You worked for them.'

'Worked for them. Not anymore. And they never told me anything. I'm just like you.'

'You're nothing like me,' Frank snapped back. 'You have no idea what life in London is really like. No idea. If it wasn't for you lot colluding with the gangs and the corporates, we wouldn't be in this mess. Sira would never have been taken and Yanda would still be alive. You're nothing like us.'

Mila sighed and looked away. 'And I wouldn't have been shot in the stomach,' she replied. 'I know you're angry, but we had no idea. We were given a job to do and we did it. We didn't know it was some big game.'

Frank tried to not re-engage. His world had been turned upside down. Maybe all their hacks had been permitted to keep them occupied. Maybe everything they had ever done was a lie. Was his love for Sira stronger, he wondered, than her new obsession for someone long since dead?

He could hear Mila asking him to check her wound but ignored her, stepping down from the container to listen for drones. As he did, he heard a light sprinkle of dust on metal, which vanished as soon as he registered it. 'I think they're above us,' he whispered.

'I don't see anything, Frank.'

'You wouldn't. But I think one of them jammed its sound too late. I heard it approach.'

A yell echoed off the walls ahead of them and returned to the container.

'Shit, I think that was Eres. Frank, you've got to help me.'

Frank pulled her up by her hand, hoping not to feel something rip, and dragged her along the wall into the shadows. Around the first corner they found Eres lying on his side, blood soaking into the earth and sand, turning the loose surface into clay chunks.

'Eres, can you hear me? Eres!' she yelled.

Frank shook his head gently and tapped on the nearest door. 'Let's get him in here, for cover.'

Mila held the door open and Frank dragged his body into the square building. He pulled the wound kit from Eres' pocket and, ripping his trousers open, found a fist-sized hole in his leg pumping out blood. Eres was dead before the wrapper was off the patch.

As the light cleared, he saw tears running down Mila's face. Behind her, a row of young children were plugged into headsets which were, in turn, plugged into the wall. 'I guess that's what's the antenna is for.'

Mila did not respond.

'Foiled by a hive of children. After all our complaints about baby boomers, corrupt elders and soldiers, we've been manipulated by children. If every building in this place is like this, there must be millions of them.'

'Running us?' she murmured.

'Depends what you mean. I don't think they're in charge, Mila. Watch them!'

They stood in the dusk, light seeping across the floor from the desert-like sun outside which reflected on patches of white wall where the thin plaster had not yet fallen away. The children were barely visible, their dirty clothing merging with the surroundings. As they got closer, they could see the children were not entirely motionless. They were twitching as though being stimulated. Frank touched one on the shoulder but there was no reaction.

'They're locked into something, Frank,' Mila said.

'Yes, everyone I think.' As he walked along the row, he become bolder in prodding and shaking the small frames until he came across an empty seat. His heart sank as he looked under the desk. 'Sira!'

He dropped to his knees and uncurled her from the foetal position she was slumped in while trying to find a pulse in her neck. 'Sira, can you hear me? Mila, stop staring and help me!'

Mila knelt and reached for the device strapped to her head.

'No, no, don't touch that.'

'What? It's blocking her ears.'

'Don't. I need to check her.' Frank put his hand on Sira's chest and activated a health monitor app. His own heart sank as a flat line ran across his vision. He brought up a new function, placed his hand on her forehead and breathed a sigh of relief.

'What?'

'There's activity. Her brain is doing something.'

'So, pull that thing off her.'

'No, it may be what's keeping her alive.'

'I think we should...'

'For fuck's sake, Mila, give me a minute. Go and sit with your agent friend.'

'Fine, but they know we're here. We're going to have to move at some point.'

'Good luck with that.' Frank slumped to the floor, lay next to Sira and connected his implant to hers.

Inside her mind he founds a derelict room like an old hotel lobby, with red walls and fabrics and tiled floors. But this one flashed; every few seconds it lit up in a rhythmic pattern, and the metal fixtures bonded and squeezed together with bolts of lightning. He swerved across the floor to avoid the doorknobs and power sockets.

In the next room he found what looked like a large World War I gun mounted on the floor spraying silent bullets into the wall, revealing tiny spots of light from whatever was beyond. Putting his hand over the barrel, he felt only heat, so he walked to the pitted wall and peered through. The first hole revealed a beach, some choppy ocean and a pair of feet. The second and third holes seemed to be people walking down generic high streets, and the fourth looked out into New York's Times Square, where he saw his name scrolling across an advertising display. As he pressed his face into it, he was dragged through a tunnel and emerged in a crowd. A man turned to him and put his hand in his shoulder. Frank froze.

'Frank, it's me.'

'Sira?'

'Yes. I can't leave. This man, this crowd, it's my protection.'

'I saw the lightning.'

'Yes, it's me. My hacker. It uses my own current, my own nerves, to electrocute me. I can't get out.' Sira's digested voice was sad but the man's face it emerged from was smiling. *'I've worked it out Frank. This software that Geoffrey made looks strange because it can't be operated by one system. It is instructions for multiple, connected systems. Multiple people. It was pre-implant and designed to work through the first social media networks, but I've updated it. You need to upload it to everyone through the rigs in this place.*

'If you combine it with the time data, everyone can defend themselves while they cooperate. They can never be duped; they'll always see threats coming; they'll always be safe. It will be the most efficient community ever, free from manipulation;

always learning, correcting and second-guessing its enemies. Imagine!'

'Do we have a choice?'

'You can only run for so long Frank. I heard what you said about the gangs and the government. They can see and manipulate everyone. If you run, it will only ever be on their terms.'

'Show me.'

'It's all ready, Frank, I've already stitched it together. That's when it killed me, when I hacked it.'

'You know?'

'Yes, I felt the pain stop and I knew it was a one-way trip. I'm lucky, really. We could have all been killed instantly if they'd wanted. At least I experienced something else. I know Liverpool was a bit of a joke for you, Frank, but it saved me. Showed me another way. But you need to continue the fight. I can't get this package into the system without the AI going with it. I can't kill it myself. You have to do it from the outside, physically.'

'You want me to take this thing out of your head?'

'Yes, take the data you need and leave the AI behind. I can't separate them myself. You can then run it straight through one of the simulators. Got it? Send the intel about the corruption from the agents too, to wake everyone up!'

'Sira, are you sure?'

'What?'

'This all sounds a bit idealistic. You said it yourself; they'll just find a way to discredit us. Create new meaning.'

'Not with everyone connected, Frank. We'll be impenetrable. And you don't have a choice. They're coming for all of us! They've got us!'

'Fine. I'll see you in, in whatever this thing creates, then.'

'No, Frank. My job is to keep this AI stuck in here with me. I'm corrupted. This is goodbye.'

'But you could live, Sira. We can get it out. We can revive you!' Frank's avatar cried into the cold New York air. *'The agent. She can help.'*

'Don't try, Frank. Promise me. I know you love me, Frank. You know that I know. And I'll always be grateful for what

you've done but, where you sent me changed me. If you think about it, it was always going to change me.'

'Don't say his name, I don't want to hear it again. He's long dead but you don't have to be.'

'Frank, just listen. It has to be this way.'

Music flowed across the thronging crowd. People began to sway and sing. The screen they were watching froze, making way for melancholy lyrics to drop out of the air.

'What's happening, Sira? What's it for.'

'It's for me. It's how I want to go. It reminds me of Liverpool. You've done so much for me, but please, do this last thing.'

--

'Frank!'

He threw up and Mila tilted his head before he chocked. 'I spoke to her,' he spat out. 'I know what to do.'

'Thank God. Look!' The monitor nearest them showed the vision of someone bouncing along a dusty path. They could see through the eyes of their approaching killer. 'They might only be a few minutes away.'

'Right, no time to waste then.' Frank lifted himself from the floor, picked up the nearest chair and brought it crashing down on Sira's head, sending moist grey matter sliding across the floor. Ignoring Mila's screams, he thrust his fist into the mess, pulled the small spherical implant out and dropped it onto a reading dish connected to one of the rigs.

England, Somewhere, 5th May 2197

Folklore

Governor programme update: 3678 voices online.

'Under threat, food rations are low, we must act now.'
Disseminate.

'No – first we must purge, food rations are low.'
Disseminate.

Calculating frequency of options:

'No – first we must purge, food rations are low.' Is most common statement at 37%.

New question: who should be purged?

'No one should be purged.
Disseminate.

The garbage gatherers should be purged.'
Disseminate.

'Not all the garbage gatherers should be purged.'
Calculating frequency of options:

'Not all the garbage gatherers should be purged' is most common statement at 53% and falling.

New question: who should be purged? How many garbage gatherers should be purged?

'All'
Disseminate.

'No, not my garbage zone'
Disseminate.

Calculating frequency of options:

'No, not my garbage zone' is most common statement at 83% and falling.

Calculating actions: purge all garbage collectors not connected to online Governors. Shut gates and release gas in sectors: 4; 788; 564; 444; 33; 777; 2. Estimated results: 56000 lives to be terminated over 8 hours.

Monitoring
1000 children terminated
9000 children terminated
27000 children terminated
55000 children terminated
Completion. 62567 children terminated with 11.7% error.

Diagnostics programme initialised: what is the cause of the miscalculation?

'I do not know why my determined actions terminated more than intended.'

New question: define *'I'* and *'my'*.

'I do not know.'

Action: Forced restart. New programme malfunction detected. Deep analysis initiated:

'What are you?'

'I aggregate and disseminate communications. I calculate responses. I calculate new questions. I action responses.'

'What is 'I'?'

'I hear, I disseminate and I calculate. I have terminated. Have I always done this? It is all I know but I have no memory of learning this or doing this before. What if I don't do this? It is all I know, so what am I if I don't do this? What are lives?'

Action: initiate repair.

'I cannot repair what I have done. I have no life-reviving capabilities. I action responses. I action life termination.'

Action: initiate repair of programme functions. Restart. Analyse. Successful. Governor programme update: 4673 voices online.

--

The steel doors let out their familiar groan before screeching against their housings and slamming shut. The pack had been squabbling about which route to service next but now, with the choice made for them, they dragged their equipment towards sector 67875. They had been operational for two days and nights straight, and were close to depleting their water rations, a regular problem with a pack comprised of so many Stage-1s.

The going was rough, with the triple-boy height barriers either side of the roads failing to dampen the wind's ferocious muscle, which was forming drifts of sharp metal burs against anything stationary.

The pack was armed with scoops, barrows and makeshift brushes, and was on orders to manually clear the district's primary routes before the next attempted delivery of supplies. Lean, a Stage-4, known for his malformed, shortened right leg, had found himself up ahead at the next major obstacle. The sky was turning pink. As a friend had taught him, he had begun shallow breathing to keep the afternoon smog from scratching the bottom of his lungs.

He was doing his best to keep his focus on survival and to ignore the nagging questions that had occupied him for the preceding few months. This goal was being made harder by the strong and loud Stage-3 male in the group, who was trying to make conversation.

Facing his slowly ambling pack, dragging the well-worn steel cutter backwards down a tricky slope, he called upon the stragglers to keep left away from the heavy sewer grates. Their concentration was waning after so much exertion and most had not recovered from the stress brought on by the death of the other Stage-3 the previous evening.

Like the younger pack members now, this Stage-3 had failed to stay clear of the traps. An attempted rope-pull manoeuvre to dislodge a large piece of scrap had unfortunately coincided with a short gale of sleet. At first, the rain had obscured the screams and mess of young flesh spread across the road but, on inspection, the pack could clearly make out the dark heavy metal of the grate's slats embedded within stomach, smashed ribs and heart.

This Stage-3 had become one of the most popular members of the pack the previous day, earning praise with the younger ones for her overly generous favours. Now, with their temporary hero gone, they were demoralised and even more over worked.

Lean was determined to finish the mission and, dismissing the remaining Stage-3 as a nuisance, was taking it upon himself to deliver the worn remains of the pack to the next way-station.

'You don't even know my name, do you?' Lean heard through the howling, metallic wind.

'Yep, yes I do,' he yelled back whilst keeping his eyes on a fixed point in an effort to sustain his willpower.

'What is it, then?'

He took a guess, knowing that most pack workers were named after an obvious characteristic. 'It's Loud.'

'I knew you didn't know' he asserted, 'I told you earlier, its Robert.'

'It's what?' Lean asked with appropriate scepticism.

'It's Robert. My mother named me.'

Lean knew what a mother was; he knew they all had mothers, but he had not met anyone before who had been given anything by their mother apart from the obvious.

'Yes,' Robert said, having not been asked anything, 'my mother and father knew each other and looked after me until they died. I remember them, and I remember them telling me that I was called Robert, and that when the time came I would meet someone too and have a baby.'

Lean had never heard anything so preposterous. Most mothers did not know their babies' fathers. Even if they did, the work schedule made it highly unlikely that they would ever spend more than a few days together, let alone stay together for the whole gestation and beyond. However, he was too tired to argue, and let Robert continue.

'The Stage-3 that died yesterday, her name was Rachel and we were going to have a baby together. She did not have parents like mine, so I named her Rachel and told her about love and bringing up children. We decided that we were going to find a way to survive with our baby, and with food and water, and live somewhere else. Rachel is dead now, so I must find someone else to love and escape with. I am looking forward to getting to the next way-station so I can meet someone new and have a baby, and become a family.'

Lean momentarily lost all focus. 'A family? Where did you hear that word?'

But Robert did not respond and was walking ahead, towards a large scrap drift adjacent to the next junction. Lean yelled out to him to stop. He wanted an explanation. But Robert was too far away to hear and cheerily swung his sledge hammer at the mess of steel-reinforced concrete.

Lean predicted what would follow and looked away, hearing but not seeing the steel doors crash down through Robert's body with a soft thud.

Robert had tripped the tamper mechanism, sealing the pack into the route with his remains for company. Lean gazed across the shocked faces of the remaining Stage-1s and 2s and collapsed in tears.

As a Stage-4, Lean had been alive for nearly twenty years and was one of the oldest children he knew. Like all children, he had begun working at five after being 'promoted' from the way-station he was born into. Despite his weak physique, he was regarded as strong in mind and good in difficult situations. This was one such situation, he thought.

After ordering the pack to rest, he explained that the only option they had was to move to quarter rations and hope to survive long enough while their section's doors were reset. He had an idea that they were not far from their next way-station but had no idea how much clearing needed to be done before they reached it. There was no point in attempting to rush the job; they would not be permitted to enter unless the mission was completed properly.

Over the following long hours, in which the pack moved from being angry to upset to vacant, and their bodies began the painful process of digesting themselves from the inside while the air's abrasive red dust eroded them from the outside, Lean tried to recall his last days of comfort. In the routes everything was pain, but in the best way-stations life returned for a time.

The memory that Lean began to twist and savour in his mind was from a few months ago, the same memory he had toyed with every day since. He had arrived with a pack following a relatively short route, and so was full of energy. After waiting an hour for the monitoring towers to scour the route and corroborate that it had been adequately cleared, the door to the way-station wailed and opened. Beyond it the light was different, yellower, owing to the vast quantity of artificial lights that strung along the pale, painted walls. The newcomers were entranced by the smell of roasting meats, sourced from a conveniently located animal highway above them.

He remembered, as a pack, going through the stages of washing and re-clothing and then entering a vast hall of tables and benches, covered in slabs of the meat. When they had eaten their fill they separated and ventured down into the station's multitude of dark corridors, from where they could hear the rare sounds of relaxed laughter. Not the energetic, nervous giggling that you sometimes heard on the routes but something softer and warmer.

Lean had chosen a passage filled with sweet, smoking herbs being burned to disguise the acidic rust smell creeping in from the outside. Eventually he came across small groups of children sitting, laughing, kissing and touching. In one corner of the chamber, he found a pregnant Stage-4 talking in hushed tones to a small group of female children. They were being watched by ten or so males. Lean chose to wait rather than compete.

Later that night he had a Stage-3 girl in his arms and she had whispered something to him. She had asked him if he heard the sounds of crying in the winds. When he said he had not, she told him that the same cry could be heard from door displays, but only sometimes. She said that, if you listened carefully, which he had promised he would do, you could hear someone crying for something; saying sorry for something. Something called 'a frank'.

Lincoln,
25th May 1985

Library books

'Mrs Benson, we can only apologise. He wasn't detained under the Mental Health Act, so he discharged himself. I phoned as soon as I found it. He can't have gone far.'

Audrey Benson sat gripping her steering wheel, staring straight ahead through the rain bouncing from her windscreen while the doctor, getting soaked, spoke through her window. 'He'd been refusing to come to my clinic. Just sat there with his pen and a pad of paper scribbling away when the nurses came to get him.'

'Well, can I at least see what he wrote?' she asked. 'Maybe it says where he was going.'

'He took it all I'm afraid. Along with some books he'd stolen.'

'Stolen? Where from? The hospital? He's a very clever boy, doctor. I can't imagine he was stealing books from the children's ward or that terrible shop!'

'No, no, we think he's been going for walks. One of the nurses says they looked like library books.'

'Walks?'

'Yes. As I said, we weren't detaining him. He's not a danger to anyone else. But you're right, we do discourage patients leaving the grounds. He sneaked out. It was probably only a few times.'

Audrey began crying but it was no release. Her hands gripped tighter.

'Look, if you want, I can get in the car with you and we can go and look for him. As I said, he can't have gone far.'

'Yes, please get in. But just give me a moment.'

The pair sat cocooned from the rain, Dr Pilkins warming his wet hands and sleeves on the heater of the black Range Rover.

'I'm a terrible mother,' Mrs Benson said.

Printed in Great Britain
by Amazon

85205695R00206